PEACE *at* BOWLING GREEN

by

Alfred Leland Crabb

THE BOBBS-MERRILL COMPANY, INC.

PUBLISHERS

INDIANAPOLIS • NEW YORK

To
four young Kentuckians:
LELAND, WADE, GARRY, AND DAVID

THE assistance of the following in the preparation of the story is worthy of special acknowledgment: Mrs. Mary Moore, Western Kentucky State Library; Judge John B. Rodes, Bowling Green, Kentucky; Dr. J. L. Harman, Bowling Green, Kentucky; Dr. Hambledon Tapp, Lexington, Kentucky; Dr. Edwin Windrow, George Peabody College for Teachers; and my wife, Bertha Gardner Crabb.

TABLE OF CONTENTS

PEACE AT BOWLING GREEN

The Settlement Begun

1803

1

THE KENTUCKY spring came early that year, and the country was filled with its sights and sounds. The crude trail along which the wagon had traveled its western course for so long had lately become better. The winter rains had stopped as by the signal of the equinox, and a warm and friendly sun had dried and hardened the clay of the road. At times, and particularly in the bottoms, the ruts slowed progress to a snail's pace, but where the ground was drier, the pressure of wagon wheels had leveled the winter-worn surface to a reasonable flatness. The reports that Jacob Skiles had heard had magnified the discomforts of the journey. He had expected it to be much worse. It, all things considered, had been a good trip.

Jacob Skiles's face bore the look of calmness and equanimity. He disliked overeagerness in other people, and he had schooled himself against any show of it. But within him there was a great eagerness to get to his new home. He kept wondering, as he had done so often on the journey, what Bill Willie Blewett had done to make the home ready for him, his wife, and his three-year-old son. On what sort of place would it be built, and how would it look? Other things were running through his mind. It was time to be working his land for summer and fall crops. It was getting time for crops to be planted, but he was by nature a methodical man. He would carry on his work with no undue haste and with the least loss of time.

The first thing to do would be to search out the land most favorable for planting in corn, though doubtless Bill Willie had already decided that. Corn grew quickly and surely when it was well tilled and there was enough rain. Corn yielded nourishing provender for man and beast. And then, for the hundredth time, a troubling thought filled his mind. He had hoped to bring much more seed corn than lay in the two sacks under the wagon seat, but seed corn was a fiercely sought commodity among the emigrants leaving Virginia for the western country. He did not have more than half of what he had hoped to bring. That made more imperative the wise choice of the land in which to plant it. Bill Willie Blewett had told him in a letter, which one of the scouts had brought, that in southern Kentucky corn ought to be sprouted by the second week in May. Skiles had remembered that, for Bill Willie had proved a canny man in his observations. Skiles had sent Blewett to Kentucky late the summer before to make ready for his coming. He would have a house ready for them, else Skiles missed a prime guess. And he would miss another guess unless the house had been provided with some surprises. Blewett had never done anything in the usual way, not even fought Indians. Even with the house that Bill Willie had built, and the country alive with the brightness of spring, the months ahead would overflow with hardships. But hardships were a regular portion of a pioneer's life. They belonged in it.

Jacob Skiles was not likely to find any hardships in the new country that would match the ones he had endured in the past. He clucked to his horses for a little faster walk. His right foot prodded under the wagon seat, and touched the sacks of seed corn, merely for reassurance. Then his foot turned and pushed against a smaller sack. It contained the seeds he had brought to plant in his new garden. A great deal depended upon those seeds.

It would be like Bill Willie to have the garden newly fenced in against prowling beasts. Perhaps the garden would be spaded too. Bill Willie was a great man for anything done in the name of eating.

The small boy sitting between Skiles and his wife spoke for the first time in an hour. "Daddy, I'm tired. How far is it?"

"Not far now, Rumsey. I guess your mother is tired too."

"Not very tired," said Priscilla Skiles, "but I am getting lonesome. You haven't said a word for I don't know how long. And Rumsey is just like you. I never saw a child that could go as long without talking."

Skiles looked around at the boy sitting quietly at his side, his calm, large eyes missing nothing. "He is tireder than he knows, Priscilla, but he will have a lot of resting time from now on. As for me, I cannot make plans and talk at the same time."

"Then stop making plans for a while. I need talking to."

"You were present in my plans, Priscilla."

"Then I need to be told about them."

"When you first spoke, I was remembering the two pints of onion sets in my seed bag. I was thinking that I should get them into the ground just as soon as I can, maybe the next day after we get there."

"Spring onions make fine eating. I am hungry for some now."

"They are a good tonic, and they go specially well with hoecakes."

"You get the corn meal and I will make the hoecakes."

"Bill Willie says the Kentuckians drink a great deal of tea brewed from the root of the sassafras. It is supposed to be a tonic too."

"I like to try new things, Mr. Skiles. I'd like to try a new home right now."

"This time tomorrow I intend for you to be trying one."

"Couldn't we keep on going? The horses can see their way at night. I'd rather be awake at home than asleep on the road."

"So would I. So would Rumsey, but those horses are tired. It is natural for horses to get tired, and with feed and rest they will get over it. But when you push a horse it gets more than just tired. Something gives way inside it. We must be careful with our horses. A lot depends on them."

"A lot depends on my husband," she said smiling. "We could get more horses."

"It's more horses that would be hard to get. Horses are scarce, specially good ones, and oxen are clumsy beasts." He sat silent, thinking. "There'll be so much to do I'll hardly know where to begin."

She sat thinking too, but her thoughts ran not ahead, but back over the journey they were about to end. "We've been mighty lucky on the whole trip. I am thankful for that."

"Mighty lucky. There have been no heavy rains since we left, and freezing weather only once. The way I make it we are four days ahead of what I expected."

"There was never another man born that I would have started out on this trip with, Mr. Skiles." She leaned forward and patted with affection the hands that held the reins. Then her mind moved to the grim possibilities ahead. "You don't expect the Indians to bother us any more?"

"They could, but I don't expect it. I think they have learned their lesson. Good God, I hope so!" He spoke with such sudden and unwonted violence that the horses mistook it for a command and shifted to a faster walk.

Again her hand was touching his, affectionately, restrainingly. "There are things you should forget."

He said nothing and the tenseness relaxed. He steadied the team across a shallow branch and up the opposite bank.

"Home!" she said. "Home! It is thrilling just to think of it."

They had been traveling for two days through The Barrens, called that because over a long stretch of time the Indians in the early spring had fired the countryside, finally killing off all timber and undergrowth. The heavy mass of grass had been green the summer before, but frost and freezing had turned it to a winter brown. They were leaving The Barrens then, for the distances were dark with heavy woodlands, and thickets and clumps of trees were reappearing in the fields.

Skiles turned back to his wife. "I've said it before. Let me say it again. We are moving to Kentucky to stay. There's nothing to be gained by moving often. There has to be some moving, but some people move so much it gets to be a habit with them. I do not expect us to move ever again. What roots we have, I want us to put them down here. We will live pretty hard for a while, but we are staying in Kentucky."

"Whatever has got into you, Mr. Skiles? Who said anything about leaving?"

"And I want Rumsey to stay on here after we are gone, and I want his children to stay, and their children. That was my feeling when we left Virginia. I have it still deeper now." He sat silent for a while. His wife and son regarded him wonderingly. Then he changed the subject. "I've been thinking that sometime we may want to start a store at Bowling Green. We'll wait and see how things are there."

"I'd like to see inside even somebody else's store once more," she said. "I thought we were going to farm. If you are going to have a store, what are you going to do with all that land?"

"We are going to use it. Farming is a good way to live, but it is a poor way to make money. No, we won't start a store for a while. We will wait and see how things are. Bill Willie Blewett thinks that Bowling Green will grow into a large town someday. If so, a store started soon ought to do well. But I am going to start farming tomorrow, or I hope I am. I am anxious to be at it."

"I hope we have good neighbors. Good neighbors are mighty important."

"I don't expect to have any living close. The place isn't that well settled yet. You are right, Priscilla. The wrong kind of neighbors can do a great deal of harm. It will be my aim to be neighborly. My guess is that you are lonesome for a talk with a woman."

"I am. It seems like a year since I saw one."

"If I can find a woman anywhere who is any good, I want to hire her to help you get started. You can talk while you work. If there is one anywhere close, Bill Willie will know about her."

"Thank you, Mr. Skiles, but I'll do all right." She fell into silence, meeting with practiced movement the lurch and sway of the wagon.

"We have been lucky indeed. All the rivers and creeks low for the fording, and ferryboats waiting where they were deep. There have been places where we might have been held up a month, but we have never had to stop for anything. That sun is just about down. It is time to begin looking for a place to camp for the night."

"I am not tired, Daddy," said the boy.

"Well, I am," his mother said, "but I never did want to be at home in all of my life as much as I do now."

"We will get everything done and go to sleep early. We will be on our way by the time the sun is up tomorrow."

They came to a creek. It was a large creek but they got across it without any trouble. The bottom was firm, the water clear, and not in any place over fifteen inches deep. The trouble lay in climbing the ridge on the opposite side. The horses were panting in great heaves when they reached level ground, and the sweat was showing on their sides.

A half mile farther on they came to a good place for camping. It was at the base of a sheltering ridge. They tethered and fed the team. Then they fried the side meat and warmed the bread made the day before. They ate with relish and for a few minutes sat and watched the dim light fade in the west. Skiles moved things in the wagon and leveled a space on which they slept soundly till the darkness began to thin the next morning. For breakfast there was more of the warmed-over bread, some sausage smoked back in Virginia, and coffee made from their scanty store. Only the rim of the sun was showing above the eastern horizon when Skiles clucked to the team. Then they were moving on the final stretch of their journey home. The early morning was filled with the softness of spring and birds were all about them with their flutter and song.

They drove for half an hour in silence. The morning was tender and misty and the woods and thickets had become sprinkled with the whiteness of dogwood blooms. It was the woman who spoke. "I have wondered a lot of times why you have so much faith in Mr. Blewett."

"He saved my life once, and once I am sure I saved his. We have been close to each other for a long time. He has never disappointed me. I don't think he will this time."

"I hope you can still say that tomorrow."

"I think I will be able to." He changed the subject. "I'll do what I can to help, Priscilla, but at the best you will have a hard time of it for months. When you move into a new country there's no way to get around that. Bill Willie is a jack-of-all-trades, handy at most anything. I expect him to have a house ready for us to move in. I am sure that it won't be much of a house, but it will keep the weather out. It will do us for a year or two. I gave him the money to buy some things with, a bed, a table, some chairs, some things for cooking, and a cow. I'll be surprised if he hasn't attended to it better than I could. He is a canny man at a trade."

"How much farther do you think it is?"

"I'd guess ten miles, and I might miss it that much either way. I've tried to keep track, but it is not easy in a strange country. Bill Willie said there was a creek not far from the place. I don't guess it was the one we crossed."

"I hope it was." Her husband felt her suddenly grow rigid. "Mr. Skiles, there's a man coming yonder."

"I suppose he can tell us how far we have to go yet."

But Skiles shifted the reins to his left hand and took the rifle from the rack and laid it at his feet, spreading his coat to cover the sight of it. He hadn't expected any trouble from robbers, but it was a possibility to be ready for.

The man came on, riding in a slow canter. He saw the wagon and spurred his horse to a faster gait. With his free hand, Skiles lifted his rifle for easier use. His wife seized his arm, breathing quickly. Then she felt her husband relax. "That's Bill Willie now," he said. "We must be getting close to home."

"Thank goodness," she said.

The man on horseback drew to a stop and sat there unsmiling, imperturbable. "I wasn't expecting you till long towards night, or maybe tomorrer," he said calmly. "You musta hurried. I hope you're feelin' all right, ma'am."

"I am feeling very well, thank you, Mr. Blewett. It hasn't been hard traveling, at all."

"And the young feller, he looks healthy."

"Rumsey hasn't complained a single time," answered Skiles. "I am proud of him, and of his mother too. How did you figure out so well when we would get here?"

"I wasn't too certain about it, on account I didn't know what sort of weather you was havin'. I figgered it accordin' to the weather we been havin' here. I was goin' to start lookin' for you in an hour or two by sun. Things is ready for you to move in."

Jacob Skiles glanced with significance at his wife, then looked back at Blewett. "I expected that you would be ready for us, Bill Willie."

"The house ain't what you woulda wanted, ma'am, but I reckon you can live in it, for a time, anyhow."

"I like it already," she said. "Let's be going. I am anxious to get to it."

"How far is it?" asked Skiles.

"Not more'n a half a mile. I was on my way to see a woman about helpin' Mrs. Skiles for a few days, but I reckon I'll wait till after dinner to go see her. We turn offn the road up here apiece. You foller me."

He turned his horse, stopped, looked back at Skiles, then rode back along the trail by which he had come. He was a small, knotty man, roughly dressed but oddly clean. His face was the color of outdoors, and gnomelike. His deep-set eyes were as bright as from disease.

"Oh, I do hope the house is a little nice," Mrs. Skiles said softly.

"Daddy, where's a house?" the boy inquired.

"It's not far, and it is ours. It's your house, Rumsey, to grow up in. It must be yonder. He's turning off the road."

Bill Willie turned off the road to the left. He stopped to wait for Skiles to turn. The road along which they drove then was but a wide spacing between the trees. There were some marks of travel on it, but very few.

A hundred yards farther on Bill Willie stopped and pointed. Then the Skileses saw their new home. The woman's exclamation told of her pleasure. She looked long at it, then turned back to the spread of the country that stretched away to the west. She filled her eyes with that prospect and turned again to the house. It was perhaps fifty yards from where she sat in the wagon. The house was on an elevation that seemed to dip gently away in every direction except to the south. To the south the land was level and thick-wooded. There was a spreading maple tree in front and slightly to the left of the house. Opposite the maple tree was a towering cedar. The grass in front of the house was far advanced in growth and greenness. The woman looked long at the house and her eyes were warm with pleasure. It was larger than she had expected. It was, as she knew it would be, built of logs, but no coarse and slovenly workmanship showed in those logs. They were large and smoothly hewn. A massive chimney of mortar and limestone rose above the roof on the end nearer the maple tree. The door was in the center, and at the right of it a window, the size of which also surprised her. There would be more light in that house than she had expected. There was only one room in the front, but the house was so tall that she knew there would be a great deal of space in the attic. She could see from the angle from which she viewed the house that another room was at the back. That, of course, would be the kitchen. The pointing in the spaces between the logs was neat and trim. A faint curl of smoke was lifting from the chimney as from a fire all but burned out.

She heard her husband saying, "Bill Willie, if that house is as good as it looks, you are even a better man than I thought you were."

Blewett's face changed not one whit, though his deep-set eyes warmed. "Better go see for yourself. You might want to go back."

"That's a good idea," said Skiles, climbing down from the wagon and walking around to his wife's side. "If we are going back to Virginia, we ought to get an early start. Let's go see for ourselves, Priscilla."

The three of them walked up the little rise to the house, the boy holding gravely onto his father's hand. Priscilla Skiles's eyes never left the house as they approached it. But her husband's eyes moved away long enough to see a fenced-in lot in which a spotted cow grazed contentedly. His wife was the first to open the door. She raised the hand-whittled latch and pushed it open. She stood there, pouring all of her vision into that little chamber. The floor was clean and she could see that it was smooth when matched against the pioneer homes she had known. Three cured deerskins were scattered about on the floor. There was a fireplace wide and deep, and a few embers were still alive. She could see a bed back in the room, its sides threaded with rope and quilts spread upon it. Where had Blewett got those quilts? Under the big bed was a trundle bed, for the boy, of course. And there were quilts upon it too. She went inside, followed by her husband, Rumsey still holding fast to his hand. Priscilla Skiles saw a door at the far side of the room. She walked quickly across and pulled it open. She gasped with pure pleasure at the sight of her kitchen. It too was well floored. In the middle of the kitchen was placed a table fully as good as the one she had left in Virginia. On the hearth was an assortment of kettles and cooking things. A cedar bucket, bright in its newness, sat on a shelf by the side of the door. From a peg at its side swung a drinking gourd. From one end a door led out into the yard, and in the other end there was a small window. Two chairs were placed at the table.

"You are a faithful man, Bill Willie," she heard her husband saying.

Blewett's face relaxed into as close an approach to a smile as he was accustomed to make. "Glad you're suited," he said.

"I am much more than just suited," said the woman. "I have been wondering all the way from Virginia what sort of house we would have. My husband was right about the sort of man he said you were."

"Got to do right by a feller who's kept me out o' jail as much as he has."

"You haven't been in jail here, have you?" A worried look was in Skiles's eyes.

Blewett grinned this time. "It ain't my nature to stay out, but I jest ain't had the time. I been busy."

"Daddy, is this our house?"

"It is our house, Rumsey. This is where we are going to live."

"I don't want to move any more. I like the house."

"Think no more of it, son. We are going to live here as long as your mother and I are alive. And that's a promise."

"It's a promise, Rumsey," said the mother.

"What do you think we ought to do first, Bill Willie?"

"I'd say the first thing to do is to get unloaded and the stuff in the house. Then I'd start plantin' the garden. You got the seeds, ain't you?"

"All I could get. Not enough. I have some potatoes to plant and some onion sets."

"I never set eyes on better ground than this is. Your garden is ready to plant. It's a little late to plant onions and potaters, but they'll raise some. I've been talkin' to some of the fellers who raise crops aroun' here. They say you ought to expect a cornfield to raise more things than jest corn. They plant punkins and runnin' beans after the corn is knee-high. I expect you ain't got time right now to listen to all the things I've heard. I reckon we better get the hosses unhitched and the wagon unloaded."

"How long have you had the cow?"

"Bought her last Friday. Brought her home yestidy. She's a purty good milker. It's been a long time sence that youngster teched a drap o' milk. There's some in that crock on the table." He turned to Mrs. Skiles. "There's one thing you will like about the place, ma'am. It's got the best spring water I know of, and plenty of it. There ain't jest one spring; there's three. And they are not fifty yards from the house. Come here and let me show you." He led them into the yard and pointed. "Right there by them poplar trees. Runs steady summer same as winter."

"I like a named place," said Priscilla Skiles. "We'll call this Three Springs."

"It's a purty name. Sorry I didn't get a barn up, but I fenced in a horse lot, and there's a holler place under a bluff yonder that the hosses can stay in when it is rainin'. Let's unhitch the hosses so they can rest while we tote the plunder inside. I expect you'd better put the onion sets and potaters where we can get them. They're goin' to be in the ground afore night."

They unhitched the horses and stripped the gear from them and turned them into the horse lot that Bill Willie had prepared. It was the first freedom the horses had had since they left Virginia. They stood uncertain and stolid for a few minutes, then walked to a patch of grass and began grazing.

"Many people around here?" asked Skiles.

"Some, not many. Several have moved in lately."

"What about our neighbors?"

Blewett, who was lifting a leather trunk from the rear of the wagon, stopped and looked at his employer. "There is things about them all right," he said grimly. He pointed to the south. "Lank Motley lives a mile that way. He meddles in everybody's business but ifn his house was afire he'd leave it to help put yours out. The closest one this way—" pointing to the north—"is Elvis Grider. He's a curious one, a schemer I call him. I guess I ain't a good jedge o' folks but I'd count my fingers after every handshakin' with him, and it wouldn't surprise me none to miss a few. Mrs. Motley's a right neighborly woman. All I'll say about Mrs. Grider is she married the right man." He bent and pulled the trunk high on his shoulders and went on toward the house.

While he was gone Skiles loosened the things in the wagon and piled some of them on the ground. When he came back Skiles said, "We've been so excited about the house that we've forgotten something. Where are you going to live? What have you got ready for yourself?"

"Yonder's my cabin. I got it fixed up jest like I want it." He pointed, and Skiles saw the little house a hundred yards away, partly hidden by the land's curvature.

They spent the rest of the morning unloading the wagon and carrying the things into the house. The boy played out in the yard. At intervals he would come inside, look solemnly around, then return to his play. The two horses, not quite sure of their new freedom, would stand for a while apparently in deep meditation, then sedately proceed with their grazing. Skiles and Bill Willie carried everything into the house, and, as nearly as they could, placed things in their proper positions.

On their last trip Mrs. Skiles said, "I guess I'd better fix some dinner for you. We haven't got much right now but it is filling."

"I didn't aim for you to have to start cookin' this soon." Bill Willie went to the kitchen hearth and took the top from a kettle. "This here is hominy, ma'am. People here eat it a right smart. I got it at Mr. Hardcastle's store in town. It's already cooked. Jest needs a little warmin' up. Them is stewed squirrels in that other kettle. They need warmin', too."

The meal was the first relief the Skileses had had from wagon fare since they left Virginia. They ate with heartiness and at length.

Presently, Bill Willie stood. "Let's get your potaters and onions planted. It's so warm that it's liable to start rainin' any time, and they ought to be in the ground."

"Mr. Blewett, how far is it to a store?" asked Priscilla Skiles.

"A little the rise o' three miles. There's three stores in town now, but one of them is out at the edge o' town this way."

"Mr. Skiles, could I go to it before night? We need a trip to a store."

"Bill Willie is right about the planting, but I guess you are right about going to the store, Priscilla. We'll work awhile and then quit in time to go."

Jacob Skiles knew how to plant onions and potatoes. Bill Willie Blewett was an expert with the hoe. Skiles cut the potatoes into pieces for planting. Blewett hollowed out the row with his hoe, and Skiles planted the potatoes, spacing and placing them carefully in the row. The boy was having great sport, walking uncertainly along behind, then running around his father to the furrow ahead. Bill Willie came behind, covering the potatoes to the desired depth, and smoothing and patting the top of the row. The soil was soft and pliable and had the look of fertility. Often Jacob Skiles took up a handful and looked at it with assurance. They finished the potatoes, and then planted the onion sets.

Skiles straightened up from the final planting. "We have now planted in Kentucky soil," he said whimsically. "I suppose that makes Kentuckians out of us."

"Yessir, you can vote now," said Bill Willie.

"We'll get to work in earnest tomorrow. My wife is hankering for the sight of a store. Well, she deserves anything she wants. She didn't whimper once on the entire trip. The boy didn't either. She shall go to the store. Which is the best one?"

"All three is purty scrubby. Mr. Hardcastle's is as good as any, and I think he does have more things. But you have to watch him like a sparrer does a snake. He'd cheat his grandpa if the old man give him a chance. You go out to where you turned off the road this mornin'. You turn to the right and go about a mile. Then you take the left fork and it'll lead you right to Hardcastle's store. While you're gone I'll go see that woman about helpin' Mrs. Skiles. You want me to, don't you?"

"I certainly do. What is it, Bill Willie?"

"You havin' comp'ny," said Blewett in his dry tones. "Elvis Grider. I halfway expected he'd be comin'."

The man hitched his horse, apparently with meticulous care. Then he tested the knot to make sure, turned and walked toward them in short, mincing steps.

Skiles walked to meet him. "Good afternoon, sir. I am Jacob Skiles." He held out his hand.

"I fancied you were Skiles," the man said in tones that curiously matched his steps. "My name is Elvis Grider. I live a mile in that direction." He pointed to the north. "We welcome you to Kentucky. It has the makings of a great state. It is a backwoods place now, but it has promise. The day will come when it will match Virginia." His eyes were upon the horses in the lot. "Your team stood the trip well."

"They are sturdy animals. This is real neighborly of you, Mr. Grider."

"I trust there were no undue hardships on your journey."

"No, we were greatly favored. Good health, good weather, not a breakdown for the wagon, not a ford deep enough to stop us, a good house to move into. And now, your friendliness. Kentucky appeals to us. We are indebted Bill Willie Blewett for many things, specially this house. I am sure that you have already made his acquaintance."

"I have seen Blewett often," Grider said. His friendly manner had changed subtly. It was almost as if he had said *too often*.

"I have no more trusted friend than Blewett. I sent him to Kentucky eight months ago to get the place ready for us. Our arrival, because of him, has been much the more pleasant."

"A capable servant, no doubt."

"I employ him and pay him wages, but he is not a servant at all." It seemed well to shift the subject. "How long have you been in Kentucky, sir?"

"Five years in all. I stopped in Lincoln County two years, then came on here. This suits me better."

"I have been here six hours and I feel suited. This looks like good ground."

"It is good ground, some of it excellent." Grider's next question was asked idly. "How much do you have title for?"

"About six hundred acres."

"That's a great deal of land. I fancy you will sell off some of it."

"I do not expect to sell any of it. Good land should be sold only in an emergency. I intend to farm every acre of it just as soon as I can."

"I rode by on the chance that you had arrived. I hope you keep on liking Kentucky."

"I take your visit kindly, sir. Won't you come in and meet Mrs. Skiles?"

"I shall reserve that pleasure for later. It is a busy time at my place. Good day, sir." Somewhat stiffly Grider held out his hand. Skiles took it. Then Grider untied his reins, pulled his horse around, mounted and rode away with never a glance at Bill Willie Blewett.

Skiles watched the man ride out of sight. "You are an observing man, Bill Willie," he said.

Blewett almost smiled. "Count your fingers," he said. "Four bits says you ain't got 'em all."

It was Skiles's turn to smile. "Have you no concern for our friend? There are times when I accumulate fingers."

Not everything had been removed from the wagon. Jacob Skiles climbed inside and handed a saddle and riding bridle out to Bill Willie. "Put that on the sorrel."

He went deeper into the wagon and reappeared with a bridle and a woman's saddle. The horses were enjoying their rest but it was interrupted. Soon the Skileses were riding along the well-worn trail toward the village of Bowling Green. There was enough of the sun left to give them an hour of daylight at the store. Then they would come back through the gathering dusk and early darkness. It was a quiet and gentle countryside through which they rode. The air was softened by the vague fragrance of things in early bloom. The distant hills showed dimly through a film of springtime haze. The trail rose and fell with a sort of billowing effect.

"I like to live in a place like this," she said. "I don't feel tired at all."

The boy rode behind his father as he had so often on their trips in Virginia. His large, wondering eyes were full of the sights about him. Then he thought of something. "Will Daddy stay home more now?"

"He will, Rumsey. He has promised it."

"I have a home now," Skiles said. "I intend to stay at it."

"We are lucky to have Mr. Blewett," she said. "But I think he is lucky to have you. Tell me, Mr. Skiles, how did he ever get that awful name."

"His father wanted to call him Bill, and his mother insisted on Willie. Neither would give up. So they settled it this way."

He said nothing for a while, then continued musingly, "I remember the first time I ever saw Bill Willie. There had been a fight at Covington, and Bill Willie had beaten a man rather badly. I got there in time to see the last of it. The man Bill Willie had thrashed was a common loafer, and he got what he had needed for a long time, but they lugged Blewett off to their filthy jail. I thought the matter over and went to see him. It wasn't easy to do but I talked them into letting him go. I learned that it was the third time he had been in the jail within the month, and all for fighting. He never drinks or carouses but he has an Irishman's love for an honest fight. That was when he started working for me. When he came on early last fall he promised me that he would fight no one till I got here. I told him if anyone jumped on him to fight back, but to stay peaceable if he possibly could. I don't think he has had any trouble, but I can guess where he would like to have some."

"You mean the man who was here awhile ago. I saw him from the window. I saw that he left without looking at Mr. Blewett."

"I don't know the whole story; in fact, I don't know any of it, but there is something between them. Bill Willie had the same look on his face that I saw back in Virginia. It will come out at the proper time."

"What did you think of the man?"

"The man is Elvis Grider, and he lives somewhere out this way. Well, you might say that I was inclined to sympathize with Bill Willie."

They passed no one on the entire trip to Bowling Green. Skiles

pointed to a house back in a grove of oak trees and said he guessed
that it was Grider's. They came to the fork in the road. The observant
Rumsey tugged at his father's coat sleeve and pointed. A man was
plowing far back in the field to the right. The newly plowed ground
showed dark in the afternoon sun.

"We'll be plowing ourselves tomorrow, Rumsey. It is time for corn
to be planted. I don't look for any killing frost, at any rate not after
we get ready to plant."

"Corn is a pretty growing crop. It is pretty from the time it comes
up till you gather it. I like to pass a corn patch and just look at it."

"So do I, but corn is good for a lot more things than to look at.
Bill Willie said fifteen acres are ready to be plowed, but I am not
sure we have seed for that much. We have got to buy some more
stock. We need some cattle and some sheep and some hogs, and I am
going to get out as soon as I can and look for them. And these two
horses can't do the work I have in mind. I am not going to use any
oxen. They are too clumsy to suit me. The more crop I can raise the
more stock I can carry through the winter. I have been looking at this
grass. It ought to make good winter pasture. It seems as if we need
more of everything."

"We can't have everything at once, Mr. Skiles. A farmer in a new
country has to grow up like a boy does, a little at a time."

They passed a house, and then another. They were nearing the
village. The distant tinkle of a cowbell sounded as music. "What have
you in mind buying, Priscilla?"

"I guess I want to see more than I want to buy. A woman just likes
to see things she could buy if she was of a mind to. There are some
things we need. A respectable house can't get along without soap,
and I want to buy some. I'd like to have some molasses for sweetening, and the bacon and corn meal we got here with won't last long.
Rumsey is growing so fast he eats as much as you do."

"What about some dress goods?"

"I'm fixed all right for clothes, at least till we get settled."

"I suppose they have preaching here. If they do we'll go Sunday."

"I've got preaching clothes. Soap is what we need most."

"I guess that is the store yonder." Two minutes later, they reached
it. The store was a double log cabin with no front porch such as the
stores generally had back in Virginia. A half dozen hitching posts
were ranged at the side. A horse stood at one and dozed. Skiles dis-

mounted, threaded the reins through the iron ring and tied them. He hitched his wife's horse and the three of them entered the store.

The proprietor stood in the middle of the room and played the role of salesman, a horse collar swinging from his arm. His speech was loud and disagreeable.

"You can't get a horse collar as good this side of Philadelphy, or maybe Noo Orleens. I'm in the business and I ought to know."

"I ain't a-denyin' it's a good horse collar," said the customer, "but money's mighty skeerce. I reckon I'll have to hoe my crop instead o' plowin' it."

"Lissen here, Breed Loving, you've bought goods from me nigh onto two years. Name one time I ever cheated you, jest one time. I ain't a-goin' to risk cheatin' you. You're a smart man and I need your business. I wouldn't make enough profit at the price I ast you for that there horse collar to buy me a pet jaybird."

"Where'd that hoss collar come from?"

"Like I told you, Philadelphy. Best horse-collar-makin' place in the whole world. Wait here a minute, Breed. Them is strangers that jest come in."

He turned and took a step toward Skiles, bowing stiffly. "Don't ricollect ever seein' you before. Strangers, ain't you?"

"My name is Jacob Skiles. This is my wife, and this is my son. We arrived today."

"I'm Wash Hardcastle. I reckon you come from North Caroliny. A lot o' folks is comin' from there lately. Pleased to make your acquaintance, ma'am. That's a likely-lookin' lad you got. I'd like mighty well to have your trade, Mr. Skiles."

"We came from Virginia. I am afraid we won't make very good customers, but now and then we will need some things. You go ahead and wait on the gentleman. We are not in a very big hurry."

Hardcastle awoke to his social obligations. "This feller's Breed Loving. Breed's a mighty fine farmer and a good man, wuth a lot to his neighborhood. Where you settlin' at, Mr. Skiles?"

"Three miles east of here. Maybe you have heard of the three springs."

"Feller's been buildin' a house out there all winter. I heard it was for somebody else. So that's where you settlin'?"

"We moved in today."

"Neighbor o' Elvis Grider then. Lots o' fine ground out that way.

Excuse me, and I'll finish waitin' on Breed. Jest as soon as I have sold him this horse collar I'll be right with you."

He turned to Loving. "Made up your mind yet, Breed?"

"I reckon I'll take the collar. I jest about have to. Still I believe you're overchargin' me."

"Don't talk so loud afore strangers, Breed. They might get the notion you mean it."

"Wouldn't be bad for them ifn they did." He counted out the money and handed it to Hardcastle, who totaled it with care. He gave the horse collar to Loving, who nodded stiffly to the Skileses and left the room.

Hardcastle looked after him, his eyes blinking. Then he turned his shrewd little eyes appraisingly upon Skiles. "Ifn you jest got here I expect you'll be wantin' a right smart, stuff for plowin' and fixin' up the house. I'm a little short o' things right now, but I guess I can rake up what you need."

"I think my wife wanted to see inside a store more than she wanted to buy anything, but she does want a few things."

"What'd you like to see first, ma'am?"

"I want to buy some soap," said Priscilla Skiles.

"I got some soap made by a widder woman from Rockfield. Good soap, too, and good soap is mighty hard to get. I've had a hard time keeping any lately."

"How much do you ask for it?"

"Two bits a pound, ma'am. There's ginrally close to three pounds to a bar. It's good soap and cheap at the price."

"Let me see it."

"It's a good sign, you bein' particular, ma'am." He handed her a bar across the counter. "The woman that made it is particular too, ma'am."

She looked at it. Then she said, "I'll take a bar. Do you have any molasses?"

"Not a spoonful. Molasses is skeercer than hens' teeth. But I got something that's better. I got three gallons of maple sugar. Fresh too. Ain't been made over a month. You'd be special fond of it, ma'am."

"How much do you sell it for?"

"I'll sell you a gallon for a dollar and throw in the crock. Ifn you'd been livin' here a week I'd ask a dollar and a half."

She asked to see it. The storekeeper looked at her in surprise but permitted the examination. "I'll take a gallon," she said.

"I'll give this little shaver a lump free o' charge. What else, ma'am?"

She bought some thread, some needles, some beeswax, and a dozen candles. Mr. Hardcastle suggested the wisdom of buying some calico for dress goods. He claimed that he had just got it from Philadelphy, and when it was gone there wouldn't be any more for maybe a whole year. Her quick eyes had seen the calico when she first entered the store, but the prospect of a dearth of it, however long, seemed to give her no concern. He did have a skillet that she liked and needed. The price was too high and she turned away from it, but he reduced the price, claiming that he always lost money on newcomers. She bought the skillet.

He asked how they were off for side meat. She relayed the question to her husband for an answer.

"We have a full slab left," he said. "We'll use it before we buy any more."

"Right now is when you need a lot o' side meat. I hear there's a good crop o' poke greens this year, and plenty o' narrer dock and lamb's-quarters comin' on. Did you bring any chickens with you, ma'am?"

"No, we left our chickens in Virginia."

"Can't very well get along without chickens. You need 'em when the preacher comes. I hear Elvis Grider is sellin' off some o' his. I expect he'd sell you some cheap."

"We won't buy any till we get straightened out and see what we need."

"Grider's got the best in the county."

"It's time for us to be going," said Jacob Skiles. "We haven't got acquainted with our new home yet."

There was no more than ten minutes of life left in the sun when they started for home. The brightness of the day had faded and the light had become soft and caressing. A sleepy note had come into the song of the birds. Rabbits were thick, hopping along the side of the road with no show of fright. A crescent moon hung two or three hours high in the western sky. It was dim and faint at first, and the boy was the first to see it. As the shadows deepened and steadied it grew bright and clear. From a thicket to the right a whippoorwill sounded its haunting cry.

"That's a poorly kept store," said Jacob Skiles. "Even a new place deserves a better one."

"I can think of some improvements you would make, Mr. Skiles."

He corrected her. "We would make. I wouldn't trust Mr. Hard-castle very far."

She looked at him shrewdly. "So you really are thinking of starting a store."

"That's exactly what I am thinking of. But I'll not have time for anything till the crop season is over. We will take things as we come to them, but I'll be thinking it over."

"You can think a lot in that time."

"So can you. I'll need help."

"If you think it is the thing to do, I'll think it too."

"Thank you, Priscilla. Did you notice how oddly the storekeeper looked at me when I told him where we lived? He had heard something about us before then."

"I noticed that he knew that Mr. Grider had some hens for sale."

"Are you tired, Mommy?" asked the boy. "I am."

"He very seldom says he is. I am a little tired, Rumsey. I think it sort of rested me to see the store, even though it wasn't a very good one. Better not get too sleepy till you have had your supper."

"Mommy, what are we going to have for supper?"

"I don't exactly know, but if you and your daddy will let me off easy tonight I'll see that you are filled up tomorrow."

"We accept your promise," said Skiles. "We will look forward to tomorrow. Here is where we turn. It isn't far now."

But Priscilla Skiles didn't have to worry about supper that night. Bill Willie Blewett again had taken care of that need, wild greens with side meat, crackling bread, and milk from the new cow.

The next day the men worked in the fields from sunrise till after sundown. The good weather still held, and it was time for the corn to be planted. The soil was good, even better than he had thought the day before, and it lay most favorably, well beyond the southern limits of The Barrens. No annual burning had stunted or deadened the thickets or woodlands of the area. A considerable part of the section was covered with heavy timber that would be vastly helpful in putting up fences, or in erecting barns and homes.

The two men ate their dinner of boiled white beans and side meat and great slices of corn bread. Priscilla had made a cobbler out of some dried peaches that she had brought from Virginia. It was a satisfying meal.

"I went to see that woman about helpin' you, but she was off somewheres visitin' her kinfolks. Her husband said she'd be here Monday. I've heard people say she's right good at housework."

"Much obliged, Mr. Blewett. There'll be plenty of work for her to do."

The harness needed a bit of repair, and the two men worked on it while the horses rested. The boy watched them gravely.

"Just as soon as I can spare the time I'd like to go about the place. I must learn my own land. Is it plainly marked?"

"I had the surveyor run it off jest like you told me to. Yes, it's plainly marked."

Some odd tone in the man's speech caught Jacob Skiles. He stood still waiting for Bill Willie to tell him what it was.

"There's a little misunderstandin' about a piece of the ground on the east side. Elvis Grider claims it."

Skiles stared at Bill Willie. "How could he claim it? I have the grant for it."

"There ain't no disputin' that you have the grant. Trouble is he does too. Anyhow, the surveyor said the people who made out the grants got mixed up. I didn't know what to do but wait till you got here."

"How much does he claim?"

"I figger it close onto seventy-five acres."

"Which grant was issued first?"

"That's the first thing I looked to see. They were made out the same month, yours two weeks before his."

"Then that gives me priority and I'll keep it. I thought I ought to come on here when I got the grant, but that was four months before Rumsey was born. After that I didn't ever seem to be able to get started. Has Grider said anything about it to you?"

"He ordered me off when I was out there lookin' one day."

"What did you do?"

"I ordered him off too. He got off first."

"What kind of land is it?"

"Good timber. Finest cedar trees I ever looked at. Lots of good oak and poplar, and it's got a first-rate spring."

"It is my land and I'll keep it. It is time for us to get back to plowing."

2

FOR A WEEK there was no break in the spell of fine weather, and each day the world grew visibly greener. Each day more of the world burst into bloom. Each day added cheer and volume to the vernal folksong of the birds. The onion sets hurriedly thrust their green blades through the crust of the rows. The potato plants hadn't appeared yet. The men planted a ten-acre patch of corn, then moved to another field and started plowing there. Priscilla worked in the house and yard. The woman whom Bill Willie had engaged helped three days, but then felt obliged to return to the needs of her own home. The boy often went with his father and Bill Willie to the field and trudged along with them as they plowed. Then he would return to the house, his father watching until he was sure that the trip could be made safely.

On Saturday afternoon Jacob Skiles felt they could afford a brief respite from interminably following the plow, dropping seed corn, precisely spaced and placed, in the furrow, and covering it carefully with a hoe. Their work had gone well. They could afford a brief period of rest and relaxation.

So the two men and the boy went fishing in Drake's Creek. Bill Willie had been once or twice before and knew a favorable place. They let the horses rest and walked the two miles to the creek, carrying poles and bait. Rumsey carried the bait, a pewter bowl filled with grubworms which he had picked up from the freshly plowed furrows. Bill Willie claimed they were the choicest delicacy one could offer to a fish. Jacob Skiles and Bill Willie took turns carrying Rumsey for short stretches so he wouldn't get too tired to enjoy the fishing. They climbed down a rocky bank to the creek, the father half carrying, half leading the boy. The creek was a fair sight. No late rains had clouded the water and it was reasonably clear, and the shadows of the trees fell in delicate tracery on the water's surface.

They stood on a flat, projecting rock and threaded grubworms on barbless hooks. The water beneath where they stood was deep, maybe ten feet, Bill Willie thought. The sun sprinkled its rays through the budding leaves on the trees that lined the bank. The air was calm and sleepy. They fished for half an hour and not a grubworm was touched.

"Sumpin' musta happened," said Bill Willie. "Last time I was here I had to fight 'em off. They got real dangerous."

Then a school of white perch arrived and for a while they were busy taking fish off their hooks. They threaded the fish on strings Bill Willie had fixed for that purpose, anchoring them in the water, then put on more grubworms which the boy handed them, smiling broadly as he did.

"No need of being wasteful," Skiles said. "This is all we could eat for two days and that is as long as they would keep. I am glad we had this luck. I am hungry for fish."

They climbed the rocky bank, Skiles carrying one string of fish, Bill Willie another.

"You are going to have to do more walking going back, son." Rumsey by way of answer ran ahead for a piece.

"I want to go back another way," Bill Willie said. "It ain't no further."

They struck out through the woods, bearing a little more to the north, Bill Willie leading. They crossed alternate strips of woodlands and cleared fields. They came to a woods heavy with great trees.

"That's your land Grider claims," Bill Willie said.

"About the surveying—it was done carefully, wasn't it?"

"Best surveyor in the county. He run it twice to make sure. I reckon the trouble was somebody give your land away to Elvis Grider."

Jacob Skiles stood looking at the trees that towered. Then he said, "If it was made out to me first I'll keep it."

"Nothing I'd like better'n to help."

"As soon as the crop season is over we'll get this straightened out. We couldn't use the land anyhow now. When we have time we'll try to reason with Mr. Grider."

"I'm afeard it's goin' to take more'n reason."

"If the grant was issued to me first, that is reason enough. Any grant after that was merely a mistake. But we'll not bother about it till fall unless he tries to use it."

The sun was already out of sight when they reached home, but the western sky was ablaze with its light. They cleaned the fish and Priscilla cooked them all. They would keep better cooked. She made corn bread and added water to the coffeepot and set it to boiling.

But before supper was fully ready a visitor arrived. It was Mr. Lank Motley, their neighbor to the south. Skiles was washing up from cleaning the fish when he heard the man's hello ring out. He went down across the yard to where the visitor was sitting on a horse.

"Name's Lancaster Motley," he announced in tones audible a quarter of a mile. "Folks generally call me Lank. Thought I'd ride over so as to be neighborly. Ought to have before now. I reckon you might say I've been busy." He considered a moment. "Though at what I don't rightly know."

"Get down and come in."

"Can't stay but for a minute. My wife was starting supper when I left, and you know how women are about you being ready when they get ready. I would like to make the acquaintance of Mrs. Skiles. In a way of speaking, I've got some business with her."

Skiles led him into the house and placed a chair for him. Then he called his wife from the kitchen. She told Blewett to mind the frying fish, then she wiped her hands and joined her husband.

"This is Mr. Lank Motley, one of our neighbors. Mr. Motley, this is my wife."

"Proud to make your acquaintance, ma'am. My wife and me thought you would like to go to preaching tomorrow. Brother Galloway is our preacher and he can put the gospel down where it will do most good. Right now we are having our preaching at Brother Tobias Jenkins' house. It's the biggest Presbyterian house in town. We are going to build a meetinghouse after the crop is laid by. We 'most always have a good crowd. Reckon you can go?"

"We can, can't we?" Skiles looked at his wife for approval.

"I never was for staying away from preaching," she said. "It's no way to bring that youngster up. If you will tell us how to get to Brother Jenkins' place, we'll be there."

"We weren't aiming for you to go to all that trouble the first time you went, ma'am. We'll bring the wagon by and take you with us. There'll be plenty of room."

"That is real friendly of you. We'll be ready to go when you say."

"There's another thing," said Mr. Motley. "Last thing my wife said to me was that she would be expecting you to go home with us for dinner tomorrow. Won't be much to eat, but hardly ever anybody drops dead from starvation at our house."

Mr. Motley laughed heartily at his own wit. Again Skiles looked at his wife for direction.

"We wouldn't want to put you to much trouble, but your invitation is right welcome. It's been a long time since I got a chance to visit anybody."

"You can be looking for us just about ten o'clock. I reckon you all Presbyterians."

"Our folks were before us," said Priscilla Skiles proudly. "We never have missed preaching when we could help it."

"Even the little shavers like Brother Galloway. This boy of yours will understand him. Never in all my life did I see better weather. But just wait a few days and you'll hear people hollering for rain. When people holler for something it doesn't mean they need it. It just means they haven't got much of it. Guess I'd better be going or Brother Galloway will be preaching my funeral tomorrow." He left laughing loudly.

At ten o'clock the next morning, the Skiles family, prim and starched, sat waiting for their hosts. They didn't have long to wait. They heard the creak of a wagon and the sound of horses' hoofs, and a few moments later Mr. Motley's wagon came in view. Mr. Motley was driving and his wife and young daughter, Sallie, sat on the wagon seat with him. There were three chairs placed in the bed of the wagon.

Skiles turned to Bill Willie Blewett. "Take care of things," he said. "Rest all you can. We are going to work hard this week."

"There is plenty of fish in the kettle on the hook," said Mrs. Skiles. "Help yourself."

Mrs. Motley was a pleasant-faced lady, not much given to volubility. Her husband talked loudly and most of the time. He remarked on the weather, his pleasure at seeing the Skileses, and the entire righteousness of the Presbyterian Church all in one breath. Jacob Skiles helped his wife into the wagon, lifted Rumsey over into the bed, and climbed in himself. He noted that some minor repairs would have left the wagon and harness greatly improved, and that Motley hadn't completed the blacking of his second shoe.

"I've been hearing Presbyterian preachers since I was knee-high to a gosling," Mr. Motley said, "but I never yet heard one that could kindle me with the Lord's fire like Brother Galloway can. When that man preaches I kindle. They say there's a first-rate Methodist preacher somewhere down on Gasper River, but no good Methodist preacher could hold a candle to any good Presbyterian preacher." He laughed loudly, and the little girl shared heartily in his mirth.

Lank Motley bethought himself suddenly. "This is my Sallie. Isn't

she a big girl for four?" Sallie, a plump, fair-haired child, looked ador-
ingly at her father.

Mrs. Motley turned to Mrs. Skiles. "I am sorry I haven't been to
see you, but this is a busy time with us. I'll try to make up for it."

"It is real neighborly of you to be taking us to preaching. Of course
we wanted to go, but it is sort of hard to start out by yourself among
strange people."

"Presbyterians aren't strange people, ma'am," said Mr. Motley. "It
is the other folks that are strange, but not the Presbyterians. You know
what the Scripture says—what is it it says, Clara?"

"You know, Lank Motley, that the Scripture doesn't say a word
about Presbyterians."

"Of course, Clara, if you look at it that way. They don't exactly
use the word Presbyterian, but it means the same thing. Anybody
can see that. Presbyterians aren't strange people. They are the chosen
people."

"Your own brother-in-law is a Baptist. What about him?"

"Yes, and my great-uncle stole a sheep. What about him?" Mr. Motley and the little girl joined in hearty laughter at the memory of his
great-uncle's larceny.

"Now, I ask you, what can you do with a man like that?" inquired
Mrs. Motley calmly.

Jacob Skiles turned the topic away from the Presbyterians to farming. "Are you about finished with your corn planting?"

"I ought to be but can't seem to stick at it. First one thing comes
up and then another."

"You went fox hunting yesterday, Lank."

"So I did, and I made a mistake. I ought to have stayed at home
and finished that bottom patch. I would have too, but Bill Spalding
has got a new hound dog, one of the Trigg breed from up at Glasgow, or maybe it's Greensburg. Them Trigg hounds are real dogs too.
Reub Buckner says he's thinking of selling his farm and buying one.
But you might say about Reub that he's got fox hunting on his mind."
Mr. Motley laughed with gusto. "It was right exciting, but still I ought
to have got that patch planted. Now that house yonder—" pointing
with a whip—"belongs to a Presbyterian named Elvis Grider." Skiles
noted that an unwonted dryness showed in the tones.

"Is he one of the chosen people?"

"Ask him and you'll find out. I reckon Elvis was there when they
did the choosing and he put his own name down first."

"Mr. Grider tends to his own business," said Mrs. Motley calmly.

"And that's all he does do. I wouldn't trust a man who just tends to his own business. He's not a good Presbyterian. He wouldn't even make a good Methodist. Don't the Scripture say, 'Help your neighbors'?"

"He came to see us the day we got here," said Skiles.

Motley stared at him. "Well, now, that's something! But there's one thing certain, he didn't make that trip to help you, not Elvis Grider." He heard something and turned in his seat to look back. "That's them coming. Watch the way he drives by, looking neither one way or the other, just straight ahead. That's the way he always looks, just straight ahead."

The carriage, drawn by two horses, pulled around the wagon, never slackening speed. The driver and the lady on the seat with him looked straight ahead, but the boy of six or seven on the back seat looked interestedly at the wagon as they passed by.

"Yes sir, he minds his own business, and if you've got any business you'd better watch out or he'll be minding it. That is the only carriage that will be at preaching today, and I'll bet you it don't speak to a single wagon or plug horse there. That man who works for you is fond of Grider just like I am. Blewett," he remarked irrelevantly, "would be a bad man in a tussle."

"He's pretty good at anything he does."

"I get along fine with him. He has told me a lot about you. Says he would be living his days out in jail if it hadn't been for you. But except for a little spat with Elvis Grider he hasn't been in a speck of trouble since he got here. That's Wash Hardcastle's store yonder. Some folks say Elvis Grider set him up in storekeeping."

"Does the town have enough stores?"

"I think it needs another one, maybe two. We're growing fast. You ladies put on your best meetinghouse looks. We're just about there."

"We will if you will take off your fox-hunting looks," his wife answered, smiling faintly.

They saw a large log house sitting far back from the road. A number of people stood about in the yard. A dozen or more wagons were hitched in the spaces immediately off the road. There was a sprinkling of saddled horses. Elvis Grider's team was hitched under a large cedar tree apart from the others. Brother Tobias Jenkins was out in the road with a cheery greeting for all comers, assisting them in hitching if they needed it. Lank Motley introduced his friends. Brother Tobias overflowed with hospitality and good will.

"Welcome to Bowling Green. I've been here two years, and I think it is the best place to live in the world. If I can judge from looks, you and Mrs. Skiles are going to think so too. But let's be getting inside. Brother Galloway likes to start on time."

Inside the house the ladies sat on chairs and crude benches. These were all occupied, so Mrs. Skiles and Mrs. Motley sat on a bed in the corner. Children usually sat on their parents' laps. The leader of song, Brother Jess Graham, moved to the front and announced that the first hymn would be "Amazing Grace." He lined out the verses in a sonorous reading voice, then looked about him to make sure that all were ready. He lifted his right hand, held it impressively poised, and on the downbeat started the song. It was a favorite in the Presbyterian churches in Virginia where most present had learned the words and the tune. What those pioneers missed in pitch and unison they more than made up in volume and spirit. Priscilla Skiles loved to sing, and from the joy of it her voice at times lifted above the others. She saw that some were looking at her in a surprised sort of way, so she discreetly lowered her volume and sang on.

Then the preacher, Bible in hand, was standing before them. He was a tall, thin man. His eyes burned as with a fever. His hair was long and raven in its blackness. His face was covered with a great shock of black beard which made his face seem even paler than it was.

"I will read the Scripture lesson from the twenty-ninth chapter of Proverbs," he said in a voice for all of its challenge singularly sweet and appealing. "For the text of the sermon I shall use the first verse. I shall read the verse now, and before I begin my sermon I shall read it again. Listen to it. There are those in the congregation who need to hear it, to think about it, to pray about it."

It was a sermon whose power Jacob Skiles felt. He fell to wondering whether he had hardened his neck. The preacher had the art of making his words personal to his hearers, causing them to search to find whether they were under the guilt of his charges. There was a sort of literacy in his language that greatly appealed to Skiles. A sidelong look at his wife told him that she too was impressed. The preacher closed his sermon with a flourish compounded of admonition and eloquence. Then he shifted to a matter of business.

"Brother and Sister Jenkins have a hospitable and devout home, but we must not abuse our welcome. Our town is growing fast. Of those who arrive in our midst more are of the Presbyterian faith than any other, though lately some of other faiths have been arriving. It is our duty to greet them as brethren, for most of them are good people, raised in the church and happy to take part in worship. Bowling Green will not be a backwoods place much longer, and a good church building is one of the best signs that a place is moving ahead. We Presbyterians believe in good church houses, and we must build such a tabernacle here. I haven't much money, but I will give ten dollars to build a Presbyterian church in Bowling Green. That means that I will have to skimp some in clothes and in comforts. It means that my wife will have to go without some things that she wants very much. But we are happy to make our gift. Is there anyone here who will give a like amount?"

For a moment no one stirred. Then Jacob Skiles arose. "We will give ten dollars."

"Will the brother introduce himself? I did not have the pleasure of making his acquaintance before the service opened."

"I am Jacob Skiles and this is my wife, Priscilla Skiles."

Priscilla Skiles arose. "Mr. Skiles said *we* when he made his gift. I will give ten dollars too," she said calmly, though her face was flushed, "and we will give five for our son, Rumsey."

"I verily believe that the Lord had to do with your presence here this morning." The preacher's bow included the three Skiles. "Twenty-five dollars is a gift to move our hearts. We now have thirty-five dollars. That will buy a great pile of brick. But we need more than brick. We need windows. Who will help buy the windows that let the light in for our bodies even as the church itself lets it in for our souls?"

"Five dollars apiece for my wife and daughter and me," said Lank Motley.

The preacher became jocular. "Shall we permit our nice brick walls and windows to go without a roof?"

"My family will give ten dollars for the roof," called Brother Tobias Jenkins.

"We'll give three," said Brother Breed Loving.

"Amen, but we haven't got a whole roof yet, and I would have to stand under the leaking part. You wouldn't want your preacher drowned, or even wet. I saw Brother Bill Willie Blewett come in a little late. He wouldn't want any of us to get wet, would he?"

"Two dollars to keep 'em dry," said Blewett.

"Thank you, Brother Blewett. That gives you a pew in a dry place."

"I'm not satisfied with the windows," called out Brother Eliphalet Searcy. "Even if it's dry weather I don't want to have to sit next to a hole in the wall. I will give five dollars for more windows."

Mrs. Breed Loving counseled with her husband. "Two dollars more for the roof," he called.

Soon the preacher moved on to the floor, then to the chimney, then to the benches. He was clearly pleased with the generosity of his parishioners. "We have promised already enough money to do a great deal of work on our new place of worship. We will plan it and start to work on it right away. But the thought has just come to me that we have not yet provided the preacher a place on which to stand. A preacher needs a pulpit. It is both his anchor and mount of inspiration."

"My family will give twenty-five dollars for a pulpit," said the brittle voice of Mr. Elvis Grider.

"Thank you, Brother Grider. You have not disappointed me."

The meeting adjourned with appropriate prayer. There followed a few minutes of conversation. Then the wagons began to rumble along their homeward ways, and the villagers, on foot, scattered to their homes. The preacher stood out in the Jenkins yard, talking to the Skileses and Motleys.

"You started our meeting off just right, Brother Skiles. The members couldn't let a stranger go ahead without following. I knew that everything would be all right when your wife made her gift. We are greatly blessed to have you as members of the congregation."

As they drove along the road homeward, Lank Motley lifted robust tones out of a full minute of silence. "I tell you Brother Galloway is a humdinger. He knows more human nature than a fortuneteller. He knew that Elvis Grider wouldn't go in with anyone else in buying brick or a roof or floors or benches. He knew that, so he was saving the pulpit for him all the time. That preacher played a tune on old Elvis just like he was a fiddle."

The Motley house was like the Motley wagon, a bit under cared for. But the dinner was good, and the quiet Mrs. Motley was flushed from the compliments of her neighbors. When dinner was over the two children played out in the yard. Mrs. Motley showed Mrs. Skiles the quilt she was piecing. The two men sat and talked of crops.

"I would like to finish planting corn this week," Skiles said. "I wish

I had more seed. I brought all I could get, but seed corn is scarce in Virginia."

"It's scarce here too, but I guess I could let you have, say, a pint for a late patch."

"I thank you just the same, but I'll not take it. I am glad you mentioned a late patch. I'll save a little out for one."

"You can't do without a late corn patch. Late roasting ears are the best, and cornfield beans grow the best in late corn. Would you like to see my hound dogs?"

Skiles was not interested in hound dogs, but it was plain that Motley wanted him to be. He said, "Yes, I'd like to see them."

The dogs were kept in a rail pen back of the house. "I hate to keep them penned up," Motley said, "but there are a lot of foxes now, and if I didn't they would run them dogs to death. When I wanted to have me a fox race they wouldn't be fit to run. I told Reub Buckner that his dogs would make a better showing if he would keep them penned up part of the time."

Skiles asked a question, though he knew the answer. "Does Mr. Grider keep foxhounds?"

"He wouldn't have one as a free gift. No, Elvis isn't interested in anything that would keep him from being a rich man. I guess that is one reason I have decided to stay poor."

Skiles turned the subject back to something more fitting. "I liked the preacher. He is a better one than we had in Virginia."

"You can't beat Brother Galloway as a preacher, and he's a good Christian man. If somebody gets sick he beats the doctor there. Once he went fox hunting with me."

"It was a clever thing the way he took up the collection this morning. It will do me good to remember that I bought some of the brick for the church."

"I thought it was clever too, but he generally is clever. It will do Elvis Grider good to remember that he bought the pulpit. That was smart of Brother Galloway. Grider wouldn't give a lead nickel to mix up with other folks' good ones. That was the way to pull money out of him, to let him think he was doing it all. This was the first time I've seen Blewett out at preaching."

"I didn't expect him to come, but I am glad he did."

" 'Two dollars to keep 'em dry,' " Motley mimicked. "He can be right comical."

"I have gathered that he doesn't like Grider either, but he can be a closemouthed fellow. Do you know of any trouble they have had?"

"It is no trouble at all not to like Elvis. I guess it is the easiest thing I do. I don't know of any special trouble they have had. They say Blewett was a little forgetful that he was talking to a great man when they had some words about that mix-up in your land titles. I guess you have heard about that."

"Bill Willie mentioned that there was some overlapping in the titles. My title is the older, but if he insists that the land is his, I guess we will have to let the court settle it."

"They had some words. Blewett was having the tract surveyed, I mean your whole tract. The survey included some land that Grider claimed. He heard about it and went out there where the surveyor was at work. He ordered Blewett and the surveyor off. Blewett kept trying to tell him about your grant. Grider kept saying, 'Get off my land, get off my land.' Blewett got tired of it and told Grider to get off himself. And then Grider told Blewett that he was going to have him arrested. Bill Willie picked up a switch and cut Grider's horse a sharp lick across the flank, and before Elvis could get the animal quieted down, he was off the land sure enough. He tried to take a warrant out against Bill Willie, but Squire Potter talked him out of it. He said that land trouble was mighty bad for a new community. The real reason was the squire had been fishing with Bill Willie and liked him a whole lot. I guess it blew over."

"The first thing I am going to do is to try to raise a crop, but if that land turns out to be mine, I'll try to keep it."

"I'd take a look at that land every now and then. It would be like Elvis to start using it for anything he can think up. He'd do it just to get the notion out that it is really his. Maybe he will let things drift along, but I doubt it."

3

THREE DAYS LATER the Skileses' cow got out and made a beeline for her former home. Bill Willie went to bring her back. His way skirted the land under dispute. The portion that Bill Willie passed by was heavily wooded in cedar. He heard the sound of chopping among the cedars. Hot anger boiled within him. He turned into the trees and saw almost what he had expected. Two men were chopping

down a large cedar tree. Others, already felled, lay about. He walked
to the nearest chopper. The man heard him coming and started to say
something.

Bill Willie's hand flicked out and jerked the ax from his grasp. "This
ain't your cedar tree. You both get away from here."

"Gimme that ax."

"I'm a-keepin' it to pay for the cedar trees you cut down."

"Gimme that ax. Grab him, Lem."

"I don't like fellers that steal. I done said once for you to get off."

"Elvis Grider said cut cedar trees, and when he says we cut."

Lem, holding on to his ax, started toward him. The man whose ax
Bill Willie held took a step toward him also. As he crossed the margin
of the cedars Bill Willie had picked up a round sandstone rock and
put it in his pocket. He shifted the ax to his left hand, and almost with
the same motion his right hand sought his pocket. The arm inscribed
a fierce arc and the stone struck the man with a vague *plump* flush
in the stomach. With a gasp that trailed off into a sigh the fellow sank
to the ground. The ax fell from his loosened fingers and lay on the
ground. With a leap Bill Willie reached it. Then he turned to the other
man.

"Get this polecat off this ground," he said. "Drag him off. Ifn you
want the axes back, ask Skiles. I'm givin' them to him to pay for the
damage you done."

The man on the ground struggled to a sitting posture, almost frantically filling his empty lungs with air. His partner helped him to his
feet and braced the staggering man as they moved away. Blewett hid
the two axes in a hollow log and went on after the cow. He found the
animal in the lot of her former owner and brought her back. On the
way he retrieved the axes. He put the cow back in her lot and then
hunted up Skiles and told him what had happened.

Skiles listened and said, "This might get you in trouble, Bill Willie."

"It might, but I'll have company."

"You mean me?"

"No reason for you to get in trouble. I mean them two fellers that
was cuttin' down your trees."

"I expect you will be hearing more of this. Well, it had to come
sometime. I imagine they'll have reinforcements the next time they
cut down our cedar trees. There were only two things you could have
done: gone on for the cow without stopping and then told me about
it when you got back, or acted precisely the way you did. I don't know

which would have been the better." He sighed. "Yes, I think you will be hearing more about it."

"What do you want me to do?"

"Right after dinner you take a hoe and chop weeds in the first field we planted. I noticed a lot coming up there and they might get a start on us. You begin back next to that strip of woods. If anybody comes, it will be from this side and you can see him a half mile away. If you see anybody, do what you think is best. If you need help I'll give it. I doubt if Grider is willing for this to die down, but I hope he is."

4

SQUIRE POTTER couldn't talk Grider out of the warrant the second time, so he reluctantly made out a warrant charging Bill Willie Blewett with assault upon the persons of Jeff Lewis and Lem Mayhugh. He assigned a deputy to serve the warrant and make the arrest. Jacob Skiles told the deputy that Blewett was cutting weeds in the back field, but the deputy couldn't find him. He didn't try overly hard, but he did look around. Weeds had been freshly chopped, but the chopper was nowhere to be seen. The deputy rode on back to Bowling Green and reported his failure to Squire Potter.

The magistrate spat some tobacco juice out the open window. "I always said that Blewett is part eel. He's a squirmy man. Well, try once more, but don't overheat yourself. I'da liked to see Blewett chuck that rock. Still, I'm glad he didn't kill the scamp. That wouldn't do nobody any good."

The deputy made a second trip the next day. He found some more weeds freshly cut, but that was all he found. He rode back to town empty-handed. He reported to his superior.

"So he squirmed out again. Maybe your eyesight's a little teched. Personally, I don't recommend you goin' into a woods singlehanded to capture Bill Willie Blewett. He might not see it just right. This thing's going to be puzzling when Elvis really gets demanding. But I'll lay you four bits I'll be hearing from Elvis about this. What'll I tell him?"

"Tell him about the fox huntin' you've done with Bill Willie," said the deputy irreverently. "Or maybe change the subject on him like you done last week when Old Man Jim Shanks come to see you about the feller that stole his chickens."

"Maybe I could, but it wouldn't surprise me if Elvis Grider's a hard man to change the subject on. Still I guess I'd better try. Funny about you making both of those trips out there and not seeing hide nor hair of Bill Willie."

"Yesterday I didn't see nobody sure enough, but today there was a feller workin' in the field when I come in sight of it. I couldn't make no affidavit that it was Bill Willie though. Could have been somebody that just happened along. At that distance you can't say for certain who a feller is."

"I'll not deny you've got a point there. Still, I look for Elvis to be showing up before long."

Mr. Grider showed up late that afternoon. He wanted to know whether the warrant had been served on Blewett. Clearly he had his doubts. "What's a warrant for?" he asked in his hard little voice. "What good does it do? What good does a court do if it never does anything?"

"I sent Bud Holland out there two days hand running. He never saw hide nor hair of Bill Willie. Musta skipped the country when he heard we was after him."

"I thought a warrant was made out to be served if it takes two days, or three days, or twenty days. Don't we pay taxes to have it done?"

"An officer of the law can't do any more'n his best. Bill Willie Blewett isn't the only evildoer around here and I've got to do the best I can with all of them. Right now Bud is down at Rockfield where I sent him to serve a warrant on Elihu Duncan for swindling the Woodward brothers in a farm deal. It wouldn't surprise me if Elihu has skipped the country too. Geemanintally, the time we waste looking for fellers that have skipped the country!"

"You could have served that warrant on Blewett if you had tried. You can still serve it if you try. And I am going to expect you to try."

"It was a little reckless in him to tackle Jeff and Lem at the same time and both of them with axes. Both dangerous fellers, the way I have heard it. If my recollection ain't gone back on me, I've got a warrant against both of them for disturbing public worship at Providence Knob that you talked me out of serving, claiming you needed them mighty bad in your farming. I expect Jacob Skiles would be set back a right smart in his farming if Bill Willie happened to land in jail. I've tried mighty hard in my time to befriend the farmer."

"Blewett assaulted my men for doing the work I told them to do on my own land. I want them protected."

"Since you bring that up, I hear there's some argument about its being your land. I always try to do the right thing. I'll make you a proposition. If you'll bring Jeff and Lem in, I'll go out myself and catch Bill Willie and we'll try them at the same time. I'd sort of like to get all of them off my docket."

"I don't believe you have even tried to serve that warrant on Blewett."

"I haven't myself, but I sent Bud out twice like I told you. This is a right fair-sized country and we ain't got time to look in every place some evildoer might hide. My business is to preserve the peace. I don't like quarrels and rookuses. And right here and now I'm giving you some good advice free of charge. Don't try to use that land till it is settled who really does own it. I ain't saying you don't, but Jacob Skiles thinks he does, and the way I hear it he is an honest man."

"I claimed that land three years ago."

"So you did, so you did. But now there's another man claiming it. I'd ask Judge Drake to settle it. He's a fair and square man. And then I'd abide by his decision. If you say so, I'll go out and give Skiles the same advice. The way to stop trouble is before it gets started, and land trouble is the worst trouble there is."

"That land is mine. It has been mine for three years." Grider lifted a foot to the stirrup.

"Just as you say. You want me to try Jeff, Lem, and Bill Willie all at the same time? I really would like to get my docket cleared up."

Grider's answer was to swing himself on his horse and ride away. The warrant against Bill Willie Blewett was never served.

5

THERE WERE good crops in south Kentucky in the year 1803. The rains fell when needed, and after each rain there followed a period of hot, dry, growing days. Skiles and Bill Willie worked in the fields when the ground was not too wet. At other times they worked on the barn they were building, or at splitting rails for the fences they needed. They hauled field stones and built a springhouse over the largest of the springs. The cool currents flowing from the spring kept their milk and butter cool and their vegetables fresher. Skiles bought another cow and six hogs. He bought a team of mules from a farmer at Allen Springs.

"We are really going to put out a crop next year," he told Blewett. "I am going to save every ear that I can possibly spare for seed corn."

They raised an abundance of Irish potatoes and cabbages. He planted an acre in sorghum which promised ample sweetening for the winter. Lank Motley owned a sorghum mill, and was the sorghum maker for the community. It was for him a labor of affection. He had been heard to say that he wouldn't quit making sorghum even to hunt foxes. Skiles solicited his services and the second week in October was reserved for sorghum making at Three Springs. Mrs. Skiles and Rumsey hulled white beans endlessly. The boy would work fiercely for a while, then go out into the yard and walk about for ten or fifteen minutes. After that he would return to the house and continue with the shelling. There would be beans and potatoes and cabbages and corn bread for the winter. Skiles was getting four of his hogs ready for their winter's meat.

Many things were running through Jacob Skiles's mind. One of them was the enlargement of the house which Bill Willie had built. It was serving well and with a reasonable degree of comfort. Skiles wanted a larger and more pretentious home, though his wife had learned to love the place, small as it was. Another thing was the store which he planned to open in town. He had planned to open it in the fall, but the summer had been so full there had been no time for anything away from Three Springs. Also, he had not found anyone who quite suited him to manage the store. Bill Willie could but he couldn't spare him from his place. Hardcastle was getting a good deal of trade, and that always puzzled Jacob Skiles. He bought something from Hardcastle every now and then, but every time he made a purchase he decided it would be the last. Within a week or two he had forgotten the resolve and would stop in to buy something else. Hardcastle was more alert than the other two storekeepers. There could be no doubt of that. Also, his supply of merchandise was ampler. But Skiles never trusted the man and had not since his first visit to the store. Priscilla Skiles did not trust him either, but frequently was pleased by the merchandise he carried.

One day Skiles came home from town and his wife read in his face at the first glance that something had happened.

"I bought a site for the store today."

"I knew you had done something, Mr. Skiles. Where?"

"Across the street from the tavern. I had to pay a high price for it, but it is the best site in town."

"Are you going to start building right away?"

"Not till I get the crops gathered and the fall planting done. I'm in no special hurry till I find somebody I am willing to put in charge of it, but it is so well located that if I hadn't got it somebody else would."

"Mrs. Motley came to see me while you were in town. She wants me to make six peach cobblers for the basket meeting."

"I had forgotten about the basket meeting. Something was said about it at the last preaching day, but it had slipped my mind. When is it?"

"You would forget that I am your wife and that Rumsey is your son if we didn't remind you of it every few days. It is a week from next Saturday."

"I won't go unless you solemnly promise me some of the cobbler. I am puzzled whether I ought to build the store of brick or stone. There is a lot of good building stone around here."

"I like brick. And I'm to take a crock of cucumber pickles, and I won't say that the pickles don't strain my generosity just a little."

"I wouldn't have let it strain mine. I wouldn't have given more than half a crock."

"Mrs. Motley is in charge, so I will do what she says. Every woman around here is going to take something important. The main preacher at the meeting is to be a Dr. Hume from Nashville."

"I've heard Brother Galloway talk about him. He claims he is the best preacher this side of Virginia."

"The best this side of Scotland, the way I heard it. Guess where he is going to stay."

"At Brother Galloway's, I suppose."

"You are no better supposer than I am. He is going to stay at the Griders'."

"The Griders'? How'd that happen?"

"Mr. Grider asked Brother Galloway to put him at his house. That makes me think of something I've been meaning to ask you. Have you and Mr. Grider settled about that land that he claims?"

"We have never even talked about it. But he has let it alone since Bill Willie caught his two men cutting down the cedar trees. I doubt if there are many days when Bill Willie doesn't manage to pass that tract of land just to see what tricks Grider may have been up to." He paused, and then an idea struck him. "I may need some timber from there when I build the store."

6

THE BASKET MEETING was the main topic of thought and talk the next week. The section was mainly Presbyterian, but there was a healthy minority of Baptists and Methodists, and they heartily joined in the preparation. And, in unison, all prayed for clear weather. The meeting was to be held in the Covington Woods, just east of the town. There was a large barn near by in which women and children could find shelter if their prayers went unanswered. The Baptists jestingly affirmed that they wouldn't need the barn since their doctrine had affinity with wet weather. The Methodists replied that the arrangement suited them perfectly since in case of rain they would have the whole barn to themselves. If the Presbyterians gave thought to the possibility of rain, they made no mention of it. A platform was built on the margin of a cleared place in the woods. Enough crude seats were contrived to take care of the women and children and older people. The others could stand or sit on the ground.

Every home was busy preparing food and getting clothes ready for the great day. The countryside was heavy with the spicy odors of cooking. Anyone passing Brother Tobias Jenkins' house on Friday would have known, without benefit of vision, that a sheep, one or more, was being barbecued on the premises. Brother Jenkins was conscious of his mastery of the fine art of barbecuing a sheep and reveled in it. He purposed that in this instance even his high standard should be surpassed. Three quarters of a mile away Mr. Joe Madison was barbecuing two shoats. He was aware of the favor evoked by Brother Jenkins' barbecued sheep, and he resolved that there would be as much smacking of lips over his meat as over that of his neighbor. Mr. Breed Loving had killed a yearling calf and was roasting its better parts. There would be plenty of meat at the basket meeting. Mrs. Tate Hobson and Mrs. Hez Claypool were between them making enough bread for the entire crowd. Mrs. Jacob Skiles was getting her six peach cobblers ready. Her crock of cucumber pickles waited in the springhouse. Mrs. Charley Drake was baking six cakes. Her crock of pickles also was waiting. Mrs. Clint Porter and old Mrs. Younglove were each to bring a gallon of butter beans, and Mrs. Jess Spalding a hundred ears of boiled corn, broken in half. Every lady of the community was to come with the choicest product of her kitchen.

Everything was moving along fine, and Mrs. Motley was pleased at the spirit of co-operation she had found among her neighbors. It was the custom at basket meetings for everybody to bring some of everything, but she decided that the great meal would be best served by specialization. No one had disappointed her in the least, but Mr. Elvis Grider had left her puzzled. He heard her request for a barbecued young goat in acid silence. He had a flock of goats and some very fine young ones.

"No," he said in his dry, brittle tones, "I can't spare a goat, but I will bring something that will be more desirable. You may depend on it."

She wanted very much to inquire what it would be, but she said nothing, and his manner definitely did not invite further inquiry. "You will be pleased. I think everybody will be pleased."

Mrs. Motley thanked him and turned away. She would await with interest Mr. Grider's contribution to the dinner. On the way back she stopped at Three Springs and told Priscilla Skiles that there would be no barbecued goat on the tables.

"Mr. Skiles said last night that Mr. Grider would never bring anything you asked him to. Other people will bring meat, so Mr. Grider will bring no meat. Remember when the preacher was taking up a collection to build the church? He wouldn't give anything for brick because other people did. He wouldn't give anything for the roof because other people helped buy the roof. He wouldn't give for anything that he would have to share with others. So he gave the pulpit. He will think that it is his pulpit all the time. He won't have to divide it with anybody. I do wonder what he will bring."

7

JACOB SKILES had talked with Jim Bettersworth, who lived three miles south of town, about a book he had, and Bettersworth was so interested that he was promised the loan of the book. On Friday, Skiles sent Bill Willie Blewett to take the book to the Bettersworth home. There wasn't much work that was very demanding. If there had been, the nearness of the basket meeting would have dulled the incentive. Bill Willie drove out in the Skiles's new gig. He left the book with Bettersworth and was on his way home when he saw a man trudging along the trail. The man was dressed like a preacher and carried a valise in his right hand. His broad-brimmed black hat flapped somewhat rhythmically as he walked along. Bill Willie stopped and asked the man if he would like a ride.

The answering voice was heavy with a brogue and his words flavored with culture. "This is kindly of you and there is great tiredness in my poor legs. Not the tiredness of walking for I am used to that, but there is very little riding in Scotland and I have not yet got used to it here. My horse too seemed not used to such long travel for it went lame and I left it with a farmer two miles back. A ride would be most welcome."

Bill Willie was having trouble identifying the man, some traveling parson fresh from the old country, he thought. "Where would you like to go, sir?"

"I suppose to the home of the Presbyterian minister. The name, I believe, is Galloway, of whom there were many in Dumfries."

"I know where he lives. I can take you there. Blewett is my name."

"Blewett? It's a new name in my experience, though doubtless of distinction here. My name is William Hume. I live in Nashville."

Then this was the preacher for the basket meeting. "Glad to make your acquaintance, Brother Hume. You will have a big crowd to hear you tomorrer."

"I pray that my words may be worthy. My hearers will be. Of that I am certain. How long have you been in this settlement, Brother Blewett?"

"A little more'n a year. I work for Jacob Skiles."

"Ah, then I can see that Brother Skiles is greatly favored in his help. I trust that I may be honored by your presence in the congregation tomorrow."

"I aim to be there."

"It's a fair country you have here, Brother Blewett. Its greenness brings Scotland to mind."

"There's lots of good ground around here."

"And doubtless able men to till it. I never pass through a new country but that I try to forecast its appearance, say a century hence. It is a whimsical notion, my friend, but if we should be passing through here in the autumn of 1903, what would we be seeing? What strange and wonderful sights would greet our eyes? Oh, it would be changed. Change is as inevitable as sunrise. And I think it would be changed for the best. God would not agree for it to be otherwise. What fine homes would we see then? What wonderful inventions and contrivances would have wrought their marks upon the countryside?"

"Do you reckon we'll have any more wars, Reverend?"

"Who can know? There is still much evil left in man, but I do devoutly believe that he is losing the old evil faster than he is gaining the new good. But he still has enough of original sin in him to bring about dreadful things."

"That's Brother Galloway's house yonder. There he is in the back yard."

"A pleasant place. You really have been a good Samaritan, Brother Blewett."

Bill Willie drove away. The presence of the great man had left him warmed. He stopped at Mr. Hardcastle's store. Mrs. Skiles had asked him to see if the store didn't have some New Orleans sugar. A touch of it would make her peach cobblers much more tempting. The store was fairly well crowded. Some were customers, but most were merely loafers. Bill Willie caught Mr. Hardcastle's eyes and asked him if he had any sugar. If not there would be no use of him wasting the time to wait his turn. The storekeeper said he had got some in yesterday. So Bill Willie waited.

"I expect the biggest turnout tomorrer Bowling Green ever had," said one of the loafers in a loud voice. "If the weather stays good I look for three hundred people out there, maybe more'n that."

"I'll say one thing," said another, "if I was the sheriff I'd keep my eyes peeled. Pig Smith said he'd sold more licker at the tavern today than all the rest of the week put together."

"Public worship ain't no place to drink whisky. A feller's liable to land in jail."

"Jail's the place for any feller that drinks whisky at public worship. We need preachin' more'n we need whisky drinkin'. It's all right some places, but I'll help the sheriff take any feller who's had too much tomorrer."

"They say the preacher from Tennessee can curl your hair. I hate to say it, bein' as I'm a born Presboterum, but the best preachin' I hear in a coon's age was a Methodis' down on Gasper River. I need to hear me some good Presboterum preachin'."

Mr. Hardcastle then said he was ready to wait on Bill Willie. How much sugar was wanted?

"What's it a pound?"

"Two bits a pound. Make you a special bargain o' four pounds for six bits. Ain't hardly a chance you'll ever get it that cheap again. Good Noo Orleens sugar's skeercer than hens' teeth."

"Give you a dollar and forty cents for eight pounds."

"Can't do it. I got to live too."

"You liable to live out your time if you make your prices right. I recollect a storekeeper in Virginia that overcharged people, so the Lord give him lingerin' consumption and he died. I jest thought I'd tell you."

Mr. Hardcastle sighed. "Seein' as how I don't have to starve right away, and tomorrer bein' the basket meetin', I'll let you have it at your figger."

"Bought more'n you told me to," Bill Willie explained to Mrs. Skiles. "I just sort o' outtalked Old Hardcastle."

"Sugar will come in handy specially before sorghum making time. Come in the kitchen and see my peach cobblers."

"Never saw anything purtier that was made to eat," said Bill Willie after he had looked them over.

8

At DAWN the next day the sky was immaculate. The pink in the east darkened into coral, then into deep orange. The blaze spread and the rim of the sun showed above the horizon. Then it rose and bathed the world in a soft, tremulous light. The light caught on the dew-drenched leaves and grass and multiplied itself by infinity. The world became a vast concourse of light and sound. Chickens crowed hysterically. Cows bawled in the pastures and were answered by calves penned in lots. The trees were filled with a tumult of bird song.

Though the day promised warmth, smoke spiraled from every kitchen chimney. Breakfast would be eaten early so as to get the morning routine cleared for the greater routine of the basket meeting. There was a bit of hurry in everything. The stock was fed hurriedly. The cows were milked hurriedly. There was hurry in eating and in clearing the dishes. Vegetables were gathered from the gardens, and fruit from wherever available. The next day was Sunday and many homes would have company remaining over from the basket meeting.

Bill Willie Blewett took some old pieces of planking and made a sort of crate so that the peach cobblers could be carried without damage to their appearance, of which the maker was justly proud. She lifted them into the crate herself, regarding them with proper appreciation. She looked at the crock of cucumber pickles with real regret. The pioneers regarded pickles as a preventive against the scourge of scurvy, something to be given away only in case of an emergency. She laid out Rumsey's Sunday clothes on the bed. He could perform the chore of putting them on himself except for the final details, which his mother would trust to no one. By the side of her son's she placed her husband's best clothes, the white shirt ruffled and starched into a stiffness that would torment him through the day.

Bill Willie sat waiting in the wagon drawn up before the house. Finally they were ready. He had already placed the cobblers and pickles in that part of the wagon in which they would ride with most safety. Two chairs were already in the wagon. The horses dozed in the early morning sun. No one could have hoped for a finer day. There was no trace of clouds in the sky, though faint wisps of mist hung loosely against the distant woodlands. It was a day ordained for a basket meeting.

Jacob Skiles placed Rumsey in the wagon seat at Bill Willie's side. He and his wife sat on the chairs in the wagon bed. Bill Willie clucked to the horses and they moved away.

"I can't keep from wondering what Mr. Grider is going to bring," said Priscilla Skiles. "I have been trying to think ever since Clara Motley told me what he told her."

The wagon rumbled along the road, now worn smooth and dusty in places. The state of the road eased Priscilla Skiles's anxiety about her cobblers. They passed the Grider house, but there was no sight of anyone, no hint of activity. A farmer near town had cut a field of late hay and it lay curing in the sun. One sensed its fragrance with every breath he drew. Skiles's eyes rested thoughtfully on the field.

"That's good hay," he said. "I hope the rain stays off till he can get it in a stack."

"It won't rain today, will it?" his wife asked.

"There's no sign of it, except maybe an odd feel in this air."

"I noticed that too," said Bill Willie from the driver's seat.

"Don't you men notice it too much. I hate to think what a rain would do to my peach cobblers."

Her husband lifted his eyes to the sky and surveyed it casually. "It's the Presbyterians that'll destroy your cobblers, not the rain, my dear."

"Then it is all right. That is what I made them for."

They turned to the right at Mr. Hardcastle's store, and ten minutes later had arrived at the meeting grounds. Bill Willie drove up to the tables as close as he could. He threw the reins around the whip socket, then got down from the wagon and waited for the others to get down. He lifted the crate of cobblers to the ground.

Mrs. Motley came hurrying up. "I'm glad you got here early. You wouldn't mind if I take a peep at your cobblers, would you? I know they are just too pretty to eat."

"If it hadn't been for Mr. Blewett I would never have got them here in good order. He made the crate."

She daintily lifted the cloth, and Mrs. Motley's little cries of ecstasy indicated her entire approval.

"Get the pickles out, please, Mr. Blewett. They aren't pretty like the cobblers, but they make good eating."

"Of course they will. There is Brother Jenkins with his sheep. I just love barbecued sheep. Mr. Blewett, put the cobblers on that little table at the end. That is where I want them. Put the crock of pickles at the end of the long table. Excuse me, I want to see the barbecued sheep. They say that Brother Jenkins is the best sheep barbecuer in the county." Mrs. Motley bustled away toward the barbecued sheep. Mrs. Skiles looked after her somewhat oddly. Such affirmativeness was not a normal part of Mrs. Motley's personality.

People were then beginning to arrive in a fairly constant stream. The single horses and the teams, both of horses and oxen, were hitched in a near-by grove toward which the wagons circled after the food they bore had been placed properly in the care of Mrs. Motley. A hundred yards away from the tables prepared for dining was the preaching ground. The older people were already taking their places close up to the preaching stand. There was to be singing at ten o'clock, and at half after ten Brother Galloway was to preach. The dinner was to be placed on the tables and ready by noon.

"Brother Galloway generally doesn't preach too long," Mrs. Motley told her husband, "but sometimes he forgets. Do you know any way to see that he doesn't forget this time? He ought to be through by a quarter till twelve at the latest. It'd be better if he stopped a half after eleven. It takes time to get folks lined up."

"You're right, Clara, but just how would you stop him till he got ready to stop? Brother Galloway isn't exactly the man I'd holler *stop* to." He broke off and looked at the skies. "Funny. This air feels like rain, but there isn't a cloud in sight."

No mistake had been made in placing Mrs. Motley in charge of the food. It was her nature to be calm and unruffled, and to have generous thoughts of everybody. Also, she could sense quickly the mild and subtle frictions that unless properly eased might cause trouble. Her eyes, searching all arrivals, caught sight of a wagon turning in toward the tables, and just behind it a carriage.

"There are the Griders," she said to her husband. "What on earth do you suppose he has in that wagon?"

"It'll be revealed in Elvis' own time and way. I am not much interested, but if you find out let me know."

His wife met the Griders. "Good morning, Mrs. Grider; good morning, Mr. Grider; good morning, Nat. You have such a pretty carriage. Please tell me what you have in that wagon. I am famishing to know."

Mr. Grider assisted his wife out of the wagon. The boy got out by himself. "I have brought something very unusual," said Mr. Grider in his dry, brittle tones. "There is something in that wagon that has never been seen in Kentucky before. I have brought twenty fine watermelons."

Mrs. Motley started to ask what a watermelon was, but caught herself just in time. "Twenty!" she said heartily. "That will make the dinner perfect."

"I secured the seed from a kinsman in Georgia. It seemed to me that this section ought to be specially suited to growing them. I doubt if the people in Georgia can grow any as fine as these."

Mrs. Motley had very little idea as to how twenty watermelons would fit into the basket dinner, but she bowed her assent, her smile never failing.

"They were picked early yesterday morning, and we kept them in the springhouse till we were ready to come. I covered them with quilts to keep them cool. I brought two butcher knives to cut them with."

"Not many people would have thought of that. Why don't you leave them in the wagon till you are ready for them? They really will be something special. Just leave the wagon where it is."

"They ought to be eaten the last thing. I'll slice them when you get ready. I think I can cut them so as to have a piece for everybody. My cousin in Georgia raises them every year."

"Then just as soon as preaching is over you come to the wagon."

"I think I'll stay here. I'll go to preaching later in the day. I want to hear Dr. Hume since he is to be the guest in our home tonight. He was to come last night, but Dr. Galloway particularly wanted him to stay at his house."

Mrs. Motley saw her husband standing with a group of men. "This is one fox hunt I'll break up before it starts," she said grimly. To him she said, "Mr. Motley, come here a minute. I need you."

He came, a trifle surprised at her manner. "Tell me," she said. "Just what is a watermelon?"

He puckered his brow in thought. "I've heard of them, but I can't say I ever saw one. Maybe I read about them somewhere. I think it's something that grows in some hot country. What did you ask that for?"

"Mr. Grider has brought a whole wagonload of them."

"Load of what? What for?"

"What I want to know is what one is like. Is it like a pumpkin? Or is it like a muskmelon? I saw some of them in Virginia."

"What does it look like?"

"I didn't see it. He has got them covered up with quilts. He brought them for people to eat, of course. We have planned to give them out last. Was that right?"

"I'd like to be of help, Clara, but that's one question you will have to answer. Let's hunt up Jacob Skiles and ask him."

"Hunt him up for me. I'm busy. You'd think that those things were solid gold the way Mr. Grider acts about them."

"It's just about time for preaching to begin, but I'll see if I can find him."

Within two minutes he was back with Skiles. "I think you are right to give them out last," he said. "I've talked with people who have tasted them, and I am positive they are sweet. It's the first time I ever heard of them being grown around here."

"I didn't want to ask him about them, but I didn't want to make a mistake."

They were gathering then for preaching. Brother Galloway accompanied by a distinguished-looking man, obviously Dr. Hume, the visiting preacher, arrived. The two sat in chairs, at one side, up front. Brother Galloway's eyes were intent on the pages of the Bible, open on his lap. It was time for the singing. Brother Jess Graham arose from his seat and came forward to lead.

"I need help," he said. "In a way this is a Presbyterian meeting, but I have already seen twenty Methodists here, and maybe more Baptists than that. One of the Baptists is Brother Tom Willoughby, and he leads singing just as well as I do. We will have two songs. I'll lead one of them and ask him to lead the other. Come on up here, Brother Willoughby, and while I am leading this one you be picking out the one you want."

Brother Willoughby was obviously pleased. He was a short, chubby, round-faced man, and he beamed all the way down the grassy aisle. Brother Graham sounded a few tentative pitches, found the one he wanted and launched into the favorite of the Presbyterian churches, "O God, Our Help in Ages Past."

The Presbyterian part of the congregation was familiar with both the words and tune of Dr. Watts's hymn, and the singing was spirited, but carried on with becoming dignity. Brother Graham carried his singers through all four of the stanzas. He brought the hymn to a close and motioned for the congregation to be seated.

He turned to Brother Willoughby. "If the hymn had been twice as long, you would have heard some real singing. It takes time to warm up Presbyterians."

"It sounded mighty fine to me. I disremember ever hearing it before."

"Try it out at Providence Knob sometime." He turned to the congregation. "Brother Willoughby will lead us in a song of his own choosing. Let everybody sing."

Brother Willoughby announced that the song would be that favorite of the camp meetings, "Oh, Fathers, Will You Meet Me?"

The Baptists and Methodists knew it very well already, and it had about it a contagion that spread quickly to the Presbyterians. The leader started the hymn with enthusiasm, and ten minutes later closed it as one inspired. He marched up and down the open space in front of the preacher's stand, beating time with his feet, his shoulders, his head and his hands. Brother Graham held up one finger, signaling that there was time for one more stanza. Brother Willoughby nodded his understanding. He had used up *fathers, mothers, brothers, sisters.* So he moved on into *cousins.*

> "Oh, cousins, will you meet me,
> Oh, cousins, will you meet me,
> Oh, cousins, will you meet me
> On Canaan's happy shore?"

Under the leader's inspired direction the antiphonal response spread its volume far out on the tranquil air:

"By the grace of God we'll meet you,
By the grace of God we'll meet you,
By the grace of God we'll meet you
On Canaan's happy shore."

They were all singing, Presbyterians, Methodists, Baptists, singing in the fervor of wholehearted promise. Then Brother Galloway was preaching. The congregation didn't know it at first, but the preacher had an immediate motive in his sermon. The new church building was going up too slowly to suit him. A sort of building lethargy had settled down upon his people. The hospitality of Brother Jenkins's commodious house was a duller of the eagerness with which they had entered the project of the new building. They had paid the contributions they promised, but it wasn't enough. The people were poor, but less so than those from whom had come the wherewithal for Solomon's Temple. And the story of that building was the Scripture he used as the text for his sermon. He never brought the matter into direct application, but it was a dull-witted member who didn't discover the inference. He dramatized the building all the way from the cutting down of the great cedars on the side of Mount Lebanon to the unrestrained joy of the people at the completion. "Man must have a home to raise his children in. He must also have a home to let his faith grow in." Bill Willie Blewett lifted his eyes as if looking for the roof in which his two dollars were invested.

Before the benediction was said, Mr. Lank Motley announced to the congregation the proper order of dining just as his wife had told him. He chose to conclude the directions on a jocular note.

"Now you all do just like I say, and if there's a single one of you who is still hungry when everything is gone you just come to see me and I'll fix you up. The best eating you ever did in your lives you are going to do today right off those tables, and there will be some things that will surprise you enough to pop your eyes out."

The preacher brought his hearers back to a state of reverence and dismissed them.

Mrs. Motley saw the congregation erupting from the meeting place and waved her assistants into action, each in her appointed place. Mrs. Breed Loving stood at the head of the line of guides and guards. Mrs. Loving's formula, which she spoke often enough for all in the line to be advised properly, was:

"The first thing is Mr. Joe Madison's barbecued pig, then next is my husband's roasted beef, then Mr. Jenkins' barbecued sheep. Take whichever one you like best. Take you a pickle and some bread. After that we have pies and cake to go around."

Mrs. Junius Coleman and Mrs. Charles Drake stood at the meat table, subtly suggesting, subtly hurrying the line by. Mrs. Ed Younglove dipped an overflowing spoon of butter beans onto each plate. Mrs. Hobson and Mrs. Claypool served the bread which they had made. Mrs. Motley was everywhere, up and down the line. "When you have finished eating that come on back for some cake or peach cobbler."

"What's Elvis Grider got in that wagon?" a man asked her.

"It's a secret," she said smiling, "but there will be a piece for you."

Mr. Jenkins' barbecued sheep disappeared first, it being the favorite of the diners. Mr. Madison's barbecued shoat ran low, but there was still plenty of Mr. Loving's roast beef. Appetites had been whetted razor-keen by talk and anticipation, and the more robust ones came back for second helpings of meat. The butter beans held out well, but Mrs. Younglove kept her serving spoon in motion till they were gone. The last of the bread and the final portions of the roast beef were carried away on the same plates.

Mrs. Motley whispered to her husband, and he mounted a log and called for attention. He announced that the pies and cakes awaited the diners. Mr. Motley asked them to pass by the table as rapidly as possible. He said whimsically that the pies and cakes were so good that it was a pity there wasn't available a whole one of each for everyone there, but they would have to do the best they could with what they had. The diners would keep moving, please, but not crowd.

The ladies managed the pies and cakes so that they lasted till all were served. Some went back to their seats; others stood about eating theirs. There was audible appreciation of Priscilla Skiles's peach cobblers. But all the diners managed to keep the Grider wagon within their field of vision. The word had gone about that mystery was involved. Mr. Grider and Storekeeper Hardcastle sat protectively on the wagon seat. Over and over again Mrs. Motley told inquirers that what the wagon contained was a secret, but that it would be revealed soon.

Brother Galloway and Dr. Hume sat apart, with their empty plates upon their laps, and watched the Grider wagon.

"They keep saying that he has something new there," commented Brother Galloway. "I do not know that I have much relish for new things. What I want are old-time foods, old-time friends, and the old-time religion."

"But, my brother, consider. A few minutes ago you were eating peach cobbler with great heartiness. How old do you think it is? It is something I never saw in Scotland. The two songs they sang before you preached—did they become good hymns only after they were old? And you would not hold for a moment that anything of great age is ensured to be good. Murder, for instance, is just about as old as the race."

"I despise the *bad* old things as heartily as you do, but I live by the *good* old things."

Dr. Hume smiled gently. "And yet I hear that you are building a new church."

"There wasn't any other kind here. It would be a new one or nothing. I shall hope that it doesn't look new."

Elvis Grider and the storekeeper pulled aside the quilts and began lifting the watermelons to some planks laid on the ground at the side of the wagon. The melons were long, striped, and surprisingly uniform in size. Mr. Grider with a keen butcher knife cut off a thin nub from each end of the melons. Then he began slicing half-inch circles from the whole melon. These Hardcastle halved. The people crowded up as close as good manners would permit and with great interest watched the scene.

"Looks like something poison to me," said one to the man standing by him.

"Then I'll take your slice. Looks like good eatin' to me."

"Looks to me like Elvis been getherin' his gourds," said another.

"Don't you worry about what they look like. I'll eat your helpin'."

"It wouldn't look quite right to take a piece and not eat it," one of the ladies said to another.

"Well, I'm going to take a piece and I'm going to eat it," her companion said.

"So am I," said a third. "Mr. Grider wouldn't bring it to the basket meeting, or at least Clara Motley wouldn't let him if it wasn't good. I'm anxious to try it."

Mrs. Motley signaled her husband and again he played the role of announcer and interpreter. "Get in line, all of you. Ladies first, children second, and no-account men last of all. You are now going to be given something never before tasted by mortal man, at least not around here. You can always depend on Brother Elvis Grider being

first in everything. Last spring he got watermelon seed in faraway
Georgia and brought them to Kentucky, and the way they grow here
proves what I have always said—that Kentucky is the original Garden
of Eden. If I am wrong, Reverend—" bowing low to Brother Galloway—"correct me. Not being corrected, I will proceed to say that
Kentucky is not only the garden spot of the world, but also the kitchen
and dining room of the entire universe. From what I hear the watermelons of Georgia are practically runts, but just look at these that
Brother Grider raised on his own farm. There is practically no telling
what we will be raising here a year from now if we can only get people with enough sense to go get the seeds. At half after two o'clock
Brother William Hume, now from Tennessee and before that from
Scotland where it is against the law not to be a Presbyterian, will
preach, and you want to be there and get a good seat even if you have
to stand. Except Brother Galloway, he's the greatest preacher you'll
ever get a chance to hear. And the way to show that you are thankful
for what you've had to eat is to be there on time. Much obliged, one
and all."

He went over and offered his services to Elvis Grider in passing
out the slices of watermelon. The line moved swiftly and within ten
minutes everyone had his share of melon, and was eating, at first tentatively, then with growing delight. The children, under no restraint
to eat slowly and so prolong the pleasure, ate their slices quickly. Those
less curbed by discipline ran to their mothers asking for more. "I never
in all my life tasted anything as good, Mama. Is it all gone?"

"Maybe we'll have some next year. I see your daddy putting the
seeds in his pocket."

The notion to save seeds spread fast, and other men began putting
seeds in their pockets.

Mr. Hardcastle saw it and was racked by the sudden pain of a lost
opportunity. "Why didn't we save the seeds? The store could have
made a right smart selling them."

"You are in the business, Hardcastle. How did it happen that you
didn't think of it?"

"I knew there was something I ought to think of, all the time I
knew it, but it come to me too late. The way the people like them
watermelons, I could have sold the seeds for ten dollars, maybe fifteen."

"There isn't any profit in forgetting. I hope you have learned a lesson, Hardcastle."

They cleaned up the grounds, and carefully salvaged all scraps. Jeff Lewis and Lem Mayhugh went about picking up every scrap of watermelon rind and carrying it to the Grider wagon. "Good for the hogs," Mr. Grider had told them. "I wish Hardcastle had thought about the seeds."

"Mommy, I'd like to walk around awhile and see things," Rumsey Skiles told his mother.

Priscilla Skiles looked at her husband for his assent. "It's all right, isn't it?"

"Not for more than a few minutes. It isn't long till preaching time. Yonder is something I have been expecting." He pointed.

"What is it? I don't see anything."

"That bank of clouds. We are going to have bad weather before night."

In the west and southwest a drift of heavy clouds had risen above the distant treetops. "I hope Brother Hume doesn't preach too long," Skiles said wryly.

Bill Willie Blewett, remembering what he had heard said at the store the day before, had been watching alertly for signs of disorder. He saw the first then. He saw Lem Mayhugh signal to Jeff Lewis, and together they disappeared into the deep woods at the back of the tables. Bill Willie noted the leer which had accompanied the signal. So he followed, keeping carefully out of sight. He saw Lem dig into some rotted leaves at the side of a log and bring out a bottle of whisky. The two drank all of the whisky that was in the bottle, then started back to the preaching place. Bill Willie waited until they were out of sight and then went back himself. He caught sight of them sitting down on a crude seat at the back. These were the two men who had broken up preaching services at Providence Knob two months before. Bill Willie sat down on the bench by them. He saw from the corner of his eye the surprised look that overspread their faces when they saw who their seatmate was.

"You goin' to stay for preachin'?" he asked Lem.

"Course I'm goin' to stay. Ain't nobody says I can't."

"You drunk too much whisky."

"Want a dram?"

"I want you to listen to the preacher."

"What'd he say?" Jeff asked.

"Said we got to listen to the parson."

"Le's chaw an ear offn him."

Bill Willie took a long, wicked-looking knife out of his pocket. He opened the blade, laid the knife on his lap, pointing toward Lem, and shifted his coat to cover the knife from view. "You jest let out even a little holler, and I'll cut you half in two. You've broke up enough meetin's, and this is one you ain't."

Lem stared down at the coat concealing the knife. He knew it was there, its point toward him, and the invisibility of it made it all the more frightening. He knew something about the man who held that knife. He turned to Jeff. "Le's go," he whispered.

Bill Willie overheard the whisper. "If Lewis wants to go let him. The meetin' would smell better without him. You are stayin' and you're goin' to set right where you're settin' now."

Lem looked hard at the coat draped across Bill Willie's lap, and at the right arm that disappeared under the coat. He turned and looked at Jeff again. Then he slumped down and five minutes later both men were sound asleep.

Brother Graham and Brother Willoughby led in singing a hymn which their ancestors had brought from England to the colonies:

> "Arise, my soul, and stretch thy wings,
> Thy better portion trace;
> Arise from transitory things
> To heaven, thy native place."

Brother Galloway led in a long and fervent prayer. Then he introduced Dr. Hume to the congregation. Warren County, he said, was fast losing its remoteness. Only a week before a distinguished Virginian had stopped for the night in Bowling Green, and had stated positively that it was one of the most promising settlements of his acquaintance. And on that day Bowling Green was doubly favored by the presence of one of the nation's great preachers and teachers, Dr. William Hume, who was bringing for the uplift of his hearers the true Presbyterianism of John Knox himself.

Dr. Hume stood before his congregation, a small man, patrician in face and manner. His voice filled the spaces before him, and yet was neither harsh nor in any way objectionable, and his Scottish burr was music in the ears of those who heard him. He preached from a text befitting a saint and a scholar: *The spirit of man is the candle of the Lord.*

It was not the sort of text the people were used to. It challenged the hearers more than it evangelized them. The spirit or, as we sometimes say, the mind of man was the Lord's main agent in brightening up a dark world. The world was filled with dark places, and that darkness would ever remain a threat to man's progress and happiness until it was driven away by the light shed by the spirit of man, kindled by the spirit of the Lord.

Lem Mayhugh began snoring loudly. Bill Willie punched him firmly in the ribs with his elbow. "Stop that noise," he said in an undertone. "People want to hear the preacher's sermon."

Several sitting near understood part of Bill Willie's gesture and nodded their approval, then turned their attention back to the preacher. He was naming in eloquent detail some of the instances of man's spirit shedding light in the dark places. "Was it not the spirit of man that threw light upon the dark places of injustice and tyranny? Was not our struggle for independence the direct consequence of seeing how terrible is the darkness of oppression? You and your mothers and fathers traveled long and weary miles to found a home here. Why were they willing, yea, eager to do that? For many reasons. The chief one was that your spirits, your candles, were the ordained illuminators of the darkness of tyranny, of poverty, of ignorance. Your mind showed you that while God had blessed many of the poverty-stricken He had not blessed poverty itself. Your minds showed you that hunger is not part of godliness. They told you that in such a move you could add better bread, better clothes, better homes, better education to your posterity, and by the same additions enlarge God's light in the world."

The sermon wound to a close, and almost all of those present wished that it were longer. They tasted it with relish to the last syllable. Bill Willie Blewett closed his knife very carefully under the coat on his lap and put it back into his pocket. Very suddenly he became aware that the sun was no longer shining, that an unexpected darkness had settled on the world. Jacob Skiles had listened intently to the sermon, but he had been aware all the time of the dark, purplish bank of cloud that had risen far above the western horizon, stopped there and paused for a while as if giving Dr. Hume time to finish his sermon. Then it moved steadily and ominously on to Bowling Green.

No one ever knew whether the preacher finished his sermon in its entirety, or cut it a trifle short to yield to the oncoming cloud. The "Amen" of the benediction went unheard, lost in a jarring crash of thunder that seemed to shake the firmament. The dismissal was sudden and complete. Everyone left the scene with some semblance of decorum, but the second a person got clear of the little fringe of trees that bordered the preaching ground he hurried frantically for his horse or wagon. The teams were hitched to the wagons in frantic haste. The roar of the thunder then was almost continuous.

As he left, Bill Willie Blewett saw Jeff Lewis running ahead of him toward the road. But Lem was not with him. He turned and in a brief glance saw that Lem had fallen to the ground where he had sat and lay there sound asleep. Bill Willie smiled grimly. A wetting would do Lem no harm. Blewett hurried to give such help as he could to Jacob Skiles with the team. Ahead of him walked Brother Galloway and Dr. Hume, seemingly in no hurry whatever, and taking no notice of the approaching rain except that each was carrying his Bible tucked under his long coat. The trail out to the road was congested with wagons.

And then the rain hit. There was no preliminary and desultory sprinkling. It started raining in full force. It fell not in drops, but in sheets, driven ahead of powerful gusts of wind. Bill Willie swung onto the Skiles wagon as Jacob drove it by him. A tree crashed between them and the wagon in front.

"Thank God, it missed us! Lend a hand, Bill Willie. We can get it out of the way."

Skiles and Bill Willie jumped from the wagon and ran to the fallen tree, but it was too heavy for them. Song leader Jess Graham, a hulking giant of a man, came running from the wagon behind, and the three of them lifted the body of the tree to one side. Everybody was soaked by then. The day had begun so pleasingly that no one had prepared for this emergency. They passed three wagons at the side of the road, and saw those who had ridden in the wagons huddled for shelter beneath.

"That's no help," Skiles said. "They will be the wettest of all."

"Turned out to be a Baptis' meetin'," said Bill Willie wryly. "That is what we get for letting Tom Willoughby help with the singin'."

"I like to get wet," said Rumsey.

"Spoken bravely for a lad who is already soaked," said his father.

"I don't like it," said Priscilla. "I suppose I am a true Presbyterian."

The wind had stilled and the rain had settled into a steady downpour. The ditches at the side of the road flowed in swift torrents. "We'll get home all right if the branch isn't too deep," said Skiles.

Skiles kept thinking about the branch. Such a rain could make it too deep to ford, and that would block both the Motleys and him from their homes. But the water did not come above the hubs of their wheels, and they got across in safety. They found out later that they were just in time. In ten minutes after they reached Three Springs Bill Willie had a fire roaring up the chimney. Then he left for his cabin to start a fire there.

"Come back when you have changed your clothes," Mrs. Skiles called to him. "We have plenty of scraps left to make a good supper."

Bill Willie came back and they ate remainders from the basket meeting and talked of the day.

"I liked the watermelon, Daddy," said Rumsey drowsily.

"I saved the seeds from my piece," said Bill Willie, "and I wasn't the only one. I saw Brother Jess Graham savin' his. All at oncet it looked like Hardcastle come to his senses and he went aroun' pickin' 'em up everywhere. He might have some for sale next plantin' season."

"We'll plant Bill Willie's seeds for you next spring, Rumsey. It is time for you to be asleep."

A few minutes later the boy was on his bed sound asleep.

"People liked my cucumber pickles," his mother said proudly.

"Any feller that wouldn't's purty onery," said Bill Willie, "and when they turned folks loose at dinner them peach cobblers didn't have a chance. There's a lot o' people talkin' about them peach cobblers right now."

"Thank you, Mr. Blewett. Any woman likes to hear her cooking bragged on."

"The preaching was good too," said Skiles. "I kept my eye on you, Bill Willie. It was a funny thing, you sitting there by Lem and Jeff, and looking as solemn as a fox that had just swallowed a hound. You didn't have anything to do, I suppose, with them not disturbing the meeting."

"I set by 'em so as not to let anybody wake 'em up. They needed sleep."

"I don't know that the storm hurt the meeting any," said Mrs. Skiles. "Preaching was finished and people were ready to go home. Most people don't mind being out in the rain sometimes. I never did eat better roast beef than Mr. Breed Loving's."

9

THE NEXT DAY was clear and the ground was very wet, but there was plenty of wet-weather work to do at Three Springs, so industry on the place did not lag.

About the middle of the morning Mr. Hardcastle drove out to the Grider place. Grider sat on the front porch placing some very earnest figures on blank paper. He looked up and motioned Hardcastle to a chair. He finished his calculations, sat looking at his figures a while longer, then looked inquiringly at his visitor.

"Not much business at the store today," said Hardcastle with a slight note of apology, "so I left the old woman to tend to it. I heard some news yestidy."

"What did you hear?"

"Skiles has bought that lot across the street from the tavern, the one I tried to get you to buy."

"The price was too high. What is Skiles going to do with it?"

"My guess is he'll open a store. Every time he has come in to buy something he has looked around real inquisitive. A store there would cause ours some trouble."

Grider corrected him. "*Mine,*" he said with dry humor. "I saw that fellow Blewett at the meeting yesterday. Squire Potter was there too. Do you know why that warrant was never served on Blewett?"

"Can't say as I do. It ought to have been right then. Blewett's no good. Every time he comes to the store he wants to buy something cheaper'n its regular price."

"Skiles might have a store in mind. The place is growing fast enough for him to think that another one would get a good business, but it would hurt mine. How did you find out that he had bought it?"

"Eli Moss, the county clerk, told me yestidy. I aimed to tell you but that storm come up."

"I have been too easy with Skiles about that land of mine. The man who has just built a house beyond it, I forget the name, asked me last week to sell him that land. If he can pay a fair price I think I will let him have it, and he can fuss it out with Skiles. It has some fine timber on it, and that was what interested him most."

"Coleman is the name. He buys a lot of goods at the store."

"Go and see him. Tell him I will sell the land if the price is right.

Don't let the word get out. I would prefer to make the trade on the quiet."

But the word did get out, at least enough to justify Squire Potter's riding out to the Skiles home to tell Jacob what had happened. He found Skiles repairing the barn-lot fence.

The magistrate approached the subject of his mission obliquely: "Might be the best thing for me to do would be to mind my own business, but I say it's a mean man that'll knock a feller down without letting him know he's going to."

Skiles's eyes opened a trifle wider, but the expression on his face did not change. "Would I be the man who is about to be knocked down without warning?"

"That's about the way I look at it. To come by Richpond is about three miles out of the way, and I can't figger out why I done it unless it was maybe because I didn't want Elvis Grider to see me coming. Sometimes I'm a shy man."

"I am a shy man too sometimes, but I have a good memory for somebody who has done me a favor. I'll try to make the three miles up someday. I would appreciate knowing it if I was about to be knocked down."

"A little bird told me—maybe it was more than one bird, maybe it was a whole flock—that you claim some land that everybody knows that Elvis owns. Well, it was just one bird that chirped this time and it told me that Elvis was about to sell the tract to a man named Coleman, and right then it came to me that maybe I ought to tell you, so I took me a very pleasant ride around by Richpond. There isn't any prettier country this side of the Garden of Eden."

"A man named Coleman has built a house back there. I don't think he has been here very long. I have only seen him once. Did the little bird tell you anything else?"

"I got from one of its chirps that they are pretty hot at trading. My guess is it's like this. Elvis wants money bad enough, but he wants backing more. So if he sells that timberland, maybe he gets the money, and money is always pleasing in Elvis' sight. But if you stop that sale it'll put Coleman on his side, and make one more against you. Maybe that's not exactly it, but it is right close."

"I'll say the land is mine till a court says it isn't. If they are about to make a trade I'll stop it, and if Coleman blames me I can't help it. Why doesn't Coleman buy land from somebody who can give him a clear title?"

"I got the word from this little bird that he was a timberman back in Virginia. If he was, that is the sort of land that would catch his eye." He sighed. "I guess I'd better be riding back. Richpond is out of the way, but it makes mighty pretty traveling."

"I am greatly obliged to you, Squire. I can get along without that land temporarily, of course. Tell the little bird that no one will hear from me about this visit."

"One other thing. Elvis Grider's got some distant kinfolks named Dawsey that are bad eggs. They's a settlement of them, three families, up in the Mizpah country."

"What have they to do with it?"

"Plenty. They practically worship Elvis, and would cut a throat for him quicker'n you could wink an eye. Nero Harvey talked a little freely about Elvis one day at a turkey shooting. I guess he had had a dram or two. One of the Dawseys was there and heard him, but when Nero's barn burned down two days after that you couldn't prove a thing. We sent two deputy sheriffs out there and as far as they could find out, that barn just naturally set itself afire. This is a new country and right much scattered. So it's mighty hard to catch evildoers in the act, or prove it on them. Maybe Nero learned a lesson. I hope so."

"The Dawseys might be troublesome for a while, but they never last."

"They might last too long. Then there's a half dozen, or maybe more, pretty substantial citizens scattered over the country who have somehow got tied up with Elvis. Some of them I wouldn't want to be against me. I still have got the notion that since neither you nor Elvis needs that land there's no need to be in a hurry settling it."

"I don't want him selling it."

"I'll see that he doesn't sell it. Suppose we leave the case alone for a spell."

"All right, Squire, but I can't have him selling it. I'll look into that."

Skiles went to see Elvis Grider early the next morning. He found Grider sitting on his front porch making marks on a sheet of paper.

Grider looked up at his visitor, standing at the porch steps. A faintly puzzled expression appeared on his face. "Good morning. Come in and have a chair."

"Thank you, sir. I am in a bit of a hurry. I'll just remain standing."

Grider essayed a bit of humor. "Got dried out yet from the basket meeting?"

"I am drier than I was when I reached home. That was a heavy rain."

"Very heavy indeed, but it was a good meeting."

"An excellent meeting. Those melons you brought were mighty tasty. They caused a great deal of interest. Everyone liked them."

"They are difficult to raise. I hope to produce some for the market next season."

"Has Brother Hume gone yet?"

"Oh, yes. He left the next afternoon. His horse had practically recovered from its lameness. I am sure he made it all right. He is a powerful preacher."

"He preached a fine sermon."

"One of the best I ever heard. He is a man of faith and filled with learning. He might be a little deep for some. To what do I owe the pleasure of your visit, sir?"

"There is a matter on which we should come to some understanding. There is a tract of timberland back there—" he pointed—"to which we both claim title. My claim, I believe, is some older. You have been here longer. I think that we should work out some settlement."

"I have a clear title to that land, sir."

"No clearer than mine. I have consulted it lately and my grant very explicitly awards it to me. I think that we should ask a court to decide the matter."

"Why have you become concerned about it so suddenly?"

"I have been concerned all the time. I don't like for a thing to hang over. Suppose either one of us should want to sell it——"

"Which is something I may decide to do, Mr. Skiles."

"You would use poor judgment, Mr. Grider. I propose that we ask a court to decide the issue."

"Why should I go to that trouble? The land is mine."

"That will require more than your statement. Good morning, Mr. Grider."

Skiles did not go directly back to Three Springs but on to Bowling Green. He went to the office of Judge Charles Drake and was closeted with him for an hour. The judge heard Skiles and asked some questions. "I'll issue an injunction against the sale of the land, but I haven't an officer available to serve it today. Would tomorrow do?"

"It is on my way home. I'll serve it myself."

"It may be that you are letting yourself in for some trouble."

"I have had my share of trouble. I am used to it."

"I'll have it ready in five minutes."

The judge watched him ride away. The judge was frowning and gently shaking his head. "I smell trouble," he said, addressing the world generally.

Jacob Skiles found Grider still sitting on his front porch. A sheet of paper lay upon his lap and a pencil was in his hand. But he had company. A man sat near him, and Skiles recognized him, the man named Coleman. Grider was clearly puzzled by this second visit of the day. Skiles came directly to the point. "I have a paper for you, Mr. Grider." He handed the paper to Grider, then nodded to Coleman.

Grider read the full page, his deep-set eyes lighting angrily. "What is this for? Why was it issued?"

"You have read it."

"Why was it issued?"

"On my request. Good morning, gentlemen."

"Wait. Do you think I would pay the slightest attention to this?"

"I doubt if you would. The purchaser might though."

Grider cast a quick look at Coleman. "My property is my property. I shall do with it exactly as I please." He tore the sheet in two and threw the pieces to the floor.

"Isn't that a bit childish?" Skiles asked in mild tones. "Of course the judge kept a copy, and of course this has been delivered to you. Both Mr. Coleman and I saw you read it. Good morning."

He bowed slightly and walked back to his horse at the gate. He went home and worked for the rest of the week without intermission except for food and sleep. At preaching on Sunday he hitched his horse within a few feet of where Judge Drake was hitching his.

"There wasn't any sale," the judge said in low tones. "I don't think there will be this time. I suggest a lawsuit."

"All right, I will bring one."

"The courts do dally a great deal. I dare say they wouldn't exhaust themselves coming to a verdict. But your injunction would remain in force till the thing was settled."

"Thank you, Judge Drake."

"In the meantime I see you haven't finished hitching. Take your time. I'll move on toward the house. Brother Grider is likely to arrive at any moment, and it wouldn't look well for us to be seen together. Some Presbyterians have suspicious natures."

10

THE NEXT DAY Skiles went to see Will Raymond. He had decided to build his store, and Raymond was the best builder in the town. The church was nearing completion, and as far as Skiles had heard, Raymond had not been engaged for another project. He found him at the church in an advanced state of irritation because two of his helpers had finished a door an inch too large for its frame.

Skiles waited quietly until matters had quieted down. Then he said, "Do you have the time to talk with me for a few minutes?"

"Certainly I have the time. There isn't anything I can do here till that door has been got back down to size."

"I'll make one request, that nothing be said of this for the time being. You will understand why."

"I earn part of my living, Mr. Skiles, by not talking."

"Sometimes it's an honest way to earn it. A little while ago I bought the lot across from the tavern. My plan is to open a store there. I don't know when, but before too long. I will be needing a storehouse built there."

"All right, tell me roughly what you want, and I'll see if I can't make a draft to suit you. If I can't no harm is done."

Within a week they had agreed upon a plan.

The next day papers were served on Skiles, enjoining him from erecting any building on that lot, it being alleged that Skiles's title was clouded.

That night at dusk a "Halloo" sounded out at the Skiles gate. It was Judge Drake, who also had made the trip around by Richpond.

"I wanted to explain that injunction. Joe Beauchamp had been snooping around all week in the titles section. I ought to have known that Joe was up to something. Joe always is. This is the way things are. That lot of yours originally belonged to a man named Hampton. The surveyor, a man named Beck, said the description sort of petered out at one place, and that is just about where your lot is. Hampton was an honest man. He told Beck to mark the plot off just as it seemed fair and right to him. Well, Beauchamp ran into all of this, and the next thing here comes Elvis Grider asking for an injunction. I didn't give it to him right away, but then I thought the best way to get the thing settled was to let the court have it. My advice to you is to demand a settlement right away. Elvis owns a couple of tracts Hampton used to have, and that gave him some kind of excuse. Elvis won't want this settled any time soon. All he wants is to hold you up on your store. Competition is evil, is the way Elvis thinks, so let's not have any of it. You come into court and ask for a prompt adjudication. Anyhow, that's my advice. Family getting along all right?"

"Kentucky agrees with us, Judge."

"I could name the virtues of Kentucky for an hour and never stop to breathe. But that is an art I reserve for my campaigning. Funny thing about voters. There are some who never quit complaining about Kentucky, but what they want to hear from a candidate is that it is an improvement on the original Garden of Eden. You have raised a good crop, I guess?"

"Everything so far has favored us. Our crop is much better than I ever expected for the first season."

"Good sense, good right arms, and a few rain clouds. That is all Kentucky needs. How is Bill Willie Blewett?"

"Blewett's fine. Next to my wife and son and the rain clouds, he is the best help I have. He has gone to Drake's Creek for a little night fishing."

"He always interested me. He said a funny thing to me once about you. It was before you came. He said he wished you'd hurry up and get here so he could go out and have a fight."

"He promised me that he wouldn't till we got here. I haven't heard of any trouble since. Maybe he has got out of the habit."

"Not quite from what I hear of the way he manhandled those two hands of Grider's he found cutting your cedar trees down. Well, so long. It's dark enough for me to take the short way back to town without the dignity of the law running any special risk."

Skiles demanded an immediate dissolution of the injunction. He employed Carter Sims, a young lawyer who recently had moved from Glasgow to Bowling Green. He liked Sims and esteemed him a keen and astute judge of the law. Judge Drake set a day to decide the case. Elvis Grider claimed that he was sick and could not appear. Judge Drake asked Joe Beauchamp, who had brought the word of his client's illness, if he couldn't go ahead with the matter. He said that apparently Grider wasn't very much concerned anyhow. Beauchamp demurred and decision was postponed a week.

The judge told Beauchamp that the evidence would be heard then, with or without the presence of Grider.

"There are too many cases being put off in my court. If this keeps up soon the only thing we will be using the courthouse for will be to issue decisions not to use it. I don't know why in this case it is necessary for the enjoiner to be present. Besides, it has been reported to me that he was well enough this morning to ride into town to see his lawyer. This injunction will be either dismissed or made permanent a week from today. Court's dismissed."

Elvis Grider contemptuously remained away from court when the injunction came up the next week, and Judge Drake dismissed the case, though Beauchamp demurred at some length. Skiles and Raymond agreed upon a plan for the store, and Raymond went to work.

One day, Skiles dropped in at the little courthouse and asked Judge Drake about the timberland case.

The judge uncrossed his legs. "Leave it be. Don't hurry the unhurryable court. Leave it be. The price of timberland will double in ten or a hundred years."

11

THE FOX-HUNTING FRIEND of Bill Willie named Reub Buckner rode a gaunt horse into town and out to Three Springs. He hitched the horse at the side of the road and found Blewett mending some fence in one of the back fields. "Howdy," he said.

"Howdy, Reub. You out fox huntin' and got lost?"

"I can track a man same as a dawg can track a fox. Didn't have no trouble findin' you at all. Got sumpin' to tell you."

Bill Willie listened intently to his story. A crony of Buckner's had got the word from a crony of his. The Dawseys were very indignant because of the way Jacob Skiles had treated their kinsman, Elvis Grider, and they had been heard to vow proper vengeance.

"I reckon you know what that means, Bill Willie."

"I've heard about 'em. I reckon I do."

"I jest thought I'd tell you, seein' as how we've hunted foxes together."

"Much obliged, Reub, for your befriendin', and I'll get you in no trouble. I'll not even tell Jacob Skiles. I'll attend to it myself."

Bill Willie knew that the Dawseys would seek their vengeance by night. So, saying nothing to anyone, he moved into the makeshift barn in which the horses were sheltered. He fixed a pallet in the loft and slept there. He knew that, aside from the breathing and shift of the horses, the softest movement, either within the barn or near, would waken him.

Nights passed and his sleep went uninterrupted. It was on the eighth night that he was awakened. He shifted suddenly from sleep to full awareness. Someone was coming stealthily up to the barn door. Bill Willie heard the horses uneasily moving closer together. He saw the vague outline of the man as he came through the door. It was no one he knew. The loft was built into only half of the barn. He leaned out and down over the edge. He steadied himself by holding with his left hand to the top of the ladder. With his right hand he swung vigorously the heavy hickory club he had fashioned for the purpose. The invader heard the swish of the club and instinctively looked up. The club crashed against his forehead and he dropped to the barn floor without a sound. Bill Willie climbed down the ladder and ran his hand over the unconscious man. He was breathing all right. Bill Willie searched a bit farther and found what the man was carrying. It was a hatchet, sharp and wicked. Bill Willie almost gasped at its meaning. He seized the man by a leg and dragged him roughly over the door strip and out into the barn lot. He showed no sign of returning to consciousness. So Bill Willie dragged him across the lot and into a strip of woodland. And there he left the man. He went back to the barn, carrying the hatchet with him. He waited throughout the night, but if the man had companions they never showed up. Bill Willie went to the woodland at dawn, but his victim was gone.

12

ONE SATURDAY Jacob Skiles told his wife that he planned to leave on Monday on a trip that might last three or four days. He wanted to see what some of the best farmers in the county were doing. She asked if he had any particular place in mind.

"Yes, one place. At the basket meeting I got to talking with a man named Shobe from Oakland, wherever that is. I am sure he is a good farmer. He talked like one. I want to see how he runs his farm. He invited me to spend a night with him, and I may do it."

"Don't look just at the barn and the fields. Find out how his wife does her work. Find out how she makes light bread. Find out how she treats measles. Mrs. Motley's little girl is in bed with it."

Rumsey came into the room then. "Where you going, Daddy? I heard you talking."

"I am going to be Christopher Columbus. I am going to be Daniel Boone. I am going to discover new places, and I am going to bring you something back from every place I discover."

"Are you going to be away years and years?"

"No, just hours and hours. Bill Willie is going to be at work on the barn, and if you need him just call, or strike on a pan. That makes me think. I want a bell like the people in Virginia had put in the yard back there. That is one of the first things I am going to do when I get back."

Bill Willie rode with him into Bowling Green. He needed nails for the barn that they were at work on. Skiles had already explained to Bill Willie the nature of the trip he was taking, and Blewett had answered that he would watch out for things.

He asked, "When is the judge goin' to decide about that timberland?"

"I don't know. He doesn't seem to be in a hurry."

"This case looks just as good as that store-lot case. What's the judge putting it off for?"

"I hate to try to hurry him. I think that sometimes does more harm than good. We can live without it, but I think we'll get it. Give the judge time."

They reached the town. Bill Willie rode on ahead. Skiles turned to the right, skirting the main settlement. The morning was fresh and dewy, and vague ribbons of mist marked the creek ways. Most of the corn was in the shock, and Skiles nodded in appreciation of the generous bulge of the shocks. Now and then he passed a sorghum patch, the tops a deep, rich red. Sorghum was the section's main winter sweetening. Every place had its patch of turnips and late potatoes. In one field a man was cutting millet. He cut his swath with measured and powerful sweeps. Skiles had seen millet grown in Virginia, but this was the first time he had seen it in Kentucky. It was thought in Virginia to make prime hay for cattle. The sides of the road and the margins of the fields were bright with goldenrod, and the thickets were tinged with the purple of wild grapes.

Soon he was passing through some very poor country, and he fell to wondering why settlers had stopped there when a bit of ingenuity and patience would have provided land much more productive. There must, he thought, be a sort of affinity between poor land and people poor in spirit. Would such a one be happy on land that yielded abundantly? It would offer more than he knew how to take. One cornfield in a creek bottom was heavy with its yield of pumpkins. Skiles grumbled audibly with regret. It had been his plan to plant pumpkins in his own cornfields, but nowhere had he been able to find the seeds he thought he had brought from Virginia.

A man drove a wagon along the trail. He brought the man to a stop with an arresting gesture of his hand and inquired the way to Mr. Shobe's place. The man considered at length, broke himself a chew from a twist of tobacco, then gave further thought to the matter.

"The best way is to go on this road for about a mile—no, you'd get all fussed up going that way. Anybody would. It'd be puzzlin' to a Philadelphy lawyer. I've heard they's people living along there who never did intend to settle there a-tall, but jest give up tryin' to get out."

The man laughed loudly as the full value of his whimsy broke upon him. He pondered further. "Where'd you start from?"

"Three miles east of Bowling Green."

"Then you made a mistake comin' this way. Once I met a candidate for public office and he asked me the way to Eli Shobe's, and I told him jest like I told you the first time. He was a right nice-appearin' feller and I intended to vote for him, but he never did show up. Nobody ever seen or heard about him again. I reckon you must be a doctor. Any sickness at Eli's?"

"I am just a farmer. My name is Jacob Skiles."

Again loud laughter broke upon the air. "Don't that jest beat everything? I've heard Bill Willie Blewett talk about you by the hour. We had a big fox hunt last Christmas, and that's the first time I ever set eyes on Bill Willie, but I've seen him a right smart sence. Seen him at the big basket meetin', and you coulda knocked me over with a feather, him a-settin' there with Lem Mayhugh and Jeff Lewis, when I knowed he'd whopped the daylights outa both of 'em, and hated 'em wuss'n if they was two chicken snakes quiled there in his henhouse. So I goes in and sets behind 'em, wonderin' how the lion and the lamb, as the Scripter says, has took to settin' together. I got purty good eyesight, and you coulda knocked me offn that seat with a piece o' spider web ifn Bill Willie don't have a knife open in his lap, and it a-pintin' towards Lem. He kinda covered it up with his coat, but there he was, ready to start carvin' on Lem's inwards. I didn't get to see Bill Willie after preachin' on account o' that storm comin' up, but I figgered he was a-upholdin' law and order. Twice I know of them fellers has broke up preachin', but that's one they didn't. They never let out a chirp. They knowed Bill Willie wasn't a-holdin' that knife jest to keep in practice. I seen Bill Willie one time sence that, but that's a secret. The way I hear it, him and me has cooked a goose. And it shore needed cookin'. Pleased to meet you, Mr. Skiles. My name's Reub Buckner."

"I am glad to make your acquaintance, Mr. Buckner. Do you live near here?"

"Yessir, I am one o' the fellers that got mixed up down here and never could find my way out. I ain't complained though. The Lord never made any better fox-huntin' country than this. The second bend around the road is where I starve at." Again loud laughter violated the serene morning. Skiles regarded the man closely, and with a sort of shock. He had never before seen a man laugh with such heartiness, and with not the slightest shift of his features. There was something incongruous about that hearty laughter and that stony face.

"I am a poor fox hunter, but sometime I'd like to join you."

"Any time, any time. I'd call off a barn-raisin' to take you on a hunt. Was it Eli Shobe you was lookin' for?"

"Yes. I have the impression that he is a good farmer, and I'd like to see what he does and how he does it."

"Eli's the best farmer in the county. No doubt of it. When he plants somethin' it grows up and raises spendin' money. When I plant corn I do mighty good to raise some nubbins. When Eli plants corn they take a two-hoss wagon down in the fiel' and gether spendin' money. Sence I thinks of it you won't have much trouble gettin' to Eli's. Jest turn aroun' and go back to the next fork. There you turn to the right and foller the road to the river and cross at the ford. It ain't hardly deep a-tall. They's a road picks up on the other side, and if you'll jest stay on it, it'll take you right to Eli's house. You'll know it when you see it. Eli's a up and comer. Wish you had Bill Willie along. Once a feller in town called him some bad names. He didn't turn a hair. He said, 'You call me that after the first o' April!' Then he jest walked on away. The feller was a reg'lar bully. He told everybody that he was goin' to call Bill Willie everything he could think of on the second day of April, and then he was a-goin' to remove Bill Willie apart in little pieces. But I reckon he jest natchelly disremembered to do it. It was about then that Bill Willie salivated Lem and Jeff for cuttin' cedar trees on your land. I expect the feller musta heard of that. One day I seen him in town and I ast him had he been callin' Bill Willie Blewett any names lately and dismemberin' him by the inch. He shet up just like a mud turkle. I told him I was a friend o' Bill Willie's and maybe he'd like to call me sumpin'. My mind's made up the next time I see him to do some callin' myself jest to see ifn he ain't run plumb out o' spunk. You thinkin' o' bein' a candidate for sumpin', Mr. Skiles? I'd be mighty willin' to vote for you."

Skiles rode back to the fork and turned to the right. The road ran through some excellent farming country, then dipped down to a level spread of land, then finally to Barren River. The fording was comfortable. The way skirted some river-bottom fields, then rose to higher ground. A little less than an hour later he saw a brick house sitting impressively in a grove of maples. The house was a half mile distant, but he knew it must be the Shobe place. A long lane led up to the house. He saw Eli Shobe standing under a maple tree in his front yard, and at the same moment Shobe saw him.

He came with powerful strides down to the gate to meet his visitor. "Get right down from off that horse. I've been thinking about you." He whistled. A Negro boy came in a run. "Take the gentleman's horse, General Washington; unsaddle it, water it, and feed it plenty. Glad to see you, sir. I've been hoping you would come out to see how poor folks live. Come on in the house. Dinner will be ready in a little while. I introduced you to my wife at the basket meeting. She will want to see you. Oh, Lottie," he called. A lady came out of the door onto the porch. "Lottie, don't you remember Mr. Skiles at the basket meeting?"

"I certainly do." She extended her hand. "We are glad to have you come to see us, Mr. Skiles. I guess you are about starved from riding so far. Dinner will be ready in a few minutes. I think the boys are at the barn now."

"*The boys* is what she calls the four appetites that sit around our table."

"That's what I call the young men who grow something for us to put on the table. Don't I remember that you have a son, Mr. Skiles?"

"Yes, but he is at the appetite stage without having reached the providing stage. He was four a month ago."

"Don't miss any part of his growing up. It happens so quickly. It almost seems that I look now and he's a baby. Then I look again and he's a grown man. In a little while Mr. Shobe and I will be back where we started nineteen years ago."

"Only that we'll be old folks then," said her husband.

"There the boys come. Dinner will be ready just as soon as they have washed up." She disappeared into the kitchen.

The boys were husky fellows, the oldest eighteen and the others ranging downward at intervals of two years. Their names were Washington, Adams, Jefferson, and Hamilton. Skiles thought that the names had been prophetic of presidential succession, except Hamilton, and he fitted perfectly into the company of his brothers.

The table literally was laden with food. It had to be. Mr. Shobe's jest had not been an idle one. The boys were not only growing crops but growing themselves. A skimpy table might have left both stunted.

Jacob Skiles was an inquiring man. Whenever he saw anything, significant questions were born within him. He studied the food on the table without appearing to do so. Its abundance was matched only by its quality. Priscilla Skiles was a satisfying cook, but this was better corn bread than he had at home. He would find out why before he made his departure. The vegetables were the same as he might expect to find on his own table, though Mrs. Skiles usually cut the corn from the cob and half fried it in the skillet with milk and bacon grease added. There, on the Shobes' table, the largest dish was a platter of ears of boiled corn, which dredged in butter were eaten from the cob. It was so simple and delicious that he wondered why it was not served that way oftener. His patch of late corn at Three Springs would be ready probably when he returned. They would try boiling it. There was a large dish of boiled butter beans, and they disappeared rapidly under the stress of the four appetites. Not four but *six*, thought Skiles. Seven but for the fact that Mrs. Shobe ate sparingly. A fresh dish of butter beans replaced the empty one. Twice the bowl of boiled cabbages was refilled.

"We have been making kraut for two days. We had some Dutch neighbors from Pennsylvania when we lived in Virginia, and it is something we learned from them."

"I have heard of it," said Skiles, "but I have never eaten it. It is made by letting cabbages sour, isn't it? Bill Willie has been interested in it."

"Not exactly sour. We'll show you. We think it is fine for winter. All of the boys are fond of it. Pass the meat. Mr. Skiles hasn't a thing on his plate."

The meat was great slices of smoked shoulder, fried and served with red gravy. The host explained that since their supply of ham was running low their fare had necessarily been reduced to shoulder.

"We cured fifty-two hams," he said, "one for every week of the year, but now we have only four left, and it is a long time till hog-killing time again. We have plenty of shoulders and a good one tastes a good bit like ham."

Skiles ate the meat appreciatively. "This is real tasty. Before I leave here I want to find out exactly how you do the curing. I want to use my hogs to the best advantage."

"How many have you?"

"I have twenty. I expect to use fifteen for meat."

Shobe looked up from his plate. "That is interesting. You have been here since spring, and now you have twenty hogs. Most families wouldn't have that many in five years."

"Most families haven't a man named Bill Willie Blewett to push them into buying that many."

"I know Blewett, of course. He is a remarkable fellow. It's a lucky thing to be pushed like that. I suppose you have a good acorn harvest on your land. As I recall there are a lot of oak trees in that section."

"I imagine I have two thousand oak trees, and all of them loaded with acorns."

"Then you ought to have more than twenty hogs. There is fat for hogs in acorns and good flavoring too. That shoulder you are eating now was nourished by oak trees and smoked by hickory trees. Of course, they had a little corn, but mainly it was acorns. Take care of your trees, my friend." He turned to the oldest of the boys. "Going to finish that field by night, Wash?"

"By an hour by sun, Father."

"That's fine. That will give you time to break that patch for turnip greens. Two of you break it, and two of you follow, getting the seed in. Be careful not to cover them too deep."

The boys finished their dinner. They bowed politely to their parents and guest, then went out into the hall. Skiles heard them going into a room off the hall. Eli Shobe explained. "They always lie down for a half an hour after they finish eating. I find that it is good for them. Besides it gives the team that much more time for rest."

Skiles looked about the table. There was no more left than a few shreds and crumbs. The appetites had taken their due toll. He bowed to Mrs. Shobe. "I have been favored to add another appetite to your table. It is the first thing I shall tell my wife about."

"Listen," said Eli Shobe. "You are not leaving here until tomorrow. There is too much for us to talk about. I hope that you want to see my farm. Anyhow, I want to show it to you. I hope that you have a lot of questions to ask. I have some myself. We will consider that settled, won't we, Wife?"

"We are going to have chicken and dumplings and an apple cobbler for supper. Yes, we'll consider it settled."

An hour later the two men saddled their horses and started on a tour of the Shobe farm. Skiles soon saw that it was the best-managed farm he had ever seen. It was farming at its best. The fences were precise and in good order. There were a few gates that swung on heavy hand-hammered hinges; mostly passage was by stopgaps, made by setting two large posts and mortising deep holes, regularly spaced, on the inner face of each post. Poles were placed in these holes, the ends trimmed to fit the mortises. It wasn't much trouble to open and close these gaps for passing. In one field a flock of sheep nibbled passively at the turf of grass, and in another was a dozen head of cattle.

"Where are your hogs?" inquired Skiles.

"In the woods yonder. The acorns are beginning to drop."

"Do you have any market for your sheep?"

"Not much of one. There is some demand for the wool, but as a matter of fact, we use a great deal of it for ourselves. My wife is an expert at spinning and weaving. She gets some women to help her and they make practically all of our clothes. Every blanket we have, we either got from our folks when we married, or she made it. Wool comes in mighty handy. And then sheep make good eating. I doubt if you have much idea how much this family can and does eat. We can kill a sheep in the hottest weather and keep it in the springhouse till we have eaten it all. We are right now milking six good cows, and there isn't any milk or butter left over."

"What do you sell for money?"

"We are better eaters than spenders. Generally, money is a scarce article at the Shobe home. We have a little, of course. We sell a few sheep, a few hogs, and a little wheat. I could sell fifty hams if I had them, but we never have any to spare. The people in this county are great ham eaters. Next year, I am going to raise some tobacco, an acre or two, but I don't know what it will amount to. Our main need here is good roads. I guess that is true of a new country anywhere. If we had good roads, say to Louisville, or to Nashville, we could find a market for anything we raise. I heard at the basket meeting that you are going to open a store soon. Why don't you start a wagon route, say to Nashville? You'll need it. You will find out then how much we need good roads."

"I know now," Jacob Skiles affirmed. "That's a good idea about the wagon route. I'll think it over."

"And another thing. We need roads to help us get together more. A section doesn't amount to much till its people can mix and talk freely. We go to church, but there we meet only Presbyterians. The Baptists have their meetings; so do the Methodists. As long as we are separated as we are we will think and act like separated people. We need to keep on being Presbyterians, but we need to mix more with Baptists."

"My thoughts are the same. Your words are better. Do you have something in mind?"

"Yes, I do. I have heard from my cousin in North Carolina about an arrangement they have in some parts of the state. They call it County Court Day. It doesn't really have anything to do with court, except I suppose the magistrates meet then. Everybody who can make the trip comes into town that day, and everybody who has something to sell takes it along with him. My cousin says it is a great time for horse trading. Some people in his county make chairs, and everybody who does brings a wagonload in to County Court Day. They are generally sold out by noon. There is a field on the edge of his town where the people meet who have something to trade or sell. Then, of course, they stand along the streets, and talk, and go into the stores and buy things. I wish we could start a County Court Day here."

"How is it started—by some sort of law?"

"I don't think so, just by agreement. Our squires meet on the fourth Monday. That would be the best time for us. We could get the stores to offer some sort of special bargains, and maybe in the afternoon have a horse race, or some shooting matches. We would have to get word out all over the county." Shobe was enjoying his plans.

"I'm for it. Suppose we declare the fourth Monday in each month to be County Court Day."

"All right, we will. I think everybody would be for it. I'll try to get the storekeepers to offer some bargains. I'll find a field for the buying and trading. You arrange some sort of show for the afternoon. We will get everybody to help spread the news. Does that suit you?"

"It does, and I'll do my part the best I can. It would do me a lot of good to see a large crowd gather in Bowling Green once every month. It would be good for the community."

They rode on. Shobe pointed out with pride his patch of late potatoes, more than a half acre. "However good they turn out there won't be one left by March. I wonder sometimes whether we work so that we may eat, or the other way around. Of course, we will save some out for seed."

"How do you keep them that long?"

"We put about half in a cool section in the cellar, and the rest we bury. We eat the ones in the cellar first. We manage to finish them just about the time they start rotting. Then we begin on the ones we buried."

"Bill Willie has been telling me about burying potatoes and turnips. He saw some of it done here last winter."

"Also cabbage, and last winter we buried two bushels of parsnips. Have you seen the way we bury vegetables?"

"I never heard of it until Bill Willie told me about it."

"Well, we find a bank, the steeper the better. We dig holes back into it deeper than it could possibly freeze. We line the holes with leaves, or better still with straw. That helps keep the vegetables clean. We put them in on a bed of leaves or straw and then cover them with more. Then we fill it up with dirt. It will surprise you the way the stuff keeps. But we do have to be careful not to put in anything rotten."

"I'll start looking for a bank when I get home. You spoke with your sons about turnip greens. Do you mean the tops of the turnips?"

"No, this is a kind of turnip we grow for the tops. It's a lot more sprangly than ordinary turnip tops. I never heard of it till I got here. It gets big enough to eat pretty soon after the first warm weather sets in, sometimes even in February. We think it is the best greens of them all. If you would like to try it, I can let you have some seed. It ought to be planted just about now."

"I certainly would like to try it."

They came to a large branch and forded it. Then Skiles said, "I heard something in town last week. I heard that a bank is about to be opened there."

"That would be a good thing. Do you think it could make a go of it?"

"It would depend on who opens it. We do need a bank, but I doubt if we need Elvis Grider as a banker."

"Oh, so that's it?"

"Not all of it. Jim Walters is the rest of it. They are to be partners, so I heard."

"I have heard of him. Pretty hard-fisted, isn't he?" Shobe asked.

"He thinks heaven is where there will be more money."

"That is about what Elvis thinks, isn't it?"

"He thinks that heaven is where he will have more power. Bill Willie has read me a chapter out of Walters' life. He came here already rich in our sense. He settled in the southern part of the county and by sharp trading has added a great deal to what he brought. He is not interested in friends, only in money. Of course, that provides him with friends of a sort."

"Doesn't that describe Grider too?"

"Only in degree," Jacob Skiles answered. "Grider is a proud and haughty man. He would have no dealings at all with a common, onery fellow. Walters would just as soon be seen with a rascal as with a gentleman, and he would think just as much of the money he made off the rascal. I think that Elvis Grider is at heart an honest man. If he owed a debt he would expect to pay it in full, but he would be just as ruthless as Walters if you owed him one. Grider wants to be recognized as the leading man in the county. He wants people to look up to him—but at a safe distance. At this minute you would find him wearing a starched collar. Walters' clothes would be cheap; they wouldn't fit him, and they likely would be dirty."

Skiles paused, then went on. "The only thing I don't understand is how Grider can stand Walters, and my guess is that he will try to get rid of him as soon as the bank is a going concern. They are going to build a house next to Younglove's apothecary shop and run their bank there. Anyhow, that is what I have heard."

"Tell me: what business would they do?"

"I think that mainly they would have to furnish the first money themselves. There would be a little deposited, but not much. Well, they would lend money to people who need it and for security take a lien on land, or something that the bank could turn into money. I think a bank can make a profit here."

The sun was dropping rapidly toward the western rim of the woods. The air was soft but as clear as crystal. The birds were tuning for their evensong. A foxhound bayed mournfully in the distance.

"That's Reub Buckner's dog across the river," Shobe explained. "Reub usually quits work about four for a little chase, that is, if he got started working during the day. Well, I see the boys are getting their turnip seed sown. Those boys are real farmers. I am not sure that a single one of them would know a foxhound from a fox squirrel. That makes me think. I mustn't forget to give you the turnip-greens seed before you leave. Of course, you have had greens at your house, but turnip greens deserve special cooking. Be sure to ask my wife for directions. I am not much good at such things."

"Everybody else here seems to be an expert at something. Surely there is something in which you excel," said Skiles, jesting.

"There is. I am the best milker on the place. Wouldn't you like to stand by and watch me milk the cows? I see they are coming up."

The cows that ambled in bovine dignity up the narrow lane were fat and clearly ample for the four or more appetites.

Shobe turned an ear toward the turnip-greens patch. "The boys have finished. They always finish when they say they will. It would offend them for me to ask them if they had."

While they were eating supper, Wash out of a deep study inquired of his father, "What would a sorghum mill cost?"

His father smiled. "I thought you would be asking that, so I found out. The grinding mill and the pan will cost forty-seven dollars. I don't know what it will cost to have them hauled here, but not less than twenty-five dollars, likely thirty. Do you think we ought to raise some sorghum next year?"

"Yes, I do. There's a little more than eight acres in that lower creek bottom. I think you could get seventy-five or maybe a hundred gallons to the acre. The last time we were in Mr. Hardcastle's store I heard him tell you that he didn't have even a pint, and didn't know where he could get any, and that people wanted to buy it every day."

"All right, Wash. Pick out the best seed from what we raise this year." He turned to Skiles. "We have a patch for cow feed, but I think Wash is right. Everybody likes a bit of sweetening, and the handiest around here is bee-tree honey and sorghum molasses."

"Bill Willie and I thought we were about to find a bee tree several times, but somebody always beat us to it."

"We don't have much luck either. There're a lot of trifling fellows who spend most of the time looking for bee trees. Twice we have found men cutting bee trees on my land and both times we have run them off, expecting to come back the next day and get our own honey, but both times the trees were down and the honey gone. I don't blame them much. Everybody craves a little sweetening."

Adams said, "We have got some real big maple trees. Why don't we ever make any maple sugar?"

"I guess we just never got around to it, but we will next season. Don't you let us forget it, Adams."

Skiles slept that night in the room with the four boys. Two of them turned their bed over to him and slept on the floor. There was very little talk. Wash told Skiles that they would work the next few days on the fences. There were some broken rails and a few rotted ones. These would be replaced and the fence corners cleaned. After that they would start sowing wheat. Ten minutes later the four boys were sleeping soundly.

They ate breakfast early the next morning. The boys went off to work. The father milked the six cows while Skiles stood and watched.

"Before you go," Shobe said, "I want to talk with you a little more. You go and sit out there in the front yard. I'll carry the milk in and then I'll join you."

Soon he came out of the side door and down into the yard. "My wife said tell you not to forget those cooking recipes. She is very proud of the food she prepares."

"She has reason to be if it contributes any part to those four sons. Anyhow, I have not eaten better."

"I am mighty proud, my friend, to have you visit us. I liked you the first time I saw you. I like you still more now."

"Please know that those are my feelings too."

"I want you for a friend for reasons some of them personal, some of them not. Make yourself comfortable. There are some things I'd really like to talk about. I haven't the slightest doubt that it is Elvis Grider's plan to make himself the leader of this county, though sometimes it does seem to me that his methods are a bit peculiar. I have no objection to him being the leader, but I do object to the kind of leader I think he would make. You and I can take care of ourselves, but there are a good many settlers in the county who can't. They haven't any money to speak of and not much prospect for much more. They mostly behave themselves and live decently, but they don't know how to make much of a living. The chances are that they won't ever be able to do much for their children. Some of them do not live far from me, and I do what I can for them. They act like they were born to live in a sort of a rut, and I don't have much hope of getting them out of it. If things are handled right, I have a great deal of hope for their children. I like them, most of them——" He broke off, turning quickly to Skiles. "I suppose you are wondering why I am saying all of this."

Skiles smiled. "I am finding it extremely interesting."

"God knows that I do not want to be a leader any more than I have to! I don't ever expect to run for office. I do want to keep on making as good a living as I have now, but I'll be satisfied with that. But somehow I want to get the feeling that the county is getting better, growing in the way that it ought to grow, that it is being led by the people who can lead it right. There are a lot of things that we don't have and must get."

"Better roads, for instance."

"I say that we have gone about as far as we can go without better roads, and our children are suffering for lack of schools. Do you have a good idea how fast Bowling Green is growing? Faster than you think, very likely. All of the sections of the county have been settled, some of them thickly." He broke off with a little vocal explosion, then was talking again. "And they are good people, but for the best results they are going to need careful handling. I hope the bank succeeds, but I am not willing to turn them over to Grider and Walters. We must see to it that they are not turned over to them. By the way, didn't I hear that you and Grider own some of the same land?"

"My grant is older than his."

"It sounds reasonable to me that if Virginia had given the land to you, it really didn't have it to give to him. Still you can never be sure how a court will decide such things. It will come up before Judge Drake, I guess. He is a fair man, and as wily as a fox. It will be his aim to do the right thing, but a judge cannot follow simple reasoning like mine. There are precedents, and other matters to complicate his verdicts. But I happen to know that Judge Drake is no fonder of Elvis Grider than I am. The judge is a clever man. One time I was complaining to him about how slow the court works. 'I've found that often a postponement can settle things better than a verdict or decision.' That's what he said. I don't quite know what he meant, but I have the notion that he might be right."

"I'll leave it in his hands. I'll not complain."

"I guess we will all watch the new bank. It may do well, but a prolonged spell of hard times might leave it owning more land than it can handle. I am more interested in County Court Day right now." He broke off with his explosive little laugh. "County Court Day! I'm getting to like the sound of it. Suppose you meet me in town a week from today so we can work out the details. Until then we can do a lot of thinking about it."

"One week from today. I'll be there."

"The front room of the tavern at ten o'clock. When is your store going to be ready?"

"I'd like to start it by the middle of November, though it may have to be later. The building will be ready in plenty of time. The goods will be the hard part. Hauling is so poor that the other stores are having a hard time to keep in some things."

"Well, whatever happens, I hope this is the beginning of a long line of visits. Bring your whole family the next time."

13

Mrs. Skiles had finished cleaning up after dinner when her husband returned. Rumsey was sleeping soundly. Bill Willie was plowing for wheat, and Mr. Wingfield, hired the week before, was going ahead of him cutting sprouts and grubbing up the larger growth. Skiles ate a cold dinner, telling his wife of the trip as he did so. He went into the room where Rumsey was sleeping and took a long look at the boy. Then he went out into the field where the two men were at work. Bill Willie had stopped plowing; a trace chain had broken, and he was fixing it with a piece of wire.

"Have a good trip?"

"Better than I expected. There is a lot I want to talk with you about when we have the time."

"Nothing happened while you were gone. I passed that timber ground late yesterday and you still got it."

"I came by town and stopped for a while where they are building the store. What troubles me is, how are we going to get stuff here to sell? One of the regular haulers had his wagon break down. He says he is not going to the trouble to have it fixed. Says the work is too hard. What do you say to us starting a hauling route?"

"I'll go after the first load of goods," said Bill Willie calmly, "and I'll get back with it. We will have the planting finished by then. You won't need me here."

"I'll always need you here, Bill Willie, but if we can't get the goods here any other way I'll send you to Nashville."

An idea grew in Jacob Skiles's mind, to start a hauling line himself to supply his own store. Nashville, seventy miles to the south, was the nearest dependable market. There was plenty of salt available there, and it was generally supposed to be the best furniture market

within reach. There were several crude warehouses at Nashville, all
reasonably full of furniture brought on from New Orleans and Mo-
bile, smoked meat, mostly cured in Nashville, medicines and oint-
ments, produced in Nashville, and tools, also a product of the place.
He decided that if he could find a dependable driver he would buy a
team and wagon and start bringing the goods in. He met with Shobe
at the tavern at the appointed time, and after due consideration they
decided that the first County Court Day would be held on the fourth
Monday in October. They made plans in full detail.

14

OCTOBER was a month of cloudless skies. The work of the
county went ahead without interruption, and as the time passed a
great many of the people began to look forward eagerly to the great
day.

Jacob Skiles watched the weather alertly from the middle of the
week on. Rain on Monday would be most harmful, and he knew that
the rainy season was coming on. Word of County Court Day had
spread throughout the county. A vacant lot would be provided for
those who wished to trade horses or cattle or foxhounds or anything
else. The adjoining lot was for those who wished to sell or buy produce or household goods, or anything contrived at home. There would
be an auction sale at three o'clock, and Mr. Pat Curd would sell all
articles in the order entrusted him. Mr. Curd was an auctioneer of
great renown, and his auctions were held to be of both economic and
recreational value. Mr. Felix Grundy, of Bardstown, one of Kentucky's
great orators, had been secured for the main address. It would be
delivered at two o'clock from a platform erected at the east end of the
square. At such times as the platform was not otherwise in use, Mr.
Ham Vernon and Mr. Lex Spalding would play on the banjo and
fiddle. The grove next to the graveyard was cleared up for the hitching
of teams. Crude tables were set up for those who brought their dinners
with them. Mr. Art McFarland, the sheriff, would be assisted by two
deputies in the preservation of law and order.

There need not have been any worry about rain. October had been
a royal season. There had been a slow, steady, soaking rain about the
middle of the month which held the sap in the trees and prolonged
the green in the grass and leaves. It wet down the dust in the plowed

fields, and stirred the planted seed with the promise of immortality. It gave tenure to the goldenrod and the purple asters. It provided a source for the spring branches to carry their flow till the saving rains of winter set in. Since the rain there had been an unblemished cycle of golden days. The sun coursed its way through a sky untroubled even by a hint of clouds, and by night a moon moved tenderly through the same sky. What a lighted world it was!

There were five roads leading into town. In varying distances out of town these branched into smaller roads, sometimes into mere paths. Sometimes they disappeared altogether. The word of County Court Day had been well distributed. By the time the sun was an hour high people were coming in by all five of the roads. They came by all the means of pioneer travel. Some walked, giving no thought to the miles or rough roads. Some came on horseback. Ox wagons lumbered along the roads, lagging behind the horse-drawn wagons. There were a few early pretenses at carriages, driven by the richer gentry. Families ranging from five to twelve rode in those wagons, and in the wagon beds at their feet were sacks and baskets filled with provender for human beings and teams. They wore their best finery. Some who strode along the margins of the roads were roughly clad and wore coonskin caps, but it was the best they had. They carried their long rifles swung across their shoulders with easy grace. Everyone was excited and bright-eyed.

A member of the County Court Day committee stood where each of the five roads entered the town and gave directions and advice. Those who had something to sell or trade drove by the trading lot and left there one of the family and whatever they wished to dispose of. Then they drove on to the hitching lot, cared for their teams and left them tied in the shade of the maple and wild cherry trees. The first trade, a sorrel horse for a yearling mule, was made before nine o'clock, and both parties were in high humor about it. A few minutes later, a bearskin was traded for a homemade rocking chair, and a gallon of bee-tree honey for a hand-woven blanket. Lex Spalding and Ham Vernon sat on the platform at the head of the square and fiddled and strummed the banjo as though inspired. The musicians were never without an audience. Their hearers stayed as long as they felt they could. There was so much to hear, so many things to see, so much to talk about, so many to talk with that soon they had to move on, though they did it reluctantly. "Old Joe Clarke" and "Soldiers'

Joy" were tunes they loved to hear. But they moved on and others took their places about the platform.

"R'ar down on it, Lex!" one shouted. "You're my kind o' fiddler. R'ar down on it." And Lex r'ared down with a fine passion.

Sheriff McFarland stayed close to the tavern for the greater part of the day. He had learned from experience that the most strategic place to nip disorder was the place where it was most likely to start. The tavern was supplied with patrons from nine o'clock throughout the day. Most of them were fully aware that the sheriff would not bother them till they started bothering other people. Then it was his way to be a trifle rough.

" 'Spectin' any trouble, Sheriff?" inquired a bystander.

"I get paid to expect it, but mostly I get disappointed. Folks around here are right peaceable."

"Got any extry rooms in the jail?" asked another.

"Not a one. We tie 'em flat on the roof now."

"Sheriff or no sheriff, I'll drink licker when I get good and ready," yelled one in half-maudlin tones. "Ain't no sheriff goin' to stop me from drinkin' licker."

"A little and I'll say nothing. Too much will be a mistake."

"What'd you do about it?"

"First I take off the head, then I take out the vital organs, and then I work on down to the legs."

A roar of laughter applauded the details of the sheriff's routine. The man who drank licker when he got good and ready considered the matter gravely. Then he too burst into loud peals of laughter. He held out his hand to the sheriff. "Not another drap. I'm a-goin' out and listen to the fiddlin'. Any objection, Sheriff?"

"Just so you don't start playing one yourself. Come on, I'll go along with you." He accompanied the man to the square and left him listening openmouthed to the rendition of "Sourwood Mountain" then in progress. The sheriff continued his walk on down to the trading lot. Business apparently was good. He stopped to listen to a bit of banter between two men regarding a weary-looking, flea-bitten gray horse.

"What'll you take for that plug, Hez?"

"Ifn you had the eyesight of a mud turkle, Sid, you'd know that hoss is no plug. That's a fust-rate hoss that you never owned one half as good as. But to tell you the plain truth I got more stock than I'm goin' to be able to feed. It'd make you a whole lot more respectable to have that hoss where people could see it when they pass your place.

Listen here, Sid, you and me has been good friends ever sence we been in Kentucky. I tell you what I'll do, I'll jest let you have that hoss at your own price."

Sid grinned broadly. "Ain't you a little high, Hez?"

"No, I ain't. At that figger I'm practically givin' you the hoss."

15

THAT WAS THE DAY when Elvis Grider and Jim Walters opened their bank. They had worked with speed, day and night, to get it ready for the great day. The two of them sat at a pine table with Bud Cheney of the Providence Knob neighborhood, who wished to borrow some money. He explained his need to the two bankers. "Old Man Tom Shanks got more land than he can handle. There's a neck of it backs up against my place. He wants to sell it and the price is right, only he wants cash and I ain't got it. I thought maybe a bank could help me. It's good land and I need it."

Grider tapped on the table with his second finger and gazed at the ceiling. "Can he give you a good title?"

"He said he would be responsible, said he'd make anything good that turned up wrong."

"Did he put it in writing?"

"I didn't ask him to. His word is as good as his bond."

"No man's word is, but you can hold him to his writing."

"You having trouble right now about a title, ain't you, Elvis?" asked Walters. "Sometimes writin' ain't good either."

"It is my land and I expect to keep it, but my hands are tied till the court makes a decision. Titles can cause a great deal of trouble. You get Shanks to make that statement in writing. How much cash can you pay on this land?"

"I can raise fifty dollars. I'll have to borrow the rest."

"I am sure that you know we will have to take a lien on the land. That's the way a bank works."

"How much interest you going to charge me?"

"We are new at this and we will have to learn as we go along. But you are our first customer. We will make you a special rate if we can get the papers put in proper order."

Cheney left, and the two men sat watching him go out the door. "I've been over that Shanks land," said Walters. "It's a good risk."

"I am going down to the stagecoach depot," said Grider. "The coach was due in here an hour ago. The help they keep down there is both ignorant and bad-mannered. They didn't know why the coach was late nor when to expect it. I told them it had to be here by noon, for Felix Grundy was on it. It would be terrible if he didn't get here on time."

"I'll lay a dollar they didn't know who Grundy was."

"That is what they asked me, who he was. I told them and they said if he was a big bug like that maybe the driver got excited and didn't stop, maybe he just took Grundy on to Nashville. I shall complain about it. Two coaches a week, and it comes in late! Judge Grundy is staying at my home."

"I didn't even know he was a judge," said Walters.

"Oh, yes, judge, senator, several things. He is probably the most important man in the state."

"I've heard some talk about a man named Henry Clay."

"Grundy is the man to watch." A young man was coming in the door. "Come in, sir. What can we do for you?"

"My name's Steve Matthews. I want to get married and I need a little money to set up farming with. My daddy told me maybe I could get it here."

"Where do you live, Mr. Matthews?"

"Close to Dripping Springs. My daddy is going to give me fifty acres of land."

"Come in, Mr. Matthews. My partner, Mr. Walters, will talk with you. I have an engagement at the stagecoach station."

He went on his way toward the station. Halfway there he met with his two hands, Lem and Jeff. They were walking along the street somewhat uncertainly, obviously half drunk. They saw Mr. Grider.

"There he is now," said Jeff. "Go ask him."

Lem held up his hand, signaling his employer to stop. "We want a dollar," he said.

The astonished banker came to a halt, but refused to believe his ears. "What was it you said?" he asked crisply.

"We want a dollar," said Lem standing his ground.

"Yessir, a dollar," added Jeff.

"I have no dollar for you. I paid you last night."

"We done spent that money," said Jeff. "We want a dollar."

"You won't get it. Get out of my way."

"He says we won't get it," said Lem owlishly. "I think we goin' to get it."

Jeff placed himself squarely in front of Mr. Grider, but Grider pushed him so suddenly and violently with the point of his cane that Jeff staggered into a ditch at the side of the road.

"Get out of my way, both of you, and stay away from my place. You are discharged." Mr. Grider collected his dignity as best he could and proceeded on his way.

All of this had happened only a few feet away from Mr. Bill Gray's blacksmith shop and wagon works. Bill Willie Blewett was standing just inside the door. He had watched the little episode with considerable interest. He came out the door. "Tore into you, didn't he?"

"He didn't give us the dollar," said Jeff.

"He run us off," said Lem.

"Let's kill him when he comes back," said Jeff.

"Better look for another job. You fellers would starve right easy," said Bill Willie.

"Treated us like a dog and us workin' for him three years."

"You been good hands too," said Bill Willie. "Yessir, it looks like he done you wrong. He's a mean man to work for."

"And us workin' for him three years! Treated us like a dog."

"I tell you what we'll do," said Lem. "We'll get us work somewhere else. We'll get us a job with hosses. That's what I been wantin' all the time."

"I heard you both used to be purty good with hosses," said Bill Willie. "But I expect you done forgot how to handle 'em."

"Hosses is the only kind o' work I'm fitten to do," affirmed Lem solemnly. "I used to drive the stagecoach from Richmond, Virginny, to Lexington."

"I used to drive a coach too," said Jeff. "Last one I druv was from here to Nashville."

"Let me ast you, you fellers want a job drivin' hosses?"

"What you know about a job drivin' hosses? You ain't got no hosses to drive."

"If you want a job drivin' hosses, I'll get it for you. If you don't want it shet up talkin' about it."

"Go ahead and talk. We'll lissen."

"Wouldn't talk to nobody about drivin' hosses who totes a bottle or takes a dram while he's on a trip."

"You'd take a dram too ifn you'd been workin' for that old scoundrel. Go ahead and do your talkin'.'"

Bill Willie took the two men, then reasonably sober, across to a vacant lot, and they sat down on a log while they talked. In the end he employed them to drive for Jacob Skiles on the hauling line he was about to start. Of course, the employment was subject to confirmation by Skiles, but Bill Willie was sure there would be no trouble about that. They would find Skiles and have the matter settled immediately.

Then Bill Willie pronounced in series the calamities that would befall the two men at the slightest default in duty. "Ifn you do your work good, if you treat the hosses well, and get the wagons back on time, and the goods is in fust-rate order, you'll be paid good like I said. But you jest try gettin' drunk while you're on a trip, you jest mistreat a hoss and somebody'll have to look mighty hard to find enough of you for buryin'. You ast Skiles ifn I ain't pizen when I get riled up."

Fifteen minutes later, Skiles had endorsed the employment and confirmed the wages. "But I want to make sure of one thing, that you are no longer in the employ of Elvis Grider."

"I told you I heard him order 'em to stay away from his place," said Bill Willie. "They got a right to hire up with you."

"All right, your pay starts today. You will take the wagons out next Thursday. We will explain everything to you before we start the line."

Skiles continued on his round to see how County Court Day was doing. The trading lot was very well filled, and the sounds of barter were loud, aggressive, and confused. A man sitting on an outcropping stone stopped him with an upraised hand.

"Mister, how about some dried sasserfrus root? Makes the best tea in the world. Healthiest drink they is. Keeps down chills, toothache and fatal diseases. I dried it last spring, and it's better now than it was the day it was dug up."

Skiles remembered what Bill Willie had told him of the virtues of sassafras tea. He bought half the man had, and, having no other way to carry it, stuffed it in his pockets.

"Thanky, sir. Ifn I have any left I'll be back next County Court Day. I ain't done bad a-tall. I done sold two baskets o' shelled black-eyed peas."

Skiles passed two men who were haggling over the price of a hog, tied in a wagon. He stopped to listen. "I've been telling him for an hour," the buyer explained to Skiles, "that I'd buy his shoat ifn he'd come down four bits."

"All right, take it," said the owner. "Take it afore old age gets me."

Skiles moved on. He passed near the coach depot, and there in front of it on a rough bench sat Elvis Grider. He noted that Grider's carriage was waiting, his team hitched to a railing. Grider was looking so intently out the road to the north that he did not see the man passing. Then Skiles remembered why the man was waiting. The guest of honor was to be the great Felix Grundy of Bardstown. He was to speak after dinner had been eaten. Doubtless, Grider awaited his arrival. It was a bit strange that he would desert his new bank even for that honor. He wondered what Grider would say when he discovered that Skiles had employed two of his hands. That likely would add to the accumulating friction. Then he heard a bell rung with great vigor. It was the prearranged signal that it was time to eat dinner, and that all other activities were to cease. He looked back at the trading lot. All activities had stopped almost suddenly, and with one accord everyone had turned toward the lot set apart for feasting.

Skiles moved on toward the lot. His wife would be needing him. The tables were already supplied with food, and the abundance was in process of being increased from buckets and baskets and sacks. There were more families than available tables, and Lank Motley was busy putting the families into the most congenial groups possible. Mr. Motley was an authority on the county's feuds and friendships, and knew very well the ones that would make the most congenial companions. Mr. Motley's voice, practiced in the emergencies of fox hunting, sounded and all quieted to listen. He announced that Brother Galloway would bless the food spread out so bountifully before them. Brother Galloway mercifully was brief, and soon everybody was eating and laughing when his mouth was not too full.

But Jacob Skiles was troubled. Where were the Shobes? Since ten o'clock he had been looking for them. They were not there. They had, without doubt, intended to be there. The day, in a manner, belonged more to Eli Shobe than to anyone else. He looked over the lot again, but nowhere was there a sight of Mr. Shobe. At a table only a dozen yards away his wife was busy spreading food upon the table. Mrs. Motley and Mrs. Jenkins were using the same table. The food was very alluring, but he would have no taste for it until the Shobes showed up.

Then a hand was laid upon his shoulder, and there behind him were Eli Shobe, his wife and the four appetites. The two older boys were carrying large and obviously heavy baskets. They set them on the ground and all shook hands with Skiles.

"We left at sunup," said the perspiring Shobe. "We got along fine till just four miles out of town, and there the left front axle broke. Of all the times! We got it ready to move less than an hour ago. I am mighty sorry. How are things going?"

"Your axle is the only slip that I know of. And you got here, and that is what counts. Bring those baskets over to our tables. We'll make room."

Room was made. There were introductions and friendly greetings. The flimsy table creaked with the added weight from the Shobe baskets. Skiles cast another look around the lot. Everyone seemed to be eating with great heartiness. There was no sight of the Griders. Skiles wondered about Felix Grundy. Grundy's part on the program of the day was Grider's notion. He had gone to Eli Shobe with the suggestion that he be secured.

"I've heard of him," said Shobe. "He must be a mighty good speaker. Do you reckon we could get him? We are pretty short of money."

"Leave it to me. I became acquainted with him when I was on the way to Bowling Green. I heard him speak at Springfield. If the committee can furnish coach fare, I'll try to bring him. He would like to get acquainted down in this section. We will keep him at our house."

Shobe had told him to make the arrangements. Money would be got somehow to pay for coach fare from Bardstown. The people who would be there to hear Grundy would like a good speech. It would help to make the day a perfect one. And so Grundy had been placed on the program.

Bill Willie Blewett came up to the table and with him Lem and Jeff. Bill Willie was taking no chances on their defection, and they regarded their newly gained friend with obvious fondness. Bill Willie spoke to Shobe and Motley. He bowed to the ladies but tactfully refrained from introducing his two new friends to them. He passed ample portions of food to them and then stood back with them eating.

"I'm mighty sorry about getting here late," said Shobe. "Any news?"

"No special news," said Motley, "except they got the best victuals here I ever tasted."

Shobe asked, "Did the new bank open?"

"I passed but I didn't go in, but I saw two men going in. It opened."

"That plaguy axle! I wouldn't have missed being here for a whole bucketful of bee-tree honey. Did you ever see as many people?"

Bill Willie Blewett spoke up: "And they's a third of them never been here before."

"It's a good thing to start them coming," said Shobe. "From what I have heard of that man Grundy they'll like the speaking as well as the eating. They say he can have people laughing one minute and crying the next. Did you ever see people eat so heartily? I honestly believe there are eaters out there who could match my menfolks."

Mrs. Shobe said, "From the way my husband talks you would think that my boys aren't good at anything but eating."

"I didn't say that at all. They are good at a lot of things. But if any fellow wants a match at eating, I'll put any one of the boys up against him. In fact, if I had a boy that wasn't a good eater I'd disown him."

From where they stood they could see the newly laid out graveyard with a few graves even then. Beyond that the new church was nearing completion, and in the distance, beyond the church, was the square, deserted now but soon to be crowded with those eager to hear the great man sprinkle the golden air of fading summer with honeyed words and phrases. A disquieting thought struck Jacob Skiles. He remembered Elvis Grider waiting at the coach station for the orator. What if he failed to arrive? Who could be substituted? Judge Drake had some fame as a speaker, but it was local fame. Brother Galloway could preach for them. Even so, Skiles sensed that the crowd would be displeased not to hear the promised orator. He excused himself and walked to the coach station. It was locked. Elvis Grider was nowhere to be seen and his team was no longer there. Either Grundy had arrived and been driven away, or Grider had given up and gone back to the bank. If the stage had come why had Grider not brought Grundy to the dining grove? He remembered then that he had not seen Mrs. Grider during the day.

Skiles turned and started back to his friends. Someone touched him on the shoulder. He looked around.

"Name's Buffalo Strange," the man said. "We have got a lot of the best fried catfish you ever put your tongue to. I'd kinda like for you all to step over and eat a piece. We got plenty."

"That's neighborly of you," said Skiles. "I am fond of fried catfish. Where did you catch all of that catfish?"

"Where Graham Springs runs into the river. Caught 'em all on a couple of trotlines. There ain't a better fried-catfish cook than my wife in Warren County."

"You are very hospitable and sound convincing. May I have some of your wife's fried catfish? My name is Jacob Skiles."

"I've heard about you. I've fished some with Bill Willie Blewett. We got plenty. What about bringing some of your friends?"

"You are putting a strain on your wife's fried catfish. I'll go get them."

So the Skiles, the Motleys, the Shobes and the Jenkinses were proudly served fried catfish by Mr. Buffalo Strange and his wife. All testified that it was excellent fried catfish, and the pride of the Stranges was increased visibly by the relish with which it had been eaten.

"I'd better get back to our table," said Mr. Shobe. "Those menfolks of mine are likely to keep on eating even after the food is all gone. Many are the plates and cups we have lost that way."

The bell rang again. That was the prearranged signal that the speaking on the square would begin in half an hour. It was time to bring the feasting to a close, to discard scraps, and to bundle up dishes and remainders to take home. The dinner had been a success. There were some who, remembering the basket meeting, cast inquiring looks at the sky, but there was not even a smear of cloud to mar the prospects of the afternoon. The weather was October at its best. The bell rang again. That meant the speaking would begin in fifteen minutes. Time to be moving on up toward the square.

All ears were hungry to hear the great man. By then reports of his talents had been multiplied throughout the crowd, and there had been some debate as to whether Grundy or Henry Clay was the greater. Fiddle and banjo sang again from the platform though they would yield when the great man appeared. Jacob Skiles surveyed the crowd. There was no sign of Elvis Grider.

Eli Shobe shouldered his way through the crowd to where Skiles was standing. "He got here all right," he said. "I mean Grundy. The coach got in just before we began eating dinner. I saw the hostler and he said a stranger got off and went away with Grider in his carriage."

"Grider had better hurry up and get him here. These people would get impatient. Did you ever hear better music?"

Lex Spalding and Ham Vernon made a good team. Spalding was tall and rangy. His face was large and florid, and his mustache was reddish-brown, with a sweeping curl toward the tips. Vernon was short and dumpy. His face was round and pudgy, and he always seemed half asleep. Even when he was picking the banjo, his eyelids were half closed, and his expression was dull and unshifting. But his fingers flew about the strings with incredible speed. They were playing "Soldiers' Joy," the breakdown favorite of the public. They played it on and on. Then Spalding, without seeming to do so, looked across at Vernon. That meant that it was time to change pieces. They paused for a moment and Vernon twisted a key or two. Then, without seeming to do so, he looked across at Spalding. That meant his banjo was back in tune. Some sort of subtle communication existed between the two men. Neither suggested the next piece, but in full understanding they rushed into "Billy in the Low Ground." The public found pleasure in that piece too, and the musicians found pleasure in playing it. Spalding's bow darted and soared, sank and quivered. Vernon's fingers plucked and noted the strings with unbelievable facility and co-ordination. All of his fingers fused into the tune's delightful unity.

The beat of horses' hoofs and the crunch of gravel announced the approach of a carriage. It was driven by Mr. Elvis Grider. On the front seat with him sat a man of distinguished appearance, without doubt the great Mr. Grundy. On the rear seat were Mrs. Grider and their son Nat. Skiles breathed in relief. Nothing except the fracture of Mr. Shobe's right front axle had happened to mar Kentucky's first County Court Day. Spalding and Vernon must have heard the approach of the carriage, but neither hesitated the slightest in his playing. They came to the end of a verse and plunged into another. Mr. Grider turned his carriage over to a bystander to hitch. His wife and son took their places in the crowd. Mr. Grider pushed his way toward the platform, Grundy following. Judge Drake fell in with them and the three arrived at the platform. Skiles tapped Spalding on the ankle and pointed to the approaching men. But the musicians were then at the beginning of a stanza.

"I wouldn't stop a piece halfway through for the King of England," Spalding said out of the corner of his mouth. They finished the full stanza with proper flourishes.

Then suddenly they quit, and in dignity climbed down from the platform. Judge Drake, Elvis Grider and Grundy mounted the platform. Three chairs had been placed there and Grider and Grundy sat in two of them. Judge Drake advanced to the edge of the platform and held out his hand for silence—which he already had. He said that nothing of as much significance had happened in the county, and he took it to mean that while Warren was not one of the oldest of the sisterhood of Kentucky's counties it was quickly taking its place in the forefront of that great family. A kindly Providence had betokened the greatness of the day with weather unsurpassed in all of its phases. In the bleak days of the oncoming winter everyone present could remember this great day and from the memory gain needed warmth. The county was surely in the most robust of health since all of its people were present and enjoying themselves. He personally had made the rounds of the tables in the dining grove, and not in his life had he beheld such an abundance of food, of quality to give even the French great envy. The town and the county were moving forward in even step, each the handmaiden of the other. Only today a bank had opened in Bowling Green, its function to give an amplitude in living hitherto denied. He had been told that a new hauling enterprise would begin its service within the month, thus bringing the people nearer to the sources of vital supplies. It was such a town and such a county whose citizens the speaker was to address. The day was so great that it was most fitting that a man whose words were golden and whose tongue silver should speak to those assembled. He presented such a man, the Honorable Felix Grundy.

Felix Grundy was the peer of any man in the art of pioneer oratory. He knew the proper tilt of the head, the correct sweep of the eyes, the rhythmic motion of the hand in sweeping back a wayward lock of hair, without whose waywardness the picture would have been less perfect. He knew which foot to place forward, and the minutiae of its placement. All of these he compounded into his initial effect. He did it so superbly that a half gasp, a half sigh expressed the ecstasy of suspense in which the audience waited. He bowed with grace to Judge Drake, moved the bow on to include Elvis Grider. Then he turned to his audience.

"My fellow Kentuckians: My heart warms when I say those words, for when I remember that I am a Kentuckian my blood pulses faster, and my heart leaps with pride. It is the land of Boone and Harrod and Walker. It is the land of David Rice and George Rogers Clark; of John Filson and Isaac Shelby. Its gateways are the Ohio River and the Cumberland Gap. It is the land of mist-wreathed mountains and gently billowing bluegrass; it is the land of the hills and the knobs, and of the rivers lined with the very substance of life. The cold of its winters are short-lived, and the snow melts under the gentle caresses of the fragrant southern winds. The heat of its summers cannot long endure . . ."

The pressure which Grundy's oratory built up in Mr. Timothy
Elkins of Plum Springs became unbearable. Mr. Elkins loved speaking and was wont to express his approval with due audibility. He
leaned back and uttered a prolonged and resounding whoop. There
were reproving looks and shushes turned against him. Sheriff McFarland moved toward him, though slightly uncertain as to purpose.

Felix Grundy shifted his position on the platform and held up a
restraining hand.

"Ah, there speaks a true Kentuckian. The names I have called
raise rich meanings in my friend's mind and set his soul on fire
with noble zeal."

"What'd he say?" Mr. Elkins inquired of anyone in position to
answer.

His neighbor, Bird Garrity, answered, "He said if you want to make
a speech come on up there where he is."

"Ain't I goin' to get arrested? I did last time."

"That was a Baptis' preachin' you hollered at then."

Grundy was improvising on tunes the audience loved:

"Kentucky is the haven of those intrepid souls we call the
Scotch-Irish. Their veins are filled with the best blood of Old
Scotland, their souls made crystal by the Scottish lakes, their
bodies rugged by the Scottish hills, their spirits gay by the merry
hearts of Ireland. It was those same Scotch-Irish who, when
England laid a cruel hand upon their liberties, came to America
and placed deep and firm the foundation stones of our lives and
culture."

Mr. Elkins had an idea that those same Scotch-Irish had something
to do with him, so the pressure started up again.

"It was the Scotch-Irish who struck deep into the untamed wilderness, and made it a place of happy homes. It was the Scotch-
Irish who lighted the lamps of learning in our schools and sang
the songs of Zion in our churches."

Elkins exploded in a whoop, louder even than the former one. Felix
Grundy's great, luminous eyes rested approvingly upon him and a
faint smile touched the Grundy features. Timothy was cueing him

royally. Sheriff McFarland was again on his way to Elkins, and this
time he moved with decision. But he stopped, for the speaker was saying a surprising thing:

"I never in my life have been so complimented. I have lifted
my voice in many of the parts of our great commonwealth, and to
audiences of all stations and degrees. I say modestly that I have
not gone without approval. I have had smiles and nods of assent.
I have seen the eyes of my hearers brighten from thoughts awakened, but now I am left both humble and uplifted by the sincerity and spontaneity of my friend's applause. It rings in my ears
as pure music, chords sounded from the depths of the soul of a
true Kentuckian. However, it might be better to leave the unity
of my address unbroken till I have finished. I am sure that my
friend understands."

He nodded brightly to Timothy, who looked inquiringly at Bird
Garrity. Garrity answered him forthrightly. "He says you are to keep
your mouth shet till he gets through speaking."
    Elkins pondered this duly. "I'll try," he said meekly.
    Felix Grundy shifted from Kentucky's glories to Kentucky's needs:

"We are too prone to glorify a log cabin and a little patch of
corn raised by a hoe on the side of a hill. That log cabin may be
a home and the nubbins of corn sweet and succulent. But to
make Kentucky a great state that log cabin will have to rise,
slowly perhaps but surely, into the full stature of a brick house.
That hillside will have to flatten and deepen into a spreading
field. Our teachers, for all they are doing now, will have to add
to their store of understanding. Some of our preachers will have
to learn to preach better sermons than to declaim hoarsely, over
and over again, a half dozen verses from the Holy Scriptures. Our
lawyers will have to rise above the level of the pettifogger. It is
menacing for a state or a nation to stand still. If kind fortune
should permit me to return to this scene a year from now, and
there would be nothing better for me to see than that which
greets my eyes now, then I will say that you are doomed. The
only justification for tomorrow is that it may be better than today. The only reason for next year to come is that it may make
our lives freer, our spirits nobler."

Elkins was breathing deeply again. Sheriff McFarland, whose eyes had not left the man, recognized the signs of developing pressure. The sheriff was troubled. He had been as patient with Elkins as he could afford to be. He was sworn to preserve order. If Timothy sounded his whoop once more, he from that time would have to whoop in jail.

Bird Garrity made a suggestion to the sheriff. "Make him set down. Timothy can't holler when he's a-settin'."

The sheriff brightened. Maybe Bird was right. Sitting often had a quieting effect upon men.

He laid a firm hand on Timothy's shoulder. "Listen here, Timothy Elkins, you set right down there and lean against that tree. You'll be a lot less liable to land in jail."

"Sheriff wants me to set down," Timothy explained to Bird.

"You better do what he says. You'd hate to miss that big auction sale."

"One more whoop, and he'll miss it," the sheriff said. "You set right there. You can hear every word the man says. And don't get up till he's finished."

Elkins meditated upon the matter. Then he gravely and clumsily sat down and leaned against the tree. He could still hear Felix Grundy, but his pressure was weakening, and soon he was sound asleep.

The speaking was over and Elvis Grider escorted the visitor over to see the new bank. The crowd moved on to the grove where Mr. Curd was to auction off all things remaining unsold or untraded. Mr. Curd was regarded as without peer in the fine art of the auction.

Elvis Grider and Felix Grundy sat and talked in the bank's outer room. Jim Walters sat in the back room and explained to Tom Lockyear of Rockfield why it was a good thing for a man to deposit his money in a bank. Tom didn't have much money, but he wished very much to keep what he did have. A week before, his affluent cousin, Shan Cole, had had twelve dollars in his pocket, but when he reached for it there was no money there. It was gone and Shan never knew where it went.

"If I had it back," Shan had said as they stood eating their dinner, "I'd take it to that new bank. Money is safe in a bank. That's what a bank is for."

"How do you know it is safe?"

"It stands to reason. The only way you can get it out is to write a check. That makes it safe."

"Suppose the people who own the bank would steal it?"

"You could jail them."

Tom didn't want his money to disappear, so he tentatively visited the bank. "It's a good thing for you to put your money in our bank," Walters counseled him. "It helps put Bowling Green far out in the lead of most places its size."

That wasn't entirely convincing to Tom. "I wouldn't want to lose my money," he said.

"If anything happens to your money I'll make it good personally."

"That sounds fair enough," said Tom. "I'll deposit it then."

"I regard your starting this bank as very progressive," Felix Grundy was saying to Elvis Grider. "It marks Bowling Green as a forward-moving town. I fancy you have started off very favorably."

"I'd like to know how well myself." Grider went to the door to the back room, opened it and spoke for a moment with Jim Walters. Then he returned to the front room and Walters resumed with Tom Lockyear.

"I think we have done all right for the first day," Grider said to Grundy. "We have had seven men put money in the bank, and we have lent money to three. There was a man in here awhile ago talking about a big loan. Said he was thinking of starting a newspaper. My partner is talking with a customer in there now."

"A newspaper," said Grundy, chewing the words thoughtfully. "A bank could well afford connections with a newspaper, in a business way, of course."

"I am delighted, Mr. Grundy."

"A most auspicious beginning," said Grundy. "The time will come when the lifeblood of a community flows through its banks."

"Very elegant words, Mr. Grundy. I shall remember them. Have you anything you would like to do now?"

"Yes, there is. Doubtless your auction sale is going in full blast. I'd like to see it. I have a fondness for auction sales. I may say that I have learned a great deal from auctioneers."

"Certainly. I'd like to see it myself."

They walked along the street toward the auction sale. "I fancy that the County Court Day is your own idea, Mr. Grider."

"Not wholly."

Mr. Grundy's keen eyes noted the brief hesitancy. It brought to mind other things he had noticed.

"All our community needs is the proper leadership," Mr. Grider was saying. "I am very busy at a great many things, but I have found the people willing to follow."

They heard Mr. Curd while yet a hundred yards distant. He was selling a side of meat for a man from Richpond. At first all they heard was a distant flow of words fused together in a musical chant, but with little curlicues running about like a playful little dog humoring its progress by merry gambolings.

"I am selling, giving away, or paying you to take a slab o' meat so good it'll melt in your mouth, melt in your mouth, melt in your mouth——"

"Listen to that," said Grundy. "The man is an artist."

"Look at that piece o' side meat. Just look at it. Did you ever see a purtier piece o' meat, piece o' meat, piece o' meat? What am I offered for this piece o' side meat that a crowned head of Yurrup couldn't eat no better than? What am I offered?"

"Two bits," yelled a red-faced man from the crowd.

"Somebody stand up clost and ketch me if some feller makes another offer like he done. A piece o' side meat like this don't come cheap. Nosirree. That hawg went to a lot o' trouble to grow this meat. Then, the man smoked it a year with solid hickory wood."

"Then it's done ruined," said the bidder. "A year's too long to smoke it. It's done dried plumb up."

"A sweeter piece o' side meat you never set a tooth to. Whata I hear for a piece o' side meat that Gawge Washington never et any as good?"

"Four bits," yelled Tinker Grimes from Sand Hill. "I got some kinfolks I don't mind pizenin'."

"Costs more'n four bits to get shed o' your kinfolks and stay out o' trouble. Whata I hear for this piece o' meat that's dangerous for old folks to eat on account o' makin' them live too long? Offered four bits and I ain't goin' to listen no more till I hear six."

"Six bits," said the red-faced man, "and keep the porehouse doors open so I can get in quick."

"Offered six bits by that fine-lookin', red-headed gentleman that looks like he's got real good sense. Offered six bits, offered six bits, offered six bits. You men want to go home ashamed on account you ain't done right by your family? You want to see your little children settin' there hungry for side meat? Offered six bits——"

"Eight bits," yelled Tinker Grimes, "and good-by, my kinfolks."

"I sympathize with the gentleman. I got kinfolks too. They's goin' to be feastin' in your house, sir, 'cause you done bought you a piece o' fine side meat. Sold for one dollar. And now, I have right here for sale the finest baby cradle that one ever got jiggled in."

"If the baby goes with it I'll take it," called out a long, skinny man.

"I don't care if you've been all the way to Philadelphy you ain't seen a cradle as good as this'n. Stop lettin' that beautiful baby sleep on the floor. That's no way to raise a shore-nuff baby. Takes one o' these double-jinted, hand-whittled cradles to do the work. Whata I hear for this elegant baby cradle?"

The tall, skinny man wasn't done with his joke. "You goin' to sell the baby too?" But Mr. Curd ignored him. It was then that he saw Felix Grundy standing with Mr. Grider, and the sight spurred him on to nobler efforts.

"What'd this country be without a cradle? Was Gawge Washington raised a-layin' on the floor? I asts you, was he? Did Dan'l Boone roll and cry all night because his folks was too triflin' to buy him a cradle? How many o' you fine folks got real nice babies that you'd like to amount to sumpin' like that man we all heard make that speech today? Then buy this cradle so your baby can get raised right, can get raised right, get raised right. Whata I hear for this-here fine cradle?"

"I'd like to stay longer," Grundy whispered to Grider. "The man is an artist, but I am tired. That coach trip was most tiring."

"I am ready to leave. We will get my wife and son, and go out to my home. You can get a good dinner, a good night's sleep, and be refreshed for your trip back to Bardstown."

"They told me at the station that the coach is supposed to leave at ten o'clock."

"I'll bring you as I come in to the bank."

Their way led not farther than fifty yards from the tavern. A crowd of men was standing out in front of the tavern and they could see that some matter of excitement was in progress, but they made no effort to find out what it was. To the west of them, the sun was touching the tops of the trees. It had been an exciting day, and in a way a tiring day. It was time to go home.

But without stopping to investigate, Mr. Grider had no way of knowing the relevancy of the excitement in front of the tavern. Bill Willie Blewett had been an avid spectator of most of the parts of County Court Day. He had eaten an enormous dinner. He had listened with great pleasure to Mr. Grundy's speech. He had found the auction very diverting. He had had much conversation with friends, including his fox-hunting crony, Mr. Reub Buckner. But he had told Jacob Skiles that he would be back at Three Springs early enough to take care of the stock, and anything else that seemed imperative. As he neared the tavern he saw Lem and Jeff just ahead of him. It wasn't that they were unsteady in their walk, but something told Bill Willie that this was not their first trip to the tavern. The thought came to him that more trips might not be favorable to a project in which he was interested.

He quickened his steps and caught up with the two men. He laid a hand on Jeff's arm. "You done been there too much," he said.

Jeff was inclined to be surly. "What'sa matter? What's botherin' you?"

"The teams and wagons for that haulin' job is ready to go. We got stuff to haul to Nashville, and there's goin' to be stuff to haul back. Them wagons is goin' to roll. You've teched your last dram today."

"A dram now ain't goin' to hinder us from drivin' wagons day after tomorrer."

"You fellers make good hands when you got a good man to work for and no licker inside you. You both mighty lucky. Elvis Grider, he runs you off and Jacob Skiles takes you in. You can't get no better man to work for than Skiles. He'll pay you good, and right down on the barrelhead, but he don't want no whisky heads runnin' his wagons.

Them's important wagons and you done been picked to run 'em."

"What'd you do ifn we took a dram?"

"You know how you fellers liable to act when you get too much redeye in you. Them wagons is goin' to be loaded tomorrer, and I aim for you to be ready to start afore sunup the next day. No drinkin' licker till you get back from this trip."

"Come on, Jeff. Have a swig." The man who issued the invitation was big and husky. His clothes were dirty from his having lain or rolled on the ground. His face was livid from both sun and whisky.

"No more licker till you get back from Nashville," said Bill Willie, calm and flinty-eyed. His eyes flicked to the man, then back to Lem and Jeff.

"I tell you what I'll do," said the red-faced man. "I'll bring my bottle there to you, and ifn you want a dram take it. I'll chaw a ear offn any feller that tries to stop you."

He walked across the little space swinging his bottle militantly. Bill Willie stood waiting. The moment he was in reach, Bill Willie's right hand flicked out and grabbed the man's bottle. He jerked with a twisting motion and the bottle was freed from his grasp. Blewett swung it in a fierce arc and it fell stunningly upon the man's head. There was a grunt, half of surprise, half of collapse, and the man dropped to the ground with a thud. Bill Willie stood looking down at him.

Then he turned to Lem and Jeff. "You see how I feel about them wagons," he said dryly. "You goin' to drive 'em?"

For a moment the men stood in embarrassed silence. Then Jeff said, "We'll drive your wagons. No licker till we get back."

The man on the ground somewhat uncertainly maneuvered himself into a standing position. Bill Willie regarded him coldly but alertly. "You got off easy. The next time I'm a-goin' to onscrew one o' your arms and tie a knot in your backbone."

"Come on," said Jeff to his partner. "We've got to rest up for that haulin'."

The auction sale wound to a close. Everything was disposed of. Mr. Curd had convinced, persuaded, cajoled and threatened the crowd into purchasing everything offered, and mainly at satisfactory prices. A lot of swapping had been done on the trading lot. Dinner had been eaten with great heartiness and capacity. Mr. Grundy's address would be remembered for a long time. County Court Day had been a good event. Warren County was closer together than it had ever been. The first wagon, drawn by oxen, left with an hour of sun remaining. Then the wagons, the horsemen, the people on foot fell into steadily moving lines along all the roads. A near full moon lifted its pale face out of the east. When the sun had disappeared over the western rim of the world the moon's soft radiance would envelop everything.

Jacob Skiles and Eli Shobe stood apart talking. Their teams were hitched and ready to leave, awaiting only their masters.

"Everybody had a good time," said Shobe. "I'll be surprised if County Court Day isn't a regular thing from now on."

"People are fond of people," said Skiles oracularly. "They like to be with them. It is easy to be lonely in a new country. A little loneliness may be a good thing. Too much is bad. A day like today is good medicine for loneliness. Breed Loving said the new bank did a good business."

"I heard several say that. How is your store coming along?"

"It will be ready to open within a month. I am starting two wagons to Nashville day after tomorrow for goods. Hardcastle has been bragging that the store won't last a month."

"Hardcastle is a cheerful fellow."

"As much as I look forward to the store, I doubt if I am as much interested in it as I am in the hauling route. I like to think of it as a link with the outside world."

"A link with the outside world? That's a nice thought. We need links like that."

"Precisely. We need to send what we raise to a market, and to bring back the things our stores should have for sale."

"And that means roads."

"Roads and rivers. We have a river, and I expect to live to see it very helpful to the community. Except in the drier seasons we can get stuff down the river now. Of course, we would have to go to a lot of trouble to work that traffic up, but we could do it. The problem is getting stuff up the river."

"Our problem is better roads," insisted Shobe. "At least, that is our main problem."

"The river and the roads. Perhaps you are right. Perhaps the roads are our main problem, but the river is too important to neglect."

"Who is going to manage your store?"

"I will for a while. I can be spared from the farm for several months. But I will have to have someone by next spring when the crop season opens. I have thought some of asking Bill Willie to run the store, but I need him on the farm."

"He's an outside man. He wouldn't like the store. Did you ever see a man better satisfied with himself than Elvis Grider seemed today?"

"I got to shake hands with Felix Grundy in spite of Elvis. Bill Willie hired those two men of Grider's to drive my wagons today."

"I have heard the Dawseys are leaving here," Shobe said irrelevantly. "I'll be glad to see them go. You will be hearing from Elvis all right. Well, bring the family to see us any time you can. I've got the feeling I need you. I hope we can stick close together."

"A mutual feeling, my friend. And it is your time to make a visit. Any time."

16

ELVIS GRIDER drove Felix Grundy to the coach station. Then he went to the bank. Walters was closeted with a customer, but soon he came out and joined his partner.

"Did he deposit any money?" inquired Grider.

"Twelve dollars and a half. Elvis, I heard the Dawseys are moving away from Mizpah."

"To Allen County, I believe. They have bought some property there."

"What I heard was that something happened to them and they couldn't make out what it was. It is liable to make anybody superstitious for that to happen. And here's something else, Elvis."

What he told Grider made that gentleman very angry. "I missed them. They didn't come back to the house last night." His tones were clipped with outrage. "I shall not permit this. I need them. I shall attend to it right away."

He started directly to Three Springs, but met Skiles on the way to town. He held up a restraining hand. "Please send my men back to me that you hired without my consent."

"But you had discharged them."

"Inform them that they are to return to me immediately."

"I shall do nothing of the kind. You were heard to discharge them."

"Only a matter of discipline. I have used it before. They are my hands. I expect them to be sent back to my place."

"Listen to me, sir. I do not like a dispute with any man. I certainly do not wish trouble with anyone. I have had enough of it in my life. I would not go to a man's place and try to hire his hands away from him. If they were no longer employed by him and I needed them, I would engage them. These two men I have honorably engaged. They will stay with me until they are proved unfit, or until they leave of their own accord. I trust that I have made myself understood. Good morning."

"Wait. I will not tolerate anyone taking from me that which is mine. This is the second time you have tried it. First my land, and now my hands. Unless those two men are back on my place tomorrow at noon I shall hold you personally responsible."

"Mr. Grider, so many really serious things have happened to me that I am not much troubled by your anger. Once the British captured me and were going to shoot me the next morning by daylight. Late in the night such a distracting storm arose that I was able to escape. Once the Indians had me tied to a stake for burning. They had even set fire to some of the brush at my feet. But then my comrades charged them and the Indians ran for their lives. My feet and ankles were burned before my friends could put the fire out and cut me loose. Please do not think that your puny threats will frighten me now."

"I shall expect those men tomorrow."

"You will likely not see them. Good morning, sir."

At noon he told Bill Willie Blewett of the episode. Bill Willie smiled grimly. "I ain't jokin'. Ifn them fellers started back to work for that scalawag, I'd fix 'em so they wouldn't be much good to him for a month or two."

"Fighting, Bill Willie, is likely to cost more than it gives."

"I'll be keerful to keep you out of it. It was me they promised to do the haulin'."

"But what would happen to the place if you were in jail? I want you to direct the hauling. If I have instructions, I'll bring them to you and you can pass them on to the drivers. If Mr. Grider wants a quarrel, we will not meet him halfway. If he brings it to us, we will try to accommodate him. Mr. Grider was very threatening, frankly a little too threatening, I think. If he had threatened less, I would regard him more seriously. If he tries to carry out his threat, we will try to oblige him, but I don't expect it."

"Any word about that land?"

"No." Jacob Skiles was smiling broadly. "Lank Motley told me confidentially that Judge Drake told him confidentially that he was going to put off making a decision as long as possible. The judge is afraid it might bring on trouble. He is a man of peace."

"I say that land case ought to be settled."

"I don't specially need the ground, but I feel that by rights it is mine."

"Them wagons is half-loaded now. I guess I better keep an eye on them two men. I aim for them to make this trip anyhow. We've got enough barrel staves for a load going down, and you said it would be a load of chairs coming back. My notion is to get all the haulin' done we can while the weather is good."

"That's good sense. We can carry a great deal more in a wagon over a dry road."

"Not a one of the other stores has a chair. And they's lots o' people wants to buy some. Of course, folks can make them at home, but they ain't fancy enough. What they want is store-bought chairs."

"I'd like for you to go to Nashville on the second trip. By that time, the farm can spare you awhile. I want you to find out what they have to sell in the place. I believe we could do a good business in shoes. Find out if we could get them there. Old Man Daughtry is the only saddle and harness maker here, but he is never up with his orders, and there is certainly nothing fancy about the things he makes. I'd like for the store to have a half dozen really good-looking saddles. See if they have anything to sell. My wife thinks there would be a good market here for some fancy dress goods. See what they have for sale there, or are likely to have. Hardcastle's store hasn't had a grain of powder in a week. You have good eyes and ears. Use them while you are there."

17

THE WEATHER was fine. A full moon, its body of silver, but with vague inlays of gold, slowly mounted the eastern sky. Jacob Skiles and his wife sat under the tree in the front yard and talked. Rumsey stayed with them awhile, but he got sleepy and went to bed. They could hear Bill Willie hammering at something in his cabin. He was always hammering at something. The horses stamped drowsily in the barn lot. Four of them had just been bought for the hauling line. They were sturdy, broad-chested animals that knew how to pull steadily but without haste. The little autumnal things made their night music in the branches above them.

"This feels more like home than any place I have ever lived," Priscilla Skiles said.

"I have thought the same since the day we got here. I don't think we will ever leave Three Springs."

"Rumsey is growing fast," she said almost irrelevantly. "We must begin thinking about him. Bowling Green ought to have a school."

"I have been thinking about that for three months. It is one of the things to be done next year. There are a lot of things to do," he added whimsically.

"There was never a man who could do a lot of things as well as you can, Mr. Skiles."

"It would be necessary for your husband to do a lot of things to match the patterns you set, my dear."

She patted his hand. They sat in silence for a while. Then he said, "Sometimes I don't see how I can get it all done. The farm really could take up all of my time, and it would if Bill Willie wasn't so dependable. Then we are starting the store, and it would fail if I should try to be too stingy with my time. And it will take both sense and time to make a go of this hauling route."

"Maybe you are getting into too many things, Mr. Skiles."

"I won't move any till I have thought where I am going. The store will be small at first, and for the time being we will deal mainly in the things the other stores do not carry."

"Chairs?"

"Chairs and other furniture. The wagons are bringing back a solid load of chairs on their first trip. You couldn't buy a dining table or a kitchen table at any of the places. I have made trips to the stores looking for a mirror. They didn't have a one. Lamps are hard to get. A storekeeper could make a living just selling shoes, if he could get the shoes."

"You won't be able to get everything you need in Nashville, will you?"

"Not everything, but I am willing to start a wagon line anywhere within reason. I'll have to go into it carefully, and it would be foolish to start any line without trustworthy drivers. What Kentucky needs is roads you can ride over all the year around. But roads will come, I am sure of it."

"But not soon," she said.

"Nothing worth while comes soon. We always have to work and wait. I think we will be able to use the river too someday."

"Use it how, Mr. Skiles?"

"To travel on, to haul goods to market on. But before we can do that we will have to clean the snags out of it, and dredge it out deeper in places. This river empties into the Green, not far north of here, and the Green empties into the Ohio. A great many important things are going to happen in our lifetime, my dear. Some wonderful things are going to be invented and devised. There will be some things, of course, that will not turn out well. The successful man will be the one who chooses the right thing while it is still new and proceeds to use it. The new things will be coming, my dear, and I intend to watch them closely. People are not going to permit themselves to be held back too long by muddy roads and snag-filled rivers. And that is not all to watch out for. We do a great deal of work by hand now that we will find an easier way to do. Mr. Searcy's mill, for instance. I have great respect for Mr. Searcy. It is a tedious thing to grind corn in a hand-turned mill or to pound it in a pestle. Mr. Searcy built a dam in the creek so that the water as it flows over it turns a wheel that grinds corn into meal. He wasn't the first man to think of it, but he was the first man who had the getup and the ingenuity to start one here. Now, Mr. Searcy has all the work he can do grinding corn for his neighbors. When the wind blows hard it has more power than a creek. Someday we are going to contrive something to keep that power from going entirely to waste."

"I know where Rumsey gets his curiosity. He loves to sit in the kitchen and watch the lid on the kettle move up and down when the water is boiling. He is always asking, 'What pushes it, Mama?' The other day he asked me why a rock didn't roll uphill like it does downhill. That child is needing a school now."

"The other day I took him into the courthouse while a trial was going on. He watched everything very closely. On the way home he told me that he was going to make a lawyer."

"I will be proud if he does."

"He may have changed his plans by now. Children do. Maybe he will invent some of the things I have been talking about, only I just don't know what they are. The next ten or twenty-five years are going to be busy ones, and I think very exciting ones. The country is growing fast. A fourth as many people have come to Warren County as we found when we got here less than a half year ago. But some have stayed a little while and then moved on. Some of them moved to the land that President Jefferson bought from the French. I know of two families that moved to the Illinois country. But this country will grow fast. Judge Drake thinks that politics will be a very important activity in the future. He thinks that politics may become so exciting that political parties will declare war on each other and settle things that way. The judge may believe that. He kept a straight face when he said it, but I don't take it seriously."

"Do you think we might have another war?"

"There is always danger of another war. From the talk I hear we are likely to have more trouble with England, and it might end in war. I want no more war. I have enough peaceful things to take all of my time."

"I think of Rumsey whenever anybody says *war*."

"Rumsey is one reason I don't want another war. You are another reason. All of us are reasons." He was silent again for a little while. Then he said, "If our business does all right I want to build a good house for us, just as soon as we can."

"Yes, but I am liking to live here better every day."

"You deserve a better house than this one, and you are going to get it. We are going to have to buy some slaves. I hate the business, and the only excuse I can make to my conscience is that we will treat them well. We are going to be desperately in need of more help soon. I really wonder how we have got along as well as we have, but I owe it to Bill Willie. If I had another as good as he is, we could do without slaves."

"Everything is going to be all right, isn't it?" she asked a bit wistfully.

"I do not doubt it." He looked upward at the moon, then dropped his eyes to the woods and fields on which it shone. "I love the world like this," he said. "Well, it is time to go to bed."

The Settlement Continued

1 8 2 5

1

TWENTY-ONE YEARS had brought great changes to Warren County. The population was four times as large. The roads still were poor, but they had been improved to the extent that only a few of the county's sections were wholly isolated during the muddy winter months. The main roads had been given a base of heavy stones, which made the riding rough, but the people felt that it was better to be bumped than mired. The minor roads were usable during the dry season, but likely to become most discouraging to travelers during the rainy months. County Court Day was well established not only as the month's main social event, but also as a great day for buying and trading. On that day the wagons, whether drawn by horses or oxen, began rumbling along the roads by sunup. There were a few carriages and a great many of the smaller vehicles. Many of the log cabins had given way to better and more pretentious homes. There were, in the county, a few homes flavored with the quality of Virginia's best. There were a great many middle-class homes, usually two stories in height and built of sturdy planking. They were plain, but imparted the feeling of stability and reasonable comfort. There were still a great many humble homes.

Bowling Green was not only much larger but also much more bustling. There were a dozen stores, all prospering reasonably. Mr. Hardcastle's store had doubled in size. He kept a helper regularly, and on special days two. He had grown gray and weazened, but he was still alert and eager for trade. It was commonly known that the store's real owner was Elvis Grider, thought by some to be the town's richest man. The pharmacist, Dr. Younglove, not only sold drugs of all sorts, kinds, and colors, but was generally considered the town's major oracle in all of its phases. It was his custom to sell a dime's worth of bluemass and to throw in free a full chapter of the town's history, together with an indisputable prophecy of things to come. His shop was the main gathering place for the town's intellectuals, real and alleged. Jacob Skiles's store was prospering. Its principal stock had been furniture for so long that it was known generally as a furniture store. More than twenty-one years before, it had opened with two wagonloads of chairs brought from Nashville. Within a week not a chair was left in the store. For more than a score of years the two wagons had run, with varying degrees of regularity, between Bowling Green and Nashville. On the trips south they would carry such merchandise as Bowling Green had to offer Nashville. On the return trips they brought tables and chairs and beds and chests of drawers. Skiles operated four more wagons, two to Louisville, one to Bardstown, and one to Henderson. Lem and Jeff still drove the Nashville wagons. They were gaunt and grizzled men. They could handle teams with great skill and had proved dependable. They stayed away from taverns while on duty, and had developed considerable pride in their prowess with wagons. Bowling Green's original tavern had yielded to the Washington Hall Inn, which was much better than the average hostelry found in the new settlements.

The section was ablaze with political fervor, and the main issues were joined in debate at Washington Hall. It was the town's forum, and the stopping place for all men of distinction who visited in the town. There were Presbyterian, Methodist, and Baptist churches, and the new congregation, the Disciples of Christ, was considering the construction of a building. The bank was owned and managed by Mr. Grider and Mr. Walters. They had competition for a few years, but the second bank failed because of hard times and poor management. Death had long since taken Brother Galloway from the Presbyterian pulpit, but his successor, Brother Lapsley, had established a reputation as a man of eloquence and devotion. Judge Drake still sat on the bench, and he looked not five years older.

But, for all of its progress, the town's old frictions had not faded out, and new ones had been created. The people took avidly to the political issues raised before them. A fierce presidential campaign had been waged, and the citizens were sharply divided into two camps: those supporting Henry Clay, Lexington's dramatic figure, and the state's great orator, and those supporting General Andrew Jackson, the renowned hero of New Orleans. There was no concern for the other candidates. It was true that Jackson was not a Kentuckian, but his home was less than half the distance of Clay's. The battle had drawn to its crisis at the polls the autumn before, but the results had been inconclusive and were due to be settled soon by the House of Representatives in Washington. Elvis Grider was the leader of the Jackson forces in the county, and Jacob Skiles was the recognized champion of the forces of Henry Clay. Neither man spared any effort to place the power of the county behind his candidate. The county seemed to be about evenly divided.

2

County Court Day in January was bleak and threatening, and the crowd was much smaller than commonly. There was very little activity on the trading lot. Men stood huddled in groups or sought the shelter of the stores. But wherever they gathered, the conversation was Clay *versus* Jackson. The group of men in front of the Younglove apothecary shop bordered on the disorderly in their partisanship.

"What'd Henry Clay ever do? Jest tell me one thing except make speeches, stand on a platform and holler. Ain't that what Pat Curd does when he sells a bone-spavined mule? And the worse off the mule the louder he hollers. Does that make him fitten for President?"

"You'd be right, Bud, except for one thing. When Henry Clay stands up there and hollers, he's a-sayin' sumpin'. He's a-utterin' words that you ain't never learned about. Henry Clay's got a right to holler, but you, Bud, when you got sumpin' to say you ought to jest whisper it so nobody'll know how much sense you ain't got."

"Andy Jackson don't waste his time a-talkin'. When a thing needs doin' he jest goes and does it. When a feller needs shootin' he goes and shoots him, and when he's President he's a-goin' to be right busy 'cause they's plenty that needs it."

"Jackson ain't got no more chance bein' President than a peckerwood has a-turnin' into a Methodist preacher. But Henry Clay's got sense. And when he gets to be President he's a-goin' to talk them furriners right into anything he wants."

"And someday when he's a-standin' up on a platform a-whoopin' and a-hollerin' one o' them furrin countries is a-goin' to steal Kentucky right from under his eyes."

"I wouldn't mind 'em a-stealin' Kentucky a-tall jest so they took you along with it."

A lanky, black-bearded man took a few paces from the group, threw his coonskin cap on the ground and in a deep, rumbling voice said, "You fellers been palaverin' sence right after dinner and you ain't got nothin' settled yet. You palaver worse'n Henry Clay. Andy Jackson didn't palaver. He jest settled things. Ifn they's any fightin' to be done he jest fit. What I got to say is this. Ifn any Clay man here hankers to get a good whuppin' I'm a-waitin' to do it. I'm the very man to skin him and render him down for his taller. I'm the feller to take off his ears and onscrew his nose, and when I've finished with him you'll have to look twicet to see a grease spot where he used to be. I'm a-standin' here a-waitin' to start chawin' him up and spittin' him out. I got my teeth sharpened for tough meat, and I'm pizener'n a copperhead snake."

Bill Willie Blewett came out of the apothecary shop and stood listening. He walked across and stood in front of the black-bearded man. "I ain't whupped you sence last summer," he said mildly. "Ain't it about time agin?"

"Stay away from me, Bill Willie. I ain't got no fuss with you."

"How you know you ain't?" Bill Willie struck him suddenly and violently. The man staggered back, holding his jaw.

Jacob Skiles came out of the shop. His quick eyes caught the meaning of things. "Come on," he said quietly. "It is time for us to be going home." They drove away in the buckboard.

A bystander said, "When Bill Willie come out of the store and stood there listening, I saw there was going to be trouble. He's a regular fightin' Irishman."

Another said sympathetically to the black-bearded man, "Doc Younglove's got some liniment that'll help that jaw. Ask him for a rub."

Characteristically, Jacob Skiles said nothing about the episode as they drove home. He did say, "I'll be glad when the election is finished. This is wasting a lot of time."

"Henry Clay got a chance?"

"Between us, Bill Willie, I doubt it. Jackson is very popular around here just as Adams is in the East. Either Clay or Jackson will have to team up with Adams, and of course it will not be Jackson. The Atlantic seaboard is still our most powerful section. The West is gaining, but I don't think it is strong enough yet. I will say to you, Bill Willie, that which I will say to my wife and you, and to nobody else. I have my hopes fixed on four years from now. I think we can elect a Western man then. I don't believe we can now. I hope that it will be Henry Clay."

"It would have to be him or the Ginral, wouldn't it?"

"We will have to wait to see how the wind is blowing then. I would be uncertain about Jackson even if Elvis Grider were not mixed up with him. Jackson has some good points, but he has some bad ones too. I think it would be bad for us for him to be elected. It would give Grider more power in Bowling Green than would be good for the place. I doubt whether Jackson could be called a statesman—a soldier, yes, but hardly a great political leader. I think Henry Clay is one. He has several times endorsed the improvement of rivers and roads, but when I think of it, he has not been explicit enough to suit me. I would like him to come out more clearly for Federal aid to the states that need it. Let me tell you what I mean, Bill Willie. Our town and county will be a different place the day we hear the whistle of a steamboat blowing for the Bowling Green landing. That will mean that the door has been opened and we can go out in the world. Our pikes are pretty rough traveling, and they are risky. We have a heavy rain and the creek gets up so high that we can't ford it, and there we stay till it runs back down, sometimes in a day, sometimes in ten days. I am told that almost every day a steamboat passes up or down the Ohio River. We would have steamboats now, but our river isn't ready for them. If we had steamboats we could sell everything we could raise or make, and we could buy everything we need. We could buy goods for our stores all the way from New Orleans and Natchez to Cincinnati. But our river is filled with snags, and there are so many sand bars that passage is difficult, even for a flatboat. We haven't got the money to open the river for trade. It will take money from Washington. I wish Clay would say more clearly what he thinks of such improvements. But I regard him as a statesman. I shall depend on him to do that which is right."

"When is it goin' to be settled who's elected?"

"I suppose it is already settled, and my guess is that Adams is elected. It will be two or three weeks before we hear. If Adams is elected he won't lift a hand to help this section. Our river isn't in New England."

"I heard that Elvis Grider said that the Ginral will come through here on his way back from Washington."

"If Elvis said that, he has given up hope that Jackson will be elected. If he is he won't come back. He will stay there. If Elvis said that, it would mean that they too are getting ready for four years from now. Well, I'll stick to Clay." He was silent for a moment. "We had a letter from Rumsey yesterday. He passed his law examination and is going to start practicing in Bowling Green right away, perhaps by the first of March."

"I reckon Miz Skiles is mighty proud of him."

"She walks on air. She lives in the clouds. She hopes that his clothes have holes in them so she can mend them. And I expect they do. She is planning what she will give him to eat, and trying to think how she can talk with the neighbors about him without seeming too proud."

"She's got a right to be proud."

"I'll not argue that with you. Rumsey is a good boy, and I think he will make a good lawyer. I do believe it is what he has been wanting to do since that day I took him to a trial when he was just four years old. He is bright enough, and they have good law teachers at Transylvania. Guess what he said in his letter."

"I don't have a notion, Mr. Skiles."

"He will stay at home the first month and never once mention paying board. After that he will pay board or else he will move into town. We can take our choice. We have spent enough on him already, he says. His mother doesn't know whether to be proud of that or hurt. She will wind up by being proud."

"She's got the right to be proud," Bill Willie said again.

"I heard one piece of bad news in town," said Skiles. "Judge Drake has opposition for the judgeship."

"That is bad, but I don't guess anybody can beat him. Who's runnin' agin him?"

"Jess Beecham. He announced Saturday."

"He ain't got a chance."

"My opinion precisely, but there is no denying that Jess has some popularity. Besides, Judge Drake has been in the office for twenty-four years. A great many people think that is long enough. They think offices should be passed around."

"How'll Elvis Grider vote?"

"I don't know, but he will never say a word in public against Judge Drake."

"I expect Rumsey will be runnin' for sumpin' someday."

"If he does I hope we both will be alive to vote for him. I think you'd like to know, Bill Willie, that we finished totaling the books at the store today. We made a good profit last year."

"Things look all right for this year?"

"I'd say so, but there is some uncertainty. We will sell a good deal of furniture but we do need more variety, and that is hard to get. People are wanting better pieces for their homes now."

"You done all right on the farm too, didn't you?"

"That brings me right back where we started. We raised plenty for us to eat, for the stock to eat, and wool to make into clothing, but I could have fattened twice as many hogs if we had had a steamboat. The wagons have carried some pork to market, but that is a slow way. I'll guarantee the prosperity of Bowling Green when we have a better way of getting things in and out."

They were nearing the Grider home then. As they were passing, a carriage drove out at the front and turned to the right toward town. Skiles bowed gravely as he had been doing for years. Grider looked rigidly ahead as was his custom.

Bill Willie looked back with interest. "Mighty late for him to be goin' to town."

Skiles made no reply.

A few minutes later the two men reached the Skiles home. The log house that Bill Willie Blewett had built was no longer there. On its site stood a two-story brick house that Skiles looked at with pleasure as he always did when returning home. The house was well proportioned, and fitted into its site with charm. Its columns showed a dull white in the thinning light. It had not been easy to tear the log house down. Mother, father, and son had loved the place from the day they moved in, but the time came when they found that it cramped their ideals of a home. They had prospered and could afford a more commodious place. They tried to find a site that pleased them and would leave the log house untouched, but Bill Willie Blewett had been too correct in his choice of a site. Search as they did, they could find no place that bore so well the tokens of fitness. So they rented another log house a mile away and moved into it while the old one was being taken down and the new one constructed. The rented house was not a pleasant place in which to live, and it was home-coming indeed when they could move into the new Three Springs. Lights had blazed in every room that night, and all the neighbors came in to share their pleasure, all but the Elvis Griders. . . .

"It is going to be a cold night," Skiles said. "There will be a hard freeze." He didn't tell Blewett to see that the stock was well taken care of. He knew that would be done.

"It will be like old times to have Rumsey back," said Blewett.

"We need somebody young on the place. You and I have lived here twenty-two years. We are that much older than that first morning."

"I wasn't any spring chicken then."

"Sometimes I feel forty years older. I am glad that Rumsey is coming back for more reasons than merely to have him here. Someday he will have to take charge of this place. Maybe sooner than we think."

The two men stood at the gate. It had grown so dark that neither could see very well the face of his companion. He didn't have to. They had lived too close together for their understanding to be that superficial. Each one knew what the other was thinking.

"Could he run the farm and practice law too?"

"That would be for him to decide. And the store would be his too. Don't forget that. All the time the boy was growing up I was trying to make him love and understand the farm. Though I think I succeeded, he has always wanted to make a lawyer. But the farm is not to be sold, Bill Willie. This is Skiles land. He can dispose of the store if he wants to; not this farm. I love every acre of it. Three Springs is a Skiles place."

"Even the timberland?" Bill Willie approached a jest as nearly as was his custom.

"Every acre of it," said Skiles, the dark hiding the smile that softened his face. "And I know every acre of it, Bill Willie, almost every tree. I know that Elvis Grider knows it too. I have never seen him there, but I have seen his tracks. I knew they were his. Sometimes I have amused myself thinking what we would say to each other if we met there. Remember the cedar trees that Lem and Jeff cut down there? Well, the stumps are still standing. They have rotted very little. That was good cedar. I am proud of those stumps. It came about indirectly but those stumps brought us two good wagonmen. I couldn't ask for better men."

"They wasn't much good then."

"They are now. If it hadn't been for them, we couldn't have kept the store open half the time. If we ever get a steamboat and don't need the hauling routes any more, there will be enough hauling on the place to keep those two men busy. Keep that in mind, Bill Willie."

"I expect you to live a long time yet. Stop talkin' like that."

"I hope I live a long time, but I wasn't a young man when I came here."

"About the same age as me."

"The difference is you are more durable than I am. Bank your fire so your room will stay warm. It is going to be a cold night."

"I wonder what Elvis Grider was going back to town for."

3

ELVIS GRIDER drove into Bowling Green, and directly to Washington Hall. A stable boy took his horse, and Grider went inside. Logs were blazing brightly in the wide fireplace. Through the door at the right he could see that the room was almost filled with men eating their suppers. The owner of the place, Whitsitt Helm, sat at the desk. He saw Grider enter the tavern and met him. "Mr. Rodes has arrived, Mr. Grider. He is lodged in Number five."

"Then tell him I am here. We were to have a private place to eat, I believe."

"Yes, indeed. I'll have a table moved into his room, and a waiter will serve you there. I asked him if that suited him, of course."

"I suppose that is all right. It will at least be private. I will go to his room. Tell the waiter to serve us in ten or fifteen minutes."

Grider knocked on the door of Number five. It was answered immediately by a tall, thin, dark young man. "I am sure that you are Mr. Grider. Come in, sir. I am Robin Rodes."

The young man was pleasant in manner and voice, and despite his thinness gave the impression of surprising vigor. They sat and engaged in pleasantries, each studying the other as intently as manners permitted.

"I have asked that supper be served here," said Grider. "The dining room is a very public place."

There was a knock on the door. It was a waiter bringing in a small table and cloth. He placed the table, spread the cloth, and was soon back with the best silverware the tavern had to offer. He placed it and said, "I'll be right back, suh, wid yo' suppah."

"I have had reports of you, Mr. Rodes. They were favorable, I may say. Bowling Green will be benefited if you choose to remain here."

"I am a lawyer, sir, with a scant six months' experience in its practice. It is pleasant enough to live where I am now, but frankly the prospects of a substantial practice there aren't reassuring. That was the occasion of my letter to you. I had heard that you were the town's best-informed citizen, so I wrote to you."

"You noticed, I am sure, that I did not respond immediately. I wrote two letters and waited for their answers. I have a friend in the town in which you are located; one of the letters went to him and one to your professors in Centre College. I felt that their answers warranted the reply I wrote to you."

The waiter came with their supper. They ate, talking about commonplace things—Rodes' trip on the stagecoach, the continued flow of settlers into the new country, Governor Desha's difficulties with the supreme court of the state.

Forty minutes later, Grider pushed his chair back and said, "If you will remove your practice to Bowling Green, I will turn all possible legal matters your way. I am the head of the bank here, and occasionally we need legal assistance in its conduct. I doubt if your income from it would be sufficient even for a skimpy living, but it will serve to call attention to you in a very favorable way."

"Most of the practice I have been able to get so far has been concerned with land titles."

Grider smiled wanly. "There may be some of that too. Now and then, the bank needs to verify a title, but mainly your work for us would be to determine the legality of various items of the bank's business. Of course there will be papers to draw up in the proper form and things like that."

"What other kinds of practice would I stand a chance to get?"

"Of course, there is a great deal of criminal practice in our court. We are a young community and at times disorderly. So our criminal dockets are usually crowded. But, as you know, criminal practice doesn't pay very well. The average criminal hasn't anything to pay with. Collection work is more profitable. One or two of our lawyers have more land-title work than they can handle. The bank will be in position to turn a good deal of title work to you."

"I am very grateful to you, Mr. Grider. Tell me—is the community reasonably free from factions, from feuds?"

"Reasonably free. There are some here who do not see eye to eye with some others. But that generally happens. The social layers of this section are about the same as you would find in any of the state's better sections. The members of the ruling class are relatively few. There are a good many of the middle class, owners of small farms who work hard and try to pay their debts. We have some drifters who work as little as possible and generally manage to live off the community. The Bible speaks of them, I believe."

"How well is the court conducted?"

"The magistrates who make up our county court are middle-class men, but mainly honest. They would not be able to direct our affairs themselves, but we help them. I had a conference with one of them today. I found him very agreeable to my ideas."

"I meant the circuit court, sir."

"Judge Drake has been on the bench for twenty-five years. It will soon be time for him to yield his work to a younger man."

"I have heard of him. Something of a character, isn't he?"

"He is not very amenable to anything he didn't think of himself. He is not disposed to take any advice from anyone."

"A man with ideas can afford to be independent."

"I think the time has come for a change, though I would not wish to be quoted."

"Since, sooner or later, I may enter political life myself I could not afford to identify myself with any faction. At any rate, at first."

"It would serve the best interest of the bank for you not to. At least, not openly."

Rodes sat in silence for a long minute, thinking. Then he said, "I shall come to a decision in a few days. If I move here I shall do it with the idea of staying. You have encouraged me greatly, Mr. Grider."

The next morning, Robin Rodes walked about Bowling Green, observing closely the things he saw. Late in the morning he called on Judge Drake, court not being in session. Back in Harrodsburg he had heard some things about the judge that interested him.

"Come in," a voice answered his knock. He opened the door. The judge sat at a large crude table, one leg draped almost across the table top. He expertly withdrew his leg from the table and jumped to his feet. "Good morning, young man. I heard you coming down the street, but I misjudged your walk. I make a habit of listening to the sounds men make when they walk, and you sounded a lot like Eli Shobe. I thought you were Eli."

"My name is Robin Rodes."

"Oh, is it? Well, it is a right pretty name. It sounds like one you would be likely to find in a verse of good poetry. But this I will say—outside of my judicial capacity, of course—that any man who makes a sound like Eli Shobe is a respectable man. There is a firmness in Eli's walk, a sort of *I'm a-going-where-I-started-to-go* sound. My name is Charles Drake. I've been judge here since about the time Noah put out to sea. Have a chair."

"I am at present practicing law in Harrodsburg, but I am thinking of moving here. I am glad to have this opportunity to pay my respects to a judge of whom I have heard many interesting things."

"Harrodsburg? Then you must have been talking to Alex Mc-Dowell. We nibbled on Sir William Blackstone at the same time. How is he?"

"No longer nibbling. He takes great bites now. The other lawyers in the section stand aside to watch him chew."

"I don't know how good a court lawyer Alex is, but he is a born scholar of the law. I'll say this, young man, that if you think that highly of Alex McDowell you will do well here. There is room here for two or three good lawyers, at least fellows who have heard of William Blackstone. We have got too many plugs, though that pronouncement should remain within these walls. I am in trouble as it is. So you know Alex McDowell! I wish I could be as profound once more as I used to be when Alex and I decided every question that came up, finally and free of charge. The law! What a thing is the law! Omnipotent and stupid, gracious and petty, the climax of justice and the essence of tyranny, prompt in promise yet a truant in performance. The law! Where, sir, did you make your acquaintance with the law?"

"I finished my course in Centre College, sir; then for three years I read law and worked in Mr. McDowell's office."

"Oh, that was the way of it. Then you have taken full bites of Blackstone too, or I don't know Alex. By all means join us here. But be tolerant of me. I don't know what Blackstone would think of it, but it is my way to approach justice by varying routes. If sometimes my approach seems oblique, please believe that I am not serving my own gain. For instance, I have postponed the settling of a land-title contest for more than twenty years. It is a very good piece of land, but neither contestant particularly needs it. I don't think it is worth either way what a decision would cost the community. It is a ticklish piece of real estate, and I have tried to keep the claimants in suspense, and so more proper in their behavior. As a matter of fact, my invention has just about run dry. I doubt whether I can think up many more excuses for postponement. But at least I can try."

"What makes this particular case such a delicate one?"

"Well, the two men who claim the land aren't delicate fellows. Either one could be troublesome if he set his head to it, and that is what he might do if I gave it to the other. They are very different fellows, oh, most different, but both important. Then, to be truthful, I don't know how to settle it. The exactnesses of the law do not quite apply in a new country. Here's a case of the prior grant *versus* prior possession. I fear it would bring on trouble that Bowling Green can't afford, so I let it drag on. We need peace here more than either man needs sixty or seventy acres of timberland. Here I am, running on like a candidate for constable at a county picnic. What would you like to know about our noble community?"

"For one thing, is one of the claimants named Grider?"

Drake stared at him. "When did you get to Bowling Green?"

"Last night about sundown, on the southbound stagecoach."

"Then grass isn't what grows best under your feet. Yes, that is the name of one of them. But, as one Blackstone chewer to another, don't tell what I have just said. It could do harm."

"Not even a syllable. And I have found it very helpful to hear you talk. But I will tell you something, also in confidence. If I decide to settle here, and I am now almost sure that I will, part of my duties will include the legal matters of the Grider bank."

The judge stared again at his visitor, but quickly regained his composure. "Nothing wrong about that, nothing at all. Perfectly ethical, and heaven knows a bank needs a lawyer. But the conviction deepens that you are able to take care of yourself. Suppose we drop local matters for topics with ampler horizons. By this time, something of great importance has happened at Washington. Have you a guess who will be our next President?"

"You asked for a guess. I'll make one. Mr. Adams."

"It's a good guess, and I will make another. He will be the last of the Virginia-Massachusetts dynasty. The tides of leadership are fast moving westward. The next time it may be Clay, or it may be Jackson. Or it may be that both of them will have exhausted their strength before their opportunity comes. In whatever case, keep this in mind: Kentucky is in the path of that westward-moving leadership. By the way, your employer is an ardent Jackson man."

"So am I an admirer, though I would hardly say an ardent one. I admire the General greatly, but I do find him vulnerable, though in infrequent spots. But I believe I could become an ardent supporter of any man able to hold a Kentucky judgeship for more than twenty years. We don't keep them that long except for good reasons. Has your claim to the title ever been contested?"

"Twice. Once by a good man whom it was an honor to oppose. There was no honor the other time. Even when they counted the vote I felt like spitting. I may be about to encounter the same sort of opposition now, though when the time comes it may fade away."

"I earnestly hope so. I have taken up a great deal of your time, but it has been good for me. I shall make a full report to Mr. McDowell."

"Do so. I'd love to see Alex. The sight of him would whet my zeal for the law. Come on down to Bowling Green. It might be that someday I'd want to hand the judgeship over to you."

4

WHEN JACOB SKILES got to the porch that night he found his wife standing in the cold waiting for him. "You shouldn't be out here, Priscilla, it's too cold."

"There is bad news," she said. "Mr. Lank Motley is bad sick."

"I missed him in town. What is it?"

"Dr. Briggs says it is pneumonia. He was taken in the night and has grown worse ever since. I was over there two hours right after dinner."

"Is it really serious?"

"I'm afraid it is. He was delirious and talked constantly. He was burning with a fever. I'm afraid he is bad off."

"I will saddle one of the horses and go over."

"Not till you have had your supper. It is waiting for you."

An hour later, Skiles hitched his horse at the Motley hitching rack. There were two other horses standing there. He recognized one of them as belonging to Dr. Briggs. The other he did not know, though it was too dark to get a very good look at it. To his surprise it was Nat Grider who opened the door for him. His mind stirred in wonder as to what Elvis Grider's son was doing there. He had never talked with the young man, but perhaps a dozen times he had been in groups with him; always he had been surprised that the son of Elvis Grider sounded in him no discordant note.

The young man said gravely, but pleasantly enough, "Come in, Mr. Skiles. It was neighborly of you to come. Mr. Motley isn't doing

well at all. Mrs. Motley is in there, sir." He pointed to the room at
the left. Skiles stood silently in the door till Mrs. Motley saw him.

"I knew you would come to see him. Dr. Briggs is in there with
him now. He doesn't give us much hope, Mr. Skiles. The sickness
came so suddenly. He seemed as well as ever yesterday morning. We
went to preaching, and he was joking all the way back like he always
does. It rained a little while he was unhitching the team, and he got
wet, not soaking wet but right damp. But that has happened a lot of
times. He came in and sat by the fire and talked and joked, and we
didn't think anything about it. Then, after dinner——"

She was crying. He sat looking at her, and finally said lamely, "But
Lank is a strong man. He will get better."

"I'm afraid he won't, Mr. Skiles. Maybe he doesn't want to." She
was trying to control her sobs. He sat looking at her wonderingly.
"Sallie is going to marry Nat Grider." Still Skiles said nothing. He
knew nothing to say. "We never dreamed of it till yesterday after
dinner, when Nat came to ask us. We didn't know that they had ever
talked very much together. For Lank, the sun rose and set in Sallie.
You know that Lank never did like Elvis Grider. Something happened right after we came here. I never did know what it was. I always
thought he must have insulted Lank, made bad fun of him, or something, but ever since then my husband hated him. He was the only
man that Lank ever knew that he didn't like. Nat was very respectful
when he asked us yesterday. He came out like a gentleman in what
he had to say. Lank had always said that he wanted Sallie to have the
man of her choice, and that he didn't intend to meddle. And I
know he didn't. Nat got here about two o'clock yesterday, and Sallie
met him at the door. They came straight in where we were. Neither
one of us could say a word. We just sat there listening. First Nat
would talk, then Sallie would. They had made up their minds. Finally,
Lank said it was all right. I never heard his voice sound like that. I
wouldn't have known it was him talking if I hadn't been sitting there
watching him. He just sat there all the afternoon looking into the
fire, not saying anything. He didn't eat a bite of supper, and after
that he just sat there holding my hand. When we went to bed I
dropped off asleep, but it wasn't very long after that I was awake. I
knew there was something wrong the way he was breathing."

Someone knocked at the door. They heard Nat Grider come from
the back hall and open it. From the voice they knew that the man
coming in was Judge Drake. He came in and stood about, shaking

hands, but saying nothing. His face bore a strained look, for Lank Motley had long been a favorite of his.

Then a door opened and Dr. Briggs came into the room. His face was set in a rigid calm. He bowed to Mrs. Motley and Judge Drake, then turned to Jacob Skiles. "He is perfectly conscious. He heard you come in. He would like to speak with you. Don't stay long. Go in too, Judge."

The room was lighted by a single candle. Their vision steadied and they saw clearly the man lying so quietly there on the bed.

"I am glad you came, Jacob, and you too, Judge. There is something I want to say." He stopped for a moment, gathering strength to go on.

"Rest now," said Skiles in low tones. "You can tell us later."

The sick eyes looked at Skiles as if in surprise. "Now," he said, not much above a whisper. "Come up here close."

The two men moved until they were standing against the bed. "It's Sallie. Promise me you'll help Sallie when she needs it. You know about Sallie?"

"I know." Skiles turned a look upon Judge Drake which said plainly, "I'll tell you later."

"And my wife," Motley whispered. "I didn't know there could be such a good woman till I found out from her. But she won't need help like Sallie will. You'll watch out for Sallie, won't you?"

"For both of them. We promise. For both of them. You are a good man, Lank Motley. You have always been a good man. Bill Willie Blewett says you are the best man around here. I have heard others say it."

There was a wan smile on the sick man's face. "Bill Willie!" he said. Then the smile faded. "Not the best man, my friends, not a very good man, not a good provider for my wife and Sallie."

"Listen, Lank Motley," said Judge Drake: "I ought to know a good man, and I ought to know a bad one. As judge of the Warren County Court I have seen enough of both, and I pronounce you a good man. I stand behind Jacob Skiles in his promise for both of them. Here's my hand on it."

"And mine," said Skiles.

Dr. Briggs came then and motioned the two men out of the room. Before Skiles left he went and lifted Motley's hand and shook it tenderly. So did Judge Drake. Dr. Briggs followed them out and beckoned Mrs. Motley and Sallie to the sickroom. Skiles saw the woman clasp her hands in a gesture of terror, but without a word she went into the room and Sallie followed her.

"Shouldn't we stay?" Skiles asked the doctor.

"I don't think so. You are not a young man any more, and it's a bad night. If Bill Willie Blewett is feeling all right, send him. You and the Judge both come out early in the morning. You'll be more needed then. Tell Bill Willie to fetch Brother Lapsley. It would be a comfort to have him here."

All of this time Nat Grider had stood in the back hall. Mrs. Motley came out of the sickroom. "You too, Nat. Mr. Motley wants you to come in."

5

THEY BURIED Lank Motley in the Presbyterian graveyard next to the church. The bleakness had gone out of the weather, and the day had turned friendly. It was the largest funeral that Warren County had ever seen. The church was crowded for the funeral sermon that Brother Lapsley preached, and the attendance at the service at the grave was much greater. At the grave an odd thing happened. Nat Grider had stood with his parents at quite a distance during Brother Lapsley's prayer. When it was finished, Nat walked through the crowd and took his place at Sallie Motley's side. She looked around and his presence seemed to steady her. Elvis Grider and his wife turned away, went directly to their carriage, and without a backward glance drove toward home, leaving their son standing at the side of the grave, then being filled by the Presbyterian elders.

Not many days after that, Bill Willie Blewett came from town, his face a little grim. "I heard some news in town. Nat Grider's done left home, and moved to Washington Hall. It looked to me like it was goin' to happen that day at the buryin'. They say they'll be married inside of a month. Nat's not a bad boy, but this is the first time I ever heard of him using much push. I bet he surprised his dear pappy."

"We must keep in mind, Mr. Skiles," said Priscilla, "that we might get surprised sometime. We have a son who is old enough to."

6

A WEEK LATER the county was surprised, but in another way. It was surprised by a young lawyer named David Settle. He had been practicing in Bowling Green for a year, having moved to the place from Frankfort. He was a presentable young man of looks and breeding. His voice was powerful and he used it on all available occasions. He had achieved a favorable standing, but not enough in the minds of the older and more conservative citizens to warrant his announcing for the judgeship in opposition to Judge Drake. And that was what he did. Beecham's candidacy had dwindled out within two weeks, and it was generally thought that the way was clear for Judge Drake. Settle promised a vigorous campaign for the office, and he kept his promise from the very outset. The older people were aghast. Judge Drake was not only a good judge, but he was a tradition.

Eli Shobe and Jacob Skiles made a visit to Settle. It was a call, they told him, made out of friendliness. He would do himself no good at the outset of his career by opposing one of the community's pillars. It was surely not the most effective way to make the friends that a profitable career would require.

Settle listened for a while, then made a speech. He was, he claimed, duly appreciative of their interest. He was indeed grateful for it. But what was a young man to do? Twiddle his thumbs and wait for the older eligibles to drop out by process of death? He had given prolonged thought to the condition of the county, and it was his deliberate conviction that senility and near senility were the main threats to the welfare of the citizens. There existed the dire need for the vitality of youth to send the pioneer currents surging again. Judge Drake had grown too old, and the county was still too young for the partnership of the two to remain.

The two visitors looked soberly at each other. The fellow was worse than they had thought. They bowed gravely and left the office.

Settle was desperately in earnest about the race. Every Saturday he was off somewhere in the county, speaking in the tenor of his remarks to Shobe and Skiles. There could be no doubt about it. He was gaining some support. He was endearing himself to the young and unheeding.

Judge Drake met Settle on the street and held out his hand. Settle accepted it, though with some show of reluctance.

"It is all right for you to run against me," the judge said heartily. "I don't blame you at all. I'd come out against me myself if I was as young as you are. You go ahead and run, and when you are defeated run again. Don't permit yourself to become discouraged, and sooner or later you are likely to make it. I knew a man back in Virginia who had been running for office as long as anyone could remember. Of course, he got defeated, but he didn't let it bother him. He just kept on, and when he was sixty-nine he got elected coroner. I never saw a happier man. I just thought I'd tell you about him. First time you get elected I'll be around to wish you well."

"The election is the first Saturday in May. I'll be looking for you the Monday after."

Judge Drake stared at him. "You are not expecting to be elected this time, I hope. I never suspected you would think you could start out at the top. I thought you were just sort of working up to it. Well, since you are taking this thing seriously, let me give you a little advice, just about the same as I would thank anybody to give my son if he were in your place. The word I heard about your speech at Green Castle last Saturday is that you spent a lot of time telling them that I am getting old and weakening fast, but you didn't tell them how you found it out. You didn't tell them what I had done or hadn't done. You didn't tell them about a single decision of mine that had the marks of old age on it. Now, if I was you I'd prove to them that I am too old, not only by the family Bible, but also by my actions on the bench. One little slip that I made and you point out to them will get you more votes than an hour of hollering that I am getting old. I hope you keep in health, sir."

The judge bowed gravely and courteously and went on down the street. Young Settle looked at him, his eyes blinking. All right, he had been challenged. He would accept it.

7

THREE WEEKS LATER the news reached Bowling Green that the House of Representatives had declared John Quincy Adams of Massachusetts the duly elected President of the United States, and that he was already occupying the office. There were no Adams partisans in south Kentucky, and so the news was depressing. But in a few days there was further news that the victory of Adams had been due to Clay support. That left the matter still more confused in the minds of the people. Clay had stalwart support in the region, but even the most loyal wondered why he should turn his forces to a New Englander. Even if Clay couldn't accept General Jackson, there was Crawford of Georgia. Anything but leave power in a section that already had held it too long.

Even to Jacob Skiles, a Clay man, that was an unnatural union. Skiles could not see the election as favorable to the interests of the western country, particularly to the western parts of the western country. In the mind of Skiles, Jackson was a sort of firebrand, with not enough stability of temper to be committed with the guidance of a great young country. He was without doubt a patriot, and greatly concerned with the prosperity of his own people, but he did not have the intellectual poise needed in the Presidency.

Jacob's mind went back again to the problem that gave him most concern. The section of which Bowling Green was the center was suffering for the lack of trade caused by inadequate transportation. The people raised and made products for which there was little market. The wagon lines were not enough, and the few flatboats moved with slowness almost frightening. As a merchant, Skiles knew that the stores needed more to sell, particularly luxuries, and that it required all their facilities to bring in the necessities.

The Shaker Colony fifteen miles to the south was producing many things, churns and water buckets made from cedar wood, brooms, a few carriages, and in the fall great quantities of kraut which they sent by flatboat to New Orleans. They built a large water mill and supplied the Nashville markets with a good deal of wheat flour, but the output of the Shakers was always limited by lack of transportation. It was the economic blight that touched the whole section. Corn was easily raised, and that made it possible to produce large amounts of pork, but to carry it to markets was difficult indeed. Jacob Skiles had seen steamboats on the Cumberland and on the Ohio. The day the steamboat whistle was first heard on the Green and the Barren would usher in a new era for Bowling Green. Henry Clay had spoken emphatically of the desirability of improving the rivers and the roads. He had felt that Clay was the main hope for those improvements, but matters were not moving as he had hoped.

Then came the word that General and Mrs. Andrew Jackson would

stop at Bowling Green on their journey back to Nashville. The party
had stopped at various places during the whole journey, and every
place had political significance. Bowling Green had become the center of all of south Kentucky. Those familiar with the ways of politics
saw clearly that the General was using the trip for its best effect on
1828. He would again be a candidate, and, unless the course of things
veered, a formidable one. He was starting early his play for Kentucky's
support. Louisville and Bowling Green would be friendly, and so
would that tier of counties lying next to the Tennessee border. It
would be difficult for Clay to offset that. But Clay's name was potent
and his voice had magic in it. And Clay was the best chance for in-
ternal improvements. Jacob Skiles gave thought to these matters and
decided to remain steadfast for Clay.

On the third of April, posters appeared all over the town announcing the presence of General and Mrs. Jackson the following Monday.
The General was greatly fatigued by travel and political strain. He
would make no speech, but he would appear in the afternoon and
evening in the parlors of Washington Hall. During that time he would
be honored to have as many of his fellow Americans as possible call
upon him. The poster continued to relate that Kentucky had found
great favor in the General's eyes. Its soldiers had been of paramount
importance at the battle of New Orleans.

There followed a great deal of running to and fro in preparation
for the great event. Announcements were sent to Russellville, to Glasgow, to Munfordville, to Scottsville and to Franklin. There were
twenty-five veterans of New Orleans residing in Bowling Green and
Warren County. Word was sent to them, and upon each was put the
responsibility of seeing that his neighbors came to town to bask in
the General's presence. Every store window had its flag, large or small.
A large flag floated from the Courthouse. The merchants filled their
shelves with the most alluring items. Mr. Hardcastle publicized the
recent additions to his stock: an entire case of Nuns Thread, one
dozen pairs of Ladies Morocco Shoes, one case of Men's Fine Hats,
one half dozen of Large and Elegant Silk Mantles, one dozen pairs
of Gentlemen's Beaver Gloves, a full cannister of Imperial Hyson
Tea, and a case of French Perfumery, lately imported. The farmers
worked overtime in the fields so as to take the day off with more grace.

Banker Grider, Storekeeper Hardcastle, and Ewing Porter from
Smith's Grove sat in conference in the corner of the Washington Hall
parlor.

"Any danger of the Clay people startin' trouble?" asked Hardcastle.

"Might be some danger," said Porter. "They've got some hotheads."

"I don't expect any disorder," said Grider flintily. "Their candidate might want to come here sometime. They'll behave themselves."

"Specially with the old soldiers around," said Hardcastle.

"There will be a lot of people here that day. We must provide them with plenty of excitement, keep them stirring, you might say."

"Make 'em like the day and think it's the General they're likin'," said Mr. Hardcastle.

"Something like that. Of course, we want them all to see Jackson, and as many as possible to shake hands with him. But they can't all see him at once. So we will have something else for them to see part of the time. We must keep something going on. What do you suggest?"

"The new goods they have in the stores ought to bring in a lot of people," said Hardcastle. "I'll put my most attractive things out in plain view."

"Sell it in the morning," said Grider. "It might be a good thing for the stores all to close after dinner. We want everybody to see the General, get up close to him, and they can't do it in the morning."

"Why can't some of them?" inquired Ewing.

"He will have important engagements with important people before dinner. He will shake hands with everybody after dinner, not before. Another thing, you can't have a day like this free. We have got to collect some money. The bank will start it off with five dollars."

"The store will give two and a half," said Mr. Hardcastle. "Of course, we will put a notice in the window saying we did."

"I'll give two," said Porter. "You want us to do some collecting, Elvis?"

"A good many will want to give something. Give them a chance. It's a day for everybody."

"Even Jacob Skiles?" Porter asked, smiling wryly.

Grider considered. "No, I don't believe I'd bother him. It would be just as well if he was left off the list. But see everybody else, specially the Jackson people. What kind of entertainment do you suggest for the morning?"

"That's when we expect them to visit the stores."

"We have got to have more than the stores going on. This is going to be the biggest day that Bowling Green ever had. We want to please everybody."

"You can't beat fiddling and banjo picking," said Ewing. "If we can get Lex Spalding and Ham Vernon, that will be fine. They are getting a little old now but they are still good. Lex can pull a fast bow, and the rheumatism hasn't hit Ham's picking fingers yet. We might get them for nothing."

"Pay them something," said Grider. "They would be satisfied with a dollar apiece. All right, Porter, you attend to that. You get them. What else could we have?"

"You couldn't please people better than to get Pat Curd to auction something off. Pat can sure call it out."

The suggestion was immediately pleasing to Mr. Grider. "Why, we can kill two birds with one stone. We can let Pat auction off that building on Frozen Row the bank had to foreclose on. A crowd will help the bank get a good price for it. Yes, we'll get Pat to sell it. What else?"

"Plenty of free drinking water for everybody on the square. It will please them not to have to walk to the spring for it. They would be afraid they might miss something. Besides, it might be a warm day and crowds do get thirsty."

"All right, two barrels. One at each end of the square. Suppose you see Ed McGinnis about hauling it. Tell him to keep the barrels filled."

"I think that every window should have a sign in it, something like 'Welcome, General Jackson,' or 'General Jackson, A Great Hero,'" said Porter.

"That is a first-rate idea, Ewing. How about you spreading the word?"

"All right, I'll spread it. Wouldn't Gard Tandy be a good man to help me?"

"He'd be fine. I must go see the sheriff. I don't expect any misbehavior, but some may get too noisy. A little noise will help, but too much won't. I'll get him to appoint three or four deputies for the day."

"No harm in being careful," said Mr. Hardcastle.

It was a mistake for Elvis Grider to choose that day for the selling by auction of the house on Frozen Row. There would be a large crowd present for the auction, he had thought; under the contagion of Pat Curd's wit and art the bidding would be above normal, and the house would sell more favorably. Also, Mr. Curd's fee could be paid from the funds collected for the expenses of Jackson Day. But Mr.

Grider omitted one factor from his calculation, namely, Mr. Trezevant Covington. Mr. Covington's nephew, Virgil Covington, had been the victim of the bank's foreclosure. In a high flush of youthful speculation he had bought the building, and the Grider-Walters bank had aided him.

Virgil had asked his uncle to lend him the money, but the denial had been forthright. "I will not. You have no business with property like that. You don't know what to do with it. I am fond of you, Virgil, but I am fond of my money too."

"Then I'll try elsewhere, Uncle Trez."

"Maybe you'll get it, and maybe you'll lose every penny you put in it. You are too green not to. If you are willing to grow up slowly, I'll help you. If you want to rush into it, I won't."

Virgil lost every penny of it, and so the building was about to be sold. In the considered opinion of Mr. Trezevant Covington that would be a salutary lesson to his nephew. But while a little discipline would be good for Virgil, it was not good for the Covington name to be bandied about as freely and carelessly as this auction sale would require. Uncle Trez decided not to permit it. The Covington name was very dear to him. The situation had become so shaped that his attention was demanded. To call the attention of the entire county to Virgil's improvidence was a reflection on the whole family. Uncle Trez wondered if there might not be some political chicanery implied in the sale. The Covington men were Clay men. Uncle Trez would not permit the Covington name to be pilloried, and certainly not on Jackson Day. There ensued a period of wry thinking. After which, Mr. Covington rode down to Russellville and engaged the services of five gentlemen known as The Fifers, and inclined toward music in its most audible form. Mr. Philo Duncan served as director and played the fife. Mr. Duncan loved a prank as well as any man. Also, since he had once seen Henry Clay he had committed himself wholeheartedly to the Clay side. Mr. Covington had lived in Russellville briefly, and during that time he and Duncan had become good friends. The situation was explained in full, and it appealed to the leader of The Fifers. It was a first-rate opportunity to accomplish three desirable ends: to do his friend Covington a favor, to support Clay against Jackson, and to engage in a bit of exciting pranking.

"Pat Curd has got a voice like a lonesome jackass," said Mr. Covington. "Reckon you can play him down, Philo?"

"I reckon we can, Trez. Our new drummer can jar a squirrel out of a tree."

"I'll tell you what you do, Philo. You ride a stagecoach up to Bowling Green and see Elvis Grider at the bank. Elvis has got the notion he's running the day. So let's humor him. You tell him The Fifers would like to play here on Jackson Day. He'll bite at it like a Drake Creek catfish at a livery-stable fishing worm. But get him to put it in writing. Act businesslike. Tell him you want to do it in regular order, and that you can get a lot of business by just showing his permit. Be careful not to play where the General is, but let Pat Curd know he can't make a public show out of anybody named Covington. If it was just an ordinary day I wouldn't bother about it. Virgil needs a good lesson. But everybody in Warren County will be there, and that fool boy is named Covington. When Pat starts up put on the rousements."

The vivid posters were very exciting; the influence of the twenty-five veterans and the glamour of Old Hickory were most effective. In order to give the day more appeal, and to remove all excuse for staying away, County Court Day was shifted by official action to coincide with Jackson Day.

8

THE SUN had not cleared the eastern horizon when the first ox-drawn wagon rumbled into town. It had been on the road for nine hours. It was driven by a man named Moulder from the eastern part of the county. With him were his wife and seven children. Some of them may have slept during some of the better stretches of the journey, but there was nothing about them then that suggested sleep, and all eyes were shining. For a week they had lived on the prospect of Jackson Day. They would miss no part of it. They would fill their hungry eyes with its sights and their eager ears with its sounds. The stolid oxen seemed to catch a hint of the excitement and lifted their heads a trifle higher above the ground. The Moulders made their way to the hitching lot. The man arose, placed his hands on the side of the wagon bed and vaulted to the ground, landing with a sprightly show of elasticity in his knees and hips. "Mrs. Moulder and young'uns, we are here."

His wife was a practical woman. "Get them beasts unhitched, water them and feed them, and we'll eat our breakfast. I'm hungry."

"Beatin'est wife I ever had for gettin' hungry." His innate gallantry came tardily to his rescue. "But jest like all young people she can't keep her mind off o' eatin'."

When he returned from watering and feeding the beasts, his wife had performed a seven-fold chore of face and hand washing at the water trough. The second and third wagons drove into the hitching lot then, and Mrs. Moulder was overjoyed to find that one of the women was her first cousin, Callie Gilliam, who had married Rochester Grimes from Sand Hill. The cousins hadn't seen each other since the wedding five years before. Under the stress of her cousinship, Mrs. Moulder lost some of her practical sense. She and Callie talked excitedly and at the same time for the next ten minutes.

Moulder and Grimes regarded their wives philosophically. Finally Moulder spoke to his wife. "What about some breakfast? I thought you was hungry."

"Mr. Moulder, this seems like the first time I have seen Callie since she was born."

"It's been mighty tough on you to wait that long, seeing as how you was just three days old, as I've heard you say a dozen times."

"I guess I meant married. I reckon I'm just excited. I don't get away from home enough. Let's eat breakfast together. We've got plenty, and I expect Callie and Mr. Grimes brought some."

Callie and Mr. Grimes had brought some. They placed it all together and ate happily.

"Try some of this fried ham, Callie. I did a big frying last night to bring along. Mr. Moulder killed seven hogs last winter, and he's a specially good hand with the hams. His hams make the best red gravy in our neighborhood. We still got a five-gallon crock half-full of sausage at home. We fried it and poured melted lard over it. It'll keep fine that way till real hot weather. I wish I had brought some of it."

"I reckon it's jest as well you forgot it, honey," said her husband. "We're still liable to want our meals after we get back home."

"Always joking about something. What in the world is that, Callie?"

"My husband is a foraging man. That's wild turkey. I know it's a little late for them, but Mr. Grimes couldn't help it. He was walking through the woods and he saw a big gobbler running toward him, and it scared him. He accidentally had his gun along with him. Mr. Moulder, what would you have done?"

"I'da cured another ham," said Moulder grinning.

"Yes, turkey ham. That gobbler was real nice. Here's a place to put that oilcloth down, Mr. Grimes."

9

AT THAT TIME, Elvis Grider and Ewing Porter were meeting in Washington Hall. They had got to town by sunup, and had drunk some hot coffee at the tavern. They were responsible for the smooth and proper passage of Jackson Day, and they were conscious of that responsibility.

"I've done better about the collection than I ever expected," said Porter. "I've got a hundred and eighty-six dollars in my pocket."

"Fine! I expect that will take care of it."

"Guess who I got ten dollars from."

"Not Judge Drake?"

"I never saw him. He was off somewhere politicking when I went to see him. I think he would have given something though."

"Who was it, then?"

"Jacob Skiles. Oh, I didn't ask him. He met me on the street and stopped me. Said he had bought a bull down somewhere near Hopkinsville and would have to go after it. Said he thought Jackson Day would be good for Bowling Green, and he wanted to help in anything that would."

"He must be up to something. He may have a notion to get up a Clay Day and expect us to contribute. I don't think a Clay Day here would ever be a success."

"He didn't talk like he was up to anything. I used almost an hour talking with Trezevant Covington, and all I could get him to give was two dollars. I feel bad about that. He is rich enough to do better."

"I wouldn't push him too far. He made a heavy deposit in the bank yesterday. First money he's ever put in."

"And I'll lay you six bits he had a reason for it. Trez wouldn't breathe without having a reason for it."

"You arranged with Mit Stone, didn't you?"

"Mit will be at the forks when the Jacksons get there. You can depend on that."

The committee had left very little to chance. Mit Stone, the town's best horseman was stationed at the fork of the Louisville and Glasgow roads, six miles north of town. At the first sight of the Jackson carriage, Mit was to ride furiously into town, bearing the news. That would permit all last-minute arrangements to be made in time for the arrival. Ewing Porter had told him, "If you get us word a half hour ahead of time we'll put you in the history books."

At half after nine, Mit clattered up to the hitching rack at Washington Hall, threw the reins over a hook, and ran inside to where the committee was waiting.

"They are coming," he said a bit breathlessly, "and they're drivin' purty peart. Team didn't seem fagged hardly any. The road is crowded. That will hold 'em back some. There wasn't a quarter of a mile without a wagon. Looked to me like I had to ride half the way in a ditch to get around 'em. It will be thirty minutes before they get here, maybe a little the rise of it."

Then orders simply crackled from the committee's lips. No mishap or miscue must be permitted to mar the day. Mr. Grider and Mr. Porter mounted their horses, matched grays, and cantered down to the river. They stationed themselves where the road climbed the south bank and reached high ground. Two ferryboats were working furiously to get the people across. They saw the carriage drive down on one of the ferryboats. It was ferried across with speed. They saw the carriage drive off the boat and start up the road. There could be no mistaking it. The man's face was long, lean, and angular. He wore a tall, dominating, shiny hat. Even a casual observer would have noted the arresting quality of those eyes. The woman at his side was plump, dark, and obviously tired.

Grider held up his hand, and the driver, a Negro of jet blackness, drew the team to a stop.

"Welcome to Bowling Green and south Kentucky, General Jackson, and you, Madame. We are honored by your presence. I am Elvis Grider, and may I present my colleague and friend, Ewing Porter? We have been appointed to escort you to your quarters."

The General stood up in the carriage, lifted his hat with a broad sweep, and said, "This welcome, sirs, is an expression of the spirit of true Kentuckians, a noble people whether in peace or war. And now, may we proceed to our quarters? Mrs. Jackson did not sleep well last night and is greatly fatigued."

"Less so, since your welcome," said Mrs. Jackson, smiling bravely.

General Jackson turned to the Negro. "Drive on, Flag," he said.

The carriage moved up the street, Mr. Grider riding at the right,

Mr. Porter at the left. It was not easy going, for there were many vehicles and many pedestrians, and a great volume of cheering sounded continuously. They passed the cemetery, and the Presbyterian Church, then reached the square. There, the twenty-five veterans, standing ready, broke into General Jackson's favorite song, "The Hunters of Kentucky," with good carrying power and some conformity to tune. The General again arose and doffed his hat. A minute later the carriage was passing the stand on which Spalding and Vernon, both old and grizzled, were playing the sprightly "Downfall of Paris." The General turned in his carriage to see the musicians, for he always found such music enlivening.

Then the carriage drew up before Washington Hall. A carefully selected group of Jackson supporters stood in position to greet the distinguished company. There were introductions and felicitous words.

Jackson said, "Please permit us to repair to our chamber for a while. My wife is much exhausted."

"May we send some hot coffee to your room?" asked the tavern proprietor. "It is very refreshing."

"By all means. Your hospitality is most marked, sir."

Twenty minutes later, the General was back, refreshed and erect. All the rest of the morning he sat in the parlor and conferred with the local chieftains, and the theme of all the talk, whether or not explicitly stated, was 1828. Crit Alexander asked the General the unnecessary question, whether or not he would be a candidate then.

Jackson sprang from his chair, straightened himself to his full thin height and said, "Of course, I'll be a candidate then, a successful candidate, sir. I will not permit a piece of dastardly chicanery to postpone my destiny longer than four years."

Outside the stores were doing a business that warmed the keepers' hearts. Spalding and Vernon sat on their stand and played fiddle and banjo with the musical vigor of their youth, not one whit abated by the years that had settled down on them. The hearers stood listening in rapt attention to "The Cackling Hen" and "Leather Breeches." The streets were crowded, and old acquaintances stood everywhere talking of old times with a fervor deepened by the months of absence and by the human hunger to talk and listen to talk. It was more than Jackson Day. It was Old Friends Day. It was Talking Day. It was Buying Day. It was a day that memory would not let die.

At eleven o'clock a bell jangled lustily, and the ringer announced that at half after eleven Mr. Pat Curd, the town's most renowned auctioneer, would sell at auction the Covington house on Frozen Row. It was a golden opportunity to buy a house at a reasonable price and with the prospect of profit. Come to the site at half after eleven o'clock. To witness Mr. Curd in action was itself well worth the time.

A great many people started moving toward the house. Most of them were drawn by the anticipation of attending an auction carried on by Mr. Curd, a few by the hope of being able to purchase a well-located house at a bargain. Mr. Philo Duncan led his Fifers to the place and stationed them where in his judgment their music would prove most effective. Mr. Trezevant Covington and his nephew stood at one side. The nephew had not wished to come, and yielded only after continued insistence. On the way, Mr. Covington had talked blightingly of his nephew's buying more breeches than he had legs to fill. But in his own ironic way Uncle Trez wished his nephew to witness in person that the name Covington was not to be dragged in the dust.

Pat Curd hurried up, carrying in his hand an impressive document. Mr. Covington's eye caught that of Mr. Duncan and signaled him to be ready. Several of the patrons of the auction wondered casually as to the presence of the musicians, but concluded that it was merely a pleasant interlude between numbers. Mr. Rex Sublett, the sheriff, to whom Elvis Grider had managed to speak a few words earlier in the morning, came up and stood watching the scene. Trezevant Covington saw him and his anger flamed anew. He considered that the sheriff was under Elvis Grider's thumb, and doubtless had been sent by him as a safeguard. Very well. It would take more than an ordinary sheriff to divert him.

Mr. Curd cleared his throat, and suddenly his raucous voice blasted the calm:

"Ladeeze 'n' gennulmen, if any feller here ain't interested in makin' a profit, this ain't the place for him, for standin' here in the sound o' my voice is somebody who's goin' to make more money than a bald man has got hairs on his head. And I'll gorantee that in writin'. I've been up and down this old world in four directions and I ain't seen such a bargain, seen such a bargain as I'm about to offer for sale, offer for sale, situwated on the best street in the best town in the best country in the best world I ever been in, and known as the Virgil Covington proppity."

Mr. Covington's eye again caught that of the leader of The Fifers. Mr. Duncan's hand swung and The Fifers crashed into "Yankee Doodle." There was at first some lack of unanimity, but the erring player quickly readjusted himself to the beat of the majority. Mr. Duncan was nothing if not forceful, and he soon communicated his full spirit to the players. Pat Curd was caught flat-footed in a sentence identifying the property he was offering for sale. He went over it again:

"And known as the Virgil Covington proppity."

But the music of The Fifers towered over his words as an east Kentucky mountain would over a central Kentucky knob. He shook a threatening finger at the players and shouted out the beginning of a protest, but found it futile. He then settled himself into a philosophical acceptance of the inevitable. Surely The Fifers would not expect to interrupt the auction longer than required for the rendition of one piece. He was confident of his ability to recapture his audience then. Sheriff Sublett was uncertain as to the course he should take. Elvis Grider's instructions had not included anything of this nature, but he accepted Curd's pattern and stood waiting. Surely this annoying episode would blow itself out soon. But the stanzas went on and on. Mr. Duncan was charmed by the lilt and swing of "Yankee Doodle." The audience seemed to be sharing his esteem of it. He felt no need to change to another piece. He saw out of the corner of his eye that a sardonic smile was covering his friend Covington's face. That meant that his patron too liked the piece.

Soon Mr. Curd felt that the digression had gone far enough. He summoned all the power of his voice and began again:

"Best proppity you could buy in Bowling Green, buy in Bowling Green——"

But at that precise moment The Fifers added lustiness to their volume. Curd cast an appealing look at Sheriff Sublett. The Fifers were playing as if inspired, and "Yankee Doodle" was moving toward permanency. The sheriff walked across and laid a heavy hand on Mr. Duncan's arm. Philo Duncan looked around and saw who it was. He dropped his instrument so that it swung loose in his left hand. The precision of the beat of his right hand was not marred in the least. The other Fifers never faltered. They had been forewarned against this emergency. Duncan stopped the beat of his right hand long enough to take a piece of paper from his coat pocket and hand to the sheriff. The bewildered official unfolded it and read. It authorized The Fifers to play on any street in Bowling Green at any time on Jackson Day, and was signed by Elvis Grider.

"He didn't intend for you to break up an auction sale," he shouted. "Go somewhere else to play."

"Like it here," yelled Mr. Duncan. "We got here first."

"Can't help it," bellowed the sheriff. "This is business. Move on."

The tempo of "Yankee Doodle" never slackened. Mr. Trezevant Covington saw that it was time to play a card that he had been holding in reserve. He tapped the sheriff on the shoulder and asked a question that rose above "Yankee Doodle." "You thinking of running for sheriff again, Rex?"

The harassed sheriff couldn't think of the proper answer. Mr. Covington proceeded: "My cousin, Eugene, has been thinking of running. Eugene would make a good sheriff too. He'll run if I ask him to, and that man could get a lot of votes. He's right popular. He wouldn't do your race any good at all. I don't like to see people pushed around. These men come all the way from Russellville to take part in Jackson Day, and if they don't get to," he shouted hoarsely, "then Eugene is going to run."

"If they got to play," roared the sheriff, "get 'em to go somewhere else!"

"Looks to me like you bought more breeches than you got legs to fill. Keep on playing, Philo."

Mr. Duncan lifted his instrument back into service and The Fifers kept on playing. The crowd didn't know what had happened, but it was plain that Mr. Trezevant Covington had put the rabbit sign on the sheriff. The Fifers kept on playing, and Pat Curd sadly folded his document and took his departure.

Sheriff Rex Sublett opened the door of Washington Hall and walked in. Mr. Grider looked up in surprise from his conference. General Jackson was saying something with great vigor. The sheriff beckoned Grider with his forefinger. Grider arose, bowed to his conferees, bowed doubly to General Jackson, and walked across the parlor.

"I couldn't help it," the sheriff said, "you give 'em a permit."

The surprise of Mr. Grider's face deepened. "What are you talking about, Rex?"

"The auction sale. It's broken up. You give 'em a permit. What could I do?"

"Who broke the auction up? What permit are you talking about?"

"Them musicians from Russellville. You wrote them a permit to play anywhere they wanted to. What could I do with him a-wavin' that permit in my face?"

"The people elected you sheriff. You could have discharged the duties of your office. That note I wrote didn't permit them to march right into this room and start playing. It didn't permit them to break up a regularly advertised auction sale. You get right back down there and run them fiddlers off and sell that house."

"They're not fiddlers."

"Run them off and start the sale over. Where's Pat Curd?"

"He left."

"Get him back and start it over. You knew I didn't want that auction disturbed. What else did I tell you about it for? Get it started over."

The sheriff knew that he was caught. The only thing he could think to say was, "I think Trez Covington must have egged them players on. He was there."

"What was he there for? Do you suppose he wants to buy it back?"

"That wasn't the notion I got. That boy is kin to him, ain't he?"

"You hunt up Pat Curd and get that auction going. Pat can get a crowd back. You hunt him up, and tell him to sell it." Grider turned on his heel and rejoined the group gathered about General Jackson. The sheriff left Washington Hall. He didn't think there was any chance of getting the auction under way again. He did try to find Pat Curd, but he was nowhere to be found. He had gone to his home. His professional pride had been insulted. Never in his career had he been so ill-treated. The sheriff gave up looking for him, and in his exasperation arrested a man for staggering along the street singing "Yankee Doodle" at the top of his voice.

Suddenly, at noon, the crowd on the streets thinned out to a mere trickle. Almost everyone had gone to the grove where tables were prepared for the visitors who had fetched their dinners. The men went on to the second lot and watered and fed their teams. The women had the food out and properly placed on the tables by the time they returned. It was a mountainous feast that greeted the men. The women stood and guarded and distributed their food. The men moved up and down the line of tables, their eyes alertly searching for choice things. There was plenty of mutton and ham and chicken for all. A few tables were supplied with venison and wild turkeys. For some reason, it was Mrs. Eli Shobe's cucumber pickles that proved the most alluring exhibit of all, specially alluring to the men. Her stacks of cucumber pickles melted away like ice blown upon by a hot wind.

"Never tasted anything as good in my whole life," Bud Garvin from Three Forks said to Eli Shobe by way of a compliment.

"I like them myself," said Shobe, "and to be honest, I played a lowdown trick on the old lady. She thought she brought all she had, but I hid out a two-gallon crock. She doesn't like pickles, and she has got the notion from something she has read or heard that pickles breed malaria, or something, and that they stirred up a lot of business for doctors. She thought she was getting rid of all we had. She wouldn't believe it but pickles are real nourishing for grandchildren."

"Good for granddaddies too. Hand me another one, please."

"I'll tell you something, Bud. There isn't a more interesting man in the county to me than Bill Willie Blewett. He never was sick a day in his life, as far as I know, and I've seen that man eat a whole meal off of pickles."

"Where is Bill Willie? First big day I ever knew him to fail to be here."

"Maybe the late spring has got Bill Willie behind with his planting. He might not come anyhow. He is not a Jackson man."

"Neither are you."

"Not much of one. I'll not vote for him, but besides that I'll do him no harm. If they'd have a day here for Old Nick himself, the Shobes would show up and bring dinner. I won't bother the Old General to shake hands with him, but I want a good look at him."

The twenty-five veterans, having stuffed themselves in a hurry, had got together at one side and again were singing "The Hunters of Kentucky."

"I know now how they whipped the British," said Eli Shobe. "They sang them a piece. But come to think of it I don't guess General Jackson could be very mad at me. I named my youngest boy for him. I was a sort of a Jackson man then though."

Then another diversion arose, an informal but fiercely contested wrestling match between Wren Woodford of Galloways Mill and Tim Miller of Sand Hill, each being the champion of his community. After three exciting falls, Woodford was declared the winner. The crowd then moved on to the horseshoe-pitching match between Art Gray and Claude Curry on one side, and Luther Hornback and Mel Diddle on the other. That was exciting for a while, and then the crowd was moving again.

The word was passed around that General Jackson was ready to . shake hands with all of his fellow Kentuckians, but that everybody would have to conform to the demands of a line. Almost in an instant the street was congested by those en route to Washington Hall. The managers were waiting and began arranging them in a line even before they reached the tavern door. They were instructed to shake hands with the General, speak a pleasant word and then move on. The line must be kept moving. Generally, the direction was followed, though at intervals one would anchor himself in front of the General in a pose that suggested a long stay. But the eagle-eyed managers would quickly set the stationary one in motion again.

Aunt Emmaline Hendricks of Sunnyside was not disposed to cooperate very fully with the managers. Aunt Emmaline could see no difference between a manager and anybody else. Aunt Emmaline had the notion that she was kin to Old Hickory, since her grandmother's maiden name was Jackson, and since that lady had emigrated from the "Carlinas" (an o in the name was held quite frankly as an abomination by Aunt Emmaline) with the first wave of settlers. Her grandmother in many ways reminded her of the General. She had been a woman of great bravery and determination. Aunt Emmaline's grandfather was a singing teacher, and, therefore, not capable of worthwhile uses. His wife, single-handed, had repulsed any number of attacks by the Redcoats and Indians. On the way to Kentucky, the wagon had suffered a severe fracture. The singing teacher was of no help. His wife had repaired that wagon herself so that it was better than brand new. Her grandmother's sturdiness and ingenuity in that emergency had always led Aunt Emmaline to consider herself related by blood to the gentleman in whose presence she stood. The audible grumbling in the line discouraged Aunt Emmaline not at all. And, as a matter of plain fact, General Jackson seemed to be enjoying the situation. His face was flavored with amusement for the first time that day. Aunt Emmaline desired to know of General Jackson from what section of north Ireland his original American ancestor had come, and what was the date of his arrival. The management stood in a huddle at one side of the room, and a baffled look was on its collective face. It simply didn't know how to get Aunt Emmaline to move on, and it was further distressed by a suspicion that General Jackson himself was not eager for her to move on.

"I could wring that woman's neck," said Ewing Porter with great sincerity.

It was an unfortunate statement and during the next several minutes he devoutly wished he had not made it. Jordan Hendricks, a nephew of Aunt Emmaline, happened to be standing near and overheard it. "How about practicing up on my neck before you jump on a lady twice your age?" he said truculently, holding his neck in an advanced position to render the practice more convenient.

Mr. Porter recognized Jordan, and recalled several optimistic reports of his prowess in personal combat. "I didn't mean it. I was under strain. I apologize."

"It might not hurt any to keep your mouth shut before you jump on an old lady." Hendricks' voice had risen, and was curiously reminiscent of a pioneer woman repairing a wagon broken down on a wilderness road.

Aunt Emmaline heard him, though not the words he was using. She turned about and spoke to him. "Oh, Jordan, come over here and speak to General Jackson. He's kin to you."

Aunt Emmaline didn't wait for an answer, but shifted back to the General and asked him if he had ever had any kinfolks named Carson, and when he said that he didn't know of any she argued with him that he had.

General Jackson, recognizing the congestion that Mrs. Hendricks was causing, decided to take a hand in favor of management.

"I should like to talk with you, dear lady, for several hours about our mutual kinfolks, but I promised to greet everyone, even those not my kin. If you will visit us at the Hermitage we will trace our Jacksons back to a common meeting place." He pushed her gently on, and Aunt Emmaline was so overjoyed by the conversation that she did not realize that she had left General Jackson's presence till she had reached the door.

General Jackson had greeted the twenty-five veterans that morning, but they were in line again, and they too proved troublesome to the managers. The General pronounced a special benediction upon each one of the twenty-five which left the soldier so filled with pleasant confusion that he didn't know he was being hurried on till it was too late. Finally, the line made its way across the room and past General Jackson. He had redeemed his promise: he had shaken hands with and greeted everyone who so wished. He had been tired when he arrived in the morning, fatigue plainly written upon his face. At the end of his ordeal he had the look of a rested man.

"Sit down, General Jackson," said Elvis Grider. "There are some of us who would like to talk with you a little longer. This is Mr. Cuthbert Jones, and this is John Keel. Both of them had to go to Franklin to a funeral this morning and missed you then. They are among your strongest supporters, sir."

"Certainly. If you gentlemen will excuse me for a few minutes I will go see how Mrs. Jackson is faring. I'll be back soon."

He was back within five minutes. "She was sleeping soundly when I entered the room, but she awoke. She was very sorry that she couldn't take part in your festivities. I think she will be rested by tomorrow."

"We counted on you being elected, General. We are quite distressed," said Jones.

"And I would have been elected, sir, but for the blackest piece of treason this country ever saw."

"We understood that it was like that."

"I would have been chosen had I been willing to yield to their evil plans. I was approached by the supporters of Henry Clay, and offered their support if I would appoint him Secretary of State. I told them to go straight back to Mr. Clay and tell him that I would rather see the earth open and swallow all of the contestants than for it to be said of me that I got into the presidential chair by bargain or intrigue, and that I would have no part in cheating the people of the country out of an honest election."

"The country's honor can be redeemed in 1828," said Jones.

"By the eternal, it will be redeemed then."

10

TWO WEEKS LATER Nat Grider and Sallie Motley were married at the Motley home. Dr. Lapsley had made a trip to the Grider home to reason with Elvis and Mrs. Grider. They had been so unyielding and vindictive that the preacher told them as he was leaving that he had not known a father and mother so cruel. He told them bluntly that the community had no finer girl than Sallie, that her character and wit were of such quality that they only con-

demned themselves when they objected to her. Then he had walked
rapidly to the Grider gate, mounted his horse and ridden away.

They were married on a spring day at twilight. Nat had gone to
ask his father and mother to come to the wedding.

The father had looked at the son for what seemed hours. Then he
had said, "I shall never put my foot in that house. You have arranged
your future without consulting us. It is your future, not ours."

11

NAT GRIDER was a good farmer and loved farming. The
Motley land was basically good, but it had gone without care for so
long that it was greatly in need of the thought and system that are
a major part of all successful farming. Some fields had been over-
planted; some were filled with stumps and had been used too little;
the fences were in disarray; the principal barn needed a new roof;
even the faithful spring needed a drastic cleaning out. For Nat Grider
his marriage was the beginning of a new life. He accepted the farm
as a challenge, not only to his sense but to his character. He was
deeply in love with his wife, and his mother-in-law was the soul of
character. And yet, Nat's happiness was marred by one circumstance.
Once every week he went to the Grider home. Never did Elvis Grider
use blunt and harsh words to his son. He used almost no words. He
would sit in his usual chair, his flinty eyes turned upon his son. Sometimes he would say something, but something only distantly connected with their relationship. He never inquired of Sallie nor of Mrs.
Motley, nor even of the progress of work upon the farm. The mother
rarely said anything.

The Grider-Walters bank was prospering. Both men were canny
in their dealings. They guarded the money entrusted to them with
scrupulous care. They had enough foresight to be prepared for the
crises that were thrust upon them. When Nat left the home, Grider
stopped trying to conduct the affairs of his farm. He started renting it
out to various tenants. He was favored in that. He found dependable
and hard-working tenants, and the crops grew well on the farm.
Grider stopped going to Dr. Lapsley's church, but within a few months
was working with a group helping to establish another church.

12

DAVID SETTLE was a surprising young man. He election-
eered from early in the morning till late in the afternoon on Jackson
Day, taking time out only to shake hands with the General and to eat
a hearty dinner, remembering to congratulate those who had prepared
the feast.

"He's a-headin' into trouble," said Bill Willie, "and when a feller
tries to do the undoable, that's where he lands at."

"One thing David needs to learn," answered Jacob Skiles, "is that
we still have the undoables."

"And we still got limestone bluffs that folks can butt their heads
against."

About the middle of May, the *Pantagraph* carried a paid advertisement that caused the readers to gasp.

INQUIRY TO VOTERS

Isn't twenty-two years too long for a judge to leave a question
undecided? Don't the tax-paying and law-abiding citizens deserve
prompter action on the part of their judge? Consider the following.

In 1803, a tract of land in Warren County, Kentucky, was
claimed by both Elvis Grider and Jacob Skiles, having been mistakenly issued to both men. This was brought officially to the
notice of Judge Charles Drake, then as now, judge of the court.
No judgment has been issued in the case. Both men still claim
the land. Neither has paid taxes on it. The matter stands exactly
as it did twenty-two years ago. If this is the sort of dillydallying
that serves the best interests of the county, then return Judge
Drake to the bench. Otherwise, vote for

DAVID SETTLE

The advertisement brought on a great deal of talk on the streets
and in the taverns. Most people had forgotten about the dispute, and
most of the younger ones had never heard of it.

"I am on the judge's side," said Mr. Trez Covington. "I wouldn't
decide that case for one of Elvis Grider's biggest watermelons. I don't
think it would make much difference to Jacob either way, but he has
a lot of friends who wouldn't like it. Elvis wouldn't like it, and you

got to say that he has friends too, some of them as mean as poison."

But some members of the younger generation were inclined to find justice in Mr. Settle's plea. "If you want to shoot somebody," one of them said, "go ahead. The judge would never get around to trying you."

Jacob Skiles read Settle's piece and was uncertain whether to become angry or amused. He tentatively decided upon the latter. He handed the paper to his wife. "What do you think of that, Priscilla?"

She read it through slowly. "Maybe Judge Drake ought to have settled it way back yonder when we first got here, but there's no call to start up hard feelings now."

Skiles laughed. "I have had time to get used to not owning that land. When it first came up it would have made me angry to lose it. I didn't want to lose it, and I didn't like Grider. I might even have got violent about it. Do you remember Judge Drake making a trip out to Three Springs around by Richpond just to be friendly? Well, since then, whatever his decision there would have been no trouble. That showed me he was a just man. But I haven't talked about it. Not that I wanted the notion to get out that I was indifferent about it. As a matter of fact, I didn't want to lose it and don't yet, but I could take it calmly, perhaps even laugh about it. But that I will tell to nobody but you, Priscilla. I wonder what Bill Willie will think of David Settle?"

"Judge Drake is one of his favorites. I know what he will think."

"I expect I'd better talk to him about it. Bill Willie can be right tactless when rubbed on one of his delicate parts."

He went to Bill Willie's house and showed him the paper. Blewett took one look at it and vowed that on the morrow he would leave the hired hands on the place to their own devices long enough to beat Settle into such a physical pulp as to leave him heedless of judicial decisions.

"I doubt if you could think up a better way to defeat Judge Drake. He hasn't many enemies, but that would give them a rallying point. Leave Settle alone. He will defeat himself better than you could."

The second day following that, the *Pantagraph* carried another advertisement:

THE JUDGE NEEDS HELP

I have been reading in the *Pantagraph* how negligent I am. Every word of it is true. I have put that decision off year after year, hoping that I might see the true light and so be able to render a just decision that would bring happiness to earnest people like my opponent. Alas, that light has been denied me.

I would like to get the case settled, and I hereby make this proposal to my opponent. If he will write and sign the decision which seems to him to be warranted both by the facts in the case and the law, I will issue it under my authority. This is a bona fide offer. If he is so eager to get this case settled here is his chance.

CHARLES DRAKE

Settle read this, and his face grew redder with each succeeding line. He knew that he was caught. He was sure that if he accepted the judge's challenge and decided in favor of either contestant he would lose half the county. He was sure that if he ignored it he would be made the laughingstock of too many to survive. Whichever way he turned would be wrong.

Jacob Skiles handed the paper to Bill Willie Blewett and pointed to the letter. "Settle walked right into it like a mule with the blind staggers," said Bill Willie.

Judge Drake was out on the streets most of the day, and at every turn someone was bantering him: "Settle told you what to do yet, Judge?"

"Sure must be fine to have a Settle to settle all your problems, Judge."

"I wish you'd send Settle around to see me, Judge. I just can't make up my mind whether to sell that sorrel horse of mine. I need help, Judge."

The judge would reply in effect, "No sir, I never did enjoy living as much. I haven't got a trouble to my name. Settle takes care of everything."

Settle was just as brash in his letter of withdrawal as he had been in his allegations:

SETTLE IS SETTLED

Having discovered how not to conduct a candidacy for office, I wish to advise all and sundry that I do know how to practice law. Henceforth, I may be found at my office on Frozen Row. I will give my closest thought and care to all business brought me.

I have transferred my support in the judge's race to the present incumbent, whom I regard as worthy of the high honor.

DAVID SETTLE

"I like a man who can learn that he is wrong," said Jacob Skiles. "I am going to turn over the store's collecting to him for a while." "He took his time learnin'," said Bill Willie Blewett.

13

THE YEAR moved into the summer, then out of it into the autumn. Crops in the county were good except in the western part. There a prolonged drouth had wrought its harm. In August, an epidemic of typhoid fever swept through most of the homes in the Woodburn section. It ran its course and disappeared, leaving eight new graves in the section's graveyards. A revival under the sponsorship of the Methodists was held in Hobson's Grove, on the outskirts of the town. Reverend Valentine Cook was the preacher, and he was powerful in doctrine and exhortation. His voice was soft, persuasive, yet carried to the utmost parts of his congregation. His eyes were dreamy and conveyed the impression that he was witnessing a vision. The Baptists of the community joined with the Methodists, though warily at first. The more staid members of the Presbyterian church were not drawn to hear Dr. Cook, though other Presbyterians were. The meeting went on for three and a half weeks, and closed before it started to dwindle out. Dr. Cook endeared himself to the people not alone by the power of his preaching, but also by his feats in absent-mindedness. One time he was suddenly moved to leave the pulpit. He was gone half an hour. The congregation filled the time with song, led by Mr. Obadiah Harman. Mr. Harman was tiring when the preacher, red-faced and flustered, reappeared. While standing on the platform, it had occurred to him that he had forgotten to bring his wife along. So he had unhitched his horse and ridden in a canter to the house where they were staying, to remember upon arrival that she had gone with him and was at that moment sitting in the congregation. One day he was invited to supper in two different homes and accepted both. In the middle of the first supper, he remembered his acceptance of the other invitation. He hurriedly excused himself, indicating that he needed to be alone before the preaching hour. He arrived promptly at the other home where his host had all but given him up. The preacher apologized, indicating that he had felt the need to be alone before the preaching hour, and proceeded to eat a hearty supper. One night he brought a copy of Melanchthon's *Vergil* instead of the Bible which he intended. When he opened it a look of surprise overspread his face, but he quickly mastered it. His mastery of the Scriptures was so complete that he held the book open before him, his eyes apparently intent upon the page, and read the Scripture he had planned without the omission or misplacing of a single syllable. Few preachers have ever been loved in south Kentucky as was Valentine Cook.

The echoes of the revival had hardly died when Dr. Cargile Butler of Illinois appeared in town for a series of four lectures on abolition. The topic was new for Bowling Green, and the rumor was out that Dr. Butler was a firebrand. So the Hobsons would not permit him to use their grove. But he did get the use of a vacant lot in the town. He hired a helper and together they put up a makeshift stand. On Monday evening he gave his first lecture. It was plain that the man was a fanatic, but he was an orator, and he knew all the tricks of public speaking. His voice was powerful and his delivery colorful. There was a great deal of talk about him on the streets on Tuesday.

"I say le's run him out o' town," said Noah Runner to a crowd gathered on a street corner. "I got eight slaves. I claim the Bible gives me the right to them. I don't aim to have no man from up north tellin' me what to do and what not to do. People like that do harm. I say le's chase him out."

"You can never stop anything by just making people quit talking about it, Noah," answered Eli Shobe. "I don't intend to go hear him, but I would if I lived close enough."

"You don't want to lose your slaves, do you, Eli?"

"I don't have a slave to my name. I gave the ones I had to my sons. I'll say this, they are better treated than if they were free."

Reub Buckner, who was standing near, said, "I'm for you, Noah. If a man don't want no slaves, he don't have to have 'em. If he does want 'em, I claim he's got a right to have them, and I'll help salivate anybody who says he can't."

"There is no doubt that you could run him off," said Shobe. "But suppose the man is right. I am not sure you could find in the Bible any verse that says it is right to have slaves. I have hunted for it, and I haven't found it. The way I read the Bible it seems to want everybody to be free."

"I asked Brother Galloway a long time ago, and he said he didn't know any Scripture that said it was wrong to have a slave."

"I feel in my bones that slavery is going to cause us a lot of trouble someday."

"That's the rheumatiz you got in your bones," said Buckner, laughing. "What you say, Noah, about gettin' up a crowd and sendin' this feller back where he come from?"

"Better not do it," counseled Shobe. "At any rate, don't try it till you have heard him speak."

"Eli's right," said Boone Elkin. "We ought to go hear him first. If he gets too cantankerous, we can tend to him. If he talks reasonable, there ain't no use of us goin' to all that trouble."

"Besides, we might get into trouble with the law," said Homer Lowe, always cautious.

There were only a few avowed antislavery men in the section then. But not one of five of the householders of the county then owned slaves. The majority accepted it as a proper routine. Some, like Eli Shobe, in one way or another were connected with slaves. Some were dimly aware of the ominous threat hanging over the whole business.

About a dozen men, led by Noah Runner, went to find out for themselves how objectionable the man's words were. Dr. Butler had a fair audience. There were some who attended all public meetings. Then, too, the word had gone out that Dr. Butler was mighty in denunciation, and many found that an attractive quality in public speakers. Also, there was the feeling that he might go so far as to bring on a bit of sharp excitement. One would hardly want to miss that.

Dr. Butler was an intense man. There was no faintheartedness in anything he did or said. His hair was a thick, curly mass of black and gray. His eyes burned like large points of fire. They seemed never to be still, and to see everything. In an era of powerful voices his would ask no quarter.

He led in the singing of two hymns, and after that read a chapter from the Bible. Then he stood erect so suddenly that the snap was almost audible. He almost slammed his Bible shut. So might an ancient prophet have stood and cried aloud his denunciations against the people.

"Ye dwellers in Babylon, thy judgment has come. Ye buyers and sellers of gold, and silver, and precious stones, of fine linen and silk, of all manner of vessels of ivory and precious woods and brass; of cinnamon and oil and frankincense; of wine and oil; of horses and chariots; of slaves and the souls of men."

His voice thundered savagely.

". . . the souls of men. Buyers and sellers of the souls of men! God's angry judgment is upon the buyers and sellers of the souls of men. Tell me, ye buyers and sellers, where is Babylon? Where are its pleasant streets and busy market places? Where are its groves and temples? Where are its horses and chariots? Where are its vines and fig trees? Gone into desolation, and today the jackal prowls endlessly for stray wisps of food and finds them not. The land is parched and gives no increase. The stones burn and the rivers have changed their courses. The vultures fly low above the land, always searching for death. What happened to Babylon will happen to any people or place that scorns God's laws enough to buy and sell the souls of men."

Noah Runner and his comrades had deliberately chosen seats well up front, and there sat under the spell of the speaker's voice. As long as the curse remained upon Babylon they could find no major offense in what he said. There was nothing personal about Babylon. But the speaker was leaving Babylon. It might be that he was moving toward Kentucky. They would wait and see.

"Ye men and women who sit before me, Babylon is far away, and there is only desolation to show where it stood. It is but a waste of ashes left by the fires, kindled by God's anger. But that same God still sits upon his throne and looks down on the people of Kentucky as they traffic in the souls of men. He is a patient God, but His patience will not last forever. He is a kindly God, else long ago Kentucky would have been as one with Babylon."

The men in the group looked at one another, their souls not yet stirred to violence but trembling on the verge.

"How will the people of Kentucky pay for this great sin? Hearken to the prophecy of me, His servant. You will pay for it in war. Your blood will redden your fields. The bodies of your

sons will lie by your roadsides. The smoke of the burning of
your towns will hang against your hills. The cries of your be-
reaved will be carried by the winds——"

Noah Runner sprang to his feet, not knowing quite what he did.
"Reverend, what are you talking about?"

"I will tell you what I am talking about."

His forefinger swung about with the terrible austerity of a John Knox
until it rested unmistakably upon Noah.

"Have you bought and sold the souls of men? Do you own
slaves?"

"No," shouted Noah, "but I wish I did!"

"Then you are as wicked as those who do. You have purposed
in your heart to buy and sell the souls of men."

"It isn't wicked to own slaves," shouted Noah. "We are not going to
let you say it is."

"I am not the first one who said it. I am repeating what God
said. Any man who owns a slave is an evil man——"

The men arose, scrambled out into the vague aisle and made their
way toward Dr. Butler. Three men, avowed abolitionists, gathered in
front of Dr. Butler, yielding nothing to the greater number. One of
them held in his hand the handle of a broadax which he had bought
that afternoon at Hardcastle's store. Dr. Butler's voice rang out above
the angry hubbub of the men.

"Listen, you men of Babylon. I came here to speak the words
that burn in my heart, and as long as I am alive I will speak them.
But I do not wish violence. That will come soon enough. And
when it does you will all be destroyed, root and branch. I have
chosen to speak here tonight. It is God's will for me to speak.
If there is breath in my body I will speak. If you do me harm
then this is Babylon indeed."

"Go ahead, preacher," bellowed Clay Ellis, a dour hater of slavery from Rockfield. "Go ahead and we will suffer with you."

Another man came across the area in front of the stand. "I say he'll finish his speech, or there'll be a widder woman at my house tonight."

"Stay out of this!" yelled Noah Runner. "Stay out of it. You are our neighbors. We just aim to shut his big mouth."

Dr. Butler paused a moment as if in deep thought. Then he took two steps forward and his voice rang out:

"I came here to speak and I will speak, unless twelve men overcome five, which is the way they did in Babylon till the Lord tired of their tyranny. But I will bargain with you, you men of Babylon. If you will leave now, or else take your seats and leave me uninterrupted till I have finished tonight, then I will be gone by tomorrow. It is either that or bloodshed. Take your choice. Make your decision."

He stopped and looked searchingly at the four men arrayed on his side. Noah Runner looked at his fellows, and they looked back at him uncertainly.

"Let him speak," called a voice from the audience. "He can't do no harm."

"Better do like he says," growled the man with the broadax handle.

Noah Runner turned to Dr. Butler. "Is that a solemn promise?" he asked.

"It's my word."

"What you men say?" Noah asked his colleagues.

"All right with me," said one, "but ifn he's back here tomorrow night, he'll wish he wasn't."

"And anybody that sides with him," growled Reub Buckner, casting a vicious look at Dr. Butler and his friends.

Dr. Butler waited until the sounds of the footsteps of Noah Runner and his companions could be heard no longer. He raised an outstretched hand, commanding silence. He resumed speaking almost as if no interruption had occurred. His first sentence fitted perfectly into the one broken into by Noah Runner. His audience watched him in silence and with hypnotic fervor. An hour later he was speaking with no lessening of volume, no abatement of intensity. At eleven o'clock he was still speaking, but soon thereafter brought his address to a dramatic close. Most of those left quickly, but a few remained to bid Dr. Butler good-by.

"Said all you aimed to, didn't you?" asked the man from Rockfield. "When you trade with jockeys you drive the best bargain you can. Yes, I was able to combine my four addresses into two without much loss. I'll stick to my promise. I'll be moving on tonight."

14

NATURALLY, the news of Dr. Butler's maneuver got out, and Noah Runner never heard the last of his permitting Dr. Butler to give all four of his addresses. But Dr. Butler's visit to Bowling Green amounted to more than a joke on Noah Runner. It served to give form and direction to a deal of antislavery sentiment that had been existing rather nebulously for several years. It started people to talking and thinking about the virtues and faults of slavery.

"I have been thinking," said Elvis Grider to Walters, "and I doubt whether we should lend much money for buying slaves. It has been good business up to now, but somebody is going to lose a lot of money on slaves, and it might not be long off. I think we ought to have gilt-edged collateral the next time we make a loan for buying slaves."

Eli Shobe found Jacob Skiles in his furniture store. "I wanted to ask your advice on something. This slavery business has been bothering me lately. I have been wondering if I oughtn't to advise my sons to sell theirs. What do you think?"

"It's hard to say. The time is coming when we will have no more slaves. I've been convinced of that for a long time. For that reason I have not owned any. Sometimes such things move swiftly, and sometimes they drag along for years. I don't know what to tell you. I am no abolitionist. This is no moral matter with me. I believed it would be better for me to hire white people to do my work than to own Negroes and have to depend on them. I think that slavery is worse for the owners than it is for the slaves."

"I have thought that for a long time. I think that I will tell the boys to sell them if they can find good masters for them, but to be careful about that."

"It's a big problem, and the answer is in the mind of time." He changed the subject. "Rumsey is coming home tomorrow."

"How fast the years get by us! Rumsey a lawyer now, and licensed to practice in the courts. Only yesterday he was a small lad, looking at everything with big solemn eyes. I congratulate you, and specially Mrs. Skiles."

"She is a very happy woman."

"And a very fine one. I look for Rumsey to get a good deal of practice from the very first. There is a lot of law business stacked up and waiting for really good lawyers."

"We talked about it the last time he was here. He is of the idea that most cases ought never to reach court, that they can be settled that way."

"That system would be all right—up to a certain point. It could be overdone. Justice would then reside in law offices and not in the courts."

"Of course, but most cases are too trivial to take up a court's time."

"So Rumsey is a man now. Soon, he will be getting married, and soon you will be a grandfather. How the years pass! I ought to know."

Rumsey came home the next day. The day after that, he opened an office in Mr. Neale's building on the square. He had his first case within an hour. A Mr. Shanks from Clear Fork came in with a complaint against Mr. Herndon of Bowling Green. The plaintiff had bought from the defendant a slave who within a week was taken with an advanced case of consumption. The slave had died before Mr. Shanks had owned him a month. He wanted his money back. The slave had appeared a bit skinny, but no hint had been given as to any trouble. Herndon could not possibly have been unacquainted with the matter. The sale was fraudulent. Mr. Shanks wanted his money back. His apparent sincerity appealed to Rumsey.

"I'll take the case, but I want you to tell me exactly what happened. Don't leave out a thing."

Shanks told the story, and that afternoon the young lawyer went into the Herndon neighborhood and did a chore of investigating. What he found out touched his boyish face with grimness. He sent for Herndon to come to his office. After waiting several hours, he was preparing to go hunt him up when the man shuffled into his office.

"What do you want to see me about?" he asked in a surly voice and manner.

"Have a chair, Mr. Herndon." The man remained standing. "I wanted to talk with you about the slave you sold Elmer Shanks."

"I heard he was grumbling about it. He bought him fair and square. What do you want to talk with me about?"

"Didn't you know the man had consumption when you sold him?"

"I am no doctor. I knew he was skinny."

"You didn't pay him not to cough while Shanks was looking at him?"

"Who says I did?"

"I have two affidavits that I think would stand up in any court. Either you pay Shanks his money back, or we will see if they won't stand up."

"Slave affidavits no good."

"I didn't say who made the affidavits. The judge and the jury will know whether they are any good."

Herndon twisted his fingers violently. Finally, he said, "I hate to see a man lose his money. I'll give him half of the purchase money back. He couldn't ask anything better than that."

"He would like to have it all back. I think he is entitled to it. Do you want us to take it into court?"

Herndon twisted his fingers a full two minutes. Rumsey said nothing. Herndon twisted about. "It's a lot of trouble to go to court. I'll give him his money."

Mr. Shanks didn't lose his money, and Rumsey Skiles gained some reputation. Everybody knew that Herndon was a difficult man to get money from.

"Mighty clever of that young lawyer to find that out. He sure cooked Old Herndon's goose," said one.

"Herndon wouldn't have settled it even then if he hadn't remembered how Judge Drake feels about a thing like that. Yes, it was right clever."

"I got three new cases today," Rumsey told his father one night when he had been there a week.

"You are not claiming that the town needs more lawyers, are you?" the father asked jestingly.

"Yes, I am. Your friends alone will bring me all the work I can do. I have been finding out how many good friends you have here. It didn't surprise me, but it did me good to hear it. 'So you are Jacob Skiles's boy?' one of them will say. 'I wonder if you could take a case for me.'"

"You'll do all right, Rumsey. I have no doubt of it. You have too much of your mother in you to fail."

"And enough of your father to succeed," said his mother.

Rumsey Skiles laid an affectionate hand on the shoulder of each parent. "I am glad to be at home and at work. I haven't told you yet, but I am having some new competition."

"Another lawyer?" asked his father.

"His name is Robin Rodes. I stopped at a meeting of lawyers in Louisville as I came home. I became acquainted with him there. He had already chosen to settle here."

"I remember now," said Jacob Skiles. "He was here sometime in January. He went to see Judge Drake. The judge liked him. Elvis Grider was going to turn some business his way, I believe."

"If it isn't sound business, Rodes will not accept it. I have a letter from him. He expects to get here tomorrow or the next day. I am sure you both will like him."

15

Virgil Covington lived with his sister Ella in the house his father had built a mile out of town. His father and mother were both dead, and he and Ella were the only children. They were the source of considerable anxiety to their Uncle Trezevant, who was inwardly very fond of both, but who outwardly suspected both of irresponsibility and general inadequacy, and was under little restraint in saying so. Uncle and nephew rarely spoke friendly words to each other, and yet, from some subtle awareness, each knew of the other's affection.

"I am thinking about getting married," Virgil told his sister one day. "I have reached that period in life when such thoughts are logical."

She stared at him. "Good gracious, Virgil, whatever got that into your head?"

"Whatever could keep it out of my head? I know the way to get a perfect wife, and I am considering trying it out."

She laughed heartily. "Go tell Uncle Trez. He'll cure you."

"I think it is time that you come to some decision about a husband, Ella."

"Virgil Covington, are you demented?"

"Did you ever know a Covington who wasn't? The way I am going to do it is this: I am going to see Uncle Trez, tell him what I have decided and ask him to name the wife he thinks I ought to have. When he tells me, I am going to say *uh huh*, just like it suits me perfectly. Then I am going to ask him of all the girls he knows which one he thinks is the wrongest one for me. When he says which one I am going to say *uh huh* just like I can't even bear to hear her name mentioned aloud. Then I am going right over and ask her to marry me."

"Don't you do that, Virgil. She might accept you."

"Of course she would. Nobody could ever refuse a Covington. Then we would live happily the rest of our lives. I don't know why I haven't thought of that before."

"It's the sort of thing you would think of before. And then, pray, while you were living so happily, what would become of me?"

"Oh, I have thought of that too. You could cook for us."

"How utterly charming! Then I could poison you both, and that would leave me the sole owner of this property."

"Oh, no, Uncle Trez would get it. You would be no match for that old miser. He would know right off that you had more breeches than you had legs to fill."

"At least, he would be delicate about it. Do you know what day this is?"

"A Covington always knows what day of the week it is. Thursday."

"And tomorrow?"

"Tomorrow always comes on Friday. What are you driving at?"

"It's tomorrow, Friday, that we appear in court to protect our own property. Don't you remember the man who says he owns our dog? Don't you remember the clever little note the man brought from Judge Drake?"

"I do indeed. Isbell *versus* Covington, it said. Well, we will show that Isbell that he can't *versus* any Covington. I suppose we had better go, like the note said. Mother would not want us to refuse a clever invitation like that."

"Mother wouldn't want us to lose Sir Galahad either."

They had named the dog Sir Galahad the day he had appeared in their front yard. It wasn't then over three weeks old. "I remember that pup when I first saw it. I got fond of it right then," said Ella gaily. "Don't you remember? We had gone all the way to Allen Springs looking for one, and the one they had didn't suit us. And here it was in our front yard. That's the reason we named it Sir Galahad."

"I never did get the hang of that name. No, don't explain it to me. I always get confused when somebody tries to explain something to me. Anyhow, Isbell'd just as well go out to Allen Springs and get that dog. He won't get ours. I don't mind going to court at all. I expect I'd just as well get used to it. I am thinking about taking up a life of crime just as soon as I can get things straightened out here."

"I don't mind going to court either. A little excitement would do me good."

"I don't think you are going. Court is no place for a woman. Suppose Uncle Trez should see you there."

"He would be proud of me. I know something about Uncle Trez you don't."

"Then don't tell me. I know all I can and stay a Christian gentleman."

"He has bought that house, the one you almost bought."

"The one that wouldn't stay bought. How did you find out?"

"I went to see Mrs. Durbin about a fitting for my dress, and I passed Judge Drake who was out for a horseback ride, and he stopped me and told me about it. He said his guess was that Uncle Trez bought it so it would stay a Covington house."

"And that's exactly what it will stay till he gets the chance to give some fellow a first-rate skinning. I'll bet an ear he has got his eye on somebody now. What time we got to be in court?"

"The note, or whatever it was, said ten o'clock."

"My main regret is that I didn't kill Isbell when he came here trying to get Sir Galahad."

"I didn't think he was in much danger. I saw you offer him a drink of water with ice in it from the icehouse."

"Just following the example of our dear mother. And the very next thing we have to go to court to save Sir Galahad from a man who had been refreshed from our icehouse."

16

JUDGE DRAKE entered the little room which he used for an office. Ellie Davenport, the bailiff, awaited him. The judge mopped his brow, though the weather was not at all hot. "A plagued nuisance," he grumbled.

"What is, Judge?" inquired Davenport.

"That scamp Jess Isbell bringing a lawsuit to force those Covington children to give up their dog."

"They are not children, Judge. They are both grown."

"If they are grown then you are an Egyptian mummy, Ellie. I saw them standing there at the door when I came in. I'd have gone over and spoken to them, only a judge has to be mighty careful."

"You haven't any opposition, Judge, since Settle got off."

"A judge has to be careful about more things than opponents for the office. That scamp! Only don't tell anybody I said it, Ellie."

The case of Isbell *versus* Covington was called. It seemed that both sides were ready for the trial. Jess Isbell took the witness chair and was duly sworn. Questioned by his attorney, Rumsey Skiles, he testified that a pup of his, then not quite a month old, disappeared, and he had heard no word of it till one day he was passing the Covington home, and there was that selfsame pup, grown into a dog, lying in the front yard.

Ella Covington had not looked at the man while he was testifying. Consequently, she had not seen the young lawyer who was asking him the questions. But something in the lawyer's voice drew her notice. It was a nice voice, a very appealing voice. Why should such a voice be used in behalf of such a man as Isbell? Ella turned and looked at him; a startled look spread upon her face, and a sort of flush mantled it. Judge Drake, on the bench, saw the episode, and, smiling faintly, lifted his eyes to the window. Isbell told his story. He had made a second trip by the Covington home, then a third one. There could be no doubt about it. It was his dog, and one of great value. He had gone to the house and asked for its return, since it was rightfully his dog. His request had been refused. It was his dog. He needed it, and he wanted it. That was his story.

Judge Drake said that the defense would present its case and asked who the lawyer was.

Virgil Covington arose and said, "Your Honor, we haven't got a lawyer. My sister and I talked it over and we decided that we can tell what you want to know just as well without a lawyer. If that gentleman—" pointing to Rumsey Skiles—"will ask us questions, we will answer them." Virgil sat down abruptly.

Judge Drake looked at Rumsey Skiles and asked if that suited him. The surprised Skiles hesitated, looked about him, then hesitated some more, and finally said it did.

"Then take the witness."

"We aren't just one witness, your Honor, there are two of us."

"Then take the witnesses." The judge's eyes were upon the window, and a faint smile hovered about the corners of his mouth.

There was just one witness chair, and Virgil motioned his sister into it. The bailiff considered the matter, then displaced a spectator, and offered the chair to Virgil. The two Covingtons sat together on the side of the table opposite the examiner. It was then that Rumsey Skiles saw Ella Covington for the first time. Their eyes met, and he, as if from sudden surprise, hastily looked down at the table.

Soon he looked up and asked, "You are Ella and Virgil Covington?"

"Of course we are," said Ella. "You are Mr. Skiles, I believe."

The onlookers laughed. Judge Drake pounded the desk before him, struggling to maintain a becoming composure himself. "Proceed with the questioning."

Rumsey used up some seconds steadying himself. "When did you first see this dog in question?"

"Late in April, or early in May, a year ago," Virgil answered. "I do not remember exactly."

"But I do," said Ella. "I remember perfectly well. It was a clear, fine day, and after breakfast I went out on the veranda and sat there for a little while. It was the twenty-ninth of April."

"But, Ella, how can you be so exact about it?"

"I'll tell you how. That little dog came walking up toward the veranda and I went out and met it. I called you and you came from around the house somewhere, and you asked me where the pup came from."

"What has that got to do with the twenty-ninth of April?"

"Don't you remember? That was the day I went to Miriam Dulaney's birthday party, and her birthday is the twenty-ninth of April. When I left to go I told you to take care of Sir Galahad." She turned in explanation to Judge Drake. "That was what we had named the dog. Would you like to know why we decided to name it that?"

"Later," said Judge Drake, his eyes upon the window. "Continue with the examination."

"Judge, please let me ask him a question." Virgil pointed to Jess Isbell.

Rumsey Skiles started to object, but instead he sat there and looked at Ella Covington. Judge Drake nodded his head vaguely.

"Mr. Isbell, do you still own the mother of our dog?"

It was in Rumsey Skiles's mind to point out the illegality of the pronoun, but he did not get beyond a faint start. Mr. Isbell said, "yes," and then "no," then relapsed in his chair and sat looking in surprise at his attorney.

"So you do own her, and then again you don't. In either case, describe her."

Lawyer Skiles arose and inquired whether Covington had been admitted to the bar.

"Never even tried to be, and if I didn't ask the question right I wish you'd help me." He smiled brightly at Skiles. "I guess you have learned a lot about asking questions."

Skiles couldn't think of anything further to say. "Are there no further questions?" asked the judge in a grave voice, though an odd light was glinting in his eyes.

"I don't know how to ask a question, Judge Drake, of a man who owns a dog and doesn't own one at the same time. When he tried to get our dog my sister and I walked by his place three times, and we didn't see a sign of a dog except a little runty feist that looked pretty sad. Where do you think he might have been keeping our dog's mother, Judge?"

"I asked one of the slaves there and he said Mr. Isbell never had any dog except the one my brother told about."

"This is irrelevant. We will have to ignore it," the judge said.

"Excuse me, Judge, but it seemed right relevant to me," said Ella, "though I may be wrong in the meaning of the word. Words trouble me a great deal." She bowed to Rumsey Skiles. "I suppose they come easy to you, sir."

"I am of the opinion, your Honor," said Rumsey Skiles, and the words were coming easy to him, "that my client brought this action under a misapprehension. I ask, therefore, to be permitted to withdraw the suit."

"I want my dog!" shouted Isbell.

"You have already got your dog," said Virgil. "My sister and I saw it three times as we were passing your house."

"The court is not inclined to accept the evidence as sufficient to find for the plaintiff," said Judge Drake. He struck the table with his gavel. "The case is dismissed."

Isbell turned savagely upon Rumsey Skiles. "What sort of law business is this? You won't get a cent for it."

"Certainly not," said Skiles sweetly. "I'd be willing to pay you a reasonable price for this privilege."

"And there's a lot of practice I'll see that you don't get."

"Be off, won't you? I wish to congratulate the defendants."

A husky farmer came up. "You done right," he said to Rumsey. "Jess Isbell never owned a good dog in his life. He saw this dog and he heard they picked it up somewhere, so he tried to get it. You done right."

"Can't you come and have dinner with us some time?" asked Ella Covington. "My brother and I would like to thank you for saving Sir Galahad for us, and as Mama used to say you can't thank a man right without feeding him. Can you come?"

"Listen, Sister, he has just got home from somewhere and likes to be with his father and mother. Let's ask them too."

"All right. I'd like to. Your mother is such a sweet woman. I suppose we can ask them to be present while we thank you for saving Sir Galahad for us. How about two weeks from next Sunday?"

"I'll accept for them," said Rumsey. "If anything happens so they can't come I'll ride out and tell you. Where do you live?"

"Oh, I forgot. We moved here from Virginia while you were away at school. Mama always said 'From Amelia County, Virginia,' but I think Virginia is enough. I heard several people talk about you, and not a one of them said a bad thing, of course, but I never dreamed you would save Sir Galahad for us. We live—well, your father knows where. He brought a cookstove for our house out from his furniture store."

"I never did understand why your father is against General Jackson," said Virgil.

"One reason is he thinks we have a better chance to get steamboats with Mr. Clay."

"You all come right on out from preaching," said Ella. "We'll be expecting you."

That night Rumsey told his parents of the invitation. "Isn't it a bit odd," asked his mother, "for her to invite us just because you lost a case for a client?"

"Perhaps I needed some sort of consolation. They are nice people, aren't they?"

"I am sure they are, but sometimes nice people are the oddest of all."

"They are a little straightforward, but of fine quality," said Jacob Skiles. "Their father and mother died of some sort of plague the second year they were here. The son and daughter have lived on in the home place. In fact, they were required to live there by the terms of the will. Covington was a man of means, but a bit peculiar like his brother, Trezevant. He left them the place, but with a strange reservation. They were to keep the place five years, and if then they could prove that they had made a living off it they were to be given full possession of it and of all the other property he had. They have three years to go."

"Have they been making a living?"

"I think so. I think they will do all right if Virgil doesn't act foolishly again and buy another house. He got the house at a bargain, but he was not prepared to hold it long enough. So the bank got it back, but I hear that Trez has paid off the mortgage. They say that Trez knows more people by name than any man in Warren County, though he has not been here very long."

"And more about more people," added his wife.

"That's what they say. I think you did right in the trial, Rumsey, and I think you will win favor by the way you handled the case, though I recommend against turning back very often when halfway across the stream."

"We ought to have gone to see them before this," said his wife, "but somehow we never got around to it. We will be glad to go with you, Rumsey."

"Don't you think she is a very beautiful girl, Mother?" said Rumsey.

"I certainly do," said Priscilla Skiles.

17

It was on Saturday of that week that Jacob Skiles addressed a mass meeting in the courthouse, called to consider ways of improving the river enough to permit steamboat traffic. The topic was of interest throughout the county, and a considerable crowd gathered. Judge Drake presided and called the meeting to order. He introduced Jacob Skiles.

Skiles was a plain but convincing speaker. He said that he had been concerned with the issue for a long time. He was a farmer. He raised, or could raise, on his farm produce which as things were then he could not get to market. He ran three wagon routes. He made a profit from his hauling, but much less than if the roads were even in fair condition. He owned a furniture store, and it was a matter, all too familiar, to be out of an article without much prospect of having it in stock soon. The available transportation simply wasn't adequate. In his opinion, the section could not reach its due prosperity until more goods, much more goods, could be taken to market and brought from market. Bowling Green needed desperately a road to Nashville, usable in all seasons, and one to Louisville. More than half of the road to Nashville was in Tennessee. Nashville, being supplied with river transportation, was not immediately interested in the road, though sooner or later, it surely would be. The road to Louisville ran through some rugged country, which made the cost of making it a good road almost prohibitive. That left steamboats as the best answer to the community's transportation problems. "I have seen steamboats both at Nashville and at Louisville. They are marvels, able to carry an unbelievable amount of merchandise, and to travel with unbelievable speed. I saw the steamboat *Enterprise* arrive at Louisville from New Orleans, and I saw the *General Jackson* at the landing at Nashville. I tell you that if we had one steamboat once a week each way between here and the Ohio River, yes, once every two weeks, it would double our prosperity. It costs no more to carry an article from New Orleans to Nashville than it does from Nashville here, though the distance is fifteen times as great."

"How can we get a steamboat?" called a man from the audience.

"The river will have to be navigable from here to the Ohio River near Evansville. The expense of that should be borne by both the state and Federal governments. I have talked with people who ought to know about such matter, and they have told me that the cost is not prohibitive. It will cost a great deal of money, but it will bring in a great deal of prosperity to offset the cost. Not only would it help Bowling Green and Warren County, but every town and county down the river will be helped in the same way. Every farm will be able to raise more, and at a profit. Every merchant will be able to sell more, and every home will be able to have some luxuries it does not now have. I think that in twenty-five, or thirty, or forty years we will have good roads and bridges across the waterways. I am sure that it is possible for us to have a steamboat in five or six years. The river is right now our best hope."

"What can we do?"

"Cornelius Turner and Joe Underwood represent you in the state legislature. Many of you know them. Go to see them, whether or not you know them, and ask for their aid in bringing this properly before the legislature. The Federal Government will likely hold back till the state takes the lead. We need some action in Frankfort."

"We're for you. Count on us," shouted George Moulder.

"Thank you, George. And one other thing—I hope that this movement for the improvement of the river will not be given any political label. I know that there are many here who are for General Jackson. Go ahead and support the old hero. I know that there are many Clay men here. I am one of them, as most of you know. That should make no difference at all. This is for the common good."

Trezevant Covington met him as he was leaving the courthouse. "You talked good sense, Jacob," he said. "I'll talk with Joe Underwood, though I doubt if he needs it much."

Fifty yards farther on, Skiles passed Elvis Grider. He started to bow, but saw that Grider was regarding very closely the building he was passing. He remembered that Grider had not been at the meeting.

Judge Drake and Eli Shobe were waiting at the corner.

"I am an old man," said the judge, "but I have never seen a steamboat. You make one seem mighty attractive. I can hardly wait."

"Nor can I," said Skiles, "to see one on our river. I made that trip to Nashville just to see the *General Jackson*. Perhaps I shouldn't have gone. The sight of that boat at Nashville has made me all the more impatient to see one here."

"Let's make a covenant," said Shobe. "Let's all three stay alive till a steamboat lands at Bowling Green."

"I'll do what I can," said the judge, "but old age comes on quickly."

18

THE THREE SKILESES rode out directly from preaching and reached the Covington place by half past twelve o'clock. Ella and Virgil met them at the veranda steps.

After the greetings Ella said, speaking to the dog at her feet, "Sir Galahad, thank the gentleman who saved you from the wicked man so that you could stay out here and dawdle in luxury. I am sorry that Sir Galahad wasn't with me when I met you on the street Wednesday, but I didn't think of him at the time. Have you no manners, Sir Galahad? Thank the gentleman who saved you."

The dog advanced with dignity toward Rumsey Skiles, sat before him on its haunches, and held up a foot.

Skiles accepted the proffered foot, then turned to Ella Covington. "Can you train other, ah, things than dogs?"

"When I am asked."

Again he was blushing furiously.

"Come on into the house," said Ella. "It is pleasant in the parlor."

She led them inside. Priscilla Skiles uttered an exclamation of delight. "That secretary, I never saw one as lovely!"

"It is lovely. We bought it at your store, and Mr. Skiles himself brought it out and placed it right where it is now."

"It came by wagon from North Carolina. I had to charge you a lot for it, but as I remember it didn't have a scratch on it."

"It didn't. Mama loved it. I forgot to tell you that Judge Drake is coming out for dinner too. I thought it would be nice to have all of Sir Galahad's protectors here together. The judge is a dear man."

"I have wondered how he can be so everlastingly cheerful," said Mrs. Skiles. "He has lived there all alone since his wife died twelve years ago, and he is the poorest hand at choosing a servant I ever saw."

"And he never finds out how poor a servant is," added her husband. "I imagine he has more invitations for dinner and supper than any man in Bowling Green. Everybody, well almost everybody, likes the judge, but half of his invitations are to provide him with a respectable meal."

"Do the Griders ever invite him?" asked Rumsey.

"I never heard of it if they did."

"They used to invite all the important people who came here, but they have about given that up," said Priscilla Skiles.

"Let's not carry that topic any further," said her husband. "We have been careless about company lately ourselves. Judge Drake has a nephew in Logan County, a lad seven or eight years old. He is very fond of the boy, and told me recently that he plans to see him through law school when he is ready for it, and then bring him here and start him in practice."

"Yonder is the judge now," said Ella, looking out the window. "You meet him, Virgil. I'll go see about dinner."

19

PRISCILLA SKILES, who knew a great deal about food, was delighted by the quality of the food placed before them. The baked ham, set on a blue platter before Virgil, was a matter of art. She was fascinated by the ease and accuracy with which he sliced it and served the plates at his side. The maid would carry the plate to Ella, who sat at the other end of the table. She added supplements of fried corn and butter beans, and then the plates were carried to the diners. There was golden butter within reach of all. Biscuits, baked brown and piping hot, were passed around the table. A dish of cucumber pickles went the round of the table. The maid inquired of each diner whether sweet milk, buttermilk, or coffee was desired. After that, she was back with a great tureen of sliced beets, hot and deep red.

"The first cured ham I ever tasted," said Judge Drake, "was one Sabbath when I went home with Brother Jess Graham from preaching. It was in the summer, and there on the dish was a ham. I wondered what Brother Graham was doing killing a hog in hot weather. It tasted so good that I spent the rest of the time I was there asking him how he did it. Now almost everybody cures hams, though some haven't quite got the knack of it yet. Brother Jenkins told me that he cured sixty hams last winter."

"We cured twenty-six," said Virgil Covington. "That makes it all right for us to have one every two weeks. Uncle Silas cures our hams. We brought him from Virginia——"

"From *Amelia County*, Virginia," said his sister.

"I have talked with men from Virginia, Amelia County, I am sure, and North Carolina about the curing of hams," said Jacob Skiles. "It is probable that the Carolinians learned how to cure meat as they passed through Virginia. Of course, people have been drying and smoking meats for a long time, but some of the better ways they have learned only recently."

"Also better ways to cook," added his wife. "I doubt if anyone even in my mother's time ever used sorghum molasses in cooking. And yet, you must have used it in cooking this ham, didn't you?"

"We saved a three-gallon crock just for that. Don't you think it was good for the ham?"

"Excellent. It fits with the ham perfectly."

"One of the best signs of the real goodness of the human race is that it is always learning something," said Judge Drake.

"We have to spend a lot of time correcting things that we got wrong at first," said Jacob Skiles. "And, of course, that is learning. Let me give you an instance. We thought tomatoes were unhealthful things for a long time. My father and mother thought they were. They grew wild around our garden in Virginia, but we didn't touch them. They are so pretty that I hoed them out in my garden, and they got bigger and redder. The other day I found a specially big one, deep red all over. So I ate it all, and went up to the house and sat on the porch waiting to die. Well, here I am. Tomatoes are no more poisonous than those beets. It wouldn't surprise me to find that people at first were afraid of hot biscuits."

"My notion is that there is a good deal of sense in our taste," said his wife. "I think that anything that tastes good *is* good."

The final course was a deep fresh-peach cobbler. Rumsey Skiles turned to Ella Covington. "I wonder how you knew it," he said.

"Knew what?"

"That of all things to eat, I like peach cobbler best."

"Something must have told me. I have something that is all the time telling me something."

"Rumsey Skiles is a stranger around here," said Judge Drake. "Your something had nothing at all to do with him. It was transmitting a message from me."

The dinner was finished. They went back into the parlor and sat there and talked. It is often the way of summer to end on a golden note. The world was golden that Sunday afternoon, the sun resting caressingly on the early gold of the maple trees. The cicadas droned, softly at first, but with a rising note as the afternoon passed.

Judge Drake looked about him with serene eyes, then out of the window to the world beyond. "Our blessings are a rebuke to our inadequacies."

"When will our inadequacies rise to rebuke our blessings?"

"Alas, there are signs of it now. That abolitionist speaker who was here recently was a sign. We will be hearing others. I am no prophet. I am by nature a cheerful person, but I can't get rid of the feeling that some morning we will open our eyes upon a world that we have got into bad trouble. Our inadequacies will have caught up with our blessings. I pray that I may be permitted to depart ahead of that evil time."

Virgil Covington asked jestingly, "Isn't there a land case that you ought to settle before you depart, Judge?"

"I recall something since you mention it. First time I have thought of that case in fifteen or twenty years. I must have got stale on it. What's the matter with your dog, Ella?"

There was the sound of a dog whining with a sort of pleading note at the door. "That dog wants somebody. It must be that he thinks he hasn't thanked you enough." She looked at Rumsey Skiles. "Suppose you go out there and see if it isn't you he wants."

"Don't be ungrateful for gratitude, boy," counseled the judge. "Go on out and accept your thanks."

The dog kept on whining. "All right, pup," said Rumsey, smiling uncertainly, "I'll make an effort to stay on your good side."

He went out the door. They heard him speak to the dog, but it was still whining. "I'll go see what it wants," said Ella. "Maybe it is sick or something."

She opened the door and went outside. The whines ceased. Judge Drake turned to Jacob Skiles. "Tell me about my dear friend, Bill Willie. I don't get to see him as often as I'd like to."

"He is just about the same, certainly no older. I got him out of a fighting scrape yesterday."

"What kind of scrape was it? I'd turn him loose in my court even on a plea of guilty."

"Bill Willie was having a horse shod at the blacksmith shop, and a man there said that Henry Clay was a scalawag. So Bill Willie knocked him down, and left his jaw pretty badly bruised. I got Squire Coleman to let him off with a dollar fine. He gets in a fight now and then, but he has done more work in the last twenty-four years than any other man in Warren County. I never saw his equal as a worker."

"And I'll say for him that he has worked longer for one man than anyone else in the county. You are the sort of man that he needs to work for. You have steadied him and held his loyalty. About the worst thing he ever does is to knock some fellow down who ought to have been knocked down long before. There is no man in Warren County, including you, Jacob, for whom I have a higher respect than I have for Bill Willie Blewett. I suppose they got that marvelous dog satisfied," he said, casting a glance toward the door.

"We simply couldn't get along without Bill Willie," said Priscilla Skiles. "I don't care what sort of help we need, he can give it. Rumsey is having a case in your court Tuesday, Judge. One of the witnesses on the other side is a man named Chester Massey, from Ray's Branch. Rumsey has to examine him. He asked Bill Willie if he knew Massey, and Bill Willie spent the next fifteen minutes telling him things. You would think that Bill Willie had spent a year hunting up things on him. I feel sorry for him. He will think Rumsey is a fortuneteller."

"I know Massey. I shall listen with interest. I doubt if I am overly sympathetic with him."

"Rumsey will not browbeat him, or anything like that. All he will be trying to get will be the truth."

"My dear lady, you can use truth to browbeat a man with."

Ella Covington opened the door and came in. She went across to

Mrs. Skiles and asked, "Would you like to have a bunch of chrysanthemums to take home with you? We have some that I like very much."

"Why, yes, I certainly would. It is sweet of you to think about it."

Judge Drake watched the door close behind her as she left. "You have a remarkable sister, Virgil."

"One thing I like about my sister, Judge Drake, is that I never have much idea what she will do next. I lead a surprised life."

"How infinitely better than to be bored! Your crop is good this season?"

"It's good, some of it very good. The corn crop is so good that I know better than ever why we need a steamboat. I sent ten hogs to Nashville in one of Mr. Skiles's wagons. I made some profit, but it was an awful lot of worry and trouble."

"We will have the steamboats inside of twenty years, maybe fifteen. I'll be proud to give up the wagons. I make some profit out of them, and they enable me to keep the store open, but they are, as you say, Virgil, a lot of trouble. I spend much time in being concerned about them when I ought to be at ease."

"The roads are pretty good now, aren't they?" inquired Judge Drake.

"They are at their best now. The roads are dry, but rough. We take three days going down, spend one day there, and then three days on the trip back. The trip takes a week in the dry season; in the winter months I don't expect them back before the ninth day. That adds greatly to the expense of winter hauling, but we can't close down simply because the roads get muddy."

"And you have to take care of your teams," said his wife.

"Of course. Everything depends on the teams. Lem and Jeff have hauled for me twenty-three years. They have never mistreated a horse. But they have been loyal to Bill Willie, not to me."

"I must get the recipe for cooking that ham. I never before heard of using sorghum molasses in baking a ham," she said irrelevantly, "but it certainly makes it better."

"Ella would like to tell you," said Virgil. "Nothing goes on in that kitchen that she doesn't know all about it."

"How is your uncle?" asked Judge Drake. "I haven't seen him in two weeks."

"He's all right. Uncle Trez never stays sick long. When he feels a spell coming on, he gets mad at somebody and that cures him."

"You have been his medicine a few times, haven't you?"

"I keep him well most of the time."

Five minutes later, there were heard steps across the porch. The door opened and Ella Covington, Rumsey Skiles, and Sir Galahad came into the parlor. It was no ordinary entrance.

"We thought we would let Sir Galahad come in too," said Ella. "I think he has the right. He was the one that brought us together."

"That's true, in a way," said Rumsey, "but we would have got together even without him."

"Yes, but I expect he hurried it up some. Have we made ourselves understood? We are going to be married."

Mrs. Skiles tried to say something, halted, and gave it up. Her husband spoke in his level tones. "I can't say that I am very greatly surprised."

"Mr. Skiles was never surprised at anything," said his wife.

"But I am greatly pleased, and I must say that I never expected it to be announced this way."

"It is possible, of course," said Virgil Covington, "that my consent isn't required, but I'll give it before that point is brought up."

"I'll give my consent very happily on one condition," said Judge Drake.

They looked at him inquiringly. "And that condition is that you never leave Bowling Green. I shall oppose the match if there is the likelihood of your removing elsewhere."

"We'll stay, won't we, Ella?" asked Rumsey, smiling whimsically.

"We wouldn't think of leaving against Judge Drake's wishes."

"The place is too dear for its best sons and daughters to be permitted to leave. That terrible thing, alas, would tend to make it less dear."

20

IN THE EVENING, Ella Covington and her brother sat on the porch and talked. The air was bland and refreshing. The moon was lifting itself above a grove of trees at the left. The night was filled with the dull drone of the dry-weather flies in the trees. Sir Galahad slept contentedly near them. At times the dog would raise its head, look at them solemnly, then lower it back to the floor.

"You would have married someday, Ella. So I suppose it would just

as well be now. As far as the man is concerned, I think you would have
lost by waiting. I wonder how Uncle Trez is going to take it."

"Now, isn't that funny? I hadn't even thought of him."

"I doubt if even a Covington could object to a Skiles. But you know
Uncle Trez always takes a thing one way or another."

"I haven't thought of Uncle Trez yet. There are more important
things. For instance, you ought to get married, Virgil. You understand that, don't you?"

"Not as clearly as you seem to. What for?"

"Of course, Rumsey and I will not stay on here, and we won't go
out to his house. You remember Papa's will, don't you? You can't
stay here by yourself and make a living on the place."

"That's a cold-blooded way to look at it."

"It's a sensible way to look at it. You know perfectly well that you
are going to marry sometime. What have you to gain by putting it off?
Name one thing. Just a little more than two weeks ago I had never
seen Rumsey. Confidentially, I don't think we became engaged today
at all. I think it was at that trial when we saw each other the first
time. I'll have to take Sir Galahad with me when I leave."

"Better leave him here. You won't have any place to keep him where
you are going."

"Where I go, there Sir Galahad goes." She sighed. "What did I
ever do to deserve a husband like Rumsey Skiles? Tell me one thing,
Virgil."

"At the moment I can't think of one, though I am sure that several
will come to me later. Can you think of any merit whatever I may have
for a wife?"

"Not a one, but I'll think of some in a day or two."

"What about Harriet Dulaney?"

"Harriet Dulaney? You are joking, Virgil."

"I have thought a lot about Harriet when you weren't looking, Ella."

"But you know what Uncle Trez thinks of the Dulaneys."

"That answers my question. If Uncle Trez doesn't like her, I'll go
ask her in the morning."

"But, Virgil, you will have to court her first."

"How many decades, how many centuries, how many eons, may I
ask, did Rumsey Skiles court you? It all opens out before me like a
vision. You will marry Rumsey and go off somewhere to a log cabin
and live there with Sir Galahad. I will marry Harriet, and bring her
here to our ancestral home which we built after arriving here from

Amelia County. Here she will attend to my every want, such as bringing in the firewood, and we will be very happy together. I'll ask her tomorrow, and if Uncle Trez says a word I'll wring his withers."

"I couldn't be better pleased, but don't rush into it. Give yourself time to consider it, a half day, or even better a whole day."

Virgil gave himself a whole day, but on Tuesday he was even more convinced that Harriet Dulaney was shaped by destiny to be his wife. Tuesday afternoon he rode over to the Dulaneys'.

Harriet met him at the door. "How do you do, Mr. Covington. I suppose you want to see Father."

"No, that wasn't what I had in mind."

"Mother is not here either. She went with Father to Mr. Hackney's funeral. How is Ella?"

"All right, I guess. She didn't say. How are you?"

"Just fine, thank you. By the way, I heard the strangest thing about Ella yesterday. I remember now, I am sure it was yesterday. It was the strangest thing."

"Then it's so. What was it?"

"That she and the Skiles boy who has just come back from law school are going to be married. Ann Lucas told me, but she said she had forgotten who it was that told her. But she vowed it was so. I didn't know that Ella had ever set eyes on him."

"Ella just doesn't loaf around when she's going somewhere. She's got Covington blood from Amelia County, Virginia, in her."

"Goodness, you don't mean that Ella took the lead?"

"I think they sort of took time about leading. But she did see him at the courthouse where we were being tried, something about a dog. He was prosecuting us."

"Maybe you had better not say anything so I can learn what happened."

"You got any plans, Harriet?"

She stared at him. "Of course, I have plans. Everybody has plans. What makes you ask a question like that?"

"Just wondering in my mind. Do you mind telling me what your plans are?"

"I think *wandering* is what you meant to say. Why are you interested in my plans, Virgil?"

"Well, for one thing, how would it fit your plans for us to marry?"

Her eyes grew large and the color of her face deepened. "It would be bad to joke about such a thing."

"Please don't think that I am joking. I never was more serious in my life."

"You have never given me a hint. If this is the way you feel about me, why haven't I ever known anything about it?"

"Well, you know about it now. I've just told you. I'll say it again. Will you marry me?"

She looked at him, troubled. "No," she said, "I won't. Maybe that is the way a Covington would ask, but it is not the way a Dulaney would answer. I like you, Virgil, as well as any man I know, but if you are in earnest, and somehow I think you are, you will have to give me time to find out about myself. You should have given me some hint before you asked me. Did Ella give you this idea?"

"She did not. I thought of it exclusively. But I can see how you might think this is a little sudden. I have had the idea a long time, but I wasn't in position to do anything about it till Sunday. You know that I have had to take care of Ella."

She smiled. "Or isn't it that you have had Ella to take care of you till now?"

"I'll admit that I am going to need some help."

"Both of us would need help. Have you mentioned this to your Uncle Trezevant? But, of course, you haven't. I notice that you are still alive."

"Uncle Trez snarls a lot more than he snatches. By the way, what was the trouble between him and your father? I've forgotten."

"Your Uncle Trez set his dog on Papa's fine hog, and it tore her up some. Papa thought he would go and shoot your Uncle Trez, but Mama talked him out of it."

"I remember now. Uncle Trez thought that hog didn't have any business in his garden, besides rooting up a lot of his potatoes. I remember how they fussed on the square the next Monday. It didn't do the town any good at all."

"And if I would promise to marry you, your Uncle Trez would start the war over again."

"I'll handle Uncle Trez. The minute your name is Covington I'll protect you from that old pirate."

"I've heard that a Covington is hard to handle."

"Listen, Harriet, if you will start handling me I promise you won't have a speck of trouble."

"I wouldn't marry you unless I loved you frantically. I admire you greatly, but you will have to give me time to think about it."

"How about till after dinner?"

"Three months, Virgil."

"Six weeks, and not an hour longer. We'd both be old and doddering in three months. No, we'll make it a month."

Virgil rode back by his Uncle Trezevant's and told him what had happened. For thirty seconds, his uncle said nothing. Then he exploded. "Good God! The whole Covington layout gone batty?"

"You got married once yourself, didn't you, Uncle Trez?"

"What's that got to do with it? I don't object much to young Skiles, but I am keeping my fingers crossed about him. But that Dulaney girl! Who put the notion into your head, Virgil?"

"I put it in my head, Uncle Trez, and I'm going to keep it there."

"A Covington is better than a Dulaney any day."

"This Covington isn't better than that Dulaney, and he knows it."

"Listen, Virgil, let's be sensible about this. Your father and mother left you what they had, but you and Ella have got to prove to the court that you have enough gumption not to waste it. I've been watching you, and except for that horse you sold Old Man Breed Loving, and for that house you bought on Frozen Row, you have done all right. But you have to prove to the court that you made a living on the place, a good living, a Covington living. What effect is all this marrying business going to have on that?"

"We have talked that over. Ella says she wants to step out and let Harriet step in, that is, if she is willing to step. Ella says she is sure she can live on what Rumsey makes. Of course I'd expect Ella to take anything on the place she wants when she moves. Harriet and I can make a living on the place, that is, if she will help."

"If she can make you show a little more spunk I'll feel better about her. What you need is more spunk. I'll not blame her for her daddy. What I'd like for you to do is to beat somebody in a horse trade, or sell somebody a mule with the heaves and make him pay a good price for it. You need a little spunk."

"I'll get Harriet to spunk me up a little, that is, if she's willing."

"Stop saying *if she will do this* or *if she will do that*. You can't manage a wife on *ifs*. What will you take for that chestnut filly?"

"I've told you a dozen times I don't want to sell that filly. I like her best of all our stock."

"I'll give you a hundred dollars for her just as she stands."

"That filly is not for sale. If I ever decide to sell her I'll give you first chance."

Rumsey Skiles and Ella Covington wasted no time in making due preparation for their wedding. The house they were building went up slowly, it seemed to them; rapidly, it seemed to everybody else. Rumsey was busy with his law, but he tried to save a period from each day during which he and Ella went to watch and guide its progress. But yet a little while and it would be ready.

21

BOWLING GREEN was built on hills. At the town's southern border a tall, rounded, cedar-crowned hill towered against the sky. For some reason, never discovered, it was called Vinegar Hill. From it, in all directions, spread a magnificent view of the countryside. Another hill stood as if guarding the town against approach from the east; it was almost as tall, though oddly no cedars grew on it, and was called College Hill because of an abortive attempt to establish a college there. The descent from these two hills, sharp at first, then gradually leveling off, converged into a little plateau of perhaps five acres. And there Bowling Green found its center, known as the square. To the north and northwest the land fell slowly to the river. To the north ran the road to Louisville. Vinegar Hill stood between two roads angling out from town. The Russellville and Hopkinsville road lay to the right, and the Nashville road to the left. A half mile north of the river, on the Louisville road, was Baker's Hill, tall and commanding. Across the river to the right from Baker's Hill was Underwood Hill, sometimes called Mount Ayr, and to the left Webb's Hill.

Rumsey Skiles and his father rode into town one fine fall morning. As they passed the Hardcastle store, Jacob Skiles said, "Stop a while. I want to see this. This is something I have never thought of. Drive there to the side of the road."

"What is it, Father?"

"War, my son, and here in Bowling Green. The place was made for it."

"What made you think of war?"

"I don't know. Perhaps it was the talk I have been hearing about abolition and slavery. Perhaps it was some of the complaints I have read in Northern newspapers against the South, or in some Southern papers against the North. I don't expect to live long enough, Rumsey, to see a war but you might."

"War because we have slaves?"

"There will be other things, but that will be the main reason. If there is a war, this town can't stay out of it. It is on a main road, which by then will be a better road. Bowling Green is too close to the border for either side to miss it if it tries an invasion. Armies like hills. Look yonder—" he pointed to Vinegar Hill, towering in its dark-green growth of cedar—"or there——" He pointed across the river to Baker's Hill, then swept his pointing finger around to College Hill. "Remember what I have said, son. You may see forts on those hills. I pray to God you won't, but you may. Sometimes I get frightened."

"I never thought of you being frightened."

"I try not to show it. Well, drive me around to your house and let's see how the builders are getting along."

Jacob Skiles had a knack at housebuilding, and he was greatly enjoying the rise of his son's house on one of the town's minor hills. He would sit there by the hour, watching everything with discerning eyes. Whenever he considered workmanship poor or badly directed he pointed it out without hesitation, but always with tact and generous spirit. His son knew very little about housebuilding, and his law business was enough to use about all his time. So his father's skill and interest were most fortunate. Almost every day Ella Covington came to see what progress was being made on the house. She came that day.

"Do you think they will ever finish it?" she asked, sighing.

"I haven't lost hope. I see a brick yonder that wasn't in place yesterday."

"You always say a thing so cleverly. Do you suppose Rumsey will ever become as clever as you are?"

"Much more so. He is kin to his mother."

"She is the dearest woman. Mr. Skiles, is that floor level?"

He regarded the floor with critical eyes. "It is not." He turned and called, "Oh, Mr. Atchley, come here, please."

Mr. Atchley came. He saw the flaw immediately and directed a workman to remedy it. Ella spoke to Mr. Atchley. "I want a good doghouse in the back yard. Don't waste anything that can be used in it."

"Has Harriet made her mind up yet?" asked Skiles.

"I don't think so. Virgil goes over there almost every day. I think they are studying each other."

"I could make a good guess that they will like what they learn."

22

THE GARDEN FENCE at the Covington home needed a bit of repairing, and Virgil was at work on it. He heard footsteps coming in a shuffling run and looked up. It was Thusy, so called because he had been christened Methuseleh. Thusy's work was mainly at the barn, and he was coming directly from there. His hurry was obviously the product of great distress.

"Massa Virge," he said panting, "that ches'nut filly of yours, she daid."

"Dead! What are you talking about, Thusy?"

"Yassuh, she daid. She didn't have nothin' to die about. Yestidy I let her out the ba'n, an' she jump de ba'n-lot fence, and den she jump de spring branch, den she come by de big road back to de ba'n. I put co'n in de trough for her, an' hay in de rack, but she ain't et it. She daid."

Virgil Covington reached the barn in a run. The chestnut filly lay stiff and rigid on the stall floor. Thusy was right behind him. "She look like she been daid all night."

There was no sign of violence on the filly. He remembered that the barn-lot fence was high and the spring branch wide. Something must have happened while she was jumping.

"Dat's a nice filly. Oncle Trez, he lak dat filly a lot."

He did like her a lot indeed. Virgil Covington remembered his uncle's very words, "A hundred dollars just as she stands." He stood there, a half smile upon his face. Maybe Uncle Trez would buy that filly after all.

Thusy stood at one side wondering at the strange look on Virgil's face.

"Thusy, get some of the other men, and drag that filly over here by the fence. Stand her up there and tie her so she stays standing. Tie her so she looks like she is standing there alive. You understand me?"

"Yassuh. You feelin' all right, Massa Virge?"

"First time I have felt real spunky for years. Hurry up and do what I told you. I am going over to Uncle Trez's just as soon as you get her tied."

"Yassuh, you goin' to tell Miss Ella about dat filly?"

"She's in town building a house. You do what I told you."

"Sho' will." Thusy's conviction of the basic insanity of the Covingtons' deepened. He went about his task, shaking his head, shaking his head in grave doubt. He was still shaking his head when Virgil left for his uncle's.

Virgil Covington rode up to his Uncle Trez's home. That gentleman was sitting on his front porch reading a newspaper. Almost the nephew's spunk failed him, but he steeled himself to his purpose by remembering his uncle's words.

"Uncle Trez, come here. I want to talk with you."

Trezevant Covington folded his paper and placed it on a little table at his side. He then strolled down to the gate. "What you got on your mind, Virgil?"

"You still want to buy that chestnut filly, Uncle Trez?"

Uncle Trez eyed his nephew suspiciously. "You in some kind of trouble, Virgil?"

"Not a thing. Just got a trading notion. You remember what you offered me for her? 'A hundred dollars just as she stands.' You can pay me now and go get her."

"You joking or mean business?"

"Give me a hundred dollars and go get her. She is yours."

"I guess I got that much money in the house. I'll go see."

He returned and counted out the money. "Go right on over and get her," said Virgil. "I got to go to town to see how Ella is getting along with that house she is building."

Uncle Trez nodded, smiling grimly. He knew that chestnut filly was worth considerably more than a hundred dollars. He had got a bargain. He wondered what Virgil was going to do with the money.

The two slaves who went with him ran for their lives when it finally dawned upon Uncle Trezevant that he had been made the victim of the lowest trick ever played on a human being. He looked long at the chestnut filly standing so lifelike against the fence. Then his outrage died away and he broke into a chuckle.

"First time I was ever certain that boy had any Covington blood in him. He's got some spunk after all."

23

Robin Rodes was making a good start at law. He had been given a few cases by the bank, but mainly trivial ones. Rodes was very tall, very thin, and generally of an ascetic appearance, except that his mouth at the corners tended to turn upward, and that his eyes could show unmistakable signs of laughter long before any show of amusement reached the rest of his features. His speech, especially in its formal phases, was tinctured with his classical education. It was he who introduced the name Justinian into the procedures of the Bowling Green courtroom. That left Judge Drake puzzled till he looked the name up that night in his reference books.

On one occasion, his preoccupation with the classics made him the butt of a long series of jokes. He was arguing a case before a jury, the foreman of which was a pudgy blacksmith named Ike Lay, who liked nothing better than to ask questions in season and out, and to let loose his peals of Gargantuan laughter. Robin Rodes lifted his six-foot-three splinter of classical flesh before the jury, and as a prelude to his argument, rendered a long quotation from Homer. "As you all know, it was Homer who said that——"

And that was as far as he got. The foreman called out in his gravelly voice, "Homer who?"

That threw young Rodes off balance, but he rallied and said, "It was Homer who said it."

"I asked you Homer who. You said we all knew he said it. I've been thinkin'. I know three Homers, and there wouldn't a one of them said that. If I know the Homer you're talkin' about, I sure can't put my mind on him."

Judge Drake saw that the decorum of the courtroom was getting out of hand, so he thumped his gavel and said, "The counsel will proceed with his argument."

The judge later in the day offered the lawyer some sound advice. "After this don't use such talk unless you are reasonably certain that some of them do know. Your Homer is practically a stranger around here."

One day Robin Rodes received a formally phrased note inviting him to come to a reception to be given by Miss Harriet Dulaney at her home, in honor of Miss Ella Covington and Mr. Rumsey Skiles, who were to be married in December. Supper would be served. Rodes had heard of the Dulaneys, but had only a vague knowledge as to who they were. He remembered hearing Ella Covington mention Harriet, but the mention was not in detail. Rumsey Skiles had become his closest friend, and he had several times been in the company of Ella

Covington. Only the afternoon before he had walked to the house which was being built for Rumsey and Ella. He found them both there, with Rumsey's father and mother. The house was nearing completion, and alert eyes could see its very charming possibilities as a home. Rodes said as much.

"Don't look at me when you say that. Of all concerned, I have had least to do with it. It was built with my father and mother's money, and with their very practical advice, and under the power of Ella's inspiration. I think I can live in it creditably, but I couldn't plan it."

"My husband will be no jack-of-all-trades," said Ella emphatically. "I don't want him to know what to do if the fireplace won't draw, and I don't want him to fix the door when the hinge comes loose. He is a good son and a good lawyer. I want him to be a good husband. And that is all."

"No more will be asked," said Jacob Skiles. "I will send Bill Willie to show his fireplace how to draw, and to fix his hinge. By the way, Ella, I heard in town today that Virgil had sold his chestnut filly to his Uncle Trezevant. The way I heard it, it is the funniest thing that has happened here since the foreman of the jury wanted to know who Homer was."

"I tried to tell him," said Rodes, the corners of his mouth twitching, "but Judge Drake wouldn't let me."

"Reub Buckner told Trez today that his best foxhound got bitten by a snake and died, and that he would like to sell it just as it stands."

"Didn't Homer say that it is good to give a community something to talk about? If he didn't, he missed a good chance."

"How many of our young ladies have you met, Mr. Rodes?" asked Ella.

"Far too few, if you are a reasonably good sample. When I came here I made a resolve that I would go to the Presbyterian church on Sundays, and that all the other time I would give to my practice, if I could only get the practice. I have been lucky. I like the church here, and I am having my share of practice. Did you have any particular young ladies in mind, Miss Covington, or were you speaking generally?"

"I had some in mind. You be sure and come to our wedding. All the special ones will be there."

"May I sit in an elevated place and look them over?"

"I doubt if that could be arranged. Rumsey and I will be the ones to look at, you know."

"Are there any other young ladies in town who could build a house with good hinges and chimneys that draw?"

"There are several, if they had the proper encouragement."

Robin Rodes went to Harriet Dulaney's reception. Harriet was standing at the entrance to the hall and next to her stood Virgil Covington; then Ella Covington and Rumsey Skiles. And, beyond that, it seemed to Rodes, a parlor filled mainly with young ladies. He passed down the line slowly, speaking pleasantly with each.

"We have heard a great deal about you, Mr. Rodes," Harriet said as he passed her. "Rumsey says you are the best lawyer in Bowling Green, and I never knew him to be wrong about anything, including his choice for a wife."

"I never did find out who made the choice," said Virgil Covington. "I'll say this for my sister: if she had decided on him, he wouldn't have had the ghost of a chance."

"That is one of the Covingtons' best traits," said Harriet.

"I'll tell you exactly how it happened," said Ella. "We both decided at exactly the same instant. The same flash of lightning revealed it to us both."

"Is there plenty of lightning in Bowling Green?" asked Rodes.

"All that is needed. There are a half dozen young ladies in the parlor languishing for the sound of your voice."

"If they give him the slightest encouragement he will make them a speech," said Rumsey. "Be careful, Robin. Don't start your address, 'And as you all know, ladies, Homer once said——' "

"Let them ask. I know which Homer it was now."

Of the girls who languished in the parlor, Louise Potter was dark, taller than the average, and carried herself with a regal bearing. Clara Mitchell was small, fair and pert, and her sky-blue eyes danced continuously. Sally Hines held Rodes's glance longest of all. She was dark and slender and quiet. She did not chatter as did most of the others. When she spoke it was in the tones he wanted to hear. Her expression was a strange but delightful compound of mirth and sadness. Emma Loving was plump, red-haired, and her frequent laughs revealed beautiful teeth. She wielded a fan vigorously, though the day was not overly warm. She looked up at the tall young man standing before her. "How do you do, Mr. Rodes? How do you like Bowling Green?"

He replied that he had never liked it as well as he did then, but she was already back in conversation with Claude Moorman, a languid young fellow whose father owned the town's main brickyard. Rodes spoke briefly to Seraphina Sumpter and Jefferson Spalding, who stood near a window and argued with animation whether or not the country would have another war soon. Seraphina insisted that never again would man pay so cruelly for the errors he had made or the problems he had to solve. But Spalding claimed that man needed a war at least once every generation to keep him from becoming too cowardly and spineless, that courage was man's highest gift and war its chief developer. Seraphina asked Robin Rodes for his opinion. He knew a quotation from Homer, and started to use it, but stopped.

Instead he said, "War does encourage bravery and noble deeds, but I fear that it is a great multiplier of widows and orphans."

Seraphina shook a reproving finger at Jefferson. "There," she said, "you would want your wife to become a widow so that you could die bravely."

The argument was still going on when across the room Rodes saw two with whom he was already acquainted, Sallie and Nat Grider. Rumsey Skiles had told him their story, and he had found it so appealing that he had thought of it often. Neither Nat's father nor mother had been to see them, and though Nat sometimes saw his father in town, they never paused for long. Nat didn't come to town often. He was too busy trying to reclaim the Motley farm, making improvements that ought to have been made long before. He had spent that morning cleaning out the fine spring that had been neglected too long, but there was no trace of the morning's work upon him. Nat Grider was fastidiously clean. His interest and industry were the encouragement his wife and her mother needed. The house was quietly becoming one of system and taste. Rodes crossed the room to them.

"I remember so pleasantly our meeting at the church."

"I love that church," said Sallie. "My father loved it dearly. The first time I ever saw Nat was there."

"Rumsey has told me about your father. I wish I could have known him. Ella Covington told me about you two. The way she told it made me feel lonesome."

"It's a curable feeling," said Nat a bit wistfully, looking with affection at his wife.

"Nat is lonesome for my sake," said Sallie. "His parents didn't approve of me. I do hope that they were not right."

"I should say that anyone who doesn't approve of you is wrong," said Rodes.

"Amen," Nat agreed heartily. "Anyone at all."

Harriet Dulaney came across the room to them. "Surely, Mr. Rodes, your place is not with elderly married people, however charming they may be. We will shift girls, but not names. You will like Sally Hines."

"I hope that Sally is as nice as this one," said Rodes, bowing and following his hostess across the room.

"You are to take this Sally in to supper. Aren't the Griders precious?"

"I shall offer a prayer for his parents to come to their senses."

"He deserved better parents. Come and speak a word with me before you leave. I want to know what you think of Sally Hines."

Presently they went in to supper. The dining room was beautiful with a great cascade of autumn flowers in the center of the table. There were a cluster of purple asters at one end of the room and a great bunch of goldenrod at the other. The guests were served fried chicken and slices of ham whose rich redness was becomingly flecked with white. There were mashed potatoes, baked into a brown fluffiness, and of course butter beans. The hot biscuits were pleasing beyond the experience of Robin Rodes.

"You must try some of Papa's sorghum molasses," said Harriet Dulaney. "That is Papa's pride. Every year he tells our molasses maker that he must make it as good this year as he did last or he will shoot him. I don't think Papa really would shoot him, but he might. Papa can't stand poor molasses. Papa says that when the Lord made food He practiced up on everything else, and finally got around to hot biscuits, butter, and sorghum molasses. And right there the Lord stopped. Even He couldn't improve on that."

It was a chance to argue that Jefferson Spalding would hardly miss. "Downright sacrilegious! I say that if your sorghum molasses was perfect the Lord still could improve on it. How could He be omnipotent if He couldn't?"

"The molasses they have here is mighty fine for arguers, Jeff," said Virgil Covington. "Take some."

"I never argue," said Jefferson coldly. "I only present logic."

"Such as how good a thing for a country a war is?"

"There will be a war all right. God Almighty is not going to let this country be turned over to the cowards."

"Is that logic?" asked Nat Grider gently.

"Just part logic," said Robin Rodes. "I have no doubt that war helps us set some of our finest patterns in sacrifice and idealism——"

"Exactly what I claim——"

"But war sets other patterns too, and some very ugly ones. As I see it, one trait of war is that it magnifies the personal character of the soldier. If he is brave, war sharpens his courage. If he is a thief, war makes a pillager out of him."

Nat Grider said, "That has the sound of logic to me."

"Let's not talk of war," said Rumsey Skiles. "Getting married is a far more tempting topic."

"You speak prematurely," said Spalding. "You have never been married. You wouldn't accept your evidence in court, would you?"

Seraphina moved closer to Spalding. "You ought to have made a lawyer, Jefferson. I have said so a dozen times. I sometimes think you are wasting your talent, selling glass to make windows out of."

"We couldn't remain civilized without windows. They keep things from being hid. They put life into public view. Windows are one of our greatest advances. Now you take the savage——"

"I would rather have the sorghum molasses," said Virgil Covington. "Pass it, please."

"Papa would like to hear you say that, Virgil," said Harriet.

"I am sorry I haven't said it before. I covet his favor."

They ate the ham and fried chicken and butter beans and mashed potatoes and sorghum molasses and hot biscuits. But Harriet ate very little. It was almost as if she was listening for someone to arrive. Twilight was settling down on the world outside the windows.

"Listen," said Jefferson Spalding, almost breathlessly. It was a whippoorwill lifting its mournful call in the grove beyond the garden. "That's a sure sign of war. When you hear a whippoorwill, sooner or later, there will be a war."

"How about marrying?" asked Claude Moorman. "When you hear the girl of your choice accepting your proposal of marriage, isn't that a sure sign that, sooner or later, there will be a little private war?"

The servants came, bringing cake and sillabub. Virgil Covington turned to Jeff. "Isn't anything that tastes as good as this some kind of sign?"

"It certainly is. It is a sign that every spoonful and crumb will be eaten, and don't you go to complaining about my logic."

"I never heard of you using any before," said Claude Moorman.

"How long have you been in town, Mr. Rodes?" asked Sally Hines.

"You have searched out one of my weaknesses. Just a little more than three months."

"Sometimes people who have just come have an advantage. They don't know as much about us."

"Is that logic, dear lady? If it is, I crave the disadvantage of knowing more about you."

"All of us have heard about you. They say you are a good lawyer."

"Not yet, though I do hope to become a reasonably good one."

"When you were little did you act as if you were going to be a lawyer?"

He looked at her in surprise. "How does one who is going to be a lawyer act when he is little?"

"The reason I asked you that is I have a right young cousin named Tom Henry Hines. Half the time I am sure he is going to be a lawyer. He can beat his own father in an argument. The other half, I know he will make a soldier. When he goes out to play he is always organizing the young boys to fight a mock battle."

"It won't be mock very long," said Spalding. "Mark my words."

Harriet Dulaney toyed with her cake and sillabub. Suddenly she pushed her plate back and stood. The table became quiet. Of course, she was going to present the two guests of honor.

"You are my dear friends, every one of you. You are one another's dear friends. The happiness of Ella and Rumsey adds to your own happiness." She took her fork from her plate and moved a crumb of cake with it. "But I am more selfish tonight than I have seemed." She was again moving her fork about. Then she straightened up. "Weeks ago Virgil Covington asked me to marry him. I didn't answer him then because I didn't know how to. But I know now. If you still wish it, Virgil, I would like to be your wife."

Virgil Covington's face turned not red, but white. He knew well what to say, but the speech would not form.

"I have told this to my father and mother," Harriet continued, still toying with her fork, "and it pleases them. I have told no one else. I have chosen this way to announce it because I thought it would please a Covington."

Still the words would not form. "First time I ever saw a Covington speechless," said Jefferson Spalding.

No one else said anything. There was hardly the sound of breathing. Virgil Covington got to his feet. His eyes were shining, the blood was back in his face, and he was no longer inarticulate.

"I am not speechless. I just don't have anything but ordinary words. This occasion is worthy of better ones. I will do the best I can with what I do have. I accept the charming offer you have made me. But as you said yourself, Harriet, the idea was mine to begin with. Your answer is the sweetest thing I ever heard of. And another thing, you haven't a chance to back out. This was done in the presence of witnesses. It would be most illegal to back out now, wouldn't it, Lawyer Rodes?"

"She wouldn't have a chance," said Lawyer Rodes.

"Wonder if his Uncle Trez will be the best man," Jefferson whispered to Seraphina. "If so, it will end in a war."

The Settlement Disrupted
1861–1862

1

RUMSEY SKILES and his wife sat on the veranda at Three Springs and watched the summer sun fall behind a grove of trees on a western hill. The day had been cloudless and not too warm. The air was melodious with the vesper song of birds. A mockingbird in the great maple poured out a flood of ecstasy, as if the world knew no trouble. From the stubble field, beyond the road, quail sounded their clear call. In the barn lot five hundred feet away a cow lowed with a sort of plaintive satisfaction. Two fields of corn were in view from where they sat, and the last rays of the sun, filtering through the leaves of the distant trees, touched with pleasing contrast the gold of the dead tassels, and the dead brown of the corn blades. Somewhere, hay lay drying in the sun, and the quiet smell of it was reassuring. Fat cattle grazed leisurely in the meadows.

The Skileses owned no slaves, but a dozen Negroes lived on the place and were paid wages for their work. One of them, sitting in the yard of one of the houses, was singing a bit uncertainly, but with deep feeling, "My Old Kentucky Home."

"Where did Dan learn that?" asked Rumsey Skiles. "I have heard it only once before, and that was in Louisville."

"A Negro has more ears than you can see," said Ella. "Come and sit close to me, Rumsey. I need you."

He lifted his chair and placed it touching hers. Her hand lay upon his arm.

"Thank you, Rumsey. Thank you for living. Thank you for everything." He saw that tears were in her eyes.

Life was good that summer of 1861 in south Kentucky! Crops were abundant, and the trade in town was brisk. Generally, the people could look full-eyed at prosperity. But, for all that, there was strain in their hearts, a strain that sharpened and grew more obvious as the days passed. Since the early spring, they had been haunted by the sounds of distant guns and marching feet, the distance narrowing as each day faded.

But marching soldiers and cannon could not have raised all the tension. The prospect of actual conflict could not have been half so terrifying as the disunity which gravely threatened to divide the people, was dividing them. Even then, some of the young men of the county were enlisting in the armies of the North, and more in the armies of the South. Old sores were deepening and new frictions were growing. There were men in Bowling Green who within the month had broken off a lifetime of friendship. Such rumors were abroad, such suspicions unallayed, that the sober-eyed officials had discontinued the holding of County Court Day, or any other large and public gathering. The place was growing afraid of itself.

But on that day the Rumsey Skileses had reasons to live apart from the omens and quarrels of war. They had due reason to be very happy and a little sad. On that day, Jane, the youngest of their four children, had been married to Jackson Shobe, son of Adams Shobe and grandson of Eli Shobe. Immediately after the wedding, they had gone directly to their home on the Shobe farm, near Oakland. Jackson Shobe was a farmer as all the other Shobes had been. But Jackson was the only Shobe remaining. All of the others had died ten years before in one of those calamitous pestilences that sometimes laid waste to Southern communities. Eli Shobe and his wife, full of years and strong deeds, had died almost a decade before that. When they died, Washington, in the clanlike manner of the Shobes, moved into his parents' home, and the others lived in houses erected on the place. There had never been any division of the acres or other property, except that entirely personal. It belonged to all. And then, in two tragic days, it belonged to Jackson, a lad of sixteen, left unscathed by the disease.

Jane's was a good marriage. It satisfied both father and mother, both of whom believed that Jane could not have chosen more wisely. The three sons had already married and gone from home. If Rumsey and Ella Skiles were happy, they were also a bit sad, a bit lonesome.

"We are back where we started, Ella. Have you thought of that?"

"Oh, no, we are not. We have four children—fine children, Rumsey—four in-laws now, and five grandchildren. Is that no gain?"

"If you wish to look at it that way, let me add something. I am much fonder of you now than I was that December day I married you. Nothing can take away from me the memory of three dozen happy years with you."

"Rumsey, you are becoming sentimental."

"Not becoming. I have been so for three dozen happy years."

"I never needed you quite so much as I do now. I am going to miss Jane a lot. This house seems so big. I almost wish we had back the little house we built for our wedding."

"The house you built, Ella."

"When I didn't know what to do, or which way to turn, your father did. He was a very dear man, Rumsey. I'll never stop being thankful for your parents. They were very precious to me."

Far away to the northwest sounded the rich blast of a steamboat. "That is the *Gasper River*," Rumsey Skiles said. "When I hear it blow I always think of Father. You know, that boat is eighteen years old, which I guess is old for a steamboat, but it has the most beautiful whistle on the river. Do you remember my father pulling the whistle rope?"

"I remember everything that happened that day. I remember just how you looked, and the cravat you were wearing. The boat was expected to reach the landing about ten o'clock. So your father and mother and you and I got there early. I have never seen him so excited."

"He had been looking forward to that day for more than twenty years. He had lived for that day. No one could know the work he had done to speed its coming."

"Or the money it had cost him. He told me a little about what he had spent on it."

"Mother got almost as much interested in it as Father, but she was never one to talk much."

"When we got to the river the boat wasn't yet in sight, but there were several already there, waiting for it. I'll never forget the look on your father's face when the boat came round the bend. He seemed to feel that it was his life's climax."

"It was," said Rumsey gravely. "Two days later he was dead."

"He was, I believe, the best man I ever knew. I never knew your father to do an unjust or little thing, and I never heard him use a cruel word. I have sometimes thought that if he had been a little less patient he might have lived longer. He kept himself too tightly closed."

"How favored I have been! What else could I ask for in my parents, in my wife, and in my children?"

"You might add that you have met with great favor in your profession."

"With your help. I will not say that I am a wise lawyer, but I try to be an honorable one."

They heard the whistle of the *Gasper River* again. "It is blowing for the landing now. I remember it carried twelve dining tables on that first trip. They all went to father's store. I have eaten lately from two of those tables. The homes considered them prime boasts. They were delivered in Bowling Green on the first regular steamboat."

"I wonder what the boat is bringing this time?"

"Guns!" he said with unwonted violence. "Rifles, that is what they brought the last trip. Ella, haven't we lived too long?"

"No, we haven't. It isn't like you to ask that."

"Nothing is like itself any more. Here we sit and watch the world go to pieces, and there is nothing we can do about it. We have three sons, all fine men. Have we raised them to be soldiers?"

"I pray not, Rumsey. I also pray that we have not raised them to be cowards."

"The main uses of courage are outside of war."

"Your father saw this coming on a long time ago."

"I know. I remember very well one time when we were going in to town, he had me drive to one side of the street and stop. And there he pointed out to me what was likely to happen in Bowling Green if a war came on. I didn't then find much importance in what he was saying. I do now."

"A hundred times I have heard him talk about the war he was sure was coming. It may be too late now."

"It is too late. It is too late when that steamboat my father loved begins bringing rifles into Bowling Green."

"For which side, Rumsey?"

"For either side that can pay the freight. Good God, the whole thing is unnatural! At first, we thought Kentucky had a noble mission, and that was to set a pattern of peace, of calm thoughtfulness for the other states, to persuade them against their wild courses. But all of that is gone now. The Southern states are out of the Union. Kentucky trembles in the balance both ways, and that is worse than wholeheartedness. I know that now. Tom Henry Hines is with the Southern troops, and his dear friend, Ples Matlock, has joined under Buell. Those boys were inseparable. Look what has happened."

"What about our own boys, Rumsey?"

"McElroy hasn't said anything to me, or to anyone else as far as I have heard, but living where he does would likely turn him to the North. Wells favors the South. How strongly, I don't know. I am sure that Underwood favors the North. I am certain that Jackson Shobe will be in the Southern army by Christmas. Good God, Ella, have we lived too long?"

"Isn't it a little irreverent to say that the Lord lets us live after He should have taken us?"

His voice was contrite when he answered her. "Of course you are right, Ella. You always are. I didn't know that it was possible for me to be so depressed as I have been."

"I know." Then to change the subject she said, "Wasn't Jane lovely? Jackson Shobe is a lucky man. I have never known Jane to be selfish about anything. She can be headstrong but never petty. Even if she is my daughter, I'll say that I never saw a sweeter bride."

"Yonder is Bill Willie. I apologize for what I said about us being too old."

Bill Willie turned in at the front gate and came up the walk. He had passed his ninetieth birthday, but he was alert and sure in his movements. He paused at the steps, his hat in hand. "Good evenin', Miz Skiles, evenin', Rumsey. The hay in that back field is turnin' out good. I expect we'll finish rickin' it tomorrer. Miss Jane shore looked sweet at her weddin'. Mighty nice-lookin' couple. Any news from the war?"

"Motley Grider left town today to join the Northern army," said Rumsey. "His parents are taking it pretty hard. Aunt Mat Jackson told him to his face that what he needed was a good switching."

"Ain't Aunt Mat a caution! Jeff Davis ought to get her to learn him how to be a fust-class Rebel. Mighty funny how things turn out sometimes," Bill Willie mused. "Motley is the spittin' image of his granddaddy, the way he looks and the way he acts."

"He is not like either one of his parents. They are good people."

"That's so for both of them, and people don't come no better than his granddaddy Motley."

"I have heard many say that," Ella said, "though I don't know that I ever saw him. I remember her mother very well. People thought well of her."

"You never did care for Elvis Grider," Rumsey said to Bill Willie.

"Never did like a hair on his head. I ginrally go to funerals, but I didn't go to his. Him and me got on different sides before you all come. He was a schemin' man, and a funny thing is his partner out-schemed him. He took Jim Walters into the bank because Jim had scrimped up a lot of money, and Elvis needed it in his business. But I reckon Jim started schemin' the day the bank opened, and ever' now and then, he'd scheme a little more. He jest natchelly out-schemed old Elvis. He put the rabbit sign on him. Jim musta been workin' on that thirty years. Elvis seen what was comin' so he done the best thing he could do and died. Then Jim moved in—farm, bank, ever'thing, lock, stock and barrel."

"I heard some talk before Elvis died. After that I heard plenty of talk. Do you suppose that Walters and I ought to get Judge Bell to hurry up and give a decision on that land, or would that be rushing things?" Rumsey Skiles smiled at the thought of it. "It hasn't been in the court quite sixty years yet."

"Judge Drake told me oncet that he was goin' to decide that case some year or other, but I reckon it slipped his mind. Never heard him mention it again 'fore he died. He was a good judge, though. Now I look for Motley Grider to stir up a peck o' trouble. He's a born troublemaker." The old man shook his head. "Anybody heard any-thing from Tom Henry Hines?"

"His cousin, Mrs. Robin Rodes, told me after the wedding that she had a letter from him yesterday. Of course, he is with the Southern troops. Robin, Junior, told his parents that he was going to join the North."

"Mighty bad mixed-up. I don't reckon they'd take me. I heard you couldn't get in unless you was under eighty-five."

"You are considered pretty able in a fight, Bill Willie."

"I whupped a man the day I was eighty-two. I sort o' hated to do it, but he needed it. I used to think fightin' was mighty important, but I know better now. Ain't nothin' counts but workin' hard and havin' friends." He walked away toward his little house at the back.

"My father was good for Bill Willie," commented Rumsey, "but Bill Willie was just as good for my father. I would have no use for this place without him."

A little later, the Virgil Covingtons dropped in for a few minutes of visiting. They knew that the Skileses would be lonesome.

"We just wanted to talk about Jane," said Harriet, who despite the years that had put gray in her hair, moved with vigor, whose face was unwrinkled and whose eyes were bright. "I have been seeing brides

206 *Peace at Bowling Green*

all my life, and I have never seen a lovelier one. I wish her grandfather and grandmother Skiles could have lived to see her today."

"So do I," Rumsey said. "But they would have been very old."

"The sight of Jane would have cured that." Harriet smiled. "I feel years younger."

"I heard the *Gasper River* coming in," said Virgil. "I never hear that boat blow without thinking of your father."

Then upon the gentle evening air was borne another sound, that of a railroad train blowing for the bridge. It whistled frantically with little short gasps, as if to make sure that the bridge was still there.

"How that would please him too," continued Ella. "Any sound or sight that meant things were moving into Bowling Green, or out of it, was music in his ears and beauty in his eyes. We were talking about the first arrival of the *Gasper River* earlier today."

"Nothing that happened yesterday is as clear in my memory," said Virgil. "You wouldn't think from how fine everything was at the wedding today that war could reach us tomorrow."

His wife reproved him, "I told you not to talk about war. This is Jane Skiles's wedding day."

"I know you did, dear, but how can you keep from it, the way things are?"

"It's all right," said Rumsey. "We were talking about it ourselves just before you got here. Have you heard any late news?"

"There was news on the telegraph wire late today that the Yankees have established a camp in Garrard County. They don't intend for the state to remain neutral."

"There is not much comfort in neutrality. Frequently it is the neutrals who suffer most."

"You think a lot of the time, Rumsey," said Harriet. "If there is a war, how will it turn out?"

"There is a war, and I haven't thought any in a month, maybe a year."

"Virgil and I are greatly troubled. If the war should come here, I doubt if we would know what to do."

"When you find out, let me know. I am troubled too. Geographically, we are halfway-betweeners. If we lived in Georgia there would be but one thing to do, and that we could do. If we lived in New Hampshire, our duty would be crystal-clear. Here we are close to both sides. We have friends in both armies."

"Not only friends," said Virgil Covington, "but members of the family. When there is a crowd of my family present, I never open my mouth except to eat or talk of the weather. Anything else would start trouble."

"Jackson Shobe favors the South, doesn't he?"

"Yes, Harriet, and I am certain that is what Jane wants him to do. They have talked it over many times. He will be in the army by Christmas. Is that to be a large camp in Garrard County?"

"The dispatches didn't say. My notion is that they have put it there to hold central Kentucky for the North. They'll try to put one in southern Kentucky next."

"Tell me what the war is about," said Ella Skiles. "What are we fighting battles for? Is it to free the slaves? Didn't President Lincoln say that he had no intention of interfering with the slaves in the states?"

"He did, and I believe that he was sincere in it. But we have moved fast since he said those words, and he has been carried along by the rush of things. It is hard to understand the right and wrong of that business at Charleston, or that terrible affair at Bull Run, and it is almost too late to try to. Lincoln couldn't stop it now, nor could anyone——"

"I'll not let you talk that way," said Ella. "Things are not that hopeless."

"In such a crisis, there is only hope when God takes over."

Harriet Covington sighed. "Whatever happens, I'll never forget how sweet Jane looked today. Your menfolks are handsome enough, Ella, but Jane is downright lovely."

They drove away a few minutes later. All of them had tried to keep the talk cheerful as befitted a wedding day, but the war would edge in, filling their minds with grim prospects. The night was quiet and gracious. Rumsey Skiles and his wife sat on the veranda, saying little, not even listening to the sounds of the night. Sleep could not tempt minds filled with such a variety of things. The veranda faced Bowling Green, three miles away. The gaslights on the main streets would burn until ten o'clock, and they could see the vague blur they cast. They could hear the occasional clank and rattle of a switch engine down at the depot. Twice while they sat there carriages passed, moving south. Doubtless, people from the Richpond neighborhood on their way home from visits in town. Often friends passing would call out their greeting.

But the veranda was not lighted, nor was any part of the house.

Lights had blazed in all the rooms the night before. Ella and Rumsey Skiles had given a great dinner for Jane and Jackson. Two of Jane's brothers, Wells and Underwood, had been there with their wives. The third brother, McElroy, lived in Saint Louis, and could not make the trip. But he had written Jane a letter that she would treasure all of her life. Uncle Trez Covington, in his late eighties, had been one of the liveliest of guests. A long generation had brought no major changes in Uncle Trez, except that he had become a bit shrunken and walked with the steadying aid of a heavy cane.

"You are getting a nice boy in Jackson," he had told Jane, "a little overserious maybe, but nice. If he doesn't suit you, you can always trade him for a better one."

"Pay him no mind, child," counseled Virgil Covington. "He is always thinking about a trade. He would trade anything. There have been fifty times at least when he figured on trading me off."

"And I haven't had an offer yet," chuckled Uncle Trez. "That's all I'd need."

Harold Drake, nephew of the old judge, referred obliquely to a joke of long standing, "Would you sell Virgil just as he stands?"

"At any price at all and make a profit."

And so the talk had run, mostly gay, sometimes serious when a hint of war would creep in. At one point, matters were becoming heated.

Ella Skiles had said, "Give Jane and Jackson a little time in their home, and then go see them. Some of you have never seen the Shobe house. I think it is one of the grandest in the county. It is the sort of a house that will never grow old."

Then Seraphina Spalding, tactless as usual, had said, "Suppose Jackson has to go off to war—will you live out there, Jane, or come back here?"

"We can't let the farm go unused," Jane had said. "If Jackson is away from home, I will stay there and manage it." Ella had felt very proud of her daughter when she said that.

For an hour longer, Ella and Rumsey stayed out on the veranda, saying nothing, just remembering. They heard the switch engine at the depot whistle hysterically, then rattle to a bumping stop. Rumsey Skiles stood. "It is time to go to bed, Ella. I have an important case in court tomorrow."

2

THE *Gasper River* did not depart the next morning as scheduled. Word came that the locks on the river had been too badly damaged by blasting to be used for passage. The boat would have to wait at Bowling Green for further orders. Then people heard that the locks had been ruined by order of the Confederates. The reason was revealed in a copy of the Nashville *Dispatch*. The *Gasper River* on a recent trip had brought a full cargo of rifles, and these had been concealed somewhere in town, awaiting use by the Yankees. The Southern sympathizers argued that the boat could bring materials for their side too. Why sacrifice that convenience? But the river ran north to Evansville, to Saint Louis, to Cincinnati. What assistance for the South could be expected from those quarters? If the war should spread, the river would be of much more help to the North. General Simon Bolivar Buckner's order to destroy the locks had been given deliberately. The damage to the upper lock was found to be superficial, and it was repaired quickly. For a while the *Gasper River* made daily trips to Morgantown, twenty-six miles down the river. The boat carried heavy loads down the river, goods that had reached Bowling Green by rail and been consigned to landings down the river. Upstream the main commodity was lumber produced by the mills at Morgantown and Green Castle and Woodbury.

And so matters stood in the autumn of 1861. The farmers harvested their crops, but didn't store all of their corn in their main cribs. There were reports daily of raiding parties from both sides. Corn was a prime favorite of these foragers, and they always carried wagons. The more discreet farmers of the county, moved by these reports, built other cribs in obscure and inaccessible places. In these, they stored half or more of their yield. The better farmers sowed more wheat than usual, and made preparations for increased crops of everything for the next season. War was always hungry for crops.

Early in November, General Buckner sent notice of his intention to occupy Bowling Green with his army. He planned to erect such fortifications as were necessary to protect the section in case of invasion from the north. He promised the citizens the least possible interruption to their daily routines. Under the existing conditions, he could not permit any hindrance to the army in its assigned tasks. It had been the plan of the South to respect Kentucky's neutrality, but the status of neutrality had been violated by Northern forces, and consequently the South could hardly be expected to regard with fidelity the state's border lines.

On a Monday morning, the leading citizens gathered in the courthouse to consider solemnly their plans for the future. Rumsey Skiles acted as chairman. And that was fitting. No one had heard him speak a partisan word in the whole unhappy issue. He read aloud General Buckner's message and proclamation.

"It all means," he said in his cool, precise way, "that Kentucky is at war. I have never thought there would be any way to stay out of it. We have a great many people who favor the South. That has been their way of life and thought. We have a great many friends and neighbors who favor the North. We have already contributed soldiers to both armies. Undoubtedly, there will be a great many more. But our homes are here. We are neighbors. Undoubtedly, there will be friction and strained relations. But we must let the battles be fought by soldiers on the fields, and we must learn to abide by both defeat and victory. We must come to realize that a man can favor either side and still be a gentleman. We want no spies here sending out reports to either side.

"We learn that General Buckner is coming up from Tennessee with a detachment of Kentucky troops to occupy our town. All of us hate to have the town so disturbed by the activities of war, but there is nothing we can do to prevent it. We will be fortunate indeed if General Buckner's is the only army brought to Bowling Green. Our very location will tempt armies. It is my strong suggestion that those who stay here as citizens play the part of citizens, and no other part. Are there any questions, or does any citizen wish to make a statement?"

Frisbee Cherry, a known Northern sympathizer, stood. "We have been told time and again that Kentucky is a neutral state, and that we would not be invaded by either army."

"We have indeed been told that," said the chairman gravely, "but as a matter of fact, Northern troops have already invaded Kentucky and established a camp on our soil. It is possible that Kentucky will take neither side officially, but both sides will use Kentucky, and we might just as well face it. There is no earthly way to keep them out."

"All right," said Cherry, "but are we to pay the bills of both sides while they are in the state? Will these Rebels—" he looked about him and decided to change the word—"Southerners raid our cribs to feed their horses? Will they take the meat from our smokehouses?"

"We have been promised that they will not. In war promises are usually kept at first, but forgotten if it goes on long enough. I do not anticipate any pillage under General Buckner. My information is that, while he is a soldier, his word can be trusted."

"Why are we meeting if there is nothing we can do?" asked Ed Hampton.

"So that we may understand the situation, so that under this stress we may behave with due discretion. It will be annoying, of course, to have the work of this army going on near us. We may be stopped from using some of our streets. A great many objectionable things may arise. It is plain good sense to accept them with all the grace we can summon. Anything else will only make matters worse."

"How long is this army expected to be here?"

"I have no idea. Maybe just a little while, maybe as long as the war lasts. You can have no less knowledge of that than I, Ed." He paused, thinking, then was speaking again, "I might say that I have lived here all of my life. This century and I were born the same year. I came here with my parents when I was three years old. Except for the time I spent in Transylvania College, I have not been away from here many days. I speak both modestly and truthfully when I say that my father and mother helped build this town. My wife and I have reared our children here. Almost all of our friends live here. This is our home. We do not plan ever to have another one. I cannot conceive of a section more gravely stricken by war than this. Most of us have blood kin on both sides. All of us have dear friends in both armies, and we will have more. For us, there can be no real victory except peace. For us, divided as we are, there can be no good news except that our friends still live. We shall have to play this war out with such restraint and dignity and good will as we can possibly have."

He sat down and the minister of the Baptist church arose. "I have only a weak, human mind," he said, and his voice was hoarse from emotion, "and so I do not understand God. I do not comprehend His purposes till in the fullness of time they stand revealed. I do not know toward what end God is moving us now, but I do know that God is not wasting His time, nor piddling with the substance of our lives. Every word that Brother Skiles has said is good. Hearken to it and leave the end in God's hands."

They went soberly back to their homes, and to the work that waited them there. Rumsey Skiles found that Bill Willie Blewett was burying cabbages and turnips, except those he had stored in a cool place in the cellar for immediate use. The potatoes were already in the great ridge that was to be their winter home.

"It has been a good cabbage season," said Bill Willie. "Taters and turnips fair, but it's the best cabbage year I ever seen. There's five crocks of kraut in your cellar, and better kraut I never tasted. Kraut goes mighty good with backbones and spareribs. We got at least ten bushels of cabbage in there now." He pointed to the fresh mound. "I guess we're jest about ready for winter to set in: plenty o' firewood ready, barn loft filled with fust-rate hay, two cribs o' corn, more'n a bushel o' shelled beans, four bushels o' dried apples, and one o' dried peaches, fifty gallons o' sorghum——"

"Anything in the smokehouse?" asked Skiles, smiling faintly.

"Enough to last till we get good hog-killin' weather. We'll have fifteen hogs ready when it turns cold."

"Plenty of feed for the cattle, I suppose?"

"Plenty. I'm a-goin' to start haulin' the fodder to the sheds tomorrer. I bet you don't know what's been goin' on here lately."

"Working a little on the side maybe." Again the faint smile.

"I'm a bread eater. I could live offn bread by itself, corn bread or flour bread, it don't make me no difference. But I jest natchelly got to have my bread. There's a lot o' scalawags in any army, and you can't tell when they'll be thievin' aroun'. So I got that carpenter that helped build the crib out in the woods, and while you and Miz Ella was gone to preachin' Sunday, we fixed a secret place in the attic to hide meal and flour in. You might say the ox was in the ditch, and this carpenter knows when to keep his mouth shet. You let me get three or four sacks o' meal and flour and put it up there, and I'll feel a lot safer about my bread."

"Take all the corn and wheat you need to the mill. I wouldn't want you to be stunted, Bill Willie. Better take it right away."

"Had a visitor while you was gone to town."

"Anybody I know?"

"Trez Covington. He wants to buy that red bull. His bull has got the hollow horn, or somethin', so he needs another one. I told him he would have to see you, and he said he would rather trade with me, said you was liable to cheat him out of his last dollar, said he knowed he could trust me."

"So can I," Rumsey said. "We don't need that bull—anyhow, that is what I heard you say a month ago. You go ahead and trade him. I will try to do what is right by whichever one is left alive."

"It'd be right amusin' to cheat that old buzzard out o' the last strand o' hair he's got left on his head."

"You'll run a risk, Bill Willie. Don't forget that he is my wife's uncle."

Ella Skiles had come out on the veranda in time to hear the reference to the prospective sale of the bull. She was laughing heartily. "Virgil is the only man who ever beat Uncle Trez in a trade. You two youngsters would be no match for him."

"That red bull is a mighty good bull," said Bill Willie meditatively. "That is a long sight better bull than Trez Covington is used to. I think it would be a right good thing if we could fix it so afore he dies he could say that he had had one bull that wasn't a scrub."

"When is he coming back?" asked Rumsey Skiles.

"Tomorrer. I told him I'd ast you what you'd take."

"Whatever you do, Bill Willie, will suit me fine. I have an important case in court tomorrow afternoon, but I'll hurry home to hear about it."

Bill Willie and two of the hands were replacing some rotted posts in the garden fence when Trezevant Covington arrived the following morning. Bill Willie told the men to continue with their work and went out to meet his visitor. It was a clear day and the feel of frost was in the air. Covington flung himself from the horse with all the sprightliness of youth. Bill Willie asked him if he wouldn't come into the house. "A glass o' milk is mighty refreshin' after a hard ride."

"You call three miles a hard ride? But I reckon it would be for a man as old as you."

"I walked out to Providence Knob to preachin' Sunday. Had a real good time. Got to feelin' sorry for people that have to use a hoss every time they leave home."

"Why didn't you say something to me? I'd have lent you a horse. That is too long a walk for a man that is feeble." Trez Covington's eyes were twinkling.

"Didn't want a hoss. Had a good time jest a-walkin' along and a-thinkin' about things. How about you walkin' out there with me sometime? Preachin' is real good."

"I always go to my own church."

"I don't blame you. It's close. Besides, I guess you ride even to it. The folks both done gone to town. He had some business he couldn't put off, and she's gone to visit awhile with Miz Robin Rodes. From what I hear, she's ailin' some."

"Worrying about that boy of hers in the army. Did you ask Rumsey about that bull?"

"Yessir, and he said that seein' as how that bull would still be in the family, for me to make you a special price of thirty-five dollars."

"Thirty-five dollars!" Trez almost shouted. "You misunderstood me. I didn't say anything about buying all the stock he has got. You ought to have told him I just wanted the bull."

"That bull has got blood in it. And another thing, that bull has got sense. That bull took it mighty hard when Lincoln was elected. I thought for a while we was a-goin' to lose it."

"I wouldn't pay thirty-five dollars for Lincoln himself."

Bill Willie sighed. "It's jest like Rumsey Skiles said: your stock is a-lookin' a little run-down, and here's a good chance for you to sort o' build it up. That bull can practically read and write. You would be surprised how smart that bull is."

"How did it find out that Lincoln was elected? Read it in the New York *Tribune?*"

"We don't get that paper. I told it, and jest like I am tellin' you, it made that bull mighty onhappy. That's a real Southern bull."

"Why don't you sell it to Jeff Davis?"

"He ain't no good man with a real fine bull. You want me to show you what a Southern bull this one is?"

"Bill Willie Blewett, what are you talking about? You sound to me like old age has got you."

"I'll prove it to you what a real Southern bull that is. Now you look at that gate. You can see it opens out due south. Yonder is the rest of the cattle." He pointed to the right. "Natchelly, you'd think that bull would go up where the others are. And he would if I didn't remind him what direction that is. I am goin' to put this rope on him so he can't get away, and I'm a-goin' to ast him what kind o' bull he is. You jest watch."

He looped the rope around the bull's horns. He opened the gate, holding firmly to the end of the rope. "His name is Ginral Jackson," Bill Willie explained to Covington. "Now, Ginral, I'm goin' to ast you which kind o' bull you is. Ifn you're a Northern bull, you turn to the right when you go through that gate. Ifn you're a Southern bull you keep goin' straight ahead. I'm a-leavin' it to you."

"And you'll jerk a little the way you want it to go."

"You jest watch close and see ifn I make a sign. Now, take your choice, Ginral."

The bull didn't even look at the other cattle grazing up to the right. It continued exactly as it had come through the gate.

"Wait a minute. That just happened. Try it again."

Bill Willie led the bull back into the lot. "Now, Ginral, I am givin' you another chance to show this gentleman that you ain't got a drap o' Yankee blood in you. I'm a-goin' to open that gate agin, and ifn you a real Southern bull you keep goin' straight ahead. You understand me, don't you."

General Jackson walked majestically through the gate, and kept going with not a fractional shift in course. Trezevant Covington looked at the cattle grazing up on the rise to the right. Then he looked at General Jackson, and then at Bill Willie Blewett.

"You put on a good show, Bill Willie. I'll buy that bull though I think I am being cheated out of the nine teeth I have got left. You are a strong young fellow. You walk out to Providence Knob to preaching. I guess you wouldn't mind just walking along and thinking a little, and help me get that bull to my place."

"No trouble a-tall. I need me a little stroll. I expect you'll find it right tiresome, jest a-settin' on that hoss, but I guess it's about your only chance to get there. I'll get the Ginral there for you. Wait here till I get my hat."

He hitched General Jackson to the gate and went inside the house. A minute later, he was back, wearing his hat, and in his hand he held a lump of salt which he gave to a very eager General Jackson.

"Don't you reckon you ought to have a little snack to eat?" asked Bill Willie. "You look all frazzled out to me."

Trezevant Covington grinned. "This horse of mine has got real Southern blood in it. It's a real Rebel horse. It will carry double in case you give plumb out."

Bill Willie Blewett handed Rumsey Skiles the thirty-five dollars. "I mighta got a little more, but I let Trez off easy, seein' he's a member of the family."

"I didn't need that bull. Twenty-five dollars would have been enough. How did you raise Uncle Trez that high?"

"You might say that the saltin' place had sumpin' to do with it. I'd been keerful not to let that bull have any salt since yesterday mornin'."

3

ONE MORNING a week later, Nat Grider passed by with sacks of wheat flour in his spring wagon. Rumsey Skiles was starting to town as Grider drove by the gate.

"You have made an early trip to the mill."

"I didn't want to take any chances. The soldiers got to town last night."

"General Buckner's soldiers?" Rumsey asked.

"The town is filled with them. I was afraid they would take over the mill, so I hurried to get my grinding done."

"That was commendable foresight, Nat. I think I will ask Bill Willie to take some corn and wheat to the mill sometime today. Were there many there?"

"They were coming in when I left. I saw Tom Henry Hines on the street. He was wearing a gray uniform. Here for a last visit to his folks, he said. We spent a few minutes very pleasantly. He told me he was leaving tonight, but of course he didn't say where he was going. I am glad it wasn't Motley he met. They never did like each other."

Skiles left word for Bill Willie to make the trip to the mill. Then he rode on to town. Nat had been right. The place was crowded with soldiers. They were dressed in a wild scramble of uniforms, with little exactness in color and not much concern about fit. But they seemed cheerful enough, and twice they broke ranks for Skiles to pass through. He went directly to his office and wrote a letter to General Buckner, asking whether he might assume that his coming to and going from work would be unhindered. He then settled into the legal work before him. For a while his mind held to its proper focus, and the questions that arose were quickly answered. Then his attention weakened. His lawsuits faded out and in their place were the soldiers he had passed that morning. What were they doing in Bowling Green? Their presence on the streets of the city was incredible. Such a state of things must not be permitted. Then his mind cleared, and he knew there was nothing unreasonable about the presence of those ill-clothed soldiers. It was war that was unreasonable, incredible, unthinkable. But incredible or not, war was their lot. God alone knew when strife would cease and the happy days of peace return. He couldn't get his mind back to those legal forms on his desk before him. So he closed the desk and rode up Bridge Street to Vinegar Hill to see what was going on there.

A great deal was going on. The brow of the hill lying nearest town had been cleared of the fine cedars that had been there for generations. The boughs had been chopped off and burned in great, roaring, crackling fires. The logs were being stacked for further use. Skiles dismounted from his horse and stood watching the soldiers put the logs into stacks. An officer, obviously in charge, saw him and came up.

"I played on this hill when I was a small lad," said Skiles. "I imagine that I have been up in most of those trees. Am I trespassing?"

"Why, not at all, as long as you don't get in the way. I like trees, and I hate like fury to cut one down. War is bad medicine, any way you take it. I wish the Yanks had not forced this on us, but people have to defend themselves. My name is Happy Watts. I can't complain because I have been trained for war. I am the youngest graduate West Point ever turned out."

"My name is Rumsey Skiles. I am a lawyer here."

"A good one, I dare say from your looks. Well, I have a hundred men up here and half of them don't know which end of an ax you cut with till you show them. I suppose I'd better get to showing them."

He smiled pleasantly and moved on. Skiles looked about him and flinched at the terrible wound that a hundred men had inflicted upon his favorite hill. The sounds of shouting and chopping were deafening. Skiles mounted his horse to ride away. At the head of Bridge Street, he reined in his horse and sat there looking at the town beneath him. He could hear chopping and shouting on Grider Hill, farther in toward town, and to his right. Skiles flinched again. That was a beautiful elevation, not so high as Vinegar Hill, but more suited to homes. He knew that they were at work on College Hill, but the view was obstructed and it was too far away for the sounds of chopping to be heard. They would be making fortifications on Baker's Hill across the river. To the right of Baker's Hill he could see Mount Ayr, on the summit of which was the home of Warner Underwood. It was one of the country's finest homes. The site was well suited for fortifying, though it was not likely of much military significance. It would, Skiles thought, be sheer vandalism to require it, so gracious and fine was the home on its crest. But Underwood had been frank and unrestrained in his partisanship for the North. His position was well understood. The place might be in danger.

The courthouse clock struck four. It was time for him to be on his way to Three Springs. Supper would be ready by the time he reached there. As he rode down Bridge Street, he met Shade Gossom, the owner of the mill.

"Have you done any grinding for Bill Willie today?" he asked.

"A fair wagonful. There will be bread at Three Springs, Mr. Skiles, war or no war. I was just going up to see what they are doing on Vinegar Hill. Have you been up there?"

"I almost wish I hadn't gone. They have destroyed the finest cedars in south Kentucky, and I don't know for what."

"It will be more than trees, Mr. Skiles. This place has got its share of headstrong Northerners. I am going to run my mill as long as I can get grinding for it, and not open my mouth about anything except meal and flour. It would be a lot safer for the milling business if everybody was on one side or the other."

"Better for everybody. Better for the town. Any other news except the forts they are building?"

"Yes, the recruiting office on the square is filled. It looks like every Southerner came in town to enlist just as soon as he got word the army had got here. There is a full company of them already in down there now."

It was only a few squares out of his way, so Skiles rode by the recruiting office. Shade Gossom was right. The enlistment station was doing a flourishing business. He pulled his horse to one side and stopped. Fully fifty men were lounging there outside the office. There was Franklin Beck, whom a dozen times he had helped out of fighting scrapes. The boy wasn't good for much besides fighting, but for his father's sake—his father was a steady and industrious farmer out in the county—Skiles had been able to keep him out of jail. Franklin had always called him judge.

He saw Rumsey sitting there on his horse and grinned. "This is one thing you won't have to get me out of, Judge. This time I got the law on my side."

"That's fine. Keep it there."

"Don't expect to be in more'n three months, six at the most. The Yankees ain't got a chance."

"Not many of us have," said Skiles soberly. "I wish you good luck, Franklin. Make them a good soldier."

"All I ask, Judge, is a chance in a good battle."

"Franklin Beck!" bawled an orderly. "Inside." The boy grinned at Skiles and disappeared inside the office.

"Remember me, Mr. Skiles?" The young man had arisen from the curb and was standing close to him. Skiles could not at the moment identify him, though the face was familiar. "My name is Phillip Chandler. I have preached at the Methodist church here several times."

Then Skiles remembered the man. He had met and talked briefly with him at a Methodist conference held at Woodburn the year before. Brother Tully Napier, of the Bowling Green Methodist church, had invited him out to the conference, and had driven by Three Springs and taken him in his gig. Brother Napier was a hale and hearty man, and loved a joke dearly. He told Skiles that he had asked him to go because the blood of the Methodists was getting too thick and needed a little Presbyterian thinning.

The faint smile appeared on Skiles's face. "Have you ever tried sassafras-root tea? It is a good thinner."

"It's our favorite drink, and it leaves our blood thicker."

"Then I'll stand by my Presbyterian doctrine that your blood is predestined to a thickness. But I'll be delighted to go to your conference with you."

Rumsey Skiles had found the conference refreshing both to his body and spirit. The basket dinner spread by the ladies of Rockfield was well prepared and of great quantity. He had told his wife that evening that in all of his sixty years of life he had never seen so much fried chicken as was in plain view at Rockfield that day.

"I imagine you altered the view some, Rumsey."

"What would you have done with that chicken so good and those Rockfield ladies urging you on?"

The main sermon at the conference had been delivered by the great Dr. John B. McFerrin of Nashville. Its thunderous eloquence had set Rumsey Skiles's thin Presbyterian blood to coursing through his veins at unwonted speed. It was then that he had seen Phillip Chandler, sitting one row ahead and just across the aisle. The young man sat there transfixed. There was upon his face the look of one exalted, and his eyes shone like stars. The fellow was obviously so deeply moved by the sermon that Skiles felt impelled to know him. Later, in the churchyard, Skiles saw the young man standing at one side, his eyes still on Dr. McFerrin who was in spirited conversation with a group of Methodist dignitaries. Skiles walked across the intervening space and held out his hand. "I should like to make your acquaintance. My name is Rumsey Skiles."

"The lawyer from Bowling Green?"

"I practice law there. This has been a fine conference."

"I live in Glasgow, and they say there that you are one of the best lawyers in south Kentucky. I hope to become a Methodist preacher. I could ask of God no greater boon than to be just a faint shadow of Brother McFerrin. I hadn't heard that you are a Methodist, Mr. Skiles."

"I inherited my Presbyterianism all the way back to Scotland. But I covet for us Presbyterians the vigor of you Methodists. Have you preached any yet?"

"Just a few sermons in places selected by the presiding elder."

"Give me the opportunity to hear you sometime."

"Not till I am better than I am now. Then gladly, Mr. Skiles."

The episode came back to Rumsey Skiles, as he sat there on his horse. Chandler had preached a sermon at the Methodist church at Bowling Green, but Skiles had not known of it till later.

"I wish I had known of your engagement here. I would have deserted the Presbyterian church that day."

"I didn't blame people from staying away who did know of it. Brother Frogge is a much better preacher than I will be for a long time, maybe ever. I can preach a little and I know a good deal about sickness. I want the army to take me as a chaplain."

"How is it that you are so well acquainted with sickness?"

"I felt there was a war coming on and I have gone with Dr. Strother on all of his trips for the last two months. There has been a lot of sickness. I have studied the Bible between trips," he added proudly. "Do you think they will take me?"

"I don't see how they can refuse. When you have time write me a letter."

Skiles turned his horse and started away. Then he stopped, dismounted, and hitched his horse to a paling fence. He walked into the recruiting room past the orderly, who looked at him in some astonishment but said nothing in protest. An officer sat behind a table.

Skiles spoke to him. "I am an attorney in the city here. My name is Rumsey Skiles. I wish to speak with you about a man waiting outside to enlist."

"Yes? I am Colonel Lillard."

"The man's name is Phillip Chandler. He wishes to enlist as a chaplain and as a medical attendant. I recommend him strongly."

"How long have you known him?"

"A little more than a year."

"Is he related to you?"

"Not in the least."

Colonel Lillard made some notes on a paper. "We have not enlisted any as chaplains, and I am not sure that we have any official instructions about them. Perhaps we have been negligent there. When he comes in I shall give him special thought because of what you have said."

4

SKILES rode home at a brisk canter. Ella would be wondering why he was so late. He could hear the sounds of chopping on Vinegar Hill and College Hill. His way home ran not far distant from Grider Hill. There were not many trees in that section, and he heard no chopping. But there was a great deal of shouting to horses, and he could hear the sounds of iron scraping against rocks. They were using teams to throw up breastworks there, and making a lot of fuss about it.

He fell to musing as he rode along. Bowling Green might indeed become the South's main bastion of defense against invasion from the north. Its location, its topography, added to that strategy. If an adequate army was placed at Bowling Green, and its rear and flanks protected, then the Federals simply could not pass it. There were Baker's and Underwood hills to take the first shock of the advance and, unless the assault was of major force, to withstand the enemy altogether. There was the river, winding its serpentine coils about the countryside, itself a strong defense. There were College Hill and Webb's Hill providing strong secondary defenses. Finally, Grider Hill and Vinegar Hill, though the latter would not be very helpful until the enemy was already in the town. And then it would likely be too late. It occurred to Rumsey Skiles that it would be good military judgment for General Buckner to concentrate his forces on Baker's Hill. This was high and rugged and commanded the entire area over which the town might be approached from the north. He smiled at the thought that he was committing himself to Southern strategy, when it was generally understood that he had declared himself a neutral. Could the tension become enough to force him to one side or the other? If so, which side? There was the stuff of a prophet in his father. Jacob Skiles had foreseen this tragedy. Thirty-five years before, he had felt its inevitability. He had envisioned the coming of the steamboat long before any other citizen of Bowling Green had given thought to it. And when the *Gasper River* had arrived at the landing, his mind had moved on to the railroad train. He hadn't lived to see the train come into the town, but he died knowing that it would come.

Rumsey remembered the counsel his father had given Bill Willie about the war:

"I think you will still be alive, Bill Willie, when the war breaks. You are tough and wiry and can hold off disease for a long time. I have felt weakness inside me lately. I do not think I will be here that long. But you will, Bill Willie, and this is the advice I give you: take no sides. When two of your best friends fall out, take no sides, but pray for sense to come to them."

"If it was only two friends I wouldn't take no sides, but suppose all my friends was on one side, wouldn't I have to take it too?"

Rumsey remembered that his father had been silent so long that he thought he wasn't going to answer Bill Willie. Then he had said very soberly, "You can pray for sense to come to them, Bill Willie."

Rumsey Skiles thought that being a neutral in time of war could be a very lonely thing. How could a man settle it when his heart went with one flag and his mind with another? He knew that if two or three decades could be subtracted from Bill Willie, he would that day enlist on the side of the South. With Bill Willie, all of the subtleties and complexities were resolved, and only the simple issues remained. What business did the North have with a fort in Charleston harbor? Virginia was a Southern state. The North had got what it deserved at Bull Run.

Rumsey Skiles knew that his wife favored the South, but with a few reservations. Most of her best friends were on that side, but not all. He did not know what his sons would do, and in a way, he dreaded to find out. The oldest, McElroy, was thirty-five years old, too old to make a good soldier. He had married a Baltimore girl, and they lived in Saint Louis. Underwood was thirty. He lived in Russellville, and had a good furniture store there. Wells, the youngest of the sons, lived in Glasgow. He too was engaged in the practice of law. Rumsey thought that it was odd that his father had been a wholehearted farmer. He had run the store for profit, but his heart was in the work on the farm. But his father had not bequeathed his passion for farming to anyone. Without Bill Willie he, Rumsey, would be no farmer at all. His three sons had no interest in it. But he would keep Three Springs intact as long as he lived. He couldn't even guess how much longer Bill Willie could be depended upon, but Blewett had a fine young man, dependable and sturdy, coming on to take up where he had to leave off. Bill Willie was taking great pride in the man, but he would not give up the farm at Three Springs till he had to. His understudy would have to wait that long.

The Skiles men might not answer the trumpets, but Jane's husband, Jackson Shobe, would. Jane could run the farm while he was at war. She'd be able to do it, too. She had her grandfather's knack for farming and love of the land.

Rumsey Skiles was thinking these things. Something caused him to look up, and there before him was Three Springs. He had daydreamed for three miles. There was Ella waiting on the veranda in the twilight. She saw him coming and came down to meet him. "Where have you been? I was beginning to think that you were staying with the soldiers."

"The army isn't so bad off that it would take me. You will have to endure me for a while yet."

"I can see that you have something to tell me. Let's eat supper first. It isn't getting any warmer."

They sat at the table and ate their supper, served by Aunt Martha, whom they had taken over when they had moved back to Three Springs. Aunt Martha was no slave. She was endowed with a deep sense of quiet humor. She would say, "I sometimes wisht I was a slave so I could res' some."

And Ella Skiles would answer, "We will fix that all right, Aunt Martha. We will give you a half hour off one day next year."

"Yes'm, Miss Ella, and dat's de day you will invite a whole houseful of company."

Rumsey Skiles did not eat with much relish. The food was good as always. But he was greatly stirred by what he had seen that day. He knew that he had seen a tragedy. Was the war coming to him, his family, his town—the war that had begun months before? He was not used to trouble. His life had not been touched by the gravities that he knew harassed other men. He loved the town and the county with all the intensity of his quiet soul. He loved his way of life. Was it about to end? The vision of those murdered cedar trees kept rising before him. Was that the sign of the end, of some sort of end?

"If you will only look, Rumsey, you can see that I am here," his wife said gently. "For five minutes, you haven't said a word to me. Bill Willie went to town today, and he told me what is happening there. That is what you are thinking of, isn't it?"

"Yes, Ella."

"He had to wait at the mill for an hour to take his turn at the grinding, so he went down to the post office to see if there was any mail. I guess he didn't go directly, for he saw a great deal. He got a Louisville paper. It had a lot of news in it about the Northern soldiers. It looks as if they are coming this way."

"Mist' Rumsey, what is de matter wid you?" grumbled Aunt Martha. "You ain't eat enough to keep a fishing worm alive."

"I am no fishing worm, and I rarely eat on Tuesdays," he said, smiling feebly.

She went back into the kitchen, grumbling as she went. Soon she was back with a piece of fried ham, a fried egg, and a plate of hot biscuits. "Looks like I got to move yo' breakfus' back to supper to get you to eat."

"Thank you, Aunt Martha. Breakfast does taste better."

When he had finished his breakfast, they went into the front room, and Ella brought him the Louisville paper. It was filled with references to the treasonable action of General Buckner in occupying Bowling Green. It mentioned several skirmishes that had taken place between the Union and Confederate forces in the Munfordville area, the motive of both sides being the control of the railroad bridge across Green River. If General Buckner intended to move against Louisville, he would need that bridge. If it was Buell's plan to lead his forces against Bowling Green and Nashville, he would have to use that bridge. The skirmishes were but a token of the determination of both armies to control the bridge. The paper editorially called for an immediate movement against the Confederates in southern Kentucky and Tennessee.

"There is no getting around it, is there?"

"We are at war, Ella," he answered soberly.

"How long will it last? Do you think long?"

He resorted to the only answer he had. "God alone knows. It may well become terrible. The North is much the more powerful. The only chance the South has is to end it quickly."

"Then if it goes on a long time, we will lose it?"

"I do not know how to say *we*, Ella."

She was silent for a while. Then she spoke with an urgency that he had not often heard in her. "I want the family together once more. I don't suppose McElroy and his family can come, but I want the rest. I don't care how long they stay, a day, a week, whatever they can. But I want them here together. Can't we have them, Rumsey?"

"It had better be soon. A great many things can happen now."

"Sunday? No, they couldn't make it by then. A week from Sunday."

"We'll get them to come on Saturday, for a full day Sunday. If they can't stay any longer, they can leave early Monday."

"Could they have stopped people from coming by then?"

"I doubt if by then, but it could happen."

So letters were written to Underwood and Wells and mailed early the next morning. Rumsey had a client from Oakland who was coming to see him the next day, and he could very conveniently carry a note of invitation to Jane and Jackson. Ella and Aunt Martha and other sundry help spent the rest of the week getting the house in shape for the visit. Court was not in session just then, but Rumsey worked diligently in his office to get matters in hand for a relaxed week end. The hands on the farm knew that something was about to happen from the way Bill Willie worked them. There were a great many conferences between Ella and Aunt Martha as to food. Aunt Martha knew the preferences of the entire family.

"Dat Wells, he's a turnup-green eater. Miss Jane, she eats 'em, but she ain't relish 'em like he do. We'll have turnup greens from dat fresh patch. Lucky thing dat Mist' Bill Willie put in dat late roast'n'-ear patch, but the ears ain't much big. Underwood he could eat his whole size o' roast'n' ears."

"Are we getting plenty of eggs?"

"Plenty means a right smart with all o' them havin' chillun except Miss Jane. Yes'm, we can make out wid de eggs, and we gettin' plenty o' milk."

"We will need plenty. I remember how fond Underwood's children are of boiled custard."

"Jest like dey daddy. When boiled custard seen dat boy comin' it jest natchelly dwindled out."

"Maybe we can keep them from starving. Anyhow, we'll try."

5

UNDERWOOD AND WELLS and their families arrived Saturday afternoon. An emergency in farm work kept Jane and Jackson from leaving Oakland till early Sunday morning. But they could make the trip in two hours. Wells came first with his wife and two daughters. Lena, aged six, bounced from the carriage and inquired where her grandpa was.

"Won't I do till he can get here?" asked Ella. "He is upstairs primping."

"You'll do for me, Grandma," said Caroline, aged four and a half.

"Grandpa is what I came for," announced Lena, with a touch of superiority.

"I came for both," said their mother and proved it by a warm embrace.

Rumsey Skiles came across the veranda and down the walk, adjusting his clothing as he came. Lena met him and swung firmly from one of his hands. Caroline took a death grip upon her grandmother's hand. Rumsey disencumbered himself long enough to include his son and daughter-in-law in his fond welcome.

"If I am not permitted to hug you, Wells," said Ella, "I suppose I may be allowed to cook for you. Come on in. Someone will take your team and bring in your valises."

"Grandpa, what are those soldiers doing on the road?" asked Lena.

"Grandma, I saw them too," said Caroline.

"There were millions and thousands of them, Grandpa. I counted them."

"I counted them for you, Grandma."

"We will consider the soldiers later," said Rumsey. "I am looking for Ruth and Underwood at any minute. You need to rest up a bit."

They went into the house. The visitors freshened up. The two daughters changed to clothes unmarred by thirty miles of travel. They all sat on the veranda, for a faint fringe of summer still lingered. A half hour later, Underwood and Ruth and their two sons, aged five and three, arrived. Ruth was dark of hair and eyes, a lovely young woman in a wistful sort of way. Her two sons were quiet and appealing children. They greeted their grandparents quietly and pleasantly, and then retired to the immediate presence of their parents.

"Where is Jane?" Underwood asked, for his sister had always been the apple of his eye.

"Something interrupted. They can't come till tomorrow."

"Not the soldiers?"

"No, not the soldiers—yet. I think it was some emergency on the farm."

"Unplanted turnip seed would be an emergency to Jane. I wish I liked selling furniture as well as I think she likes farming."

"Jane got the right husband," said Ella Skiles. "I dare you to keep the conversation off farming twenty consecutive minutes when they are present."

"I am afraid that time will soon develop a substitute topic," said her husband.

"Even then, it will be the farm for Jane."

They walked on toward the house, Lena holding tightly to her grandfather's hand. She turned to her uncle Underwood. "You see any soldiers?" she asked.

"I am afraid it will be a novelty soon to go anywhere and not see soldiers," said Rumsey Skiles. "They are plentiful here."

"Go to your rooms and rest awhile," said Ella. "We will call you in time for supper. This is to be one of the most important visits I ever had."

"I have already rested," said Lena. "I want to talk to Grandpa."

"Talk with him all you want to, but don't get your mind off supper. Aunt Martha and I are trying to make it a good one."

The supper was a good one, all the way from the roast of beef to the sorghum pie, one of Aunt Martha's major achievements. Lena ate so much that the questions she asked her grandfather for an hour came at long intervals. Caroline's radiant affection for her grandmother was temporarily dimmed. The two grandsons ate heartily, talked very little, but saw everything. The younger son sat in a tall chair at his mother's side; the older one at his father's side in a chair built up by a pair of bulky cushions.

Ella Skiles looked at the younger boy. "I am glad to see another Skiles in that chair. Lately it has not been used enough."

"Grandma, may I eat in it sometime?" asked Caroline.

"Indeed you may, and before you leave this time."

"Grandpa, take Asher out of it, and let me eat in it now," said Lena. "I am a Skiles. I got a right to eat in it."

"It is all right, Lena," said Ruth. "Asher wouldn't mind. He is sleepy. He is willing for you to have the chair now."

"I am not willing," said Caroline firmly. "I asked for it first, Grandma."

"I don't think any of you need to use it right now. It is only a chair for eating, and we have finished our supper."

The older boy asked one of his infrequent questions. "Are you all going to talk, Grandpa?"

"I suppose we will talk some, Murray."

"Then I want to sit and hear you."

"I trust that our talk will be intelligent enough to interest you, son."

"He is not your son," corrected Lena. "He is your grandson."

"I will try to hold that in mind, daughter."

They sat for a little while out on the veranda, for the early night was warm. Rumsey Skiles, though he had not intended it, turned the talk toward war. He was telling them of the martial law that General Buckner was gradually putting into the rule of the town. He had heard a great deal of talk during the day, and it remained foremost in his thoughts.

"I wish that some of our dear friends would talk a little less. They say General Buckner is going to make it hard for the citizens who are openly for the North."

"It is hard not to fight when you feel a thing very deeply," said Wells. "I can't imagine Jane becoming suddenly silent."

"Jane has strong convictions, and so has her husband. It might cause them trouble."

"I should prefer to be for the South," said Underwood, "but a little more reluctance on its part would have strengthened my favor. On the other hand, the North has acted a bully. I shall for a while remain neutral."

"General Buckner's superior officer, General Albert Sidney Johnston, is expected to arrive next week. He will take charge of the forces here. Bowling Green may become one of the best-fortified towns in the country. I have heard that is General Johnston's ambition."

"It's not a fantastic notion," said Underwood. "The hills and the river help. In a sense our town is a gateway to the South."

"I suppose that I am a coward," said Rumsey Skiles. "I have passed my three-score years, and yet I have never seen a fist fight, though in a way I have lived in the midst of fighting. I am as little acquainted with violence as anyone I know. And yet my father, in his early life, lived by it. I have never seen more than a stray Indian, and yet he missed only by seconds being burned at the stake. He saw all of this coming on long ago, and he would have been ready for it. He would have reasoned out which was the right side for him to take, and he would have taken it. He would have made no fuss about it. You couldn't have told by looking at him how deeply he was feeling. And yet he would have been on one side, and he would have been giving it all the help he could."

"Which side, Father?"

"I don't know. His manner of thinking would have turned him toward the Union. I am sure that he would have rebelled against the very idea of secession."

"On the other hand, he was raised in the South."

"He was at heart a Southerner, but even so I doubt if he would have accepted a divided nation. But he has been spared this. We haven't."

"I shall remain a neutral as long as I can," said Underwood.

"And when the time comes that you can't, what then?"

"I don't know. I am more like you, Father, than I am like Grandfather. I could easily answer your question if you asked me what I would do when I became convinced that one side was entirely right, or even almost so. But for me, the thing teeters like a plank on a seesaw block. Now one side is up, now the other."

"You can't settle it tonight," said Ella Skiles. "Let's all go to bed. Jane will be here early tomorrow. It will be a big day."

The night was very still. The stars were large and bright. No vague blob of light diluted the darkness on the horizon toward town. The war had left the street lamps unlighted.

6

JANE AND JACKSON were there before nine o'clock the next morning. "It was the wheat," Jane explained, after she had embraced her kinfolks by turn. "We thought at first we could get done sowing by noon yesterday. We are a little late as it is. We let you know as soon as we saw we couldn't. I never saw you people look better. Underwood, you are getting younger. I'll declare you are. This would be perfect if McElroy and his folks could be here. Isn't marrying an odd thing? In a way it is uniting folks, but in another way it is separating them. If none of us had ever married, we wouldn't have got to make this trip. We would already be here. No, you wouldn't be here, Jackson, and you wouldn't, Ruth, and you wouldn't, Clara, and none of these sweet children. So I guess it is all right as it is. Jackson, get that basket of turnip greens out of the carriage. It is poor Wells's favorite tonic, and he does look so bad. I just know he hasn't been tonicked enough."

Rumsey Skiles smiled faintly but fondly. "At least, marriage hasn't separated you from your powers of speech, Jane."

"Indeed it hasn't, and Jackson is the best listener in Kentucky, aren't you, dear?"

"I keep in practice."

"Come on in the house." Ella Skiles put her arm around her daughter. "We can't keep Aunt Martha waiting for these turnip greens. I am glad to see them. She ravaged our garden yesterday, but there wasn't enough. Your tonic will be ready for you at twelve o'clock, Wells. Goodness, what a basket! We haven't got a pot on the place that will hold half of them."

"That is not all greens, Mother. I thought poor Underwood might need some roasting ears. I brought a dozen of the best. When Jackson Shobe raises corn, nubbins haven't a chance."

"I am very fond of roasting ears, but I am not yet a horse, as you have suggested, Jane," her brother protested.

"I'd expect you to divide with the others, but I insist that my main thought was for you."

"Go out there and speak to Aunt Martha. Then come back here. I want to tell you what our plans are for the day," Ella said.

"I'll be right back just as soon as I give Aunt Martha directions about poor Wells's tonic."

"Sometimes I feel sorry for Jackson," said Ella Skiles, when Jane had gone from the room, "but not often."

"I remember one Friday afternoon, when we were in school," said Underwood. "The teacher on Thursday had asked Jane to talk about potatoes at the Friday afternoon exercises. Rather, he asked her what she would like to talk about, and she promptly said potatoes. It surprised not only the teacher, but every pupil there. But he said all right, and the next afternoon he did call on her. She had learned everything in the world about potatoes. And she told it. I remember the first hour or two, but I never did know when she quit. The teacher didn't live long after that. Poor fellow."

"We have more company coming for dinner," said the mother. "I have asked Robin Rodes and Sally, and of course Virgil and Harriet, and Uncle Trez will be here."

"My word!" said Underwood. "Is Uncle Trez still alive?"

"You might outlive Uncle Trez, Underwood," said his mother, "but it will push you."

Jane had returned to the room. "No, it won't be easy for you, Underwood, but, of course, you can try. Uncle Trez gets older all the time, but I doubt if he is much nearer the grave than he was the day he was born."

"We are to have another mature gentleman with us. I have asked Bill Willie to have dinner with us."

Again Underwood expressed great surprise. "Does Bill Willie still eat?"

"We would go to church today," said Rumsey Skiles, "but for the fact that we have no minister. We have called one but he has not yet arrived. There is no rector at the Episcopal church, and both the Methodist and Baptist churches will be crowded. I imagine that three fourths of all General Buckner's soldiers are either Methodists or Baptists. At noon I will read a chapter from the Scriptures. I have it selected. I cannot read it very well, but it will be appropriate."

When all of the families and all of the visitors sat down at the Skiles dining table, extended at great length, there was no food on the table, only the china and silver and some autumn flowers. This but followed the custom of Jacob Skiles, who when he read the Scriptures at the table would have no food yet placed upon it. "When God's word is read," he had said, "I want nothing to distract anyone from hearing it with both the heart and the mind." And his father's example was in Rumsey's mind as he read slowly and deliberately the twenty-eighth chapter of Genesis, which with great power and tenderness treated of the family. No one, not even the children, spoke or moved while he was reading. When he had finished and closed the Bible, it was Jane who said, "How beautiful!"

Then Aunt Martha and Aunt Martha's daughter, Hephzibah—called Hep for short—moved swiftly into the dining room. Aunt Martha carried a baked ham on a platter and placed it before Rumsey, and at the same moment Hep placed a platter heaped with fried chicken before Ella. They disappeared into the kitchen and a moment later were back with an array of vegetables, tureens filled with cornfield beans, new sweet potatoes candied with New Orleans sugar, turnip greens boiled with hog jowl, corn cut from the cob and fried in bacon grease with sweet peppers, onions stewed in cream. There were three kinds of pickles. There were two baking dishes of spoon bread, and a platter filled with hot biscuits. There were pressed-glass preserve stands filled with peach and gooseberry preserves. For dessert there was a choice of damson cobbler or oversized servings of cake and boiled custard, the latter Aunt Martha's special tribute to Underwood.

"If McElroy and his family were here, it would be perfect," said Jane again.

"Perfect here at Three Springs, yes, daughter, but three miles from here they are cutting down cedar trees that have been growing for three hundred years, and for no other purpose than to make it easier to kill men."

"Perhaps to kill men, but for what? I will tell you—to save Three Springs and Bowling Green and Kentucky from invaders. There never was a time when men were not cutting down cedar trees to save their homes from tyrants——"

"Jane, could I bribe you to change the subject with another piece of cake?"

"Yes, Mother," said Jane contritely. "I have told Jackson a thousand times that I talk too much. Which one of you did I get it from?" She looked from her father to her mother and back.

"Neither one," said Rumsey Skiles. He smiled faintly. "I have heard that in the days of Henry the Eighth there was a Skiles who talked too much—well, a little freely."

"I like to hear a Skiles talk," said Jackson Shobe.

"I like to hear her too, but I repeat the point. It could do harm in wartime."

"There's just one man here who is old enough to talk all he wants to—that is, besides me," said Trez Covington.

"I expect I'm that feller," said Bill Willie from down the table, "but when people gets real old like us and knows what not to say they're jest natchelly entitled to keep their mouths shet too, and I think I'm going to do a passel of it for a spell now."

"You thought about doing any trading with the army, Uncle Trez?" asked Virgil Covington. "Maybe you could sell them some of your beef cattle just as they stand."

"That's the trouble. You don't sell anything to armies. When they take a notion for a steer or a hog, they just come and get it. Soldiers carry guns instead of cash. I suppose, Virgil, you were hinting at that trick you thought you played on me a long time ago. You didn't take me in. I saw through that all the time. It was my way of putting a little spunk into you. It worked too. I hate to think how you would have turned out if I hadn't taken the trouble to spunk you up some."

"Grandpa, I am hungry," said Lena.

"I am starving, Grandma," said Caroline.

"We would miss you two girls from the table," said Wells.

"I can't help wanting a piece of the ham that Grandpa sliced," said Lena. "I have eaten every scrap you gave me."

"The fried chicken is better," said Caroline. "Grandma gave the pieces."

"Rumsey, will you serve Lena a piece of ham? I'll help Caroline to another piece of chicken."

The two boys observed this but said nothing. They ate their dinner quietly and with dignity.

"Aunt Martha, don't let Wells get low on his tonic," said Jane.

Rumsey Skiles's mind was still on the soldiers. "How many soldiers, Robin, would you say General Buckner has in town?"

"I have heard ten thousand. Anyhow, too many! When you want to go somewhere, you usually find the streets blocked. You can't walk along the pavement."

"Do you really believe the Yankees are moving this way?" asked Virgil Covington.

Rodes chose his words delicately. "I would say that sooner or later the Federal troops will arrive in Bowling Green."

"Then that would mean a battle here?"

"Unless General Buckner retreats."

"Then there will be a battle," said Jane sharply. "He will not retreat."

"We will all be neutral here today," said Ella Skiles, her eyes restrainingly upon Jane. She knew then that the family reunion to which she had looked forward so fondly would have to be managed with care. Robin Rodes and Sally were friends of long standing, but it had been a mistake to invite them, for Robin Third was away with the Federal troops. Jane would find that difficult to overlook. Furthermore, Jane and her two brothers did not regard the issue with a common thought. The men would not unreservedly come out for the cause of the South. Jane would speak her mind without restraint or evasion. Jackson would endorse without hesitation whatever Jane said. The conversation must be kept on food or farming or anything except war.

"Maybe you would like to know, Sally, that Jane brought this corn from her home."

"Then I like it all the better."

"I have never eaten a better dinner, Mother," said Underwood.

"I went up on College Hill and watched a company of soldiers eat their dinner," said Uncle Trez. "It wasn't a dinner. It wasn't even a snack. I don't know how they do their work with the victuals they give them."

"Most people eat twicet too much," said Bill Willie. "I know I do, and you do too." He looked across the table at Uncle Trez. "A spoonful of nothin' would be about all you need, the work you do. What'd them soldiers have to eat?"

"A boiled scrub potato, a piece of fat meat that you had to look at three times to see it, a little chunk 'of hardtack, and that was all."

Bill Willie looked across the array of food before him to the head of the table. "Tell him what you all had to eat on the way from Virginny. You was along. Tell him ifn he got weakly, or anything. You can feed a soldier so that he's not worth a dime as a fightin' man."

"If I was starving like they are I would fight too," Uncle Trez said.

"Our troops will win battles because they are right," said Jane, "and food won't have much to do with it."

Jane caught her mother's imploring look and relapsed into silence.

"I have the notion, Jane," said Uncle Trez, "that they made a mistake when they got General Buckner. You are the one they ought to have picked."

"There are two kinds of dessert," said Ella. "Aunt Martha will pass both around. Take your choice."

"Better tell me beforehand," said Uncle Trez, "so I can make up my mind which one and not take both."

"Take both, by all means, Uncle Trez. One is a damson cobbler and the other is custard and cake."

"After what Bill Willie said, I don't think I ought to take but one. I suppose I'll get along better on the custard and cake. But I intend to keep an eye on that old walking famine to see that he doesn't take both!"

When the dinner was eaten, they went out on the veranda. The children played out in the yard. The day was unseasonably hot.

"This air has the feel of rain in it. What are you going to do now, Jackson, since you have your wheat planted?"

"I have a lot of fence that needs straightening up, Uncle Trez. I'll start on it the first thing."

A man rode in a gallop up to the gate. Rumsey Skiles saw that it was Hubert Horsley, the magistrate from the Graham Springs section. Only something imperative could cause Horsley to come in that hurry. Rumsey started out to meet him, but Horsley threw his reins over a post and came walking rapidly up toward the house.

"What is it, Hubert?"

"The Yankees. There's a raiding party of them up somewhere about Dripping Springs. They are out stealing horses. One man who saw them said they must have over fifty now. Some of us thought we ought to warn people."

"Warn us to do what?" said Uncle Trez.

"Hide your horses till they are gone. They might not get down this far, but they could. Everybody might just as well fix up a place to hide his horses till this blows over. Hide them out in the woods, under a bluff, anywhere so they can't find them too easy."

"Isn't there some danger from Confederate raiding parties?" asked Robin Rodes.

"Jackson," said Jane sharply, "we'd better be going. That is our section. I don't want the Yankees to get our horses."

"Reckon we'd better hide ours?" asked Bill Willie. "I can get them out of sight in a half hour."

"We'll not bother yet awhile. This party won't reach here, and if another gets close, we will hear about it in time. It was really thoughtful for you to let us know, Squire. Won't you have something to eat? We have just finished our dinner."

"I would be much obliged for a bite. I am a little hungry."

"Where were the Yankees the last time you heard of them?" asked Jackson Shobe.

"This side of Rocky Hill, the word I had. They were coming this way. It seemed like they knew how people stood. They weren't taking any Yankee horses."

"We had better get home by sundown," said Jane. "We can stay an hour or so yet. Let's you and me, Wells, take a walk as we used to."

Jane and her brother went out the gate and turned down the road toward Richpond. "That's an odd thing," said Underwood, watching them. "Jane and I have always loved each other like a brother and sister, but I don't think we ever took a walk together in our lives. Wells used to think he would make a farmer, and he and Jane would talk about it by the hour. He got over it, but she didn't."

"Maybe that's why she liked me," said Jackson Shobe. "Jane is as good a farmer as I ever knew. She knows when everything should be planted, how it should be cultivated, and when it should be harvested. She is an expert judge of a hog or a horse or a cow. The hens at home never laid much in the fall. I don't know what she has done to them, but ours are laying now."

"Ifn you all will excuse me," said Bill Willie, "I will go and get me a nap. I always sleep awhile after dinner on Sunday. I'll watch out for your hosses. Much obliged, ma'am, for a mighty good dinner." He left and went on toward his house.

"Bill Willie must be failing pretty fast to pamper himself like that," said Uncle Trez.

"Bill Willie is not going to sleep," said Rumsey Skiles. "It's the first time I ever heard of him taking a Sunday-afternoon nap. My guess is that he will be getting ready to move the horses if the Federals get closer."

Uncle Trez said that he would have to be leaving soon too. He also had some horses.

Not long after that, Jane and Wells returned from their walk. "What do you think?" she said gaily. "Things have changed a lot. I tried to get Wells up on farming, and he quoted Horace on me, or maybe it was Homer. I think it was Homer."

She kept an alert eye on Robin Rodes while she was speaking, for she was hinting at an old joke that was a favorite among the families.

Rodes smiled wryly and asked, "Homer who?"

"Tell him, Wells. I never did know which Homer it was."

Squire Horsley came out on the veranda. "Mighty good eatin'," he said, smacking his lips. "If the Yankees show up again we'll get you word, Mr. Skiles. Us Southerners got to stick together."

He got on his horse and rode away. A look both puzzled and troubled was on Rumsey Skiles's face.

7

JANE AND JACKSON left for home. The others sat and talked but the joy had gone out of it. There was something preoccupied in the words they used and their manner of saying them. Something had weakened the zest of the reunion. The Rodeses left in midafternoon. Uncle Trez rode away just behind them. Underwood and Wells and their families were prepared to stay till Monday morning.

By ten o'clock low, sullen thunder was rumbling among the river hills and widespread areas of the sky were brightened by the lightning's warm, sad glow. The clouds mounted deliberately. An hour later the lightning had changed to brilliant, serrated streaks, and the thunder was a continuous roar and crash. The children had long since gone to bed and were sleeping soundly. The others sat in the parlor. Perhaps there were things waiting to be said, but the fury of the storm put them out of mind. They heard the wind strike, and the creak of the trees in the yard outside as they twisted and writhed. The wind died for a few moments, only to gain strength for a more prolonged assault. They heard the sharp *clink* of hail against the windows, and its muffled rattle, striking against the roof. When the thunder and lightning and wind had made ready for the rain, it fell with a great splash against the house. For a half hour the wind and the rain searched with savage cunning for any weak place in the roof, or windows, or wherever a joining might occur in the wooden parts. A person could have read almost from the illumination cast by the flashes of lightning but he could not have spoken, for his voice could not have been heard above the thunder. Finally, the thunder faded away and the wind sank into an occasional murmur, leaving only the rain, which fell steadily throughout the night. It was still raining on Monday when dawn revealed a drenched world.

"I suppose Jackson is at work on his fences by now," said Wells at breakfast, trying valiantly to introduce a note of cheer, "and Jane is instructing her hens on the fine art of laying."

"Poor Jane," said Ella Skiles.

"Why do you say that, Mother?" asked Underwood.

"She told me that she expects Jackson to enlist by Christmas. I want you children to write to her every chance you get. She will need it."

"She knew this might happen. Why did she marry when she did?"

"Answer your own question, Underwood."

Underwood's wife said, "I can answer for him. If he were in Jackson's place and I in Jane's, we would both want to marry."

"Perhaps you are right, my dear, but it does seem almost like a way to provide Jane with widowhood."

"Don't say it, son. I am troubled enough already. I must tell you the rest of it. Jackson and Jane have talked it over, and now he is working almost day and night to get the farm in order."

"What will Jane do?"

"I will tell you," said Wells, "I will tell you what she will do. She will run the farm while he is gone. She will do both her work and his. She wouldn't think of anything else. Sometimes this war seems like a nightmare to me."

His father said, "It has been a nightmare to me, Wells, since I saw those cedar trees on Vinegar Hill lying there like soldiers dead on a battlefield."

Wells's wife tried to divert the gloom. "What did you all think of last night during the storm?"

"The war," replied Rumsey Skiles. "What else could one think of?"

Two hours later the two families left for their homes. Rumsey, hoping to tempt them to stay a little longer, mentioned that they might have some trouble with the creeks. But his sons thought that even if the creeks were up, it wouldn't take them long to run down to a fording level.

"Don't wait for us to ask you specially," said their mother. "This is your home. You don't need an invitation. Your father and I will be needing you."

They drove away, the father and mother standing at the gate, watching until they were hidden behind a bend in the road. Aunt Martha stood on the veranda, waving a brawny arm, and dabbing with a kerchief at her eyes. Bill Willie stood out in the yard of his little house, and he too was waving good-by to them. There was no glimpse of the sun that morning. The clouds had yielded all their moisture, but there was no break in the chill grayness.

8

ON THAT DAY the first violence occurred in Bowling Green. It was then that the Confederate forces started throwing their breastworks across the rear premises of Mr. Theron Finn, on College Hill. Mr. Finn, a staunch and outspoken Unionist, ordered the soldiers off his place. The sergeant in charge had been advised repeatedly to use tact in such instances. He informed Mr. Finn that he was merely obeying orders, and that if he wished he could make complaint to his superior officer.

"Where's General Buckner? Bring him here," Mr. Finn shouted.

"Sorry, Mister. Lieutenant Garrett is back there. You could see him."

"You get off my place, and bring General Buckner here. Right now."

Sergeant Miller was not by nature a patient man, and his tact was a matter of thin veneer. "Mister, I don't know General Buckner from Adam's off ox. I never set eyes on him and I don't know where he is. He wouldn't come here if I hunted him up and told him to, and I ain't going to do that. You two soldiers in that ditch, a shovel ain't something you hug. It's something you dig with."

"This is my property," shrilled Mr. Finn. "I own it. You get off, all of you."

Sergeant Miller recaptured a faint fragment of his acquired tact. "Mister, any time there ain't a war on and you order me off, I'll be off by the time you get through ordering. When there's a war on, you jest don't pay no attention to fellers that say they own the property you're working on. You soldier with that pick, stop using it like you are suffering from some fatal sickness. You better get well."

Mr. Finn looked with bloodshot eyes at his violated premises. He walked back to his house, went into the hall, and took a single-barreled pistol from a drawer. He returned to the soldiers in the back yard. Very mistakenly he leveled the pistol at Sergeant Miller whose attention at the moment was elsewhere. "Get these men off my place."

Sergeant Miller turned about, saw the pistol, and lunged after it. He caught the bullet in his shoulder. At the same time one of the soldiers struck Mr. Finn on the head with his shovel, using more force than had been his practice in shoveling dirt.

Sergeant Miller stood holding his wounded shoulder with one hand, and looking down at the unconscious Mr. Finn. He turned his mild, blue eyes on the soldier who still gripped his shovel with militant fervor.

"Thank you kindly, Private Speck. I plain don't know what to do with this feller." He touched Mr. Finn with the toe of his boot. "Maybe I'd shoot a feller too who was digging up my yard. What do you say do with him, Private Speck?"

"I say for you to get that shoulder to a doctor, Sergeant."

"Has this army got a doctor? I never heard of one. Maybe I better go and see the lieutenant, like this feller wouldn't. He'll know what to do."

"Why don't you send for General Buckner?" asked Speck blandly.

"This shoulder is starting to hurt. I better see somebody. You all keep on digging this ditch while I am gone, only you might work a little harder while I am not looking."

The army did have a doctor, and he treated Sergeant Miller's shoulder. He said that the wound wasn't serious, but he ordered the sergeant to rest two days. Sergeant Miller considered that amount of rest excessive. He was back with his men in an hour.

"I never expected to see you again except at your funeral," said Private Speck. "A couple of soldiers come and toted the man away. He still wasn't hardly at himself. He spoke language onfitten for one of Jeff Davis' soldiers to listen to. I see you got your shoulder fixed up something fancy."

The word of the episode spread throughout the town and tended to harden men in their already committed positions. *The Southern soldiers were common robbers who ruthlessly seized private property for their own selfish purposes.* Came the antiphonal response: *Any man who would accept the cause of tyranny forfeited all rights to property.*

In the course of a few days, Mr. Finn was released from the tent in which he was held as prisoner. He listened surlily to stern admonitions, then went home to find that the completed chain of fortifications ran diagonally across his back yard. He should have known by then that in time of war an individual hasn't much of a chance against an army, but Mr. Finn was never one to learn quickly.

The breastworks grew till a chain of six hills bristled with them. They stared out grimly as if daring the North to test their strength. The raiding parties kept reappearing in unexpected places, but for the time none came nearer than the one which had reached Dripping Springs. General Buckner had some raiding parties canvassing the livestock resources of known Yankee sympathizers in the Green River country. General Buckner was ordered by his superiors to destroy the bridge at Munfordville. It was a difficult order for the general to relay. It was his home town, and the people were proud of the new bridge. So he issued the order with some revisions. The order was to destroy one pier of the bridge, but not all of it. It would be easy to rebuild after the war, and the damage done would hold the Yankees off just as effectively as would complete destruction.

9

BUT NOT ALL of the anxious glances of Generals Johnston
and Buckner were turned northward. Word kept reaching them that
General Grant and Commodore Foote were massing forces for an
assault upon the defenses of the Cumberland and Tennessee rivers.
The generals were painfully aware of the vulnerability of those rivers.
The Tennessee gave access southward from Paducah through Kentucky, then south and a little east through Tennessee and into Ala-
bama. There it turned eastward to Decatur and Chattanooga. The
Cumberland left the Ohio at Smithland, twelve miles up from Paducah. Its course through Kentucky closely paralleled that of the Tennessee, turned to the east through northern Tennessee, then turned
back into Kentucky. At the Tennessee line the rivers were separated
by a narrow neck of land only twelve miles across. There the Confederacy chose to place its major resistance. A fort named Henry was constructed on the Tennessee, and a fort named Donelson on the Cumberland. The site of Fort Henry seems to have been ill chosen. It
possessed few of the advantages that the fort soon was to need. The
location of Fort Donelson was much wiser. The invaders would find it
more difficult to conquer. But at both places there were a lot of brick-
making and very little straw; there were more diggers than picks
and shovels, more riflemen than rifles. The telegraph wires to Richmond burned with pleas for the necessaries of war. More promises
came back than tools. Colonel Randal McGavock, of the Tenth Tennessee, rode his thoroughbred saddle horse, Tenth Legion, to Bowling
Green to see if assistance could come from there. The troubled look
deepened on the faces of Generals Buckner and Johnston. They desperately needed building supplies themselves. And even then General
Buell was repairing the wounded pier of the Munfordville bridge.

On an early Monday morning Jane Shobe rode at a fast canter up to
the gate at Three Springs. Her father had just come out on the veranda on his way to the office in town, and her mother had come as
far as the steps with him. They saw Jane before she reached the gate.
Something was wrong. They watched their daughter as she came half
walking, half running up to the house. There was no fright on her
face, only a sort of startled pride.

They knew then what it was, but they asked in one voice, "What is it, Jane?"

"It is Jackson. He has gone with the soldiers."

They did not ask which soldiers. They knew. "When, Jane?"

"About sundown, yesterday. They came by about three o'clock and talked with him. They went on to some other places. Jackson was ready when they came back. I think they are going to Tennessee, though they wouldn't say for certain."

"Come in, Jane, and eat some breakfast."

"I ate breakfast before I left home. I wanted to tell you and Father." She paused, then continued slowly. "Jackson and I reviewed all our plans while the soldiers were away. We had talked them over many times before. Mr. Howell, on the place, is a good steady man, and his son is a good worker. We can get other hands when we need them. We will get the work done. You understand, don't you, that Jackson had to go? He felt that way."

"We understand, Jane," said her mother. "Come into the house and rest awhile. I am not willing for you to start back till you have eaten something and rested. You are going to need all your strength, child."

"All right, Mother, but I can't stay long."

Rumsey Skiles stayed at home till his daughter rode away, her head held high. "The war has come very close, Ella." His eyes moved toward Bowling Green, three miles away. "God help Sally Rodes," he said. "A son in the Northern army, a cousin in the Southern!"

"God help all of us, Rumsey. We will be needing it."

"They have put the Confederate state capitol at Bowling Green. I think it was a bad thing to do. What good can it do the Southern cause, and it will make things much more difficult here. The North will be vengeful about that."

The autumn turned into winter. Gradually but surely, the war threw its coils more tightly about the section. Gradually but surely, life lost its old freedom and charm. Gradually, old friends drew apart, farther apart. The majority of the people sympathized with the South, but the partisans of the North were just as vocal, tended just as much to violence.

The Meadows home on the Russellville pike flew the Stars and Bars from its front gatepost. Across the pike, not half a mile away, was the McGinnis home, and from its front gatepost rippled the Stars and Stripes. Two sons from the Meadows home were in the Southern army. One from the McGinnis home was with General George Thomas. Some of General Buckner's cavalrymen rode down the lane to the McGinnis home and, without bothering to dismount, shot the flag down. The family had another flag, and early the next day, as it floated above the gatepost, the same soldiers rode along the pike. The leader dismounted, removed the flag, tossed it to a comrade. "Keep that as evidence," he said.

He walked rapidly up to the house and rapped on the door. An old man, the grandfather of the lad with Thomas, answered the summons. The sight softened the complaint he had planned to make. "Do not put a flag back there," he said, and turned back to his men. He knew from their sounds that the old man's words were defiant, but he did not catch their content.

The McGinnises saw the Southern flag was still lifted above the Meadows gatepost, and their long friendship, which lately had been weakening, stopped altogether. It was that way with a great many neighbors in the section. Irresponsible and shiftless men on both sides stole what they could from their neighbors on the other side and charged the theft to patriotism. The traditional friendliness of the people broke into factions.

By Christmas the community was stirred with bitterness. The Underwood family was one of economic substance and intellectual distinction, but its members spoke their minds with reckless regard to safety. It had from the first been a Union family. The Underwoods and the Skileses had been friends for a generation, and Rumsey Skiles had named a son for the family. A report of the Underwoods' undisguised partisanship reached General Buckner. It was important enough to bring on a conference with General Johnston. Immediately the home of Warner Underwood, one of the section's finest, was required for use as Southern quarters. And that but opened other fountains of bitterness.

One night Virgil Covington said to his wife, "Harriet, we have got to do something about Uncle Trez. He is talking too much. He is going to get into trouble."

"Nobody yet has stopped Uncle Trez when he wanted to talk."

"Then he had better stop wanting to. If he doesn't he's likely to find himself in one of General Buckner's jails."

"Not that old man, Virgil."

"Well, maybe not jail, but something that would bother him a lot more. Uncle Trez has got a lot of good stock, and there isn't a thing that the Southern army would appreciate more than some good horses and beef cattle."

"Do you mean they would take his stock?"

"You just ought to listen to the way President Jefferson Davis would applaud it. Yes, they would take his stock."

"What has he been saying?"

"That he would be glad when the Union troops got to Bowling Green, the way the Confederates have been treating people. When he said it, he was thinking of the Underwoods. Jefferson Spalding heard him say it, and about a dozen others. It will be God's mercy if that doesn't get to the Confederate officers. And that might mean that some of our Confederate friends would get beef to eat for a few days."

"I expect you had better go talk with him about it."

"I did for an hour this afternoon. Uncle Trez used to have some sense, specially business sense. I think he is going to pieces. He said the Lord gave him his tongue to talk with and the Lord wouldn't like it if he stopped using it. I tell you the old man is breaking up."

Harriet sat thinking. "Maybe you ought to help him, Virgil. He has three or four of the best horses in the state. He really would go to pieces if he lost them. It would be bad for him to lose his cattle, but a lot worse to lose his horses. I heard that Claude Moorman took his horses to the Richards down in Simpson County to keep the Yankees from getting them. Couldn't you hide Uncle Trez's out somewhere till things blow over?"

"I told him I would, but he won't let me. I tell you he's going to pieces."

"Then don't ask him. Take them away some night."

"Where could I take them?"

"I don't know, but there must be some place. It would kill Uncle Trez for anything to happen to his horses. He could stand losing his cattle but not his horses. You have got to help him. Virgil, are our horses in any danger?"

"I don't think so. I have kept my mouth shut till my jaws are rusty. General Buckner has promised not to disturb the property of people who are neutral."

"It isn't quite like us to be neutral."

"No, it isn't. But what else could we be? We are getting old, at least I am. We have friends on both sides. We have no children. What else could we be?"

"If we had a son, we wouldn't be neutral, Virgil."

"That is another reason for wishing we had one. I don't like being a neutral. But what else can I be?"

"I have just thought of it," she said excitedly. "Take Uncle Trez's horses to the Duncans at Rockfield. They'd be safe there."

"The Duncans are Southern people," he said.

"They *are* Southern people. Everybody knows that. That's the last section the Yankees will get to. Besides, no one would ever look in that pasture field down on Clear Fork Creek."

"And all the people in that section are pretty good people. I don't believe there is a one who would report that Uncle Trez's horses were there. Harriet, that's a good idea. I'll speak to Uncle Trez about it. I believe I will go over there now."

He found his uncle entirely unco-operative. "Those are my horses," he said emphatically. "I don't owe anybody a red cent on a one of them or, as far as that is concerned, on anything else. Those horses are going to stay right here, and I'll shoot the first Rebel who lays a hand on one of them."

"I would be a little careful about using the word *Rebel*."

"Oh, I won't use it in public, but that is my barn yonder and my barn lot and my pasture. And those are my horses."

"That is what Mr. Theron Finn thought about his back yard."

"That was a crime, the way they treated Theron. He's not in any more trouble, is he?"

"They have him back in a tent that they are using for a jail. He had a pile of rock that he had picked up from his premises, and the other night he carried them and dumped them in the ditch the soldiers had dug. It was his property, all right. But he *is* a prisoner of war."

"Well, these are my horses. I'm going to keep them right here, and I have got a loaded gun on the rack in the back hall."

Virgil saw that it was no use trying to convince his uncle that discretion was a large part of current virtue. That night after midnight he saddled his horse and rode to his uncle's. He hitched his horse at the lot gate and went into the barn carrying three halters. The horses knew him and offered no resistance.

He led the three as best he could along narrow roads, by a circuitous route. He went through the Blue Level country. Surely there would be no soldiers abroad at that hour. He came back into the main road at Providence Knob. But he stayed on the pike only a few hundred yards. He turned to the right along a country road and continued along it about three miles. Then he turned into a lane at the left. It led to the Duncan house, a quarter of a mile away. It was full daylight then, and Hector Duncan was standing on the front porch. He saw a man riding up to his gate and leading three horses. He went out to meet him.

At the gate, he recognized his visitor. "Virgil Covington, what on earth are you doing here? Which side are you stealing horses for?"

Virgil explained the situation to him. "I know it is an imposition, but that crazy uncle of mine would be almost certain to lose his horses, and that would simply mean that we would have to bury him."

"We can't let Uncle Trez be buried yet awhile. We can put them in that meadow down on the creek. I don't think they will be bothered there, and the best thing about this community is that nobody tells anything that would get his neighbor into trouble. The grass is pretty good, and I have a couple of haystacks close. I doubt if you would get them back in as good flesh as they are now, but I'll see that they don't starve. But, for heaven's sake, don't let Uncle Trez chirp where they are."

"He won't know. I am not going to tell him."

"What are you going to tell him?"

Virgil Covington smiled sheepishly. "To tell the truth, I hadn't even thought of that. I guess I will have to tell him where I brought them. I can't let him think that the Confederates got them during the night."

"You had better tell him something. If he thought they got his horses, he would be sleeping with Mr. Theron Finn in no time at all."

"You heard about Mr. Finn?"

"We heard the day it happened. I had been expecting something would happen to him. If they let him out again, he will be right back with them the next time they look."

"Uncle Trez is a stubborn man. If he learns that his horses are here, he may be coming after them any time."

"He and his horses both would be safer if he didn't."

Virgil pondered over the matter all the way back, and decided to tell his uncle immediately. He dreaded telling him. "He will have a spell of the cramps," he said aloud. "I have got to lay the law down to that old man."

The matter worked out oddly, and almost disastrously. At breakfast, Uncle Trez was startled by a sharp, imperious rapping at his front door.

"Somebody must have got snakebitten from all that racket," he said to Napoleon, his ancient servitor. "See who it is."

He was back in a brief minute. "It's de soldiers, suh."

"Soldiers! What do they want?"

"Dey say dey got to see you, suh."

"Soldiers! Tell them to wait till I finish my breakfast. Soldiers!"

"I 'spect you bettuh go talk wid 'em now, suh."

Uncle Trez looked at Napoleon for fully a half minute. Then he pushed his chair back and walked through the hall toward the front door. He saw that one soldier was standing at the door and that seven others waited on horseback at the gate.

"Yes, what is it?"

The soldier studied a paper he held in his hand. "We have here a requisition for use in the Confederate army of three horses which you are reported to own."

"Three horses! Get off my place."

The soldier had been ordered off places so often that it merely bored him. "Go on to the barn and get them," he called to his companions. He ignored Uncle Trez's further explosions, and turned and walked back to the gate. He took the reins of his horse from one of the soldiers, then mounted and followed the others toward the barn. Uncle Trez followed, emphasizing his sense of outrage at every step.

One of the soldiers came out of the barn just as Uncle Trez and the leader of the squadron arrived. "There's no hosses in there," he called.

"You didn't look good," said the leader. "It says *three horses*. You go look again."

"There are three horses in there," said Uncle Trez, "and they are my horses. Don't you touch a one of them."

The men came back. "There isn't a horse in this barn. There is plenty of empty stalls, but no horse."

Uncle Trez ran and stumbled by the soldiers. His quick inspection showed that the stalls indeed were empty. He turned upon the leader. "You have got my horses already."

"We were sent out here to get three horses," the soldier said. "We have never seen this place before. We don't know what has become of your horses. It looks to me like you heard we were coming and hid them out. If you did, we will find them."

He spoke to his men. They divided into groups of two and started a systematic search of the outlying fields. "I think I'll stay here where I can keep an eye on you, old man. I don't know what shenanigan you might be up to." He climbed to the top of a rail fence, made himself secure there, and gave philosophic thought to the ways and phases of the universe.

Anger dammed up the flow of Uncle Trez's statements. He started to the house running. It was firmly in his purpose to shoot the soldier sitting on his fence.

Nap met him at the door. "You be keerful, suh," he admonished. "You ain't as young as you used to be."

"All I want is that gun in the hall rack. Get out of my way, you rascal."

"Found out about your horses, Uncle Trez?" asked Virgil Covington, rising from one of the windows through which he had been watching the episode.

"They have stolen my horses. Don't you try to talk me out of shooting that scoundrel sitting on my fence."

"If they already have them, what are they looking for?"

"They want to steal them again, and I won't have it. This is my place. I'll kill him just to let them know they can't trifle with me."

"Quiet down, Uncle Trez, quiet down. Nobody has stolen your horses. I warned you about this the other day. You weren't interested. You didn't even listen carefully to what I said. I came last night and moved your horses to where I think they will be safe."

"You took them?"

"Right after midnight. I spent the night with your horses."

"You didn't get my consent to take them anywhere."

"And I am not going to tell you where I took them, at least, not for a while. But I am going to tell you that when you act like this you are inviting trouble. They would have taken the horses if they had been here, and you likely would have succeeded in getting your barn burned down besides."

"It is my barn!"

"Yes, and it's Warner Underwood's house, but he is not living in it. When they come back from their search, tell them that you have no idea where your horses are—and you don't. You tell them that the last time you saw them they were in the barn. And they were. If you don't do what I tell you, then you can take care of your own stock from now on. They will be back soon, and when they ask you questions, you tell them what I told you to. And don't use the word *Rebel* once. I'd hate to see them burn down your barn, and that might put them in the notion to burn down your house too."

"Well, I'll not tell them. It's none of their business where those horses are."

"I don't believe I'd mention that either. They are sensitive people."

A little while later, the leader returned to the house. Uncle Trez met him.

"Do you know where those horses are?"

"I'll swear I thought they were in the barn when you went out there."

"That's the way he acted to me," said one of the soldiers.

"Did you take or send your horses somewhere else?" persisted the leader.

"I don't lie the first time, young fellow."

The man pondered. Then he said, "All right, I'll report back at headquarters that the horses are gone, and that under oath you said that you had nothing to do with moving them and that you do not know where they are. I expect it would pay you to be careful." He glanced casually toward the barn. "Things out here would burn right quickly." He mounted his horse and they rode away.

Uncle Trez looked at his nephew and chuckled. "When a man is named Covington, he can think up things. Looks like I bought me another filly just as she stands."

10

BAD NEWS CAME. General Buell's engineers had repaired the bridge at Munfordville, and the enemy was massed only a little more than forty miles away. Information thought to be dependable held that for every two soldiers in the section wearing gray, there were three wearing blue; that for every rifle available for Southern use, there were three ready to be placed in Northern hands; that for every piece of Southern artillery, the North had four. And the wiser Southern heads knew that the odds on the rivers were pretty desperate.

Late one day, Jane arrived at Three Springs. She had received a letter from Jackson, who was at Fort Donelson. He had secured permission to make a visit home. It was his plan to arrive that night sometime between dark and midnight. It would be safer for them to meet at Three Springs than at their home, that being more exposed to the Northern troops. He would make every effort to be there.

Jane and her parents ate supper and talked. Everything was in good order on her place. There had been no visits from the Yankees, though they had foraged two or three times not very far away. Her stock was in good order. Her horses were reasonably fat, and her cows were giving so much milk that she had to feed a lot of it to the hogs. At the end of every mouthful of food, and almost at the end of every sentence, she would look anxiously toward the door. It was a long way to Fort Donelson, but she knew that Jackson would use every effort to reach home at the soonest possible moment. Jane wanted to know what the news was in town. She said that the Yankees might just as well have it then for all the news she got. Her father and mother could tell her of a great many rumors, but not much unquestioned fact. It was true that the soldiers on Vinegar Hill had been transferred to Baker's Hill across the river, leaving the fortifications on Vinegar Hill only half finished. But Baker's Hill would be the more strategic since it towered directly in the pathway of the oncoming Yankees. The fortifications on College Hill were completed, and of them the Southern officers were duly proud. Jane said she could see the reason for fortifying Baker's Hill, but it had always seemed to her that the only use of Vinegar Hill would be to protect Tennessee. She asked about Mr. Finn. Had he been released? He was at the moment at liberty, but the Confederates would have him back almost any day. His family had been moved out of their home on College Hill.

"If he can't behave himself, he belongs in prison," said Jane stoutly. "I had a letter from Underwood the other day. I was ashamed of him."

"You mustn't say a thing like that," said her mother sadly.

"He said that he was sorry to hear that Jackson had enlisted. Jackson has more patriotism in his little finger than Underwood has in all of him. I mean it."

"I will not have you make such rash statements. It is not fair to Underwood, or to you, or to Jackson."

"I am sorry, Mother." She turned her eyes quickly to the door, but it was the wind that had rattled it.

The father sought to turn the conversation to another direction. "I am proud of the part the churches are playing in this crisis. The pastors have been fine. There are more soldiers in town now than citizens."

"Mr. Middleton, our neighbor, said that Dr. Smoot had got into some kind of quarrel," Jane said.

"He is my pastor, and I like him. But he is often unwise in his speech, and it is a wonder that he hasn't got into more than a quarrel," Rumsey said.

"He tells the truth," said Jane.

"Truth can be pretty brassy, Jane, and silence can be golden. Sometimes his sermons are more of an exhortation for the South than anything else, and some of his best members are Unionists. He has offended several uselessly. If the Union forces take Bowling Green, I fear that one of their first acts would be to close our church."

"They will not take Bowling Green, Father," said Jane sharply.

"I don't expect it, Jane, but it could happen. Brother Ray of the Baptists and Brother Frogge of the Methodists, though both Southern in sentiment, always preach sermons that a Union man could listen to without discomfort. The Catholic congregation, though likely the most evenly divided of all, manages its worship very carefully. Father DeVries holds the respect of both sides. The Episcopal church is without a rector just now, and most of its members worship with us."

"Aunt Martha is visiting her daughter tonight," said Mrs. Skiles. "Jackson will be hungry when he gets here. I'll go get some hot supper ready for him." She went into the kitchen.

Jane turned to her father. "You don't expect the Yankees to capture Bowling Green, do you?" She was almost pleading.

"No, I don't expect it," he repeated, "but I am trying to prepare my mind for it if they do. There's Jackson now."

But Jane had heard the footsteps before he had, and she was at the door by the time her father had finished speaking. She ran across the veranda and flung herself into her husband's arms. "It has been a hundred years since I saw you, honey, and if you had been any later, I would have gone crazy."

"I have thought about you every minute since I left, Jane."

"Come in the house. I want to look at you."

"Good evening, Jackson," said Rumsey Skiles from the dark doorway. "Ella and I want to see you too. When you have greeted each other duly come on in."

Ella came from the kitchen, walking fast. "Didn't I hear something?

Why, Jackson, you have got here. I am so glad. Welcome to your home, Jackson."

Jackson kissed her on the cheek. "That's for you." He kissed her the second time. "And that is in memory of my mother."

"How lovely! Aunt Martha heard about you, Jane, though I can't imagine how she did, and she is back."

Aunt Martha waddled into the room. "I got to see 'em. I got to see 'em both, specially dat Jane lamb."

"Look for Bill Willie any minute now," said Rumsey Skiles, smiling faintly.

"Don't strain your eyes," said Bill Willie from the doorway. "The minute I heard that hoss comin' I said, 'That sounds jest like Jackson Shobe,' and I knowed ifn it was, his hoss ought to be in the barn and fed good. Howdy, Jackson. Howdy, Miss Jane."

"Howdy yourself, Bill Willie," said Jackson. "Good gracious, you are getting younger."

"Started cuttin' another set of teeth the other day. Ifn I was old enough I'd jine the army." He left to take Jackson's horse to the barn.

They all sat in the dining room while Jackson ate a trencherman's supper. Jane rarely took her eyes off her husband.

"When will the war be over, Jackson?"

He looked at her in pained surprise. "Not very soon, Jane. I don't see any signs of it being a short war."

"Can you hold the rivers?" Rumsey Skiles asked.

It was like Jackson to answer in the fewest possible words. "I don't think we can."

And all three of them looked at him, shocked by the brutal simplicity of his words.

He saw the look on their faces and added, "I have never seen Fort Henry, but I have talked with those who have. They don't expect it to stand two days against a serious attack. The Yankees will try to capture it first. After that, can't you see the position that will put us in at Fort Donelson? I don't believe they could ever capture the fort solely by a river attack. But if the Yankees take Fort Henry, that puts their whole army behind us, and the river in front. Can't you see where that will leave us?"

"I see," said Rumsey Skiles.

"Don't let them capture you, Jackson," said his wife, her hands tightly clasped. "If you see they are going to capture the fort, leave right then. Don't let them capture you."

"If there is anything I can do honorably to keep from being captured, I will. I promise you that, Jane. There's another thing that troubles me. Our supplies are in a dreadful state."

"How far is it to Fort Donelson?" asked Jane.

"The way I count it, about eighty miles. I left yesterday just before dinner. I had good luck with the ferryboat at Clarksville. Some of the road is bad, but I have a good horse. We made good time."

"You did, indeed," said Rumsey Skiles.

"There's one thing I have learned, Jane," Jackson said brightly, "and that is to sleep on a horse. I think I must have slept two hours last night. That is a smart horse. When we'd come to a fork in the road, it would stop and I would wake up, and as soon as we got started again, I'd go back to sleep."

"You must be dreadfully tired."

"No, I am not, but I am afraid that horse is."

"Don't bother about your horse. Bill Willie will take care of it. Can you stay several days?"

"I have to be back Tuesday by noon so I'll have to leave late tomorrow afternoon. The weather might get worse. Jane, I have news for you. I have been made a sergeant."

"They don't know you very well, or it would have been a colonel, at least."

"What you have been saying troubles me," said Skiles. "As I have studied the South, it can't very well do without the rivers. What will it do to us here at Bowling Green if you lose the rivers?"

"If that happens we will lose south Kentucky, and almost all of north Tennessee. Jane, how is the farm?"

"I hate to tell you, Jackson, but there isn't a thing wrong with it. Well, I guess it is all right to tell you. You had everything going so well that it kept on going."

"You are the one who has kept it going. But you don't look it. I can imagine what you have been doing, but it has left no marks. When did you leave the place?"

"Three o'clock, but I didn't come down the pike. We hear that the Yankees are likely to be showing up there."

"Have any been around home?"

"None nearer yet than Dripping Springs, but we keep hearing that they have fixed the bridge at Munfordville. That isn't good for the nerves."

"Jackson must be dreadfully tired, Jane. Aunt Martha has your room ready."

11

Sunday morning was chill, and there was a drizzle of rain in the air. There were fires blazing in all the fireplaces when Jane and Jackson came down. The father and mother sat in front of one of them, the father reading a newspaper that had found its way into Bowling Green from Louisville. It was a Union paper, filled with reports of successes, and with forecasts of other triumphs, particularly on the rivers. It carried a scathing condemnation of General Buckner, a number of the particulars of which Skiles knew to be untrue. When he heard Jane and Jackson coming down the stairs, he folded the paper neatly and put it in a bookcase out of sight. They were troubled enough already.

Jane was bothered by the glimpse of the weather she had had from her window. She went immediately out on the veranda. The drizzle of rain had stopped, but it was colder. Something in the look of the clouds warned her of snow. She went back into the house.

"You must leave earlier than you had planned," she told her husband. "It is going to snow."

"Snow doesn't bother me much. I have spent whole days in it."

"It would be all right if you were gathering corn back at home, but from what you said about the roads, this isn't like gathering corn."

"Perhaps I should be going a little while after dinner."

"It is a long ride, and a lot of trouble just to stay that little while," said Ella Skiles.

"It is worth it."

He left about two o'clock. For some reason, his wife was more troubled than she had ever been. Jane's brightness and vivacity had not often been absent but they were then. The weather was part of it. It was a long way to Fort Donelson and over some miserable roads. The clouds still bore the look of snow. She couldn't keep from thinking of the things Jackson had said about matters at the river forts. Jackson was a hopeful man. It was his nature to be. There must be some truth in what he had said. She had brought food from home for him, rather more than he could easily carry. She put what she could in his saddlebags and in bundles to be tied to his saddle. They were up in their room, getting him ready for departure.

"It is a cruel world, isn't it, Jackson? I might never see you again."

"It is possible," he said soberly. "It would be possible if I were at home and went out to gather corn. Things like that have happened."

"One hears of something like that maybe once in a lifetime. But listen to me, Jackson. You are not gathering corn. I know you, Jackson. If there is a battle, you will be in the front of it. I don't know how I could live if you didn't come back to me."

"I know you, Jane, and I know that you would live, and I know the work on the farm would go on. I know that you would do it with your head held high, remembering me. But we'll not talk of that. Someday the war will be over and I will be back."

"You might not, you might not," she said fiercely. "The farm will go on because I know you would want it to go on. I will be farming for you, Jackson, and your son will be with me."

"Or daughter," he said softly.

"Son. And his name will be Jackson. He will make it easier for me."

"It is not like you to talk this way, Jane."

"It is not like me to feel this way. I wish the sun would come out one minute before you leave. I'd like to see it just as a sign. Just one minute! How tall and fine you are! What did I ever do to deserve you as a husband?"

"You gave the right to be. Beyond that, I didn't ever do much to deserve you, Jane."

She looked out the window. "The sun! It is shining." They looked at the sun in silence for a few moments. Then a cloud covered it. "It is time for you to be going, Jackson."

She watched him ride away. At the bend of the road, he drew his horse to a stop, and looked back at her, standing there at the gate. He could see her father and mother, standing together on the veranda. Near them stood Aunt Martha, and down in a corner of the yard Bill Willie Blewett was waving a handkerchief. Jane was waving one too. Jackson Shobe sat there for a moment. Then he drew his horse around, and a few seconds later they could not see him at all. A half hour later Jane left for her home. She rode rapidly, for she was in a hurry to get home. It was there that she seemed closest to Jackson.

12

One morning two weeks later, young Thomas Henry Hines, then risen to captain, rode up to General Albert Sidney Johnston's headquarters at the Underwood house. He went inside, and introduced himself to General Johnston.

"I am glad to see you, Captain. General Buckner gave me a very favorable account of you. You wear the look of a bearer of news. What is it?"

"The Yankees are across Green River, General Johnston."

"It was a mistake not to destroy that bridge completely. How did you learn it?"

"I saw them myself late yesterday. The bridge isn't entirely repaired, so they had to cross in single file and slowly. They would stop at intervals and examine the repairs. I guess they are all across by now. I didn't see them bringing any supplies over, and I didn't see any sign of supplies on this side. I'd say they will be there for a few days longer, maybe a week. But, sooner or later, they will be moving."

General Johnston turned to a map on the wall and immediately found Munfordville. "There it is. It is not far enough away. How many men would you say they have, Captain?"

"I couldn't see the main body of them. It was behind a woods, kept there purposely, no doubt. I saw them with my spyglass from a knob a half mile down the river. I thought you ought to know about it, so I came as quickly as I could. It gave me an excuse to come home for a few hours."

General Johnston's eyes were still on the map. "Two weeks at the most," he said musingly. "Thank God, some of that road is wretched."

"You might be able to stop them from Baker's Hill, sir."

"Slow them down, Captain, not stop them. And merely to delay them might cost us too much. Captain, we are caught in a trap. I can say that to you because from various dependable sources I am assured of your patriotism and discretion. I know about the division in your family, and if anything that adds to the respect I have for you. We are caught in a trap. General Buckner, who is now at Fort Donelson, communicated with me by telegraph wire twice yesterday. The enemy is moving against Fort Henry on the Tennessee. He doesn't think it can hold out two days. He is hopeful about Fort Donelson, but I am not,

if the enemy captures the Tennessee River fort. And if Fort Donelson
is captured, we haven't a chance here. The Yankees have planned and
timed this most cunningly." His eyes were back on the map. "Thank
God for that bad road. It will give us time to decide what to do."

13

BEFORE THE WEEK was over, a message announced the mel-
ancholy news of the surrender of Fort Henry to General Grant. General Albert Sidney Johnston was a trained soldier, with the imagination
of a leader. He knew what surrender meant. He could envision, almost
with the vividness of physical sight, the Union gunboats turning about
in the flooded waters of the Tennessee. They would reach the Ohio
River at Paducah. They would steam up the Ohio for a dozen miles to
the mouth of the Cumberland and there turn their prows toward Fort
Donelson, a hundred and twenty-five miles away. The gunboats would
make the trip in less than a week. General Grant would move his foot
soldiers across the neck of land separating the rivers, timing his progress so as to arrive with the boats. Then the siege would begin. How
long could the fort hold out, pounded from the river by the cannon
on the gunboats and from the rear by the riflemen under Grant? He
answered himself, flinching with pain at the thought of it. Not more
than ten days.

And after that, what about Bowling Green? It was caught between
the jaws of a vise—Buell from the north, Grant from the south. Something had gone wrong. Many things had gone wrong. They had started
going wrong when General Thomas defeated the Southern army at
Fishing Creek in southeastern Kentucky. That freed the Union troops
for the advance on Bowling Green, with no fear of Confederate troops
in their rear. Then the North should not have won Fort Henry so
easily. Something had gone wrong there. All he could do now was to
wait and see and be ready. And waiting too often meant losing.

Captain Tom Henry Hines rode out of Bowling Green along the
Louisville pike. Late the same day he came back with the word that
Buell was marching southward and that his advance guard was at Horse
Cave. And on the same day another scout arrived to say that Fort
Donelson was under siege. For a long time General Johnston pored
over maps spread out on a table before him, and they gave him no
comfort.

A conference was called, and Generals Beauregard and Hardee sat about the table with him. Beauregard inquired what General Tilghman had done to strengthen Fort Henry during his command. The question went unanswered.

"Have you given up the possibility of saving Fort Donelson?" Beauregard asked sharply.

"No," said Johnston with equal sharpness. "We shall use every means of saving it, but the situation is precarious. We might as well admit that."

"That puts the situation here in a peculiar light." Beauregard's Gallic accents were edged with irritation.

"It does, and that is the reason I have asked for this conference. If Fort Donelson can defend itself successfully, the situation here would remain unchanged. If it should fall, then we must leave here, and immediately. What I mean is, if it should fall, these troops must be beyond Nashville before the Yankees arrive there. Anything else would be disastrous."

"It is disastrous as it is."

"How, sir, would you have directed the matter differently?" asked Hardee. His tones were even, but his face was flushed.

"Not being familiar with conditions here, I cannot say. But it will be tragic to lose Bowling Green."

"War itself is tragic, General Beauregard. We shall not retreat from Bowling Green unless it becomes necessary to save the army."

General Beauregard hesitated. Then he said, "You have my best wishes. I have been ordered to inspect the troops at Columbus. It is time for me to be moving on." He bowed with military precision and left the room.

General Hardee looked at General Johnston and said, "Wasn't that the first time he mentioned an order to inspect the troops at Columbus?"

General Johnston said nothing. The two generals sat in silence, studying the maps before them.

General Johnston raised his tired eyes and looked across the table at Hardee. "I fear there is confusion at Fort Donelson," he said, "and part of it is my fault. Perhaps it was a mistake for the three commanding officers there to be placed together. I am greatly concerned."

An orderly came in with a message for General Johnston. He looked at it, closed his eyes for a moment as if summoning courage, then tore it open and read it. He sat looking through the window at the winter weather outside. He read the message again and handed it to General Hardee who read it carefully, word by word.

"This means that we will be leaving here?"

"What else could it mean? The Yankees will be in Nashville within a week after the fort is surrendered. We must be safely beyond Nashville by then," he said again.

"And start developing other battlefields?"

"Certainly. We will select them with more care and staff them with more compatible leaders."

Again he studied the maps, then lifted his eyes to the window, and sat in thought. "I would say, General Hardee, that the next battle will be fought not far from there." He placed a pencil upon a spot on the map. "Not far from there, General Hardee," he repeated. He turned to Captain Ferguson, who was sorting the papers on the table before him. "Captain Ferguson, make out orders for the men on Baker's Hill to be brought into town and joined with those on College Hill. The same, please, for the men on Webb's Hill. When the men and supplies are safely across the river, the bridges are to be destroyed." He looked at General Hardee as if asking for support.

"It is the only thing to do," said Hardee sadly. "There is no way to avoid it."

"Are there orders for the men on College Hill, General, and the other places?" asked Captain Ferguson.

"No." General Johnston paused in thought. "But there will be tomorrow."

14

RUMSEY SKILES hurried back to Three Springs. His wife had not expected him till later in the day. She saw him hitch his horse and come rapidly up the walk. Something was wrong.

She met him on the veranda. "What is it, Rumsey?"

"They are moving the soldiers from Baker's Hill into town. When that is done they are going to destroy the bridge."

"Destroy the bridge? Why?"

"The report is that all Confederate soldiers will be transferred from here to some place farther south. The report is not verified, but it makes good sense. Buell's army, so it is said, is this side of Cave City."

"What does it all mean, Rumsey?"

"It means that the Yankees will come into Bowling Green unopposed. They can get across the river with pontoons. But if the bridge is destroyed, that will leave Jane at Oakland, with no chance of getting into town. She shouldn't stay up there by herself. It could be dangerous for a girl of Jane's spirit. She has four horses and two mules. With Jackson in the Southern army, they would go quickly. I want them brought here. Bill Willie will know where to hide them. I suppose we'll have to risk Jane's cows and hogs. They would be just as safe without her, and she would be safer here than trying to protect them. I am going to ask Bill Willie to go up there right away. She can drive the trap back and bring whatever clothes she needs. He can ride one of the horses and get the rest here somehow. He is an expert at such things."

"You know how Jane is. Do you think she will come?"

"I think she will when Bill Willie explains things to her. If the Yankees overrun those sections, she shouldn't stay. I know that it is best for Jane to be here. I'll go see Bill Willie now."

Bill Willie shared his belief that it would be better for Jane to be at Three Springs, anyhow, "till things blow over," as he put it.

"That may be a long time. Can you manage the horses?"

"I reckon if Virgil Covington can take a herd to Rockfield, I can fetch a few down here."

It took Bill Willie an hour to persuade Jane that it was wise to go to her father's home. Her statements were similar to those of Uncle Trez in like circumstances. It was her farm, there was no mortgage, the taxes were paid. What kind of a country was it that didn't respect true and honest ownership? But Mr. and Mrs. Howell, who lived on the place, supported Bill Willie's arguments. They would stay and carry on the work with no less care and industry than if Jane were there and in close observation. If desired, they would move into the house so as to offer it added protection. They would watch after everything. There might be some trouble, but they would do the best they could.

Jane stood in deep study. Then she said, "All right, I'll go. I don't expect to be away longer than a few days, certainly not over a week or two."

"It might be longer, Miss Jane," said Bill Willie. "Pack up what you need for a month. Better make it two. If we can get you back sooner, we'll do it. I expect you are going to be a right smart trouble to your folks."

Jane grinned with old-time heartiness. "Then I'd better take a little money to pay for my board. I'll be ready in an hour. You and Mr. Howell get the stock ready. It will be worth going, Bill Willie, just to see you take them."

"Where is the Yankees now?" asked Mr. Howell.

"I don't know prezackly. A man said he thought the first of them was this side of Rocky Hill Station. I expect they'll be comin' down the pike tomorrer."

Jane drove slowly along the lane that led to the Louisville pike. It was muddy, and there were some deep holes. Bill Willie followed only a few yards behind. At first, he had some trouble with the animals he was leading. They managed to get in one another's way, and several times Bill Willie had to stop and clear up the confusion into which they had got themselves. But he worked out his system, and soon they were moving freely, though they always crowded the lane. Fortunately, they met no one till they reached the pike. There they almost gasped at what they saw. The pike had been reasonably free of travel when Bill Willie had gone out not much more than two hours before. Now, in the short stretch of the road that was visible, there were not fewer than a half dozen vehicles lumbering southward. Most of them were carrying various articles of furniture. Trunks and sacks were plainly visible in all of them. Behind two of them, a man rode a horse and led two others. A patient cow tethered to the hind gate of a wagon ambled along after one. The pitiful sight could mean but one thing. The Yankees were hard behind them, and they were moving southward toward some sanctuary. Some, Jane thought, would know where to find one. Others, she felt sure, merely hoped that by some chance one might be discovered. How long would they be gone from their homes? Jane could no more than guess about their prospects or hers. And what would they find when they all returned to their homes? The home untouched, as it was that winter day they moved out? Or a sprinkling of ashes and nothing more? The grim faces of those who rode in the wagons were eloquent with fear.

In time, Jane and Bill Willie were passing Baker's Hill. They could see only a few soldiers on its top. The fort that had been the pride of the soldiers who built it given up to the enemy, without even a token protest! It was a new form of hospitality, thought Bill Willie, to spend three months constructing a fort for the exclusive use of the enemy! He puzzled at the irony of it.

At the bridge sentinels stopped them and made inquiries. "We are going to my father's house, three miles east of town," said Jane. "My husband is with your comrades at Fort Donelson. These are our horses. I didn't want to take any chances of the Yankees getting them."

"You got here just in time, ma'am. We are going to tear up this bridge at daylight tomorrow. Just keeping it open now to help folks like you get across. War's a shame, anyway you look at it."

Jane started to answer a bit hotly, saying that all the shame belonged to the Yankees for trying to conquer a free people, but she felt Bill Willie's eyes restraining her. There were several men standing at the bridge. The wrong one might be among them. She had already told them all they needed to know.

One of the soldiers impudently called out, "Why ain't you in the army, Grandpap?"

Bill Willie looked him over coolly. "If you had more grandpaps in your army, you boys wouldn't have to blow up this bridge."

The soldier's comrades laughed appreciatively. "You got your answer, Ed," said one. "Take your medicine."

They drove up Bridge Street, past the Presbyterian church and on to the square. Jane drove ahead in the trap, and Bill Willie came behind with the stock, now under good control. Bowling Green was too much concerned with its long train of woes to pay much attention to such sights. There were a great many wagons on the streets, citizens starting on their journey to the south, anywhere to get out of the way of the advancing blue hordes. A woman on horseback passed them, riding at a gallop. She was dressed in a black coat and hat, and a black veil covered her face. Jane's quick eyes caught a glimpse of the woman. Something about her was familiar. She called to Bill Willie, asking who the woman was.

"That's Miz Nat Grider. She got word yesterday that Motley was killed in a battle in the mountains somewhere. I reckon she's been to the telegraph office to see if they got any more word about him."

"Motley was never any good," said Jane.

"Not much, ma'am, but he's dead now."

"You are right, Bill Willie. I'll never say anything bad about Yankees again except the living ones."

"Miz Grider's a fine woman. So's Nat. Your mother went over to see them this morning."

They turned out the street that led to the Three Springs road, and forty minutes later they were at home. Mrs. Skiles had Jane in her arms by the time her feet reached the ground. "Jane, honey, I am so grateful. We need you here with us."

Rumsey Skiles reached them then. Though he was never a demonstrative man, he joined in the embrace. The tragedy of some of the things he had seen in town left him bleak inside, and the presence of his daughter eased and soothed his mind. He and Bill Willie talked a moment about the horses, but Bill Willie had already decided where to put them, and his decision was quite agreeable to Skiles. Jane's stock was led back to a woodland lot with a shed. The Yankees would have to be quite in earnest to look back there.

Jane, at the continued insistence of her mother, ate a few mouthfuls of supper. "Tell me, Father, what will all this mean? What will it mean in the war?"

"It means, Jane, that your side has made some costly mistakes. We will have to wait to find how well it can learn from them. It means, also, Jane, that very likely Tennessee will become the battlefield of the war."

"Then the war is moving south. Tennessee! Where Jackson is!"

"Jackson is a soldier, and a good one. Good soldiers lead dangerous lives."

"He knew that all along, Father, and I know it now. Let me tell you two something: Before Jackson left, he and I went out to the Shobe graveyard, and we marked out exactly the places we are to be buried. They are under a maple tree that ought to be living for two hundred years. Something might happen to Jackson, or it might happen to me. We tried to think about everything. I remember something Jackson said while we were there in the graveyard. He said, 'Jane, if you die next week, and I live fifty years longer, it will be a widower that they bury.' Wasn't that sweet?"

"Your father never made me a promise like that," said Ella.

"Oh, I wouldn't hold him to it, but I do think it was sweet of him to say it. Yes, Father, I know that anything can happen. I know that Jackson may be wounded, or even killed, in the war. I have been spending my time bracing myself for whatever comes. I would like for Jackson to be spared till next August. He will have a son then."

"And there would be even more need for him to be spared after that," said her mother. "Jane, you are not leaving this table till you have eaten a little more."

Jane nibbled a little longer. Then she asked if any word had come from the boys.

"We have had letters this week from all of them. They seemed well enough, but troubled, of course." The mother did not mention that two of the boys had stated their belief that the Union would win quickly and easily.

Bill Willie came in to mention that the woods lot was what Jane's stock had been hoping for as far back as they could remember. Anyhow, they acted that way. He glanced at Jane's plate and bent an accusing look upon her. He said that it looked to him like the Shobe stock had better appetites than its folks. He asked if Skiles had had any word as to the welfare of Uncle Trez's horses at Rockfield.

"I saw Uncle Trèz in town yesterday. He said that Virgil had been down to see his horses the day before. They were doing fine, though he guessed he would have to sell a couple to pay for their board. He said that he would have gone with Virgil, but one of his knees was stiff and paining him. He said that, sooner or later, he guessed he would go to pieces like you have."

"Why don't he jest give up and save time, with all of his ailments and sufferin'?" asked Bill Willie.

"I never see Uncle Trez but that he brings you up. I have the notion that right now one of his main ambitions is to outlive you, but between us I don't think he has a chance."

15

There was a great deal of sickness in the various Southern camps, some of it severe. The details and casualties of the battle of Fishing Creek were still dribbling into Bowling Green. There had been sharp skirmishes in Virginia and Missouri. A large bulletin board was prepared and placed in the courthouse. Upon it were placed the late bulletins and a list of the dead. There had not been many, but usually there was a crowd standing before it to see what new names had been added. Five Warren County names had been placed on it Friday. The war was getting closer. It had come to the Griders, to the Meadowses, to the Shankses. Those two lists in parallel columns, the one Confederate, the other Union, were searched daily by every family with reason to dread what possibly might be found there.

At daybreak, following Jane's arrival at Three Springs, both the road and railroad bridges were destroyed. Eight hours later, the vanguard of the Union forces arrived. They saw immediately that there would be no crossing of the river except in driblets, and they knew that could be dangerous. Five hundred of them went into camp on Baker's Hill to await the arrival of the main army.

"They ain't been gone from here long," one said. "This rock is still warm from them settin' on it."

"Nice chaps, to have left us this good a fort," remarked a comrade.

The next day, two thousand more Union troops reached Baker's Hill. The officers looked at the wrecked bridges, at the swollen river. Scouts were dispatched both ways along the river to look for flatboats. The party searching down the river found one four miles away. With herculean efforts they towed and paddled it to the landing at the foot of Baker's Hill.

"Tie it up and leave it there," said General Mitchel. "We have got to find out what is going on in town before we send many soldiers across."

But the crossing would be unbearably tedious with a flatboat. So the engineers set to work on a pontoon bridge. General Mitchel sent four of his most experienced scouts into Bowling Green to find how matters really were. He stood on Baker's Hill for hours, searching the streets and hills of the town with his field glass. He couldn't quite make out what he saw. There were no soldiers in sight. He could see none on Vinegar Hill, none on College Hill, none on Grider Hill, and no figures moved about on the nearer Webb's Hill. The streets seemed almost deserted. Trees interrupted his full view of the courthouse, and he saw only occasional passers-by around it. He didn't understand it. Were the Confederate troops waiting in ambush for his men to cross the river? If so, where were they? He swept the entire range of the town and got no answer. He had directed his scouts to go five or six miles down the river before attempting a crossing, and then to work their way into town from the northwest. There wasn't much protection he could provide the engineers who worked on the banks of the river. For twenty-four hours the general was baffled by the obvious, and then his scouts came back with the report that no soldier was left in the town or its margins. They had left on the fourteenth, marching southward. But still General Mitchel was not wholly reassured. He ordered the troops to enter the town with great caution, and with skirmishing units marching on ahead. Shots fired from Baker's Hill fell ahead of the troops for proper covering.

The town was a lonely place. More than half of the citizens had left, and most of the others remained close at home. The streets were rough and rutted. The houses bore the marks of war. Some of the fences about the homes had been torn away. Firewood had been scarce for both soldiers and citizens. Some buildings had been caught in the artillery fire and were burning. The smoke added to the grimness of the entrance to the town. When the officers were fully certain that none of the Confederates remained, they proceeded to station the men in the forts the Confederates had built. By nightfall campfires burned on every hill about the place.

One week from the day that General Tilghman had surrendered Fort Henry, the Confederate soldiers had marched away from Bowling Green. The day was cold and cheerless, and there was anguish and sometimes anger in the hearts of the soldiers. The soldiers from Fort Grider formed the vanguard. They were followed by the units from Webb's Hill, then College Hill, and finally those from Baker's Hill. The wagon trains fell in at the rear. The columns marched rapidly out the Nashville pike. The soldiers were tired and some of them were sick, but they doggedly kept their places in the lines. What was the need for such rush? They had heard that the Yankees were advancing on Bowling Green, but almost all the things you heard in a war were not so. There were some who kept on demanding why they hadn't defended the town instead of turning tail in such a cowardly manner at the first hint of the approach of the enemy. The business of an army was to fight, not to run away.

Corporal Roy Bettersworth, marching in the rear ranks under Hindman, pointed to the left where a clump of buildings could be seen. "That's Richpond where I live. I never thought I'd be handing it over to the Yankees free of charge." There were tears in the boy's eyes.

At dark they caught up with General Breckinridge's troops. They bivouacked two miles south of Franklin near the Tennessee border. It was an unhappy army, and during the night the weather steadily grew worse. They had no fires and very little food. The snow was two inches deep when they resumed march the next morning.

16

IN MANY WAYS, fortune smiled upon the invading Union army. The officers didn't know how long they would remain in Bowling Green, but they wouldn't have to go to the trouble of building fortifications. That had been done for them. They moved into quarters and homes that had been vacated by the withdrawing Confederates. The troops had their regular allotment of food, but it was supplemented by stores which the Confederates had not succeeded in destroying. The agents of the commissary went about canvassing near-by sources of provisions. They visited Trezevant Covington and found his nephew, Virgil, with him.

"How many hogs do you have?" Uncle Trez was asked.

"Thirty-two, and I am going to keep them."

The questioner said, "Thirty-two," and made note of the number. "Do not dispose of any of them. We may need them. Of course, you will be paid for them."

"Whose price?" snapped Uncle Trez.

"Ours. How many horses do you have?"

"None. I got rid of them when I heard you were coming."

Virgil Covington said suavely, "My uncle is ninety years old, and not very able to care for his stock. I advised him to make some disposition of them a month ago. In times like these, there are always irresponsible people—I make no reference to men like you—who pilfer when the opportunity offers. So I made the suggestion, and he agreed."

"Has he any beef cattle?"

"A few cows. They are winter-poor, and certainly would make poor beef."

"Where do you live?" the agent asked Virgil.

"A half mile yonder. I'll ride over with you if you wish."

"How many hogs have you?"

"Eighteen. Four ready to kill. I have disposed of my horses except the one I am riding. I have only milk cows. I'd like to sell about three gallons of milk a day. Of course, you can have it at your price."

The man made more notes. "We are obliged for your co-operation. We may need your hogs. Keep them ready for us. What is your name?"

"Virgil Covington, and this is my uncle, Trezevant Covington. Is there any assistance I can lend you?"

The commissary men rode away. They circled Bowling Green, stopping at many places.

In the afternoon, they came to Three Springs. They found Bill Willie Blewett at the barn. "Who owns this place?"

"Mr. Rumsey Skiles owns the place. He's a lawyer in town. I jest work here."

"How many hogs have you?"

"Who's a-askin'?"

"We represent the commissary general of General Mitchel's division."

"We've got four hogs a-fattenin' and one old sow with seven pigs."

"Do not dispose of the four hogs. How many horses have you?"

"Two. One is in the barn here, and Mr. Skiles is drivin' the other."

"How many beef cattle?"

"We got rid of three. All we got left is four cows and a little calf."

"Which side do you favor?"

"Mister, I'll be ninety-one years old my next birthday, and that's a little old to be takin' sides."

The representative of the commissary made marks on paper and rode away.

Disturbing news had become a matter of routine. Rumsey Skiles heard during the day that the fighting around Fort Donelson was becoming desperate. He had heard repeatedly that there was very little chance of saving the fort. That, of course, would mean the capture of Jackson Shobe. But the tragedy was more imperative than that. The names of three Warren County boys had been put on the bulletin board in the courthouse that day, two killed and one wounded. All three lived out in the county, and Skiles knew the parents of the two boys killed. In fact, he had done legal work for both. A messenger had been sent to each of the three families. Skiles had been afraid that the Union officers would object to the bulletin board, and to the crowds that gathered before it, but so far they had taken no notice.

Bill Willie told him of the visit of the representatives of the commissary. "I am gettin' terrible forgetful," he said. "I jest natchelly forgot to tell them about Miss Jane's stock, out in the woods we fenced in, and while I was a-forgettin' that, I jest went ahead and forgot to tell them about our stock we moved out yesterday. When you get to be as old as I am, you can't depend on your recollection any more."

"I trust your memory will bring us into no trouble, Bill Willie. The Yankees have taken charge of the town. They have filled the town with notices telling people what to do and what not to do. A large number of Confederate soldiers were too sick to leave with their comrades, so our people took them into their homes. One of the orders is a command for every home caring for a Confederate soldier to make a full report to their headquarters. Every family with more than a month's supply of food must report the surplus. Every person owning any sort of firearms must bring them immediately to a place designated. Anyone found guilty of any violation will be required to take the oath of allegiance, not to mention other penalties."

"I expect my recollection has went into a decline. That stock is goin' to stay where it is. There's a creek runnin' through the woods, and there's a bluff that more than fifty cows could stand out of the weather in. We got a haystack not a quarter of a mile away, and it's right well hid too. We went to a lot of trouble to raise that stock, and so did Jackson Shobe. I am not goin' to tell anybody anything, and I'll mess up anybody who does."

"My mouth is sealed too, Bill Willie."

Jane, pale but bright-eyed, came into the room then. "Is there any news, Father?"

"There isn't any good news, Jane. The fighting is pretty sharp at Fort Donelson."

She was silent a moment. Then she asked, "Are the Yankees mistreating people in town?"

"I wouldn't say that they are. There are some hard rules being posted, but when your enemy conquers you, he is entitled to make the rules."

"The enemy hasn't conquered us."

"I fear that Bowling Green might be regarded as conquered territory. The general opinion is that Fort Donelson will be taken."

"I can't believe it, Father. I can't believe it."

"It would not mean necessarily that the South has lost the war. I still think that it is going to be a long one."

"That will mean that Jackson will be sent to some war prison."

"If the fort is captured, it will mean that. But prisoners of war are frequently exchanged. A prison camp is bad, but it isn't the worst fate. I'll not keep it from you, Jane. Two Warren County men were killed at Fort Donelson yesterday morning——"

"Jackson . . . ?"

"No. I would have told you that sooner. I don't think you knew either of them. I saw their names on the bulletin board at the courthouse."

"Tell me, Father, do I have courage to look at that bulletin board?"

"You have the courage, Jane, but I want you to stay here. I will go in town each day as long as I am permitted. I will bring you all the news I can get."

"If he is taken away as prisoner of war where would it be?"

"Somewhere north of here. Perhaps Chicago, perhaps Indianapolis. There is no way to know."

"Would he be back by August?"

"It could very well be, Jane."

Her mother opened the door then. "You two come on in to supper."

17

ALL OF THE FOLLOWING day the crowds about the bulletin board were so thick that they had to take turns to get up close enough to read it. Although it was biting cold, the door of the courthouse was kept open and an armed guard stood there, watching closely those who came in and went out. All coming into town were stopped, searched and questioned before being permitted to proceed. Guards at the river checked closely those who came from the north side. One poor fellow from Bristow, whose brother was at Donelson, forded the river above town, crossed yards and climbed fences to get to the courthouse. But it was the jail he reached instead. It took him two days to talk his way out.

The crowds that the bulletin board drew to the courthouse were proving an irritation to the authorities. So a notice was issued that no more Confederate bulletins would be posted after noon of the sixteenth of February.

Word of this action reached Dr. Younglove in his pharmacy within an hour. It angered him. At three o'clock he was in the presence of General Mitchel, having got there by sheer audacity. An orderly called the pharmacist's name. General Mitchel looked up from a little desk. "Yes?" he said, with a faint note of impatience.

"You know my name. I was born here. I have been in the drug business here for a quarter of a century. My father was in it before that. Every grown man in Bowling Green, and in the county for that matter, knows that I am entirely Union in my belief. But I want to tell you, General Mitchel, that there are a lot of good citizens in this town who don't see it the way you do at all. This is a good town——"

"Come to the point."

"As I said, when you interrupted me, it is a good town. The people are civilized. They know that there is a war on. So do I. I have got good friends and customers on the other side. When the war is over, they will come back home, and I hope they will be my good friends and customers. If you tore one of their houses down to make some sort of fortification, I wouldn't say a word. That's the way a war is run——"

"What is it you want?"

"For one thing, a little common decency. I want that bulletin board put back in the courthouse, and I want respectable people given the right to come here to see if their sons' names are on it."

"Do you mean Rebel soldiers?"

"I mean the respectable sons of respectable people who are in the wrong army. This is no war between hyenas and wolves. Decent people are fighting on both sides, and when one of their boys gets killed the least thing we can do is to announce it in a respectable manner. I want that bulletin board put back in use."

General Mitchel looked at the pharmacist with some interest. His impatience was no longer visible. "As a matter of fact, Doctor, this is the first time I have heard of the bulletin board. I suppose it was discontinued because the crowds it drew caused some risk. You can understand that we can't afford crowds congregating about town."

"I do, if they are gathering for idle or mischievous purposes. That isn't what I am talking about. These are poor, distressed people that I am talking about. They only want to read the board and find if their sons are still alive, and then go away quickly. As it is, we can get the news only when somebody can get through to Clarksville and send it from there. They have worked out some sort of system for that. Even so, I doubt if we get half the list, but it is something for these poor people who otherwise might not get any news for months. I am only talking about the dead and the badly wounded. It is something to which a respectable Warren County father and mother are entitled."

"I sympathize with that, Doctor, but I dislike to veto the decisions of my staff. They do not make them without good reasons."

"Then I will put the bulletin board on my store front and take care of it myself."

"We could not permit that, Doctor."

"I am as good a Unionist as you are, General Mitchel. You may get ready to take me to your prison. Good day."

General Mitchel sat looking at the old man leaving the room. He called an orderly. "I have been told that a Mr. Warner Underwood is the town's leading patriot. I wish you would find him and bring him here."

A half hour later the orderly returned with Warner Underwood. The general asked his visitor to be seated. Underwood, a man of striking appearance, sat with a grace observed by the alert eyes of General Mitchel.

"I will take only a few minutes of your time. Do you know a Dr. Younglove?"

"Very well, General Mitchel. He is one of our more substantial citizens."

The general told Underwood of the visit of the pharmacist. Underwood smiled and said, "That is the only kind of aid he would offer the enemy, but if he decided to do it, the threat of prison would not stop him."

"We could stop the telegraph company from accepting the news, or if he insisted upon doing it we could station a guard at his store."

"In a way, you have asked my advice. I will give it. Withdraw the order discontinuing the board at the courthouse. That will give no aid to the enemy. It will be, as Dr. Younglove says, a civilized act."

General Mitchel considered. "For the time being," he said, "we will permit the bulletin board in the courthouse to be used."

Underwood left. An officer was admitted. "What is it, Colonel Early?"

"The men are getting a bit out of hand, sir. There was a good deal of drunkenness and some pillaging. I suppose it is a bit of splurging. They haven't been in town in a long time, and they just lost their heads."

"We can't permit them to lose their heads. Patrol the streets tonight very thoroughly. Send any special cases to the guardhouse. And, oh, yes, Colonel, continue the use of the bulletin board in the courthouse. The fathers and near kinsmen of Rebel soldiers may consult it if that is their business in town. They should be gone in half an hour. There must be no congregating and no communication beyond mere greeting."

18

THE BOARD went back up. Fathers of Confederate soldiers stood within a few feet of fathers of Union soldiers as they searched the neighboring bulletins. Charlie Howard of Cedar Valley and his neighbor, Wes Upton, stood and read those lists. They had been close friends, but were no longer. Upton's eyes were on the Confederate lists and Howard's on the Union. Upton gasped, his face drained of all blood. He had found his son's name. The other man found a name too. He stood there a moment, his hand clasping tightly that of his three-year-old son. Then he said to Upton, "You want to get home as quick as you can, Wes. Will you ride with us in the spring wagon?"

The man hesitated, his eyes still upon that bulletin. "Brother George has been wounded," Howard said.

"Thank you, Charlie. I'd like a ride."

The Skileses had not been expecting company, but at three o'clock, Aunt Mat Jackson arrived. Aunt Mat had not permitted her advanced age to weaken her horsemanship. She rode in a gallop to the gate. Ella Skiles met her at the door. "Come right in, Aunt Mat."

"I hear Jane is here. I'd like to see the child."

"We sent for her just before they destroyed the bridge. I'll get her."

"So that was where Bill Willie Blewett was going that day on the pike. I had been out to the Jefferson Spaldings to see Madeline. She went to her father-in-law's the day Jefferson Junior went away with the troops. I am trying to visit all the young wives whose husbands are off with the colors. It keeps me busy, but it's my duty."

"Have you been to see Cynthia Wright?" asked Mrs. Skiles, an unmistakable twinkle in her eyes. "Her husband left week before last."

"I have not been to see her, and I will not go to see her. I am visiting the wives of *our* soldiers only. There are too many Yankees here. Let them go to see her."

Jane entered the room. "Why, Aunt Mat," she said, subtly resisting a violent embrace, "how nice it is to see you!"

"I knit socks for the soldiers in the morning and visit their wives in the afternoon. That is my duty as I see it. You are proud of your husband, aren't you, child?"

"I am dizzy with pride. I have been that way since the first day I saw him."

"You are lucky. You married a nice boy, and of course he joined the right army. I could shed tears for poor Millie Osteen. She didn't have to marry a Yankee. Mary Combs used good sense like you did. So did Ruth Morningstar. They say Tom Henry Hines is turning out to be the smartest spy in the Southern army. Some Bowling Green girl ought to have married him while she had the chance. I've been worried, Jane, about your brother, Underwood. Are you sure his heart is right in this war? It's too bad Virgil and Harriet never had any sons. They would be on the right side."

"I think so much about Jackson I don't have time to think about anybody else."

"Jackson's heart is right. His father's heart was right. His grandfather's heart was right. I saw Jackson before he was three months old, and I knew right then that he was all right. I am gifted that way, praise God."

"Are you gifted enough, Aunt Mat, to know when I'll see him again?"

"You will see him, child. If not before the victory, then after it. I don't guess I can stay any longer. I just wanted to encourage you, Jane. I must stop to see Amelia Gerard on the way back. She is downhearted, but she needn't be. Her husband's heart is all right." She turned to Mrs. Skiles. "How is Bill Willie Blewett? He looked right peart the day I saw him on the pike. They say he and Trez Covington are running a race to see who lives the longest. Tell them I am in the race too. I expect to attend both of their funerals."

Aunt Mat left. She wasn't halfway to the Gerards' before another visitor arrived. Ella Skiles took one look at the new arrival and sighed in relief because Aunt Mat had gone. The visitor was the wife of young Robin Rodes. She and Jane had been friends from childhood, but naturally their friendship had cooled a bit since Robin had joined the Union forces. Ella Skiles saw the look on Jane's face. "I think you should see her for old times' sake. You needn't talk about the war."

"I will remember her as things were a year ago. Elizabeth was one of my best friends then."

Jane met her at the door and greeted her pleasantly, though there was a restraint which would not have existed a year before. But in the midst of her greeting, she stopped short. "What is it, Elizabeth?"

"I just had to see someone, Jane, someone who is not on our side. Robin has been wounded."

"Oh, I hope not badly."

"He was shot in the leg. I don't guess he will die, but it frightens me, and nobody on our side could give me the comfort I need. I just had to see you, Jane."

"How did you find it out?"

"They have put the bulletin board back in the courthouse. At first,

I heard they weren't using it at all. Then I heard they were using it for our side only. But it is for both sides now. I went to see Dr. Briggs and he said a leg wound generally wasn't very serious. What do you think about it, Jane?"

"The doctor would be right. Did you read all the names?"

"Robin was the only one I knew, though there was a soldier named Miller from Sand Hill on the other list. He was killed."

"Can't I get you a glass of hot milk? You look a little peaked."

"You are sweet to think of it, Jane, but I will not take it. I came out here because I needed a little comforting about Robin. But there was something else. I wanted to ask if we can't be friends again after the war is over? I have been thinking about it several days, but I didn't quite have the courage to come till I saw that about Robin. Do you think they will let him come home?"

"They might. I have heard of them doing it. Yes, Elizabeth, I want us to be friends."

"Have you heard anything——" She stopped and said, "I must be going now. You don't know how much it has helped me to see you. I feel a lot better about Robin than when I came."

The door to the other room had been open the width of a finger. Rumsey Skiles, who sat there, though making no effort, had heard every word that was said. He sat there, looking into the fire and a mist came before his eyes. What a ghastly thing was war! Those two girls for more than fifteen years had been dear friends. What was this barrier that had been suddenly thrust between them? He was proud of Jane. She had made no error, though at the first he had been terribly afraid that she would. He was proud of Elizabeth Rodes for the things she had said, and for the things he knew she hadn't said. Perhaps it would be a long time before Elizabeth Rodes came back to Three Springs. There wouldn't be much visiting from then on. There would be too much concern for the bulletin board in the courthouse for that. He found that his eyes were still misty.

He rode into town the next morning, but at ten o'clock he was back at Three Springs, and the news he bore had wrought deep sorrow upon his face. He hitched his horse and ran up the walk to the veranda. Jane and her mother sat in the family room, working with scissors and needle and thread. Jane lifted her eyes when her father opened the door and came into the room. She saw his face and knew what it was that he had to tell. And, at the same moment, her mother knew too.

"Father," said Jane, her voice sunk to a whisper. "It is Jackson, isn't it?"

"Yes, Jane, it is Jackson."

"Dead," she said in a whisper. "Jackson is dead."

"The notice said, 'Seriously wounded.'"

"Wounded," she said, "seriously wounded. He may still be alive. I must go to him. I must."

"I knew you would say that. I'll say no word against it. It is what your mother would do if I were at Fort Donelson and seriously wounded. But let's think about it for a little while."

"And while we are thinking, Jackson may die."

The mother took a step and placed a hand upon her daughter's shoulder. Rumsey Skiles looked first at his wife and then at his daughter. "All right, Jane, I'll go with you."

"No, Father, I want you to stay here with Mother. I'll need you both when we get back."

"Virgil Covington would go, Jane."

"I want Bill Willie to go. Send for him, Father. He loved Jackson."

"Isn't Bill Willie too old to make that trip?" asked her mother.

"Send for Bill Willie, Father."

Bill Willie came. Skiles told him of the news on the bulletin board. Jane asked him to take her to Fort Donelson.

"Yes'm," said Bill Willie. "I feel mighty sorry about Jackson. Maybe it's not bad. I can be ready in half an hour. We'll go in the spring wagon and take some beddin' in the back. I reckon I can find a piece of oilcloth to cover it with. We sort o' short o' good horses, Mr. Skiles. Don't you reckon I ought to go to the woods lot and get one of them?"

"Get Charlie," said Jane. "He was Jackson's favorite. Charlie would like to be the one to bring Jackson back."

"I'll go get him. You have the beddin' ready by the time I get back, and a little something to eat. Take plenty o' clothes. It's cold now, and it might get worse."

"Do you know the way, Bill Willie?"

"I can find it, sir. Was the fort still a-holdin' out?"

"It surrendered sometime last night. I was so troubled about Jackson that I forgot to tell you."

"Even when you get there, how will you find Jackson?" asked the mother.

"We will find him, ma'am."

"We will find him," echoed Jane. "Hurry back with Charlie, Bill Willie. I'll be ready."

She sank into a chair. "Oh, Jackson, Jackson," she said, pleading as if in prayer. "Jackson, wait till I get there."

The Settlement Regained

1865

SPRING WAS AT ITS BEST that day. The sky was clean-swept, but its deep blue was dimmed and softened by a purple-tinged haze that was everywhere—against the hills and thickets, over the fields, hanging gently and caressingly against the sky. It softened the stark white of the dogwoods that gave brightness to an April world. The graveyard vine that lay heavily upon and between the Shobe graves had lost its winter dinginess, and again was alive with the buoyant green of spring and thick with purple, star-shaped flowers. Everywhere the trees were clad in the garments of spring or poised to put them on. The birds that thronged the trees, or hopped gaily about on the ground, knew that it was spring again, and their songs swelled into a chorus of praise. All of the sounds that greeted the ears were tuned to spring: the plowmen calling to their teams, the tinkle of a cowbell in a meadow, somewhere in the distance the casual, deep-throated bay of a foxhound, a train engine sounding long and mournfully for the station at Oakland—all fused into the unity of spring.

A wooden bench had been placed in the graveyard. The grave nearest it did not bear the maturity of the other graves about. On the bench sat Jane Shobe and at her side a boy nearing three. He did not understand what the graves meant, but he did understand that his mother did not want him to run and scamper about, as was his way at home. For some reason she wished him to sit quietly at her side. She held in her hand some lilac blooms that she had broken from a hedge at the side of her yard, less than a half mile away. A cardinal sat on a maple bough not a dozen feet distant, its head cocked to one side, and watched with bright eyes.

"Listen, Jackson," Jane said to the child, "I want to tell you something. You will not understand what I am saying. Maybe you will understand better than I think. Anyhow, I want to talk to you a little while. That is your father's grave there. You never saw him, but I am going to tell you about him so often that you will almost think you did. I don't want you to grow up thinking that he is somebody far, far off. He believed in the South very deeply, and so did I. We married after the war started, but neither of us thought it would last very long, a year at the most. Things got worse, and he decided that it was his duty to enlist. I thought it was too. He went away to the army, son, but once he came back to see me. We talked a great deal about you, what you would look like and how we would love you. Your father didn't come back any more, son. My father came home one day with the news that he had been wounded. Bill Willie took me to Fort Donelson where your father was. You know Bill Willie, don't you?"

"Bill Willie," said the boy, his eyes bright with recognition.

"I don't know how we got there, Jackson. I don't want you ever to forget Bill Willie, son. I don't believe anyone else could have got me there in time. And we did get there in time. Your father was still alive. I know that he was spared that long so I could see him once more. We talked mostly about you. He was weak, and he would rest awhile so that we could talk again. And then the time came when he wouldn't ever talk any more. It was Bill Willie who brought us back."

"Bill Willie," said the boy again, nodding his head.

"And we buried him in that grave there. It was very cold that day, and the sun wasn't showing at all. I was terribly tired and heartbroken, and sometimes when Dr. Smoot was talking I thought I would die too. Then I knew that I wouldn't. I would live for you. I knew that your father would want me to. And then the sun came out, and that was a sign to me that you would soon be here and that everything would be better. We have had a hard time of it, Jackson, and there have been some very bad days for me. If it hadn't been for you, I don't suppose that I would ever have got through them. But everything seems all right now. The war is over and I don't think you will ever see another one. I pray to God you won't. I don't know what is going to happen, but you and I will be together. Sunday we are going to see your grandfather and grandmother. They are good people, son. You are going to be proud of them. You are going to be proud of the Shobes too. You look like the Shobes. You are one of them. Take these flowers and put them on your father's grave. Right over there. Put them down right there. That's right, Jackson. We must go back to the house now. There is a lot of work to be done."

Far in the distance, all but hidden by the haze, were the Edmonson County hills. In the southwest, Cook's Knob stood in faint outline. There seemed fitness in the scene: the haze, the hills and knobs, everywhere the white dogwoods, the misty spring sky above, the plows threading patiently across the fields, the birds throbbing their joy from meadow and bough. Spring had come, and not only spring, but the beginnings of peace.

2

"GOOD MORNING, Uncle Trez," said Virgil Covington heartily. "I was feeling a bit empty, so I said to Harriet, 'My dear, I need a little cheer, so I believe I will go over to Uncle's and let him thank me for saving his horses during the war. With the war and everything on his mind, he has been too forgetful to do it up till now.' I can't say that she was for the idea tooth and nail, but she gallantly stood aside, and here I am."

Uncle Trez leaned heavily on his cane. "So it's thanks you want. Took you all of a couple of hours, didn't it? Haven't I been stepping in and saving you from one fool thing or another since the day you were born? What would you have amounted to if I hadn't kept my eyes on you day and night?"

"Certainly nothing less than a governor. But I forgive you for your negligence, Uncle, as one Covington should another. Feeling pretty spry today?"

"If I felt any better I'd send for Dr. Briggs. Got your corn ground broken yet?"

"Not yet, but I expect to before the week is over. How are those new hands turning out? Are they good workers?"

"I think they will be all right when their boys get back from the war, so they can stop worrying. They were in Virginia, and I suppose they'll have to hoof it back. I don't expect them before the middle of the summer. We need them right now."

"How are your horses doing?"

"Just skin and bones. First fellow I hear telling about what a hard time he had during the war I'm going to tell him to shut up. He'd be a long sight worse off if he had been a horse. That war was sure hard on horses. With both armies looking for horses for the generals to ride on, it got so a horse was in real bad luck."

"The horses the generals rode weren't any worse off than those hidden out in fields. At least, they got something to eat every now and then. Five times I moved those horses of yours, Uncle Trez. Every time it looked to me like they were in danger, I'd go down and take them somewhere else, and every time the picking was poorer. That last six months at Blue Level was mighty hard on them, but at least you got them back."

"Much obliged," said the old man, grinning wryly. "Now don't go around saying you haven't been thanked. How are you off for feed now?"

"I am not off at all. I just haven't got any. I haven't got an ear of corn, but I have got a little fodder and enough timothy hay for a month. Grass ought to be pretty good by then. It will be the Lord's blessing if this turns out a good crop year."

"The trouble is a lot of stock don't have enough strength to raise a crop. It will take two years to get things back in order."

"Two! We'll be lucky if we can in five. Make it ten. Tom Henry Hines is back in town. I saw him yesterday."

"Then the excitement isn't over yet. What is Tom Henry going to do now, start the war all over?"

"He is starting up his law practice again. He is opening an office next to Jimmy Younglove's drugstore."

"Sounds like the law is more in danger of being violated than practiced with Jimmy and Tom Henry next door to each other. Any word from Robin Rodes yet?"

"Elizabeth looks for him home in a month or six weeks. He limps a little from his wound, but seems to be in good health. I saw Jane Shobe and her little boy the other day. She had been out to Three Springs to get some sorghum seed."

"Jane has had a hard time. How does she look?"

"Considerably the worse for wear. Jane has done a man's work, and a woman's too, for almost three years. Of course, it shows, but she keeps cheerful. The boy is a handsome fellow."

"I've the same as got no feed. I'll make you a good price on that chestnut horse."

"It has been almost forty years since I sold you that filly, and still you won't give up. I have told you I haven't got a grain of corn. In a year or two, I'll buy your filly, but I am not going to watch it shrivel up on my hands."

"Tell me what a war is for," said Uncle Trez in shrill tones. "Just tell me. Suppose you won it, what good would it do? But I never heard of anybody winning one. You think you have won it till you count up and then you know you have lost it. That is what will happen to the Yankees. A man is a fool that will have anything to do with a war."

"I'll not deny a thing you have said, Uncle Trez, but there is something in a war that people like, even people who are going to starve to death, and that is excitement. There is nothing that stirs up as much excitement as a war."

"I haven't got much time left, not more than fifteen or twenty years, but I do want it to be peaceful. I don't want anyone to shoot a squirrel out of a tree in my hearing. It will make me think that we are starting another war. But I don't want to die till stock and people have had enough to eat."

"Then I am afraid we will put off digging your grave for quite a while. I just thought I'd drop over and see how things are."

3

By MAY Bowling Green was a strange mixture of beauty and desolation. War had left no mark on the sky above, or on the things that bloomed everywhere. The clouds gathered and the rains fell, as if evil had no part in the world. But the homes had a worn and tired look, and the streets were rough and pitted with deep holes. A great many of the trees, formerly the town's major ornaments, had been chopped down for campfires. There were no sleek horses hitched to the carriages that bumped along the streets, and the carriages were no longer a symbol of prosperity. The clothes that the people wore had long ago outlasted newness. Lately there had been few new clothes to buy, and very little money to buy them with. What little money the people had was used for immediate things, such as food and medicine, when they could be had.

In the matter of food, the farmers were under less stress than the people in town. Even those who raised meat had very little of it, for the foraging outfits of both armies had been ceaselessly busy, with the special favorites being pork and beef animals. The more canny homes had a little cured meat, salt bacon and shoulder, frugally doled out. Now and then a ham swung in the attic, but it was regarded as something precious, and saved for a feast day. Sometimes a calf was killed, or a sheep. It was parceled out among the neighbors and eagerly eaten. Everybody raised potatoes. Those stored in cellars or barn lofts were usually gone by New Year's, eaten or spoiled. Those buried in great mounds might, under favorable conditions, last two months longer. The milk supply of the county had dwindled with the supplies of hay and corn. The marauding parties had taken so many of the chickens that eggs had almost disappeared from the kitchens. Corn meal and wheat flour afforded the base of life for the people. It was ground soon after the grain was harvested. It was hidden in the driest place the house afforded, and at intervals carefully treated against weevil and mold. There was an instinctive desire for anything sweet. Sugar simply didn't exist in Bowling Green and Warren County. The average man would have sold five years off his life for a gallon of sorghum molasses. The people had learned to beat the opossums to the persimmons that clung on the boughs or dropped to the ground, for there was a very choice sweetness in the flesh of the persimmon.

There was one very edible thing of which people seemed to have plenty, black-eyed peas. At a political rally, held a few years after the war, the speaker paid a fervent tribute to black-eyed peas: "Our preserver in the days of our tribulation, our strength in time of weakness." At the basket dinner, served at the rally, at least a half dozen ladies came to him, bearing servings of black-eyed peas, and he gallantly ate them all.

No one had any coffee in Bowling Green now except the Boswells, and the report was that they had it regularly. No one had seen them have coffee for the simple reason that the Boswells never had company. Clyde Keller, who worked at the freight office during the early days of the war, vowed that he had helped Mr. Boswell load a hundred-pound sack marked "Coffee" into his spring wagon the same week that General Buckner occupied the town. There had been some talk of violence among a few who hadn't been forehanded, but nothing had come of it. The Boswells lived in a small stone house built like a fortress. Even if they had the coffee it would have been no easy matter to take it. No one liked the Boswells, and they apparently didn't care.

Aunt Mat Jackson had some coffee—almost two pounds—when the war was over. She had made a standing offer to serve a cup to every returning Confederate soldier who stopped at her house.

"I had that coffee, most of it, when the war began, but I dedicated it to the cause. I have never touched a drop of it. General Buckner had a cup of it, and so did General Cleburne. I liked him fine, but Buckner was a little haughty. Still, I think his heart was right. There have already been eleven boys by, mostly one at a time. I wish you could have seen them when they tasted that coffee. I'll keep on giving it to them as long as it lasts. You can't do too much for a man when his heart is right."

Sassafras-root tea was the usual hot drink for the spring, though some dried the roots and used them all the year. Turnip greens proved a real blessing in the late winter and early spring for those fortunate enough to have a patch. When the day was good in April and early May every untilled field near the town was likely to be dotted with greens pickers. Most of them were children, but they had been trained to know lamb's-quarters, narrow dock, dandelion, and wild mustard. The long winter had made fresh things seem doubly desirable. Spring onions were eaten eagerly, not only as a food but also as a tonic. People needed both.

Grover Atkinson was the acknowledged humorist of Bridge Street. "If I had me a fishin' pole, a line, a hook, a sinker, some bait, some corn meal, some bacon grease, and some salt and a little spare time, I'd go and ketch me a mess o' fish. I'm hongry."

Dr. Smoot, of the Presbyterian church, saw clearly that without a great deal of hard, backbreaking work there would be no redemption of the South. He preached a sermon, using a text taken from himself instead of the Scripture. "We must work and pray and wait." But almost everybody was hard at work. Some worked who were not able to work. Indeed, there were some so weak that they shortened their lives every time they laid hands to a hoe. Many were bitter and sullen, but that would tend to pass when life again found its normal level.

4

EVERYONE, except a very few, looked older than he was. Rumsey Skiles looked older than his sixty-five years. The troubled times had left their marks upon him. One night, it seemed to Ella, the lines of care were more deeply etched than usual. She knew something was disturbing him specially and immediately and inquired what it was.

"Robin Rodes got back last week. Yesterday he resumed his practice. Tomorrow he and Tom Henry Hines oppose each other in a lawsuit. They are bitter enough against each other without that. I am worried about it."

"What's wrong with them being on opposite sides in a trial?"

"Nothing is wrong that wouldn't be wrong about anything that put those two men on opposite sides again."

"Human nature is an odd thing," she said. "If they were total strangers they would be a little stiff and that would be all."

"They are not strangers. In a way they are kin. And that makes it worse."

"I remember Aunt Mat Jackson said she expected trouble between them."

"They were friends, and that makes it the more dramatic. They are both sensitive, high-strung men, and each one feels that he has to justify his choice of an army before the other."

"Aunt Mat said also that she hoped if they did have trouble Tom Henry would win. She said his heart was right. What is this case?"

"Cephas Miller and Plural Flora, both from the Richardsville neighborhood, have had some dispute over a land boundary. I doubt if the land is good enough to warrant going to court about it, but they have got all stirred up. To make matters worse, Miller's son was with General Forrest throughout the war, and Flora's son with General George Thomas. Tom Henry Hines is representing Miller, and Robin Rodes is Flora's lawyer. Maybe nothing will come of it, but there has been a lot of talk. One thing is certain, there will be a full courtroom when the trial comes up."

"I am sorry," Ella said. "Things have been dying down. This may stir up hard feelings all over again."

"It very well could. That is my fear. Bowling Green never had a brighter or more likable man than Tom Henry Hines, but in war or out, Tom finds it difficult to remain at peace. He was fond of trouble before. I fear he has learned to love it now."

"When they were small boys, Tom Henry and Robin were inseparable and always in a fight. Can't the judge postpone the case for a while?"

"Not unless he is asked to do so, and that isn't likely to happen."

"I have the notion that Robin would like to avoid any trouble right now if he could without seeming to. His family aren't fire-eating people, but they are certainly watchful about their honor. I think Robin would prefer to be quiet now, but, like any Rodes, he would turn into a roaring lion if he thought his honor was in danger."

"And if it is a case of honor, Elizabeth will back him up."

"She might even get out ahead of him a bit."

"Tom Henry and Robin will both be armed, of course."

"Tom Henry will, but I don't know about Robin. I doubt if he carries a weapon now, but he might tomorrow."

5

JUDGE RODNEY DRAKE was a colorful figure as the presiding officer of the court. He could be droll and whimsical like his uncle, judge of the court for many years. He could interpolate a nice bit of play acting into a court scene, or he could conduct the court with most becoming gravity. He was fearful of the day that lay before him. He had heard the rumors and he knew that they could turn into reality. He would do what he could to hold things to an even keel.

He opened the court with as much pomp and ceremony as if it had been a high court of English justice. There were a few preliminaries that demanded attention. One case was dismissed, another postponed. Then it was time for the case of Miller *versus* Flora to come before the court.

Judge Drake took a deep breath and looked about the courtroom. It was crowded with people eagerly awaiting whatever might develop. The judge sighed and gave thought to the waywardness of human nature. On the front row sat Wade Grimes, whose son as far as anyone knew was still a prisoner in some Northern camp. Why would Wade want to see any more trouble? Didn't he have his fill of anxiety and conflict? Why wasn't he at work on his scrubby little farm, doing the best he could with a bad state of affairs? The judge continued his survey. There was Whit Beck. The war had been cruel to Whit. One of his sons wouldn't be coming home at all. The other was at home with the stump of one leg healing from the disaster at Missionary Ridge. What business had Whit in that courtroom? Perhaps some deep and hidden and dreadfully ironic part of Whit still longed for conflict. There sat Madison Elkin, formerly sergeant in Sherman's army. Yonder was John Horsley, corporal under Bedford Forrest. Why were they watching so intently the beginning of a trivial lawsuit? Had the word gone out that Robin Rodes was to reopen the war on behalf of the United States, and Tom Hines on behalf of the Confederacy? Judge Drake sighed and nodded to the clerk who announced the case.

Tom Henry Hines and his client arose from the benches at the side and came forward. The lawyer motioned Miller to a chair. He remained standing and announced his readiness to proceed with the trial. The eyes of many in the courtroom searched him for sign of a pistol. To their surprise, they found none. That was odd, for Hines was supposed to go armed always. Rodes announced that he was ready for the trial. The inspection of Rodes was less searching. His intimacy with weapons was less well established.

The case proceeded peacefully, though there was an obvious undercurrent of tension. Rodes was carrying on the direct examination of his client.

Suddenly Hines sprang to his feet. "Your Honor, your Honor," he intoned, "surely the learned counsel would not deliberately betray his client into an untruth."

"You may discover on cross-examination whether it is an untruth," the judge said acidly. "You are out of order."

Rodes's face went white, but he said nothing and proceeded with the examination.

Hines sat fiddling with the walking cane he held in his hand. Then he was on his feet again. "Your Honor, the time of this court is too valuable to be wasted with such utterly ridiculous falsehoods."

Rodes rose from his chair as if propelled, thrusting his towering height into the courtroom air. With the same motion he seized a water goblet from the table before him and hurled it at his opponent. It struck Hines on the side of the head, glanced and smashed against the wall. Hines staggered but caught himself. He jerked a sword from the scabbard of his cane, and plunged toward Rodes, stabbing fiercely. Rodes quickly lifted a chair from the floor and held it before him. Hines's slender sword broke on a round of the chair. He dropped the sword to the floor and grabbed at the chair. In the struggle, both men fell to the floor, clawing and grabbing at each other's throats. The voice of Judge Drake rang out sternly. "Sheriff, arrest both of those men."

The sheriff and two of his deputies pulled the two men apart, but they were not placed under arrest.

Judge Drake was speaking again. "I declare this a mistrial." He looked at Miller and Flora, standing there confused, uncertain. "This case will not be reopened until you have secured new lawyers. The court is adjourned."

Captain Hines picked up from the floor the broken blade of his sword cane. He looked at it ruefully, then tossed it out an open window. He threw his hat into the air, caught it and yelled, "Hurrah for General Morgan!"

Across the courtroom, Calvin Underwood, younger brother of Warner, threw his hat up, shouting, "Hurrah for Fighting Phil Sheridan!"

With a peremptory gesture, Judge Drake summoned Rodes and Hines before him. "If you two don't get away from this court I will have you both disbarred as sure as sunup. And don't come back into this courtroom till you have talked things over with me."

Both men knew that the judge meant what he said. "All right, Judge," said Hines gaily. "I was ready to leave anyhow."

Rodes said nothing but followed Hines out of the room. Calvin Underwood beckoned Rodes to follow him. He led the way across the street to his office.

"Sit down, Robin. I think the Rebels would like to start a rookus. It wouldn't hurt any for us to get the jump on them." He opened a drawer of his desk and handed Rodes a pistol. Rodes hesitated. "Take it. No need of running any risk." He took out another and put it in his pocket. "There may be some Dixie boys who think you were a little hasty in throwing that goblet. I think you ought to have heaved it before you did. Let's take a walk around the square just to show them who's not afraid."

"I don't want to get into any trouble," said Rodes.

"Best way to stay out of trouble."

So the two men, Rodes very tall and thin, a veritable splinter of a man, and Underwood short, his Prince Albert coat seeming to drag the ground, walked three times around the square. There was a little jeering but nothing more. They were nearing the end of their third circuit when Aunt Mat Jackson rode her horse squarely in front of them.

"If I had a boy ten years old and he tried to show off like that, I'd tan him for sole leather. You must be expecting about two hundred Southern boys to take out after you, the way you are toting them pistols. Go on home, both of you. Your hearts aren't right."

She rode swiftly away. Underwood looked after her. "Isn't Aunt Mat a corker?" he said admiringly. "Well, since court is adjourned for the day, I guess I would just as well go on home and garden a little. I am a little late at it right now. Was Tom Henry really trying to stir up a fight?"

"Perhaps we both were, though I tried not to."

"I guess it is time for cousins-in-law to start sobering up."

Virgil Covington came walking rapidly toward them. "You'd both better go home and stay there a few days. There are some hotheads down there on Bridge Street who say they are going to make you eat the glass you broke. We don't need any trouble right now. You both go on home."

"Is Tom Henry Hines with them?" asked Rodes.

"I don't think so, but there are some even wilder than Tom. Don't you show yourselves for two or three days. It will be quieted down by then."

"I have got a little gardening to do," said Underwood, as he walked away.

"I will go if you say so, Mr. Covington, but wouldn't it be just as well to settle this thing now and get it over with?"

"Go on home, Robin, and stay there for a while."

Robin Rodes stayed at home two days. They told him that there was a good deal of parading and yelling on the streets the day of the court scene, and that the day had had its share of fist fights, but nothing worse. There were a few minor disturbances the morning of the second day, but by afternoon everything had become quiet.

But his wife was troubled. Elizabeth was young and clear-eyed, and she knew her husband. She knew that it had been wise for him to seek the refuge of home, but she also knew that the refuge, accepted too long, might tend to weaken. In the late afternoon, she took his pistol from a drawer and handed it to him.

"It is time for you to go back down town, Robin." He went and saw nowhere the sign of conflict or the rebirth of the war.

6

ON A FINE SUMMER DAY, Rumsey Skiles rode to Oakland to see his daughter. He came back to Three Springs happier than he had been in a long time. Dusk was settling silently on the land when he returned to his home. Ella was waiting for him. There was such a balm in the air that they sat on the veranda while he told her of his visit.

"I am as proud of Jane as I possibly could be. I did not see a farm in as good condition as hers between here and Oakland, and there are some good farms along the way. Her crop is in better shape than any I saw. The war did everything it could to Jane——"

"Not everything, Rumsey."

"No, not everything. She has the boy, and every time I look at him I think of my father. In fact, Jane often reminds me of him. The boy resembles his father but he looks at you just as my father did, and, like my father, he thinks deliberately and then speaks very softly. Sometimes I would think that he had forgotten. That was the way with my father. No, the war didn't take everything from Jane. It didn't take her husband till she got there to see him. Twice today she talked proudly of the hour they had together."

"The war didn't take her brothers."

"Nor her parents. I say it modestly. I say it modestly, Ella, but we belong honorably in the list of those things spared her. You mentioned her brothers. Let me say something, and you will understand why I say it. Except Wells, it is best for Jane not to see her brothers for a while yet. There is still some bitterness in her heart because they openly sympathized with the side that destroyed her husband. If nothing happens, that feeling will heal within a year or two. I think that just now we should make no effort to bring them together. The myrtle needs to cover her husband's grave a little deeper. She was dreadfully disappointed when you didn't come. I explained to her that you didn't feel like making the trip, and that I made it at your suggestion. The boy sat and listened. Then he said, 'Gamma coming next week.' "

"Gamma is going when she feels well enough. I am not young any more, Rumsey."

"Thank God for that! If you were young I wouldn't have lived with you for forty years. That makes being old worth while."

She searched for, and found, his hand. "What do you think the future has for us, Rumsey?"

"The opportunity to live together for a while yet. The opportunity to be more with our children and grandchildren. No more bad health than we can rightly and quickly recover from."

"I am not much troubled about us. At the best, the most of our lives is behind us. Our children, our grandchildren, our town, our neighbors—those are what I was thinking of. Robin Rodes's father, for instance, did a lot of good and was happy. But he is gone. What about Robin Junior? Can the world offer him as much as it did his father?"

"Robin will have to stop breaking up court and putting on childish performances. But Robin will be all right. He has the proper stuff in him. He and Tom Henry Hines both will outgrow their adolescence. Soon, I hope. I don't know, Ella, how things will turn out. I imagine we will have several years of uncertainty and confusion, perhaps three or four or five. It will take that long, or longer, to work out the bad accumulations that the war has put into our spirits. But we will get back to normal and things will move ahead."

"Jane feeling that way about her brothers—it troubles me."

"It was a war between kinfolks, Ella. There isn't anything unusual about Jane feeling that way toward her brothers. You saw the same thing here in town. You could have seen it all over Kentucky. The Breckinridges on both sides, the Crittendens on both sides, three of President Lincoln's brothers-in-law killed on the Confederate side. That is the sort of war it was. We can't help what it has brought on. We must do what we can not to let it get any worse. We must try to shape things so that it gets better, but we can't do that by forcing anything. . . . Jane asked a great many questions about Bill Willie. She thinks he is a great man."

"So do I. Anybody who could take Jane to Fort Donelson when he did and bring her back with the body of her husband is a great man. I'll stand by Jane in that."

And then, as if by prearrangement, two whistles sounded upon the evening air. One was a steamboat blowing for the bend at Clark's Landing. It would reach Bowling Green in half an hour. The other was a freight train behind Baker's Hill, blowing for the bridge across the river.

"They are paying a tribute to my father. He never lived to see a train come into Bowling Green, but he did live to see the steamboat come and he loved that moment."

"In a way, I am glad that your father and mother didn't have to live through the last four years."

"I certainly am. My father was a stubborn man, but you had to know him well to find it out. When he had made up his mind, he was not likely to yield it. My father loved peace. If he were alive now, the thing he would think about most, and plan most, would be ways to help bring peace to Bowling Green, between the Hineses and the Rodeses, the Underwoods and the Gaineses——"

"Between the children of Rumsey Skiles."

"I do not doubt but that in good time that will happen." He sighed and added, "It may be slow."

7

THE WOUNDS did heal slowly. County Court Day was re-established, it being the notion of the magistrates that the more people commingled the better they would feel toward one another. But at first it seemed only to aggravate matters. The men got together in little groups, each group being either wholly Yankee or wholly Confederate. The day had unpleasant features in both June and July. In August a dramatic episode helped to restore some of the better qualities of the day. Guy Mayhew returned to his home at Alvaton late in April after starving for three years in the Confederate army. His wife and two children and farm were there waiting for him to take up life where he had left off. But Mayhew was an embittered man. He had no heart for the plow and the hoe. He found it more desirable to condemn the Yankees luridly and futilely than to raise corn. He came to County Court Day and brought his two children. He was a little surprised when his wife told him that she wasn't coming with them, but he drove the wagon away without argument. She had decided to stay at home and plant the fall garden. Her husband hadn't seemed able to get around to it.

"If it hadn't been for the Yankees, we would have a carriage now like other people."

"But, Daddy, everybody hasn't got a carriage," protested the younger daughter. "Mr. Holland hasn't got a carriage, Mr. Claypool hasn't or Mr. Roundtree."

"They would have if it hadn't been for the Yankees. Levi Claypool used to have one."

"But, Daddy, the team ran away and tore it up. I heard you say so yourself. He had been to town and something was the matter with him."

"That was the year the war started, Maggie. If it hadn't been for the Yankees he would have a new one by now."

"I like to ride in this wagon, don't you, Jennie?"

"I'd rather have a carriage," said Jennie.

"Just as soon as the Yankees will leave us alone so I can get my mind back on my work, I'll get us a carriage."

"Will there be any Yankees at the County Court Day?" asked Maggie. "Do they look like the devil, Daddy?"

"It isn't the way they look, it's the way they act. Yes, you'll get to see one. There will be plenty of them there, acting high and mighty like they owned the town."

"Daddy, how does a man act when he owns the town?"

Mayhew reached town about ten o'clock. He hitched his team and fed it a few wisps of hay. Maggie regarded the procedure soberly. "I wish our horses would get fat, Daddy."

"We are lucky to have them, fat or poor, what with the Yankees stealing everything people raised."

This continuous reference to the thievery of the Yankees had begun to prove monotonous to Maggie. "We never had much to steal, did we, Daddy?"

"There wasn't any use of having anything. They would have got it then for sure. Their days are about over though. We are going to talk some today about what to do."

"Don't you go to getting into any trouble, Daddy. You must help Mama with the garden. She stayed at home to work on it. Don't you think he ought to help her, Jennie?"

But Jennie's thoughts were upon higher things than gardens and she did not answer.

"You two girls take care of yourselves for a while, but don't leave the grounds here. I'll come back about twelve o'clock, and we'll eat our dinner. I have got to talk to some men."

Jennie and Maggie went about the grounds. There were interesting things to see. The first thing was a tightly contested horseshoe-pitching match. Four men, two at each stob, pitched with all the eagerness and skill they could command, and with considerable advice and commentary from the onlookers. The prize was a dollar's worth of merchandise of the winner's choice, to be chosen from Younglove's drugstore.

"If you win, Curt, how are you going to spend your money?"

"For blue mass for my stock. They are a little puny," answered the man, never taking his eyes from the stob.

Jennie and Maggie watched the match for a few minutes and then moved on to other exictement. Three other children attached themselves and went along. Their second stop was at a horn-blowing contest. They saw and heard two men evoke surprising sounds from their horns while the two judges made marks on some paper.

"Ifn that's horn blowin'," said a loud-voiced bystander, "then I'm a-talkin' to you in a whisper. Twenty years ago, afore my lungs shriveled up, I coulda made them fellers sound like a sourwood whistle."

"Wait till Chris Grice blows," said the man next to him. "When Chris does his tootin' watch them clouds up there start quiverin'."

"I'd like to hear Chris blow, but, let's see, there's nine other blowers before him. I'd like to see what else is going on."

Jennie and Maggie decided similarly. They stopped next at the bass singers' contest. Each singer who completed the full stanza of a song got a copy of the Methodist hymnal, and the one adjudged best got a pitch pipe of fine quality. Jim Grubbs, the singing master at Woodburn, was the judge. It was a popular contest, but the two girls wanted to see everything and moved on. In so doing, they lost their three companions, who were charmed by the contest.

"Yonder's Daddy," said Maggie, pointing. Mayhew was standing in the center of a group of men, all gesticulating, he most furiously of all.

"I know what they are talking about," said Maggie sagely. "Yankees! Jennie, why are Yankees such mean people? I'd like to know."

"I don't know," said Jennie languidly.

"I don't believe people could be as mean as Daddy says they are. Jennie, look at that man. He's as high as a tree."

"Tall," said Jennie.

"I reckon he's had a sickness. He don't walk like a sick man, though. I never did see a man as high."

"Tall," said Jennie.

The man so described was Robin Rodes, commingling among his county neighbors, seeking to become better acquainted with people whose votes someday might be helpful to him. He stopped for a few moments at the horseshoe tournament, and shook hands with some patrons of the art. He saw a few clumps of men standing apart from the activities of the day, and knew that the war again was in progress. He deliberately avoided them. They were committed to the continuance of unpleasantness and discord. He saw Tom Henry Hines stop and make merry with a group a short distance away. He recognized one of the men as Guy Mayhew, who had done jury service the year before the war opened. He had heard that Mayhew was one of the most bitter and outspoken of all the returned Confederates. He saw Mayhew and Tom Henry Hines shake hands vigorously. Rodes turned and walked away. He heard the horn blowers and decided to pay them a brief visit.

At that same moment, Blufe Miller was driving his wagon into the grounds. His wife sat on the seat with him, and his three children on the bed of the wagon. Blufe was late and in a hurry to get hitched. He drove up to an unused hitching rack only a little below the level place on which the horn-blowing contest was being staged. His team was a bit restless, for this was their first experience in a place so filled with strange things and people. Blufe and his family hurriedly climbed down from the wagon, shaking their legs to uncramp them from their long sitting. Miller started to unhitch the team. He had, in fact, taken hold of a trace when Chris Grice began his performance in the horn-blowing contest, less than a hundred feet away. His first blast shrieked with untrueness, rising far above the desired level, then falling below it with harassing effect on ears, human and otherwise. Finally, Chris found his proper place and remained upon it becomingly. But it was too late. Blufe Miller's team had jerked and trembled with Chris's first blast. They crouched at his second, and sprang at his third. Blufe reached for the lines and missed. He leaped for the bridle bit of the nearer horse and missed it. The frightened team galloped away, with the wagon bouncing crazily along behind.

Maggie and Jennie walked along the driveway that just ahead of them narrowed to permit passage between the trees. They suddenly heard a great noise bearing down on them. They turned and saw the runaway team. Maggie leaped with all her might, but her foot slipped upon the soft ground. Instinctively she reached for Jennie and caught her enough to pull her down grotesquely on one knee. Maggie lay sprawled at full length upon the ground. The group of men looked toward the commotion. Mayhew saw what was happening and started at a run. But he was too far away. Robin Rodes was nearer, only twenty feet away. His enormous stride served its purpose then. He reached the two girls in four or five steps. Chris Grice, knowing nothing of the trouble he was causing, started a new blast, true and loud enough to cause quivering among the little lacy clouds that flecked the sky. It added to the team's fright. Rodes cast a rapid look. The team was almost upon the two girls. Using a combined kick and push with his left foot, he pushed Jennie to the far side of the road. Frantically he reached for Maggie's foot and felt his grip tighten about it. Those horses were not ten feet away. He took an enormous spring, dragging Maggie with him, just as the team rushed by. He sank to the ground, still holding foolishly to Maggie's ankle. Maggie released herself and joined her father who reached them then.

"Thank you for saving my life," Maggie said gravely, looking back at Rodes, who was just scrambling to his feet. Then she walked away with her father and sister.

"He needn't have kicked me," said Jennie.

"Daddy, why didn't you thank him?" asked Maggie.

"I will someday. We got to get home now. I got to help your mother plant the garden."

A little later, Tom Henry Hines, who had returned to the court-house, heard from eyewitnesses what had happened.

"Whose girls did you say they were?"

"Guy Mayhew's."

"The one from Alvaton?"

"He's the one."

Hines thought a moment, then laughed loudly. "That's a joke on Guy Mayhew. We were together in the army six months, and I know him. He is the most cantankerous Rebel in the county, and now a long-legged Yankee saves the lives of his children." He laughed some more. "I wish I could have seen it. It sure is a joke on Guy. I wonder how he will take it. I believe I will go back down there. Something else might happen."

He entered the grounds ten minutes later. He could see the horse traders busily engaged on their lot. To his right a jumping match was in noisy progress. He regarded it briefly but found it uninteresting. He saw George Phalan standing near by. George had the knack of knowing about things.

"What's this I hear about Robin Rodes?"

"Saw it with my own eyes. I wasn't a hundred feet away, maybe not over seventy-five. They say Rodes got in some tight places with us Rebs, but I know now why we never caught him. Yessir, if he had kept on going like he started out, he'd be past Nashville by now. I've never seen any steps as long as the ones he took. John Morgan's best cavalrymen couldn't have stayed in sight of him."

"But what about the girls?"

"They'd be deader'n mackerels if it hadn't been for that Yankee that walks around on telegraph poles. They didn't get a scratch."

"Where is Mayhew?"

"He left. He looked like he was taking it right hard, a Yankee helping him out like that."

There was no sight of Rodes anywhere, so Hines went to his office.

Rodes sat at a desk with a ponderous lawbook open before him. He looked at his visitor in surprise and stood up.

"Robin, are you willing to shake hands with me?"

"Eager to, Tom Henry."

As Tom Henry Hines left the office, he stopped for a moment in the doorway and said, "It wouldn't surprise me, Robin, if you have done more this day to bring peace to Bowling Green than General Lee did at Appomattox."

8

RUMSEY SKILES often went to the boat landing to watch the arrival and unloading of a steamboat. Somehow, it comforted and reassured him. For one thing, it seemed to bring him closer to his father. Trade again was flowing through Bowling Green. The *Gasper River* had gone back on the Evansville run four weeks after the war closed, and its melodious whistle charmed the people on both sides of the river for miles back. It was a sturdy boat, but much in need of the repairs and refurbishing that a season of good business would enable it to have.

It came in on schedule one Wednesday morning, and Rumsey Skiles was there to meet it. He had no business there except to enjoy the boat's arrival. It could take his mind off the heartaches of the war. How gracefully the boat swung into the landing! How skillful the maneuvering of pilot Hickory Bill Moseley, himself one of the river's main traditions! Captain Ezekiel Ellis stood on the boat's deck and roared orders, which professional fury seemed to Rumsey Skiles to add to the musical overtones of the boat's whistle. Then the deckhands began to shuffle along the gangplank, carrying boxes and crates and other articles of freightage. Those they placed in appropriate stacks on the bank.

Captain Zeke saw Rumsey Skiles and called to him, "Come on up, but don't get in the way of any of them cases of the seven-year itch. I aim to get this boat unloaded before I die of old age." The shuffling deckhands giggled appreciatively. Cap'n Zeke always kept their work from getting boresome.

Skiles walked up the gangplank, staying carefully at one side so as not to slow down the unloading.

"I saw you before we landed. The way you stood there made me think of your daddy. He was a mighty fine man. If it hadn't been for him, I wouldn't ever have had this job."

"He did a lot of fine things, and that was one of them. How is your business?"

"Half a load. There's plenty of stuff to ship, but that Louisville boat that prowls up and down the lower river gets most of it both ways."

"Why?"

"I'll tell you why. The river played a mean trick on Bowling Green. It dodged it. How far do you think it is from here to the railroad? More than a mile and the road is plumb wore out. Right now, they are using a lot of lumber in Louisville, and there's a lot of the stuff around Calhoun and Paradise and Rochester. They would send it this way but for the hauling costs between here and the cars. That makes it cheaper to send it the long way around. The *George D. Prentice* carried forty thousand feet from Rochester the last trip. They can put it down at Louisville without any change at all. The river sure played a mean trick on this town. Say, down there, can't you tote that stuff a little faster? Just because you're teetotally dead with the sleeping sickness ain't no reason for you to give plumb out. There are about six of you that I am going to have to shoot to get waked up."

The deckhands grinned happily. Cap'n Zeke was in excellent form.

Rumsey Skiles was very thoughtful all of that day. The following morning, he left for Louisville on the eight o'clock train.

9

ON A SATURDAY in the early days of October, the churches of both town and county joined in giving a picnic for all returned soldiers and their friends, which meant everybody. After a careful canvass of all the available places, it was decided to hold it at Beech Bend, on the side of the river four miles from town.

The glory of autumn was in the great grove of beech trees which spread all about the picnic grounds and reached down almost to the water's edge. It was as if the weather too was celebrating the return of peace. There had been a long series of fine days. The nights had been chilly, but there had been no frost. Friday night had been definitely a time for quilts and blankets, but by ten o'clock on Saturday morning, a genial and friendly sun had spread warmth over the countryside. The goldenrod and purple asters were prodigal with their regal colors. The beech trees were heavy with leaves which shone yellow and amber in the morning sun. On up the ridge gum trees studded the hillside, their leaves as red as wine. Sumac and sassafras and persimmon commingled their hues in this holiday of color. The tall, stately mullein, proud and aloof, added its soft gray green. Everywhere were clumps of buck-bushes, their leaves dark green, their berries hinting of the red into which soon the frost would turn them. The trees were filled with birds: robins and jays and redbirds and mockingbirds. Crows circled about above the fields and thickets, sometimes drifting lazily, some-times cawing angrily.

There were only a few beech trees at one end of the picnic ground, and the contour of the space formed it into a natural amphitheater. A row of crude benches was placed there. They were seats of honor for the use of those whose immediate kin would not again come home. As far as the committee could determine, there were forty-three from Warren County who had died on battlefields or from wounds received therefrom. There were seven who had lost an arm or a leg.

The sermon would be preached in the afternoon by Dr. Quintard of the Episcopal church in Nashville. The rector had served as a chaplain in the Confederate army. He had been personally solicited by Warner Underwood, a stout partisan of the Union cause who had borne the expenses of the trip. There were several gestures like his in behalf of peace and unity. The memory of Robin Rodes's gallantry at County Court Day was still a matter of healing. There would be some who would not come because the other side would be represented. There would, of course, be natural limits to the fraternizing, but there would be strict neutrality. That was the committee's obligation. The war was over.

In a way of speaking, the war had closed in April. Peace had come in time for a crop to be raised. And that was a beneficent thing. The people were hungry. They were not starving, but they had lived too long on too little. Too often they had planted crops and gardens, only to watch them harvested by raiding soldiers on both sides. Stock generally was poor and gaunt, particularly the beasts of draft and bur-den. There was good grass in the meadows, but the horses and mules that pulled the wagons and the plows needed more than greenery. The news of peace had lifted hope in the hearts of the people. Corn could grow again in the fields. Haystacks again could stand boldly on the margins of the meadows. Kitchens and pantries again could give evidence of abundance.

But the sober-eyed among them knew that the days of which they dreamed were not that near. Those days had been lost and could be found only by long and patient search. Some, in their chronic despondency, saw ahead only defeat and ashes. But most were buoyed by hope, dim at first but brightening as the days passed. How good it was to see their friends gathering among the beech trees!

A few games got quickly into progress, but they were played diffidently. The women stood apart in groups, but each woman managed to stay but a short distance from the basket she had brought. That basket had in it food her home could ill afford to spare, an accumulation from fasting, carried on ever since she heard the day was planned. Those County Court Days of memory could not be followed in fullness, only in neighborliness and good spirit.

The women wanted some readjustment of the tables. The men made them and returned to their groups for more talk. Rumsey and Ella Skiles walked about, speaking with old friends, looking with warm eyes at the beauty spread out before them. But always they kept an eye on the entrance. They were waiting for Jane and her son to arrive. They had hoped Jane would spend the night with them, but Jane had said that it was the busiest of seasons at her place, and the best she could do was to come for the day. Really, there wasn't time for that, but she would steal that many hours and come anyhow. She wanted to see them very much indeed, and Jackson talked about them a great deal. She would get there just as soon as she could, but she feared it would not be before the middle of the morning. It was later than that when she arrived. Some cattle had broken out of the lot the night before, and she did not feel that she could leave till the man on her place found them and brought them back. Rumsey Skiles looked intently at his daughter. She was showing signs of the strain under which she was living. The boy was looking fine. He was a solemn-faced youngster whose large eyes missed very little.

Rumsey spoke to him. "Do you remember me, Jackson?"

The boy thought it over. "Grampa," he said.

"Jane, how are you?" her mother asked anxiously.

"All right, Mother. Nothing is the matter with me that a little rest wouldn't cure. You two look mighty dear to me."

Bill Willie came up. "You all go on anywhere you want to. I'll take care of the team."

"I'll get the basket," said Rumsey Skiles. "I think the ladies are keeping them over here. Treat the team right, Bill Willie."

"Jest like they was my first cousins."

The Virgil Covingtons joined them. "Hi, Bill Willie," said Virgil gaily. "I remember the time I looked as young as you do, but the trouble is I haven't been treated right for thirty-five or forty years." He nodded toward his wife. "Good morning, Jackson Shobe, Junior. I never saw a lad who looked like he had used better sense in picking out his parents, his grandparents, and likely his great-grandparents. In my long and eventful life I have somehow managed to see better tables provided for our ladies on similar occasions than the ones we have rigged up today. I have just spent two hours, expertly bossed by my wife and uncle, in trying to prop up these age-old picnic tables so that they could stand up under what is going to be put on them today."

A desolate look came over Jane Shobe's face. She was remembering that the last picnic that she and Jackson ever attended together had been served on those tables. Virgil saw the look and interpreted it correctly. "That was in the old South, Jane, when all of us were happy, or thought we were. This is the new South, and there isn't much happiness for us right now. The way I see it is like this. It is our duty to save what happiness we can out of those good old days. I don't do it so very well myself, but I try."

"Let me make a guess," said Ella Skiles. "The best basket here will be brought by a lady named Harriet Covington."

"No," said Harriet. "There will be better baskets than mine without half as much in them."

"I know what you mean," said Rumsey Skiles.

"Yonder comes a better basket than ours," said Virgil Covington, his eyes on the entrance.

A rickety wagon, drawn by a pair of scrawny mules, was turning into the park. A scrawny man and woman sat on the front seat, and between them a boy of eleven or twelve. Rumsey Skiles had recognized the man almost as soon as Covington had. He was Holland Wren from a poor little farm in the Richardsville neighborhood. The lad was the only remaining child, his two brothers having been killed on a late November afternoon at Franklin, Tennessee, less than a year before. When Wren heard of the disaster he hitched up his mules and set out for Franklin. Somehow he got through the Northern lines and to the battlefield. Somehow he found the bodies of his two sons.

Somehow he got them back for burial at the Green River Baptist church. Skiles and Covington had learned about it from Bill Willie Blewett, who had happened to see the pitiful little cortege as it had passed through town. He and Wren were fox-hunting acquaintances, and Bill Willie had stopped the man to find out what it meant. Covington was at Three Springs when Bill Willie had returned home. All three had gone to the funeral at the country church the following day. As he watched them drive by, Rumsey Skiles had taken off his hat without knowing that he did, and Virgil Covington had followed him.

"It's a better basket than ours, Ella," said Skiles.

Warner Underwood, fifty yards away, watched the Wren wagon till it stopped. He thought for a moment, took off his hat and walked toward the wagon. The boy in the wagon was handing his mother the split hickory basket. Wren was unhitching the mules.

"My name is Warner Underwood, Mr. Wren. I have never had the honor of your acquaintance, nor that of your wife. I suppose you would call me a Yankee, but I have heard that two of your sons were heroes, and it is my belief that you two are heroes too."

They said nothing, but stood looking at him, all three.

"Mrs. Underwood and I are going to spread the food we brought on that table yonder. That is my wife standing by it. Unless you have made other arrangements, we would find it most agreeable for you to join us."

He waited patiently for a reply. Wren looked at his wife. Confusion was plain upon her wrinkled face. Her husband said nothing. Finally she said, "You wasn't a Yankee soldier, was you?"

"Not a soldier, Mrs. Wren. I believed in the North, but I wasn't physically able to be a soldier."

"It wouldn't look right for us to be eatin' with a soldier that fought agin our boys."

"I understand," he said gently. "I promise you that I will speak no word, and think no word, against the South. I would like to make the acquaintance of this young fellow, and I would like to hear about your other sons. I was on the other side, but I think of them as heroes."

"They was heroes," said the boy fiercely and unexpectedly. "I wisht I'd been old enough to go with them."

"We couldn't spare you, Charlie," said the mother.

"Thank God, you do not have to spare him. Let's go over to the table. May I carry your basket?"

"Much obliged, but I wouldn't want to trouble you."

As they walked to the table, the boy looked three or four times up at the man walking at his side. The taut lines on the young face relaxed. Something about Underwood reassured him.

Gravely and with dignity, Underwood presented the Wrens to Mrs. Underwood. "You have heard of Mr. Wren, my dear. You heard Robin Rodes speaking of him when we were visiting the Youngloves."

"I remember. How nice it is for them to share the table with us!"

"That's Adolph Roemer yonder," said her husband. "I haven't seen him in three years. He was with General Kirby Smith and just got back this week. Bill Willie Blewett told me he was at home."

"If it is all right with our friends, ask him to eat with us."

The Wrens looked at the well-set-up young man with the vague Teutonic cast of features. Their eyes warmed at the sight of his tattered uniform of gray. Roemer listened to the invitation. He nodded pleasantly and came across to join them. There were introductions. Then Roemer turned to Wren and said, "I have heard a great deal about you since I got back. Not many men could have done what you did."

"I reckon it was what Bill Willie Blewett done at the first of the war that made me think of it."

"You selected a good pattern," said Underwood.

Roemer said, "I saw Frank and Hubert the day they left. Mighty fine boys, both of them. I'll miss them."

"They was heroes," said the little boy.

"So was your father. I fancy you will be too at the proper time."

"I am proud to hear you say it," said Mrs. Wren. "Mr. Wren is a good man."

"Warner, look around and see if you can't find Tom Henry Hines and his wife, Nancy. I would like to have them join us."

"My idea precisely, dear wife. It would be a pleasure to manage a Confederate reunion."

He departed, and five minutes later was back with Captain Hines and his young wife.

"A minute later, and I would have lost them," said Underwood. "Some very good people were bargaining for their company, but I had more to offer. When I told them about the Wrens, that settled the matter."

"I was in town when you came back through with your sons," said

Mrs. Underwood. "I saw you passing and something impressed me deeply. I heard that several men from town went out to the funeral."

"They was a crowd there," said the mother proudly.

"There is something fine in being buried at home," said Tom Henry Hines, "and something sad in being buried in a strange place. There were several times when I figured I was about due to be buried, and always I was thinking and praying that it be done at Bowling Green."

"All of our people are buried at Green River church," said Wren.

Hines looked Roemer over. "Looks like you got back without a scratch, Adolph."

"For three years I didn't have enough to eat two days in succession, but I didn't even have a bad cold."

"There have been several feast days in succession since you got home, I fancy."

Mrs. Underwood looked about. Other ladies were getting their tables ready for use. Tom Henry Hines lifted his basket to the table, and his wife pulled away the cloth covering it.

"My father and mother will be expecting me," said Roemer. He bowed and walked away.

"We didn't have much to bring," said Mrs. Wren. "We aim to have more next year."

"I hope all of us will," said Underwood, "but the scarcer food is the better it tastes."

"We haven't had any wheat flour for more than two years. There is some things you can't make unless you have wheat flour."

"There certainly are. We have been saving ours a long time for something like this. Farmers are putting in a good wheat crop this year. They are planting all the seed they can get. We ought to have flour next year. Boiled roasting ears! There is nothing I like better. I didn't know there were any left."

"We've got a late patch that is turning out good. If we could only have that corn warm."

"I like it better cold," said Tom Henry Hines gallantly. "How do you bake a hen to look that good, Mrs. Wren? Mr. Wren, where did you get that watermelon?"

"Raised it."

"I haven't seen a watermelon in three years. It got so there was no use planting them. They were considered public property, specially by the soldiers."

"We've had them on our place over fifty years. My daddy got the seed at a big basket meeting right after he come here. I've heard him tell about it a hundred times."

"Oh," said Warner Underwood, smiling, "I've heard about those watermelons and that basket meeting. In fact, I've eaten watermelons that descended from the meeting, but this is the first melon I've seen raised in Warren County this year."

And then, all the food having been made visible and available, a loud voice announced that Brother Lew Harman of Allen Springs would ask the blessing. Brother Harman was one of the foremost Methodist laymen of the section. He farmed when he wasn't engaged in furthering the Methodist cause. He had the voice of a native orator, distinct, carrying, pleasing. He asked the Lord, in some detail, to make the meeting an omen of peace and brotherhood, and for the food to give needed strength to their bodies. He said "Amen" reluctantly because prayer always kindled within him a glow of contentment. But he said it, because he also was hungry. Then they were eating. The tables covered a frontage of a hundred and fifty feet, and at places were six deep. Soon could be heard the unmistakable sound and chatter of people feasting.

Rumsey Skiles was not very hungry. At his table were his wife, his daughter and her son, Bill Willie Blewett, Judge Drake and his wife and two soldiers from Galloway's Mill. The table was laden with attractive and tempting dishes, but still he wasn't hungry. He nibbled for a few minutes, his eyes upon that panorama of feasting. How much reunion was there? He asked those at the table to excuse him, and then he walked about. He saw two soldiers, standing at one side, talking happily and apparently with no thought of food. It was a pleasing sight. One of them, Murray Phillips, had got back to Bowling Green only the day before. Ella had told him of Phillips' return that morning. She had heard it somewhere. The other was Rutherford Hill, who had returned home in May. They had been inseparable before the war. One was rarely seen without the other. The war had parted them for four years, and this was their first meeting. Skiles started to invite them to his table, but decided they needed talk more than they needed food. He would see that they got that later. He started threading his way among the tables again, speaking to many, tactfully waiving invitations to stop and eat. He saw one table, and noted that all who stood around it were Northern in their sympathies and participation.

He knew the grizzled giant who stood at the head of the table, and spoke to him. "Don't you think you need a Southerner at your table?"

"They are too close as it is," answered John R. Miller in cold tones.

"And yet your cousin Fred, a first-rate man, was one of them."

"He got on the wrong side. I'll wait for him to bring in fruits meet for repentance."

"How about repenting some yourself and meeting him halfway?"

"He's got you there, Mr. Miller," said the man's wife. "I am for forgiving everybody who really means it. But my menfolks was a stiff-necked lot," she went on, addressing Rumsey. "I don't know which side you was on, but have a slice of that ham."

"I was all mixed up. My oldest son is a Northern sympathizer, my son-in-law was killed on the Southern side. My name is Rumsey Skiles, and I will have a piece of that ham."

"I've heard of you. You're a lawyer, ain't you? Stay with us awhile. Maybe you can help take some of the stiffness out of my Yankees' necks."

"Your Yankees are good men. Just give them time. Thank you for the ham. I haven't often eaten as good."

The men about the table were definitely not friendly, but the woman was. There was gain in that. He walked on, moving slowly among the tables. He saw at one table the John Horsleys, the Dunk Arbuckles, and the Charles Daughtrys, all devoted partisans of the South. He stopped a moment. "This is like old times."

"The North has ruined the old times," said Daughtry. "We'll never get them back."

"We have a way of restoring ruined things. It's worth trying. How are you, Dunk? I haven't seen you in a long time."

"I am doing all right for a starving man," said Arbuckle, his mouth full of chicken. "What's this I hear about the Yankees getting out a ticket for the county offices?"

"Haven't heard anything of it. Why don't you come out, Dunk, for some office?"

"I've been thinking about it. I say this is a Southern county, and Southern men ought to get the offices. You like pawpaws? There are some in that basket. Take one."

Skiles took a pawpaw, thanked Arbuckle and moved on. The stiffness which had been apparent earlier was softening. He saw Dr. Younglove talking with the group at Warner Underwood's table. Something about the group drew his further attention. He saw that the three Wrens were there, and so were Tom Henry Hines and his wife. The Wrens and Warner Underwood! That was a warming sight.

Skiles started to the table, but a high-pitched voice stopped him. "What you gadding about for, Rumsey Skiles? I thought we came here to eat and not just to parade about. I guess you have got old and lost your appetite."

It was Uncle Trez Covington. He was standing by a table. He had a chicken drumstick in one hand and a piece of corn bread in the other. Virgil and Harriet were at the table, and the Cheney brothers and their wives from South Union. There were three soldiers whom he did not know standing there eating. Uncle Trez took some liberal bites and turned again to Skiles. "I wish we had some mush for you, Rumsey. It is said to be mighty strengthening for weakly people who can't do anything but walk around."

"You got your coffin picked out yet, Uncle Trez? One would come in pretty handy for a man who is past a hundred and eats like you do."

"Sue Cheney has got some first-rate crabapple jelly. Some spread thin on a piece of corn bread wouldn't hurt you."

"Not today. I have eaten Mrs. Cheney's cooking, and in part it accounts for one of my advanced age being able to walk around and think of things. I have been thinking of something I would like to talk with you about, Uncle Trez. Oh, not now, of course. But couldn't we get together a little later? I think it is really something important. This is a fine dinner you have spread here."

"Thinking, huh? That's something new for you, Rumsey. I'd like to hear what you got to say."

"When you have eaten everything in sight hunt me up."

Rumsey Skiles shook hands with the soldiers and moved on. The chatter over the grounds had quieted. The food was having its effect. He saw something that troubled him. The sheriff was escorting a young Confederate off the grounds. The boy was unsteady from drink. Skiles recognized him. It was Clayborne Grimes from Boiling Spring. The boy's father had several times been his client in a minor way. It occurred to him that he might be of some help, so he cut across and overtook them. "Anything wrong?" he asked the sheriff pleasantly.

"It was the order that there was to be no drinking here today," said the sheriff in his gravelly voice. "My notion was to get this boy away from here before he got himself into trouble, but I was trying not to attract any attention."

"That was a wise thing to do. I just happened to see you. You made a mistake, Clayborne."

The boy's eyes came into focus. "How did you know my name?"

"I am the lawyer who helped your father when he got into trouble with the McLemores."

"Listen, Sheriff," the boy said: "you let me go and I'll not touch another drop."

"Let him go, Sheriff. I'll be responsible for him. You and I might act worse if we had been through as much as he has."

"If you say so, Mr. Skiles, I'll let him go."

Skiles walked with young Grimes for fifty feet. "You don't have to tag around with me, Clayborne. Go on and enjoy yourself."

"I am sorry I acted that way, sir. I am just about sober now."

Skiles started back. A hand was laid upon his shoulder. It was a young, plump, clear-eyed Jewish fellow, dressed in a uniform that looked surprisingly new. "Why, Sam Nahm, when did you get back? Come and eat with us."

"Thank you, Mr. Skiles, but my folks are putting out dinner now. How do you like my uniform?"

"How did you ever come through the war with one as fine?"

"I didn't. My mother had been saving the cloth, and we made it since I got back. I'll never wear any other color but gray, and I don't want any blue or black on when I am in my coffin either. I had good health all during the war. Bed Forrest positively ordered his men not to get sick. Hope I'll be seeing you often, Mr. Skiles."

Skiles walked to his table and took the piece of cake his wife offered him.

"If cake is all you are going to eat, try a piece of mine," said Jane Shobe. "No, don't you dare to give that boy another bite. He is stuffed already. Yonder is Uncle Trez."

"I am a hungry man," said Uncle Trez. "Anything left? No, on second thought, I don't believe I will eat any more. I will just leave it for those who are not well and need it more. That cake is tempting. What have you got on your mind, Rumsey?"

"Let's go over here and sit on this rock. I am thinking about building a railroad. Would you like to help?"

"Any profit in it?"

"Yes, good profit, I am sure. And it is something we need very much."

"What kind of railroad? Would it go from somewhere to anywhere else? Would it haul anything? Or would you run it just so it could blow its whistle?"

"It would run from the boat landing to the railroad station. Listen, Uncle Trez, I went down to the boat landing yesterday to watch the *Gasper River* come in. It had a fair load, but it ought to have brought a third more. And before long there is going to be all the stuff down the river that it can bring. I talked with the captain. He said that as things are a lot of shippers would rather send their stuff around the other way, around by Louisville or Saint Louis. He said that it would all come this way if it wasn't for that gap between the river and the railroad. It is slow business hauling things from the train to the boat, or from the boat to the train. If we had the track, we could run the cars so as to require only one unloading and loading. If we could do that we could put a lot more business through this town."

"Got it all thought out, haven't you?"

"Louisville sends a good deal of freight to Morgantown, to Rochester, to Calhoun. It could then be loaded on the cars at Louisville, and changed to the boat here at the landing."

"If I didn't know better, I would think it was your daddy talking."

"Thank you, Uncle Trez. I talked with the railroad people in Louisville last week. They won't build the line, but if we will they will co-operate in providing it with business."

"Co-operate how?"

"If we will put down the line, and I mean put it down in good order, they will run their boxcars and engines over it and pay us for the use of it. I think the railroad would be profitable, and I think it would do the town a lot of good too."

"Your lips are moving, but it is Jacob Skiles's words I hear. How much will it cost?"

"Maybe twenty thousand dollars, and I think we can get twelve or fifteen percent on our investment. What do you say?"

"I am not a professional eavesdropper," said Virgil Covington from behind them, "but I will match any fellow who is. I didn't intend to, but it was so interesting I sort of forgot to announce my presence. I hope that I am forgiven."

"Indeed you are, Virgil. I was going to talk with you next. Well, think it over, Uncle Trez, and let's talk again in a few days."

"I'll think it over. I guess I could scratch up a few dollars, but I am not sure."

"Then stand aside, Uncle Trez, and let a Covington talk who understands such things. If you think as well of this railroad, Rumsey, as I gathered you do, Harriet and I will buy a few ties for it, of course, if we can get some nice used ones. It has always been our intention to get rich someday, and this seems as good a time as any."

"If my nephew has finished his address I'd like to hear what you have in mind, Rumsey."

"Then suppose you come to my office in the morning, say about ten o'clock."

Then the powerful voice of Captain Tom Henry Hines was lifted, announcing that preaching would begin in fifteen minutes. The voice which had relayed the commands of General John H. Morgan was not likely to be misunderstood. So the ladies set about cleaning up the tables and salvaging the food that remained uneaten. Those scraps would go well on the morrow.

Hearing the announcement, Rumsey Skiles reflected that in south Kentucky a preacher was always regarded as a gifted man. He was always welcome in the homes. His the best room and the best food. His sermons were always listened to seriously, even reverently. Generally, his voice was powerful enough to satisfy all hearers, and his appeal convincing. No man hurried away for home, or to take part in some game following Captain Hines's announcement. Something within the hearts of the people longed for preaching.

As he left his table, Rumsey Skiles was stopped by the look on his daughter's face. His eyes followed hers. Adolph Roemer was passing not fifty feet away. The sight of the uniform had lifted tragedy before Jane's eyes, and she was seeing her husband ride away to his death at Fort Donelson.

Her father said nothing, and for a while left her alone with her memories. Then he said, "Let's go. Preaching is about to begin." He took his grandson's hand and led him toward the grove.

He felt his wife's hand upon his arm. "I have been looking for them. I haven't seen them till now."

It was Nat Grider and Sallie. They were seated on a bit of planking in front of the stand. Nat wore a dingy black suit, and his wife was in heavy mourning.

"Let's go sit with them," said Rumsey Skiles.

His wife answered by turning an inquiring look upon Jane. Jane caught the significance of the look and hesitated. Then she brightened. "It's all right," she said. "They are good people, and Motley was all they had."

"They have had more than their share of trouble," said Ella Skiles.

Rumsey led the way, and stopped at Nat Grider's side. "Mind if we sit with you?" he asked.

Nat stood quickly. "It would please us, Rumsey. We need company today."

"We all do, Nat, specially today. Good afternoon, Sallie. May we sit with you?"

"Yes," Sallie Grider said softly. "I'd like for you to."

So they all sat on the plank seat, and after the greetings all were silent, waiting for the preacher. Somehow the strain on the faces of Nat Grider and his wife seemed to have lessened.

The people gathered quickly, and took their places in orderly manner. Bishop Quintard was one of the South's famed preachers, and, except for a few who perhaps would fall asleep from overeating, his audience would be attentive that day. The preacher had served as chaplain in the Confederate army, but no Northern soldier or sympathizer had made any complaint against his selection.

Robin Rodes led Dr. Smoot of the Presbyterian church and Bishop Quintard up on the little stand which had been erected for the preacher. Brother Jim Grubbs, of renown as a leader of song, led in the singing of two hymns. Brother Grubbs was a tall, thin man, with rounded shoulders and a hollow chest. No one ever knew where the volume of his singing came from. But the volume came, and with feeling and sweetness. Brother Grubbs's record in the war was appealing to many. His two sons had served under Nathan Bedford Forrest, and his two brothers under General George Thomas of the Union army. That created a delicate situation, but not beyond the diplomatic powers of Brother Grubbs. He gave the matter mature thought, and then brought his sons, both married and living in neighboring communities, and his two brothers together in his home for dinner. He meant to settle the matter once and for all. He made a little speech to his sons and brothers, and there was no evasion in what he said. He told them that the war was over, and that he wanted it to stay over, at least as far as his family was concerned. He hoped that he would not hear any undue echoes of it sounding in his community. He looked squarely at his sons. He told them that they had been defeated in honor, and that men of honor didn't prolong a conflict unnecessarily. He turned to his brothers and told them that they

Untitled

should esteem their victory too highly to engage in any crude and ill-tempered acts. He told his sons that he would take the side of his brothers if they were guilty of any kind of brashness. He told his brothers again that he would be found on the side of his sons unless they were guiltless of offensive behavior. They knew that he meant it, and so sons and brothers were up close that afternoon singing lustily.

That singing warmed Rumsey Skiles's heart. It was spontaneous and free of tension. Brother Grubbs finished the last stanza of "There's a Land That Is Fairer Than Day," and moved back into the audience.

Robin Rodes presented Dr. Smoot, who would read the Scripture, pray, and present the visiting preacher. That too was a good omen. Rodes had been a Union soldier, and the preacher was a Southern partisan. The rift in the church was healing. Dr. Smoot read the Ninetieth Psalm and then prayed long and fervently.

Then Dr. Quintard was preaching. His text was the last four verses of the Psalm that Dr. Smoot had read. Dr. Quintard was neither large nor tall, but his eyes shone like those of the prophets, and his voice, never forced, carried to the margins of the congregation: *"Make us glad according to the days wherein thou hast afflicted us, and the years wherein we have seen evil."*

It was a plea for peace, an acceptance of tribulation, an exhortation to work without ceasing. That was the way back, the way ahead. He preached for an hour and no one stirred in his place. Brother Grubbs led in the singing of another hymn. Brother Ray, of the Baptist church, pronounced the benediction, and in Brother Ray's hands, the benediction was no minor affair. This one grew into an abbreviated sermon, and still there was no impatience among the congregation. They were not anxious to leave. Somehow they seemed to feel that for the first time peace had come to Bowling Green.

Bill Willie Blewett waited to speak to Judge Drake. Bill Willie was old and grizzled, but his eyes and steps were steady, and no senile quaver marred his voice. "A mighty fine day, Judge, mighty fine."

"Yes, it has been a fine day. And we need fine days."

"I thought of a funny thing while Brother Ray was a-prayin'. A long time ago, I hadn't been here but about a year, a big preacher from Nashville come up and preached. Preached a powerful sermon too, but the very second he stopped there come a regular flood. I never seen such a rain. Good thing Brother Ray wasn't there for the benediction or there'da been a hundred drowned. Still, I like Brother Ray, benediction and all."

"That was a fine sermon today."

"Better'n I expected when I seen the clothes he was rigged up in. But what I have been thinkin' is that the town ought to have a place for its big meetin's and get-togethers. This is a good place all right, but it's too far from town. Besides, this place belongs to a man, and the time might come when he wouldn't want to give his consent for us to use it. If Bowling Green had a place of its own, it'd be a lot o' help to the town."

"Got any place in mind, Bill Willie?"

"Not a one, and I been thinkin' too. Well, I'll go help the Skileses get hitched."

He had gone fifteen or twenty feet when the judge's call stopped him. "Listen, Bill Willie, have you seen Jim Walters today?"

"He's here. I seen him in his buckboard a-settin' there eatin' his dinner. He didn't bring a bite with him. The McGinnises fixed up some things on a plate and took it out to him. He liked it fine. It didn't cost him anything."

"How did he look? He has been sick, hasn't he?"

"Looked all frazzled out to me. Countin' money is hard on a man. Yonder he is now, still settin' there."

"Let's go see him. There is something I want to tell him. No, you go get Rumsey Skiles and Ella. Bring them."

Bill Willie looked at the judge in surprise, but turned and departed on his mission.

Judge Drake stopped where Walters sat. "Good afternoon, Mr. Walters. How are you feeling?"

"Pretty puny. I guess I've got a touch of the malaria."

"This weather will cure it. I expect your bank will flourish now."

"On what? Who's got any money?"

"War scares money away, but it returns when the war is over. I guess you have a good crop."

"Nothing to brag about."

"Rumsey, you and Ella, come on over here. You too, Bill Willie. It was you who started me to thinking. Bill Willie thinks that Bowling Green needs a park, a picnic ground, an out-of-doors meeting place, not only for the use of the people of the town but the people of the county as well. I think I will provide one tomorrow, or rather I'll help you provide one. A long time ago, Jacob Skiles and Elvis

Grider had a disagreement as to a tract of land, approximately sixty-five acres, I believe. It got into the courts, and it is still there. At least, it was the last time I looked it up. It is a delightful place, not too far from town. It has an everlasting spring on it, and plenty of fine trees. It is an ideal place for public events and recreation. When you, Mr. Walters, took over the Grider property, that made you a contestant for this land. Unless you, Rumsey Skiles, and you, James Walters, object, I shall tomorrow issue a decision and assign that land forever to such a use. Will you two contestants sign such an agreement?"

"I will with very great pleasure," said Rumsey Skiles.

"No, I claim that's my land. No, sir, I wouldn't agree to that," said Walters fiercely.

"Then I think the simplest way to handle it would be for the court to award full possession to Skiles. There is no doubt that his grant was issued first. We'd simply let the matter of chronology settle it. Skiles then could deed it to the city and county for the purposes aforesaid."

"That's too highhanded. I couldn't agree to it."

"Of course, you could appeal the judgment, but you would only waste your time, and also lose any credit for generosity in the matter. And generosity is something you have been a little late getting around to, Mr. Walters."

"I'd have to think it over."

"There has been time for that. Come to court tomorrow, Mr. Skiles, prepared to execute the proper documents in making your assignment of this land."

"If you are going to do that, then I guess I'll have to agree," said Walters sullenly.

The judge was smiling broadly. "Tonight I'll have my former law partner, David Settle, Junior, draw up the decision. That makes the case perfect. Tomorrow I will announce the court's judgment. And that is getting rid of a case in a hurry. It has been pending just a little over sixty years. If I would only hang around Bill Willie Blewett and get ideas, I'd clear my docket in no time at all."

Rumsey Skiles and his wife drove home through the fading sunlight of an autumn day. They had waited at Beech Bend till almost all had left, so there were very few on the road. He drove slowly to savor the richness of the scene. The crops in the fields were scanty, but

The Settlement Regained 315

next year there would be more hands to guide the plows, and the teams would have more strength to pull them. The road was rough. For four years roads had gone without repairs. Another year would find them smoothed out a little. He remembered that the clothes he had noticed at the picnic were threadbare from long use. His eyes dropped to his own coat sleeves. They were frayed at the edges. He lifted his eyes to the east. It was, but for troubled memories, a view of loveliness. The war had not wrought its malice upon that view. There was Baker's Hill, tall and noble and commanding. On its crest, revealed in outline, was the fort which the Southern soldiers had spent futile weeks in building. Almost directly ahead of him was Vinegar Hill, tallest of all. He could see the great gash made where the cedar trees had been cut. He was thankful that those zealous soldiers had not cut them all. There was something stately and magnificent about a tall cedar tree, and something healing about its dark, waxen green. Those forts would for decades serve as monuments—monuments to what? Those grim outlines, etched against the horizons, would for generations be reminders—reminders of what?

How brave Jane had looked! There was in Jane an uncommon sturdiness. His father and mother lived on in Jane. And, after Jane, in the boy. That was as life should be.

"Rumsey, what on earth are you thinking about?" asked his wife. "You haven't spoken a word for over two miles. Didn't you have a good time today?"

"It has been a good day, a good day indeed. I have seen a lot of friends. I have seen our daughter and grandson. The spirit has been good, even better than I had hoped for. The food was more abundant than I had hoped for. The sermon was, I'd say, majestic."

"And you made some progress with your railroad," she said.

11

JANE SHOBE's spring wagon bumped along the rough road to Oakland. Now and then Jackson, sitting at her side, would see something that interested him, say something in his deliberate way, and point. But the boy was tired and soon fell asleep, leaning against his mother. Only a few rays of the sun were left as she was passing Bristow. At Sunnyside the dusk was thickening. The darkness had closed in by the time they reached Oakland. It was still more than a mile to her place. The sleepy hum of the cicadas murmured in the trees on both sides of the road. To the south a fox barked several times. Jane loved that road. To her it was a sort of memorial road to her husband. How often in their brief span together they had traveled it! Later she would tell Jackson about his father's affection for that road. They were passing Mr. Middleton's, and at the milking gap three cows set up a medley of lowing. From the barn lot the calves made their antiphonal response. The road dipped gently to the fording place of the little creek. How lovely was the sound of the water rippling over the shallow places! Her mind moved back and canvassed the events of the day. Only one thing was lacking, only one, the father of the boy sleeping so soundly at her side. As the patient horse climbed the opposite bank of the creek, Jane lifted her eyes. The sky was clear and warm and friendly. There was an infinity of stars, but one was brighter than all the others. Somewhere, far beyond that star, Jackson was waiting for her. There was much work to be done before she joined him. There was his son to be cared for and guided and guarded.

The boy stirred. "Mama," he said, and then he was sleeping again.

Their home was just ahead. She saw that a light was burning in it. What a kindly man was Mr. Howell! He had lighted that lamp to make her home-coming more cheerful. It was a dark world, but many were left, eager to light its lamps.

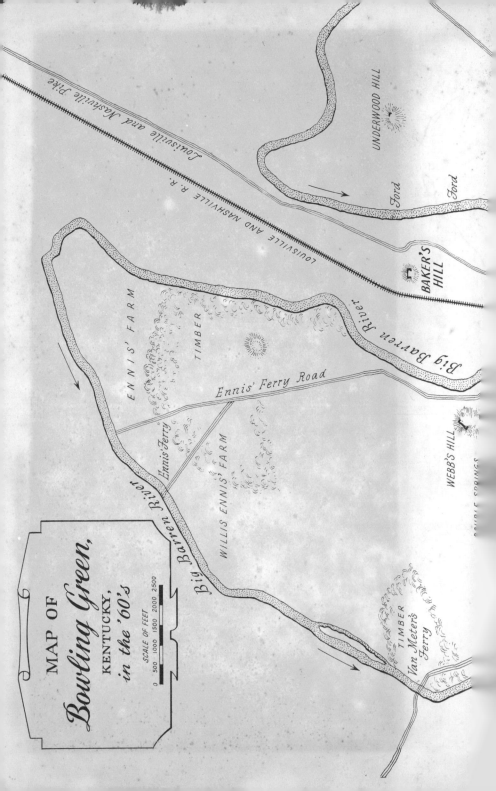

MAP OF
Bowling Green,
KENTUCKY,
in the '60's

SCALE OF FEET

0   500   1000   1500   2000   2500

UNDERWOOD HILL

Ford

Ford

BAKER'S HILL

Louisville and Nashville Pike

LOUISVILLE AND NASHVILLE R.R.

Big Barren River

ENNIS' FARM

TIMBER

Ennis' Ferry Road

Ennis'Ferry

WILLIS ENNIS' FARM

Big Barren River

WEBB'S HILL

STONE SPRINGS

TIMBER
Van Meter's Ferry